BLIND EYE

By Aline Templeton

BLIND EYE

ALINE TEMPLETON

Allison & Busby Limited
11 Wardour Mews
London W1F 8AN
allisonandbusby.com

First published in Great Britain by Allison & Busby in 2023.

A CIP catalogue record for this book is available from
the British Library.

First Edition

ISBN 978-0-7490-2937-1

Typeset in 11/16 pt Sabon LT Pro by
Allison & Busby Ltd

The paper used for this Allison & Busby publication
has been produced from trees that have been legally sourced
from well-managed and credibly certified forests.

Printed and bound by
CPI Group (UK) Ltd, Croydon, CR0 4YY

Y060734

The item should be returned or renewed by the last date stamped below.

Dylid dychwelyd neu adnewyddu'r eitem erbyn y dyddiad olaf sydd wedi'i stampio isod

Newport
CITY COUNCIL
CYNGOR DINAS
Casnewydd

05-04-23 PILLGWENLLY

To renew visit / Adnewyddwch ar
www.newport.gov.uk/libraries

For Elaine Singleton,
who wanted to know what happened to Cat.

If you wake at midnight, and hear a horse's feet
Don't go drawing back the blind, or looking in the street,
Them that asks no questions isn't told a lie.
Watch the wall my darling while the Gentlemen go by.

A Smuggler's Song
Rudyard Kipling

CHAPTER ONE

The east wind was blowing today, the wind that had an edge as keen as a butcher's knife, the wicked wind that had savaged the gorse growing near the cliff edge into surrealist shapes. There was a salty burn in the light spray it whipped up from the sea and the browned pink petals of the thrift clinging to the rocks ruffled as it passed across.

It had been a day just like this the last time he'd been here: sunlight then sudden shadows as clouds were whipped across the sky. It was a fine, bracing day for a walk to dramatic St Abb's Head, with its sheer cliffs and the surging sea below that, hour by hour, tide by tide, was eating them away. He had started out on the path from the visitor centre but veered onto the tarmac service road that hugged the cliff edge to reach the lighthouse and the farms beyond. There were a couple of groups on the same pilgrimage, and a spaniel that raced around, excited by the force of the wind blowing its ears back.

Just as there had been, that other day. As he had reached the spot where he was standing now, a car had driven up the path and parked not far in front of him – a sporty yellow Cooper S. He remembered feeling irritated – what was wrong with people? They had legs, didn't they? If everyone started bringing cars up here it wouldn't be long before it was all a churned-up mess.

The car door opened and a young woman jumped out. The wind snatched at her long blonde hair, sweeping it back from her face. She slammed the car door behind her and took off, running with a springing step straight to the cliff edge twenty feet away. Then she jumped.

He had agonised afterwards. Was there something – anything – he could have done to stop her – launched himself at her, shouted? But by the time he realised what she was going to do it was too late anyway; she hadn't paused, not to think, not to pluck up courage, as you would imagine a woman planning to take her own life would do. As she disappeared from view, he stood frozen in shock.

Then people were screaming and he had grabbed his phone just as others did the same. The emergency services were on the scene quickly and he hadn't needed to look over to make a report on the broken body on the rocks below. They'd had to call out the lifeboat to bring her in.

At the fatal accident inquiry, one of the other witnesses said that the woman had raced to the cliff edge as if all the devils in hell were after her. When it was his turn, he had confirmed that yes, she'd jumped out of the car and run, but it hadn't seemed necessary to dramatise it by saying what his own thought had been.

Beneath the windswept hair, he had seen that she was smiling, her blue eyes bright, her face eager as she ran, like a little girl who was late for a party and couldn't wait to get there.

It had been attributed to depression after the coronavirus pandemic, but in those last moments she had looked excited. What wretchedness in her existence had made a death like this hold such joyful promise?

It was afterwards in his working life that he began to be haunted by a persistent unease. Someone had told him once about The Hum, a pervasive, insistent low humming that is reported worldwide with no satisfactory explanation. Not everyone hears it, and it has driven some of those who do to the edge of insanity.

He seemed to be the only person to notice the constant trickle of nasty minor criminality, like a quiet indeterminate mutter in the background that was never quite clear enough for him to pin down. But it was getting louder.

He had come here on his day off, as if to see whether returning might in some sense lay a ghost. It hadn't, of course, but the wind ruthlessly blowing all the cobwebs away did clear his mind. What he could see now was that unless something more serious, and nastier, happened there was nothing he could do. And he was very much afraid that it would.

* * *

11

'Don't go,' Niall Ritchie said. 'It's asking for trouble.'

Sarah Lindsay looked up from her breakfast coffee at her partner. Niall was standing by the door, almost blocking it, and she felt her stomach knotting with tension. She'd always hated confrontation and she was nervous enough already about the day ahead.

'Oh, please, Niall!' she said tiredly. 'What are you talking about? We've been over and over this. I feel we haven't discussed anything else for all the months we've been waiting for the trial to call. I've made up my mind to testify because it's right and I'm not going to change it now.'

'Then you're a fool,' Niall said.

'Give me one good reason why I should.'

He raised his voice. 'I've given you a dozen!'

'For the hundredth time, that's why you haven't convinced me. Please give me the real reason – it might even make me reconsider.'

Niall hesitated. She could see his cheeks above the dark beard take on colour and he dropped his eyes. He said, 'I don't know what you mean.'

Sarah shook her head helplessly, then shrugged. She went to the door and after a second he moved aside. He was slight and not quite as tall as she was; he didn't really have the physical presence for a bully.

'You'll regret it,' he said ominously. 'We both will.'

The man in the legal wig had hard grey eyes, deeply hooded, a soft, loose mouth, a thick roll of fat round his neck and a paunch that he carried like a bandsman bearing a bass drum. His steely gaze was skewering the police constable in the witness box.

She was visibly shaking. 'No, that's not right,' she said.

'No? Not right?' He hadn't raised his voice, he'd dropped it, which somehow made it more frightening still. 'You admitted you had put it there – but it's not right?'

'I didn't, the way you mean—'

'Yet your fingerprints were on the wallet?'

She was starting to cry. She was very young, very slight and there was an uneasy movement from one of the jurors.

He noticed at once. 'No wonder you're upset, PC Moore. It's hard to disobey orders when you're being bullied. You're a very junior officer – it would be unfair to blame you when the superiors who could be expected to guide you have an axe to grind themselves.'

He wasn't gauche enough to turn his head to look towards the body of the court where DCI Kelso Strang was sitting, having given his own evidence. He didn't need to. He just carried on smoothly, 'I'm sure the ladies and gentlemen of the jury will understand your problem – and may even feel some indignation that you should have been put in this position.'

Choking back her tears, she made one more brave attempt. 'It wasn't like that—'

But he was turning away. 'No further questions.'

Tears were spilling over as she turned blindly to go. From the bench, the sheriff said, 'Wait, please,' and turned to the procurator fiscal, who shook his head, looking bleak. 'Thank you. Now you are free to go.'

Wiping her eyes with her knuckles, the constable blundered across the court room and Strang, his face set in angry lines, got up and followed her out. He'd recognised what was going to happen when Vincent Dunbar's cross-examination of his own evidence had been brief, almost perfunctory – the defence would claim that this was a stitch-up, with evidence being planted on their innocent client. There had been no way to warn PC Moore what was about to happen to her; she was only just out of her probationary year and QCs like Dunbar ate witnesses like her for breakfast – from the looks of him, with black pudding and a fried tattie scone on the side.

Moore was sitting on a bench, scrubbing at her eyes with a tissue. She stood up when Strang came over and said, 'Oh, sir, I'm really sorry—'

He smiled. 'Don't be. There's not a lot you can do when you're attacked by a man-eating tiger. Find a mate, have a cup of tea and slag him off. You'll feel better.'

She gave an uncertain laugh. 'But we'll lose the case . . .'

'Oh yes,' he said. 'It's happened before and it'll happen again. It just means that a small-time ned got off with it but he won't be able to resist doing it again and we'll get him next time. Forget about it.'

As Moore left, looking reassured, Strang's own face darkened. Sure, losing a case was all part of the day's work but it was the slur on his own integrity that stung. He valued his hard-won reputation as a decent copper and he'd been traduced in a public forum, with no right of reply.

One of the court officials came over to speak to him about a trial diet that would be calling the following week and before they had finished their conversation he heard cheers, rapidly suppressed, from the courtroom. He withdrew to a corner as Dunbar, sweeping his client along with him, came past in a little procession with his jubilant friends.

Disgusted, Strang followed in their wake and found himself coming up to the outside doors beside a young woman wearing an academic gown over a dark suit. He'd noticed her sitting on the bench behind Dunbar; she was tall and perhaps a little too thin, but she was vividly attractive, with fair hair and very blue eyes.

He stood aside to let her go in front and she said, with a slightly mocking smile, 'Thank you, DCI Strang. Generous, in the circumstances.'

It would be more dignified to smile insincerely and let her join the well-wishers outside but he was too angry.

'Perhaps I could ask you to tell your principal that nothing – nothing! – was planted on his client and that I deeply resent the implication.'

She skirted Dunbar's noisy group, going out of the Edinburgh Sheriff Court and onto the Royal Mile. Then she turned to him, still with the same mockery in her smile, 'Good gracious, Chief Inspector, you don't think Vincent Dunbar would stoop so low as to defend an innocent man, do you?'

He was surprised into laughter. 'Oh, of course I know, really. It's just hard to take, being smeared like that when you take a pride in honesty.'

'Dirty work, down here at the coal face. And to be honest, it doesn't get a lot dirtier than Vincent Dunbar.'

Her frankness was astonishing. 'But you're working for him?'

'I wish! I'm an advocate's devil, unpaid, and he's my devil master. Beggars can't be choosers and if you get an offer, you don't turn it down.'

Strang looked at her with interest. They were just passing a smart cafe and he said, 'I'm needing a coffee. What about you?'

'Above my touch,' she said ruefully. 'Every credit card I have is maxed out.'

'Have this on me, to demonstrate my forgiving nature. As long as associating with a police officer won't wreck your street cred.'

She brightened up. 'That's really kind. And anyway, I like cops. My mum was one till she retired.'

'Come on then.' He held open the door. 'You know my name, but I don't know yours?'

'Catriona Fleming. Cat,' she said, and led the way over to a table.

Driving on the motorway when you couldn't see wouldn't be smart so Sarah Lindsay couldn't even give way to tears as she drove home down the A1 to Tarleton. It had been a horrible, horrible experience. She'd given truthful, straightforward evidence, at considerable cost to herself, but she'd been made to look like a police stooge and a fool.

A fool. That was what Niall had said. But he hadn't just been talking about what would happen to her in the witness box; there was something else that he wouldn't tell her. What was the secret he knew but she didn't? She gulped, scared now.

What was getting clearer and clearer was that their

relationship was doomed. In the first lockdown they'd been stuck, each in their own one-bedroom flat, which had been miserable; they hadn't really been ready to move in together before, but now it suddenly seemed the obvious thing to do. And as if that wasn't risky enough, they'd had a sudden rush of blood to the head and decided they'd move to the country as well. Now Working From Home was a Thing, there was nothing to stop them.

They were both city folk but Niall had always talked about organic farming and after they'd watched his old DVDs of *The Good Life* so often that the discs started hiccupping, she'd let him convince her. The need to save the planet was becoming more urgent all the time; there was something romantic about making such a direct contribution.

Prices for flats in Edinburgh were high at the time they sold and with a combined mortgage they'd been able to buy Eastlaw, a little sheep farm that wasn't much more than a small-holding, from a retiring farmer who had run down the flock – and the house – before selling.

Starting with forty sheep had seemed manageable and after taking a course to get an organic farming certificate, Niall had been fired with enthusiasm. There was a bit of arable land too and liberated rescue hens would produce free-range organic eggs to sell.

Sarah had certainly been more wary but they wouldn't be relying on the income for subsistence; she had a home-decorating consultancy and Niall was an accountant for a large business and worked almost entirely online anyway. The farm would be like a hobby for him and she'd pictured herself rosy-cheeked, bringing in baskets of fresh eggs and bottle-feeding orphaned lambs. To breathe country air would be wonderful, especially here, surrounded by gentle green hills and woodland, with a view up the coast as far as Tantallon Castle on a clear day.

It was a clear day when they came to look at Eastlaw. She'd gripped Niall's arm and said, 'Look out there! This is just – just idyllic!' She would swear there hadn't been a day like it since.

Intoxicated with the view, they hadn't been bothered by the dilapidated state of the house that went with it. 'Oh, we'll do it up gradually. It's fun just camping,' she'd said airily to visiting friends who, while impressed by the outlook when it was visible, obviously felt it didn't entirely make up for primitive plumbing and open fires as the only source of heating.

It wasn't fun now. Organic farming was exhausting because everything had to be done the purist way, without recourse to pesticides or chemicals, and squashing bugs by hand rapidly lost its appeal. The sheep all seemed to be hypochondriacs, going into decline at the slightest excuse, and since you couldn't just give them antibiotics it meant expensive vet's visits. Sarah found, too, that she absolutely hated hens; despite their fluffy appearance they had nasty sharp beaks and so ruthlessly enforced the pecking order that a miserable victim would often be left all but featherless and the only kind thing to do was put it out of its misery. Niall hated despatching them but she'd told him he was the farmer and her job was merely to cook it – which wasn't too arduous, the poor creature being pretty well oven-ready anyway.

Discovering that rats liked eggs and ignored humane traps was almost the last straw; it wasn't long before they were bitterly regretting their decision. Niall's employer's business folded and hers dried up. They'd be destitute now if Gresham's Farms, an umbrella company for organic farms that supplied all the big supermarkets, hadn't taken them on, promising a guaranteed market for what they produced.

A certification officer had come round not long after and gave them top marks for integrity, if not for husbandry, and mercifully Jimmie Gresham had been quite happy with that, even if Sarah couldn't see how they were ever going to make it pay. With only Niall and the animals for company, she'd often thought she should have paid more attention to what she'd felt when they were watching *The Good Life*: that if she'd been Barbara Good married to the irritating Tom, she'd have killed him.

Once the virus was in retreat, she'd managed to get a cheap lease on a little shop in Tarleton to sell decorative furnishings. It barely washed its face but it gave her an excuse to escape the farm and she'd been hoping it would be a way to make local friends.

When, to her astonishment, Doddie Muir had the nerve to come into her shop and ask for a 'retainer' to keep an eye on it and protect it from 'trouble', unspecified, she'd laughed in his face. 'Chancer!' she'd said. How confident she'd been then!

He wasn't a threatening figure – bald, fairly slight,

with a receding chin – and it had seemed a quiet little town. So it was quite a shock when she found the paintwork on her shopfront scraped and scarred one day. The following week a stone was thrown through the window.

She wasn't confident after that. She asked around and, suddenly, the shopkeepers who'd been friendly enough before were less forthcoming. They didn't, apparently, know what she was talking about, though it was clear they were lying.

Eventually the quiet Asian lady, Mrs Patel, who ran the small convenience store next door said, 'It's not that much, you know. Easier just to pay.' And she didn't want to say anything more.

Niall had taken the same attitude. It left her feeling helpless and when Muir slimed his way in next time, a sly grin on his face, she'd talked terms. It wasn't 'that much', really. But everything had gone so badly wrong for them lately that even 'that much' meant giving up something else. She could have gone to the police, of course, but she hadn't any confidence that they'd take effective action – or at least, not until her shop was totally wrecked. There was no way she could find the money for repairs.

It was only when a senior policeman from Edinburgh, DCI Strang, had turned up on her doorstep that she'd mentioned the problem. He'd accepted her offer of a cup of coffee – a tall man, good-looking apart from a jagged scar that disfigured the right side of his face.

He'd wanted to know if they'd had any problem with farm machinery being stolen and she'd given a hollow laugh.

'Such machinery as we have is the sort we'd probably have to pay someone to take away.'

He'd laughed too, but warned that stealing quad bikes and even tractors was big business and suggested that it might still be as well to keep them secure. He was very easy to talk to and the conversation soon drifted on to her real problem.

He was interested immediately. When she'd explained, Strang said, 'Well, as you've obviously realised there's no way we can mount a twenty-four-hour guard outside your shop. You can always install security lights and a camera but I think you'd probably only get pictures of a stocking-mask, which wouldn't be much help. If you have the stomach for it, we could set up a trap. We give you marked banknotes, you give them to him and we take it from there.'

'Oh, I've got the stomach for it, all right,' she'd boasted. 'Anything to stop his nasty little racket.'

She'd naïvely thought that in court all she had to do was tell the truth about what had happened, not appreciating how cleverly truth could be reshaped by an advocate at the top of his game. He hadn't even suggested Sarah was lying, just that she was stupid, which felt worse.

Her neighbours were antagonistic now. They had wanted no part of it and obviously felt that as an incomer she had no right to cause this sort of trouble, and it was hard to be robust when a cheerful greeting was met with silence and a glare. And Doddie Muir, who hadn't bothered her since the police got involved, would be free to slither in next week, probably with an increased demand. He'd be feeling vindictive and she felt sick at the thought.

Now she'd have to go home and listen to Niall saying, 'I told you so.' Her heart sank as it always did when she turned off up the little road leading to Eastlaw.

From the first, she'd been horrified by the farm next door. The dogs that spent their time tied up outside with only a dilapidated wooden hut for shelter upset her, and the way the yard looked, with abandoned implements rusting where they stood and empty plastic bags left lying till the grass grew up round them, made anyone coming to visit them think they lived in a slum.

Ken Blackford, the farmer, was coarse-featured and coarse-tongued, mocking the new townie neighbours and their daft ideas. His, he had pointed out at their first meeting, was a farm, while theirs was a small-holding, inviting her to ask the difference.

'A farm makes money and a small-holding doesn't,' he'd said, and roared with laughter at the tired old joke.

The thing was, he was right – his farm was thriving, despite the disorder. His sheep produced twins and even triplets that could then be sent off to market while Niall's flock struggled even to keep up the numbers once he'd sent off his quota of lambs to Gresham's.

'Ken was born to it,' Niall said bitterly, 'and I'm having to learn the trade. And if you're prepared to use every chemical in existence it's easier, even if it's poisoning people and the environment at the same time.'

Of course, they were at a permanent disadvantage because you had to charge so much more to break even and not enough people cared about the planet to pay more for their food, when it came right down to it. It was a constant strain to meet their commitments, let alone make any serious profit. When they'd lost the turnip crop they'd been growing for winter feed to a plague of cabbage root fly, Jimmie had stepped in with a supply at cost, but that had still been money they couldn't afford to spend.

It was the rats that really got to her – those hideous, squirmy bodies and scaly tails that wriggled through her dreams at night. There were feral cats in the stackyard on Ken's farm and she'd thought they might be the answer; she put out food to tempt at least some of them over but he spotted what she was doing and bawled her out.

'They're working cats! If they can get food from you, do you think they'll bother their backsides to catch rats?'

She'd withdrawn, on the verge of tears, and from then on avoided him. He seemed to have a horrid fascination for Niall, though, and once it became legal to go back to the pub they would set off together while she sat at home miserably in the dark sitting room in front of a grudging fire – the Waterfoot Tavern was the sort of bleak, dismal Scottish pub where even if women weren't formally banned, they wouldn't want to go.

Ken was out in the yard as she drove past. Sarah didn't turn her head but she knew he was watching her, probably with the usual snaggle-toothed sneer. She gave a little shudder as she drew up beside their own house with its neatly tended garden. The inside of the house might be still a horror they couldn't afford to improve but plants had been non-negotiable.

She paused for a moment, head bowed, then reached

for her phone and texted: *Coffee tomorrow, elevenish? Please!!*

The reply was immediate. *Sure. Not good?*

Not good. She didn't elaborate; she'd tell her all about it tomorrow. Briony Gresham was her only friend and she always offered a sympathetic ear to Sarah's problems.

She switched off her phone. She had to take a deep breath and square her shoulders before she could bring herself to get out. Home sweet home.

CHAPTER TWO

Niall had gone off round the farm when Sarah had left for Edinburgh. He was feeling sick and hollow inside; she hadn't listened to him. It was such a little thing to make all that fuss about, but he hadn't been able to convince her to drop it. He'd been warned that he'd better stop her, and he'd failed.

Apart from the reason he wasn't going to tell her, he couldn't think of anything that would have been persuasive. He'd tried, 'There's a local feeling that you shouldn't be doing that,' and all she'd said was, 'Why?'

Feeling sick wasn't unusual for him: it was how he felt every morning as he went out to work on the dream farm that had turned into a nightmare. There must be an awful lot of people who, like him, were fervently wishing that they could just reset the clock to the time before the ravages of the pandemic had swept the country – many of them undoubtedly for more dreadful reasons than his. But with clear, glorious hindsight he could see this had been a terrible mistake, in every possible way. He and Sarah had been in lust rather than madly in love to start with and now they were so tired, their sex life was non-existent – at least, that was the excuse they gave. He wasn't sure they even liked each other any more.

She'd always had so much cheerful confidence. She was pretty and bright, and she was the one with the talent for business, which had suited him well enough; despite having a good head for figures he'd always been a bit dreamy – indolent, even. But in the lockdown, so much longer and harder than they had ever imagined it could possibly be, there had been nothing that she could do and it had all but destroyed her.

He was the one who'd wanted this, the responsibility for making it work was his, and he'd been forced to realise that he just hadn't the instinct for farming. He'd read all the books about it and felt all the right things emotionally – oh yes! – and he was never happier than when standing on his own land watching his Cheviots when they were safely grazing. But when it came to dealing with their day-to-day problems, he existed in a permanent state of barely-controlled panic.

Then, of course, there had been the exotic vegetables fiasco. You could charge over the odds for these and he'd prepared the ground meticulously for the planting – without ever considering whether they would be likely to thrive on an upland farm, exposed to everything coming in from the North Sea. It had been soul-destroying to see the hopeful shoots shrivel with windburn and the salty air and by then he'd missed the planting season for the crops that would grow. So no money at all, instead of the bonus he'd been dumb enough to expect.

Rats he couldn't just poison inflicted disease on the hens and sometimes even attacked the younger ones and chicks, leaving them half-dead with injuries that turned his stomach. Then there were the foxes – twelve good layers decapitated last week, after one got in through a loose plank in one of the hen houses. More money lost.

Allowing Eastlaw to join the organic farms under the Gresham's umbrella had saved them then. Jimmie Gresham had been supportive, but the bottom line still was that this was a business and the pressure of fulfilling his quotas kept Niall awake at night. He'd been worried sick when the rather sneering report on the first formal inspection – great on organic procedure, skills non-existent – came in, but Jimmie had just laughed.

'No soul, these guys! It's the farmers like you that carry the flame. You'll learn, lad!'

He'd been relieved and grateful then for his backing but every day was a painful struggle as more and more complex problems appeared and he was drawn deeper into active dishonesty. He'd always liked to think of himself as idealistic, honourable; funny to think of that now, when there were so many conflicting pressures that he couldn't even imagine what an honourable way out would be. Some days he felt as if his head was spinning.

Still, this morning at least he had jobs he could cope with; there were potatoes to lift and fencing that needed renewing down at the bottom of the hill. It was even quite a nice day for it: no wind for once, and a bit of actual sunshine.

But on the way down he saw a sheep, right at the boundary with Ken Blackford's land.

It seemed to be standing oddly, just staring into the middle distance. The sheep around it were nibbling away conscientiously; was there something wrong with it? And if there was, was it the sort of thing that would sort itself out or the sort of thing where it would need a vet – or even the sort of thing when it would just suddenly drop dead where it stood? He'd had that happen before, with all the ensuing fuss and expense.

Niall became aware that Ken was standing behind him. He turned and saw the man's patronising smile.

'You've been watching that yowe for ten minutes. What's your problem?'

He swallowed. 'Oh, just checking her out to see if she's all right.'

'You've not noticed before? That one's often in a bit of a dwam – just staring into space like that. There's folk I know the same.'

Niall laughed to cover up his embarrassment. How could Ken know his sheep better than he did himself? With exception of the ones who had a noticeable feature, like a crumpled ear, he still couldn't tell them apart.

'That's right,' he said. 'She was standing a bit longer than usual, that was all.'

As he said it, the ewe gave a little twitch, then dropped her head and began grazing. As Niall headed off to fix the fence, Ken called, 'That wife of yours – got off to the court today, did she?'

'Yes,' he said hoarsely, but didn't turn his head.

He got back to the farmhouse around four. Sarah hadn't got back from court yet and he couldn't settle to anything. He was getting more and more afraid; he didn't know what would happen now, regardless of the outcome.

He tensed when he heard her car drawing up. He was in the kitchen; he went to switch on the kettle so he could look busy and not have to meet her eyes when she came in.

'Hello!' he called as she opened the front door. 'Cup of tea?'

'Thanks,' was all she said as she hung up her coat, but from that flat, dispirited tone in her voice he could tell what the verdict had been. So would things just go back to the way they had been before? And would that be better or worse?

Niall was just so, so tired. He wasn't sure how much longer he could take it, getting more and more enmeshed and helpless. He'd always tended to ignore problems, hoping they would go away, but he'd tried turning a blind eye and it hadn't worked – it really, really hadn't worked.

It was just he couldn't see what else he could do.

DCI Strang had enjoyed 'supping with the devil', as Cat Fleming had termed it, but it was the 'not guilty' verdict he was thinking about as he drove back to the Fettes Avenue police station. It had been the sort of minor case that he wouldn't normally have been involved in; local CID would have been perfectly capable of dealing with it. He had gone there after much bigger fish. The stealing of farm vehicles was an escalating problem nationwide. He'd managed to wrap up a gang over on the west coast a few years ago and now he was following up on signs that organised crime could be expanding into this area.

Of course, quad bikes had always been an easy target for petty theft with many farmers even obligingly leaving their keys in the ignition, but larger equipment had been safe enough before. You couldn't exactly sidle up to someone in a pub and say, 'Want to buy a combine harvester?' Now, though, if you knew the right people, there was an expanding market in countries where agriculture was only just becoming more mechanised.

He'd had a hint suggesting that some of the 'right people' might just be operating from the south-east coast, with its ancient links to Northern Europe and the Baltic, and Strang had been visiting a farm where a theft had been reported and asking round locally when the George 'Doddie' Muir situation came up. Since it had been reported to him, he'd actioned it to go through, with today's unfortunate results.

As he'd said to poor PC Moore, you won some, you lost some. But he simply couldn't understand why Vincent Dunbar QC was getting himself involved in defending such a petty crime.

First and foremost, though, as he told Detective Chief Superintendent Jane Borthwick when he reached her office, he was seething about the attack on his reputation.

She was disappointingly unsympathetic. 'It's offended your vanity,' she said crisply. 'That's what's getting to you. It's hardly the first time the police have been falsely accused of planting evidence. It makes up for the occasions that you and I both know of, when one of our less scrupulous brethren has done exactly that and got away with it. You just had a nice clean pinny on and a nasty boy jumped in

30

a puddle and splashed it. The story won't be more than a couple of paragraphs on an inside page.'

She was right, of course. JB usually was. 'I still resent it but there's not a lot I can do about it, I suppose. I met his "devil" on the way out and I couldn't resist saying to her to tell her principal it hadn't been a plant and she just laughed and said he wouldn't stoop to defending an innocent man. Poor devil, I should probably say, having to work with him – she was only a kid.

'What does interest me, though, is that someone like Doddie Muir could get Vincent Dunbar to defend him. It was marked down as extortion, but Doddie's hardly the Camorra – more like the sort of bully that says he'll beat you up if you don't give him your lunch money. A local shopkeeper agreed to cooperate and got done over in court, so she'll be worried about what he'll feel free to do now. Lawyers playing games with evidence don't think about the results on the ground.'

'I doubt if you'd get your devil to go along with that,' Borthwick said. 'They look at it from the other side.'

'This one's mother was in the force, apparently. She was pretty balanced. And very hungry.'

'*Hungry?*'

He laughed. 'Unpaid and broke. She only eats at the weekends when she goes back to the family farm. I stood her a cup of coffee and she fairly tore into the scones.' He realised the boss was looking at him oddly and hurried on, 'I feel a bit guilty about the witness who was brave enough to testify – I'll need to check that the lads at Tarleton will keep the screws on Muir to make sure he doesn't give her grief.'

31

As he drove back to his house, a fisherman's cottage that looked out over Newhaven Harbour and across the Firth of Forth to the Fife coast, he found himself thinking about Cat Fleming. She had quite a mordant tongue and a refreshingly pragmatic attitude to the punters who would provide her bread and butter – 'And jam,' she had said, looking lovingly at the dollop she had just ladled onto a scone. 'And if I do it as successfully as Vince the Victorious, jam I shall have. Otherwise it's starvation.'

Kelso had laughed. He'd felt a bit like an uncle taking out a precocious niece for a treat, which was probably what had prompted him to ask if she'd like him to take her out for a feed sometime.

She'd bitten his hand off. 'Oh, please! Could it be Wednesday? Midway between weekends, so you see I'm always ravenous then.'

He was looking forward to it. But the 'niece' thought had reminded him that he was having his real niece, Betsy, for a sleepover tonight while his sister Finella and Peter, the new man in her life, went out for a meal.

After Finella's problems with Betsy's father, Mark, who had abdicated all responsibility and was even now doing time in Saughton Prison for fraud, Kelso was very protective of the women in his family but Peter seemed a pretty solid guy. Though Kelso had been on hand to stand in as a father figure, it would be better for Betsy to have someone who was there all the time.

Fortunately, Betsy seemed to have taken to Peter too, treating him to the cajoling little sideways glances, with eyelashes employed to great effect, that she'd been practising for years on Kelso. When Finella and Peter dropped her off, he was amused to see that she was enjoying having what she saw as two suitors for her favours.

'Peter lets me stay up late,' she announced with a pointed look at Kelso. '*And* I can have ice cream.'

He was impressed that Peter said firmly, 'Come on, Betsy, that was once as a special treat,' and that Betsy didn't argue, just pouting a little as she trotted off to put her suitcase downstairs in the bedroom.

'Little minx,' Kelso said fondly.

Finella smiled and Peter laughed. 'Can't argue with that. She's a good kid, though.'

Betsy came back to wave them off, then went importantly to the shelf where Kelso kept books for her.

'Now we'll choose books for bedtime after we've watched CBeebies. And I'll read the stories to you.'

He'd muttered in the past about the tedium of slogging through *Peppa Pig* and it went without saying that he was glad that his niece had learnt to read, but dear God, it was slow and boring! Insomniacs would pay good money for a recording, but if he fell asleep he'd never be forgiven.

'That's fine, Betsy,' he said. 'But let's go for a walk round the harbour and look at the boats first, shall we? It's a nice evening.'

Maybe after lots of fresh sea air she'd drop off first, but he wasn't counting on it.

When she heard Doddie Muir's key in the lock, his wife, Myrna, dried her hands on the tea-towel she was holding and went through to greet him 'Well?' she said.

'Oh aye, fine,' he said jauntily. 'Mr Dunbar saw me right.'

She narrowed her eyes. He had the sort of stupid grin on his face that she recognised immediately. 'You never drove back all the way in that condition? You're a right eejit. How good is he at getting folk off when they're caught drunk driving?'

'Oh, he'd do that right enough,' Doddie said, undaunted. 'And where's my tea? It's been a long day.' He went past her, through the hall to the little kitchen and sat down at the table that was covered with a seersucker cloth and laid with cutlery and a bottle of beer.

'It's just stovies,' Myrna said. 'Didn't know when you'd be back.' She fetched plates and began heating it up while he opened his beer and took a long swig. 'So – when are you going back to put the posh cow in her place?'

Doddie swallowed and wiped the back of his hand across his mouth. 'Off limits,' he said. 'Mr Dunbar said I'm to stay out of trouble.'

She stopped and stared at him. 'Who's he, to go telling you what to do? I've missed the money this last bit.'

He gave her a pitying look. 'He's the top man and it wasn't me paid for him, was it? And it's not just me – the word's gone out.'

'Oh,' she said flatly, slapping stovies onto his plate and setting it down in front of him. 'It's come at a bad time, then, when we're all strapped for cash. You'll have to see the boss and get him to give you overtime or we'll really be having to tighten our belts.'

Doddie scowled. 'Your belt's only just meeting so it wouldn't do you any harm. What's for sweet?'

There was a rhubarb crumble in the fridge ready to be put in the microwave but from spite she left it in there. 'There's a yoghurt if you want it.'

34

'Yoghurt!' He made a disgusted face, downed the last of his beer and got up. 'If that's all you've got for me after the day I've had, I'm off out.'

When he'd gone – to the Waterfoot, no doubt – Myrna sat down to eat her own yoghurt, her mind on what he'd said. It had been sort of a weird spell, waiting for the trial, when everyone had been kind of paralysed and she'd been looking forward to things going back to normal where everyone just minded their own business and didn't go snooping round. But an order was an order, and here in the Caddon they'd all understood that down the years, generation after generation.

Livvy Murray – DS Livvy Murray, if you please – had been feeling upbeat ever since she got the results of her sergeant's exam. It hadn't made a huge amount of difference to her daily life but it meant a welcome boost to her pay packet and she felt different, somehow. She'd tried to shrug off her previous failure, telling herself that it was just because she hadn't worked hard enough, but there had been a sneaking fear that it was actually because she was thick. Now she'd a piece of paper to prove she wasn't and it had restored her self-respect.

The pandemic had been hard for everyone and for the police, right in the forefront, dealing with people who would deliberately cough or spit in their faces, it was harder than for most. Murray had caught it early on and got it lightly – she'd had worse heavy colds – so she'd reckoned she was lucky, being probably immune even before she'd got the jabs.

There was comradeship and plenty to do in the working

day but sitting in lockdown in her tiny flat had been a depressing business, leaving her more introspective than she'd ever been before. She'd spent quite a bit of time considering what she wanted out of life.

A good police career, certainly. She'd completed the first step and she'd confidence now that she could go further. Apart from that . . .

Her social life had opened up again since the lockdown lifted and she'd even gone on a few Tinder dates, but saying she was in the police had proved a bit of a passion-killer. Anyway, no Mr Right had appeared – frankly, not even a Mr Maybe-Could-Be-Almost-All-Right, if she was prepared to cut him some slack. Most of them had come into the not-sodding-likely category.

She'd barely seen Kelso Strang over the last bit. He'd said, 'Hello! All right?' when they'd passed in a corridor and he'd made a point of congratulating her on her success, but that was all. It was high time she stopped kidding herself that he would ever see her as anything other than a not entirely satisfactory junior colleague, and after a bit of a tussle, she had. Well, mostly. It was professional respect she was hoping for, that was all – and of course she loved the challenge of being involved in the SRCS cases.

The last one, though, she'd definitely blotted her copybook. Strang had always before made allowances for her, but this time he'd actually given her a formal reprimand and it had taught her a lesson that she'd failed to learn before, about taking matters into her own hands.

Driving home after her shift, though, she was happier than she'd been for months, ever since Angie Andrews' message that DCI Strang wanted to see her about a job tomorrow. There was no indication of how long it would take; all she knew was that it wouldn't mean an overnight stay.

'It's in Tarleton,' Strang said when she reported for duty at his broom-cupboard-sized office. 'Do you know it? On the Berwickshire coast, not far off the A1, about an hour's drive as far as I can remember. There was an extortion case we lost in the Sheriff Court today – Doddie Muir, a small-time ned with a big name defending him—'

Murray had heard all about it. 'I saw PC Moore afterwards. She told me what had happened.'

Strang pulled a face. 'Was she all right? She was given a hard time.'

'She was quite – er – colourful about the QC. More hopping mad than upset, I'd say.'

'That's the way to take it. He's a nasty bit of work – I spoke to his devil on the way out and even she loathes him. I'd better explain the situation. This case only happened to come my way because I have an ongoing investigation into theft of farm machinery and I was doing a warning round of the local farms, and when I spoke to Sarah Lindsay, she told me about Doddie Muir. I was struck myself by the fact that none of the other shopkeepers who were questioned were prepared to say anything at all and I'd like to know why.'

'Scared?' Murray asked.

'Possibly. What I want you to do is go down and have a chat with the witness, try and find out what the scene is locally. You can say we're anxious to reassure her that we'll still be keeping an eye on this Doddie Muir. I may not be her favourite person after what happened but you're good at drawing people out.'

She felt a warm glow at that. 'Do my best, of course.'

'She might be more likely to open up to a woman. To tell you the truth, it's a job that could have been done by a local PC but, according to DI Gunn, the only woman who works from the Tarleton station is not, shall we say, the sort who would invite confidences.'

Murray grinned. 'I get the picture. Right, boss. Report back here?'

'You could arrange to see DI Gunn after that – you may have questions if anything arises from the interview. Remind him about leaning on Muir and ask if he's got any idea where the money for a top lawyer is coming from.'

Murray left the meeting with a warm glow. It probably felt like that if you were a Catholic when you came out from confession, assured that you had been forgiven.

'Briony! Briony!' Jimmie Gresham called on Tuesday morning.

'Yes, Dad,' Briony called back wearily from the kitchen. As she waited for his reply, she made a face, mouthing, 'Is everything in order for the party?'

'Is everything in order for the party?' he said.

When was she ever not organised when she'd been given her orders? 'Yes, of course,' she said. He was always a bit on edge when the supermarket buyers came up, but he'd been fussing about this one more than usual and she added, 'Is there likely to be some sort of problem with it?'

'No, no, not at all. Just – well, you know what Andrew's

like on these occasions. He'll pick any faults he can,' he said, coming through from the hall.

'Yes, I know.' *Just like the way you try to get one up on your brother when it's the other way round.* 'I'll check again with the caterers, if you want, just to make sure they're ready.'

'Right, right,' he said, his eyes scanning the immaculate kitchen. 'I'll get into the office, then.'

'I'll see you later,' Briony said, busying herself with checking a list. To her relief, he grunted and went off. There was definitely something bugging him, though – the guff about his brother had been an excuse.

It was days like these when she just couldn't imagine how her sweet, gentle little granny had coped with the expectations of her two large and powerful offspring – a blue tit having to minister to a pair of cuckoos.

Gran had been a mother to her since her own mother had cleared out and Jimmie had made it plain that she had to choose between going with her and staying with him. For Briony it was no contest since she'd always been a daddy's girl and whatever he did was right. Jimmie was a larger-than-life character; the fathers of her school friends always seemed vague and shadowy compared to him and she'd been proud to be his daughter.

She was proud, too, of her family's roots that ran deep in Tarleton, from the great-grandfather who was a skipper and who had been swept overboard in a storm at sea, to the grandfather who had then taken on the boat himself at the age of fourteen and given her uncle and her father the means to become the figures in the community they now were.

She could have made a career for herself elsewhere but she'd never really wanted to. As the spoilt only child, life at the farm was too pleasant for her to want to try. She'd a generous allowance from Jimmie, she could live at home and pop up to Edinburgh to do interesting charity work and meet friends while Gran did all the heavy lifting with making a home for her son and granddaughter.

Lockdown had put a stop to that, and then Gran had died. Briony, feeling all but destroyed by grief, found that Jimmie expected her to take over where Gran had left off.

It was an unconscionable shock when she found that her own wishes weren't paramount any more – not when it came to what Jimmie wanted. She'd taken it very hard indeed and things had gone a bit pear-shaped at that point. But it didn't make any difference; when she got herself back together again, Jimmie still wanted what he'd wanted before. She could make herself ill again by resisting, she realised, or she make it easy on herself and fall into line.

Her cousin Rob, Andrew Gresham's son – three years older and her partner-in-crime when they were kids – had always been her rock and they'd shared grievances as social victims of Covid who shared the same problem: fathers who used the force of their dominant personalities to impose their will.

'I'd a good business going, and everything just collapsed,' Rob had said bitterly. 'Now if I want to eat and have a roof over my head, he's got the upper hand.'

'But he's given you a proper job,' she'd argued. 'I've

just become a skivvy, organising his diary and all the professional entertaining for him as well as keeping house. If I was a boy it would be different but he doesn't rate me, despite having brought me up to think the way he does. His own comfort comes first so it suits him to keep me tied to the kitchen sink and the most I've time for is a bit of boring stuff in the farm office. Uncle Andrew isn't as bad as Dad is.'

Rob looked at her for a long moment. 'You think? Really? Just after I crawled back, we had the big confrontation – you know, the one we'd managed to avoid all these years by never having one-on-one conversations. I was dumb enough to say, "You've never loved me, have you?" And do you know what he replied?'

Briony shook her head.

'He said, "How could I? You killed your mother. A murderer before you were an hour old." Made me feel great, I can tell you.'

Briony looked at him in horror. 'That's a wicked thing to say! That could do terrible psychological damage.'

He shrugged. 'Oh, like they say, "I'm mad, me!" So I just have to get on with it. Anyway, I get on fine with Jimmie.'

He did, too. And Jimmie was like that – he got on with people, and perhaps she was just being petulant. He might be bone selfish but he'd certainly never have been cruel to her like that. Poor Rob!

Personally, though, she had no problem with Uncle Andrew, though he was quiet and a bit dour. Michelle, his second wife, was all right, though Briony was a little wary. She was quite hard, but then she'd probably had to be growing up in the Caddon among the low-lifes, and in the

Gresham family it paid not to be over-sensitive. They just had to accept that on a social evening like tonight, where comparisons could be made, a ridiculous sort of rivalry operated.

Briony glanced at her watch. Just time to make a totally unnecessary call to the caterers before going to meet Sarah at their usual cafe in Tarleton. It sounded as if she might be needing a bit of mopping-up.

CHAPTER THREE

It was nearly half-past ten when DS Murray arrived in Tarleton. Sarah Lindsay might well be at home licking her wounds but it made sense to see if she was in her shop first before driving out to Eastlaw Farm.

Her immediate impression was of a thriving town with a harbour at its heart – and a proper working harbour too, not just a marina, with what looked like a fish market at one end and quite a bit of industrial stuff and warehouses and big ocean-going ships too, tied up along the quay. Beyond it to the south was what must be the smart end – a lot of big, solid old houses as well as new 'executive' homes extending up the slope behind. Commuter land, she thought: you'd get a lot more bang for your buck here than in Edinburgh, and there was a station too. There was parking along beside the harbour so she found a space and left the car.

The main street ran along the line of the shore. Murray was always interested in the number of charity shops; they told you a lot about any town. Here there were a few, but they didn't dominate like in some places, and the stuff in the windows looked pretty good – she might even have a wee sneaky rake around later herself, if she'd time. The usual suspects like Boots and Costa Coffee featured, but there were quite a few smart gift shops as well as a couple of fashion boutiques and a very enticing gelateria. She'd noticed a caravan site on the way in so there would be tourists too, looking to spend their holiday money.

She didn't see the sign for Sarah Lindsay's shop, Interiors, so she explored a couple of side streets. Even then she didn't see it and as the main street curved uphill the shops petered out and she hesitated, frowning.

There was a narrower road that continued along the line of the shore and she could see that there was another small run of shops and crossed over to it. Here the houses were different: smaller, many of them opening right onto the street, and these shops were a bit run-down: she could see a bookies, a scruffy cafe, a small convenience store, a cheap-looking dress shop. And there, in the middle, all elegant with grey paint and white cursive writing, was Interiors.

Displayed in the window was a chair draped with swathes of what even Murray could tell were designer fabrics – the kind where if you had to ask how much it was per metre you couldn't afford it. An arrangement of silk flowers stood on a white tripod table with a classic white pottery urn on the floor beside it. There was a 'Closed' notice on the door.

She didn't know a lot about merchandising but even she could tell that this sophisticated-looking shop was in the wrong place. Admittedly, the local residents might know it was there, but repeat business for soft furnishings must be limited – how often does anyone change their curtains? You certainly wouldn't get passing trade from the visitors who might come for a browse in the classier shops. They wouldn't see anything to tempt them to cross the main road and the sort of people who did patronise the shops here wouldn't be able to afford what Interiors was selling.

Murray walked back to her car. Eastlaw Farm, next stop. You had to hope that the farm was making a living for them since she couldn't see Sarah Lindsay turning much of a profit here.

'Didn't go too well, then?' Briony Gresham said.

Sarah Lindsay's shoulders were slumped as she sat in the corner of the Rendezvous Cafe. She sat up as Briony came in with a groan.

'You could say. I've ordered coffee but if they had a licence, it'd be brandy.'

Briony sat down and nodded to the waitress for her usual flat white. 'Bad as that?'

She was – well, what Americans call 'homely', if Sarah was honest, with untidy mousy hair and a round face but she'd reached out at a time when Sarah felt she hadn't a friend in the world and been welcoming.

'Oh yes,' she said. 'Quite as bad as that. You don't realise how helpless you are in the court. This loathsome big slug of a man with a wig on could say whatever he liked but I was only allowed to answer his questions and he shut me up if I tried to explain. I ended up looking so stupid.'

'Don't tell me Doddie got off? Everyone knows about his little enterprise.'

'Yes, but "everyone" wouldn't admit it. I should have listened to you when you told me not to pursue it. Now he's just going to come back again and I won't be able to do anything about it. I'm scared, to be honest.'

Briony thought for a moment. 'He probably won't, you know. He won't be looking for more grief from the police and they'll be watching him.'

Sarah brightened at that. 'Do you really think so?' Briony was the oracle, in local matters. She'd lived in Tarleton all her life and she was totally plugged in to the local community.

'He hasn't been popular in the Caddon for drawing attention to what goes on – all the little scams and stuff. You know what they're like there.'

'Yes,' she said, a little bitterly. She knew now that taking a shop at this end of town had been a mistake: the narrow streets of the oldest part, round the original little harbour, were a sort of thieves' kitchen. 'But what I don't understand is why the victims let them do it.'

Briony gave her a cynical smile. 'Resisting isn't worth it, as you've just discovered. It's quite a well-priced and well-directed business. Doddie wouldn't try it on with the more middle-class shopkeepers. He just made a miscalculation with you.'

Sarah sighed. 'It was my miscalculation as well. It hadn't occurred to me that people would flatly deny that it was going on.'

'Ah, but you don't understand them. The rules in the

Caddon go way, way back. They have a kind of relaxed attitude to the law – you keep your head down and don't look for trouble. They're not running in the tea and brandy now, but the habit's ingrained – though actually, when I think about it, they probably are.'

Sarah pulled a face. 'I'm living in the wrong place, Briony – and I'm living with the wrong man, in the wrong business. We're broke and I'm miserable. We should just chuck it in.'

She could see the alarm on Briony's face. 'Oh, don't do that! Dad would be really upset after the way he's backed Niall.'

She'd gone too far, forgetting for the moment that she was talking to the big man's daughter. 'I know, I know,' she said hastily, adding, 'We're truly grateful to him, honestly.'

'Don't do anything drastic,' Briony urged. 'Wait till things settle down and you and Niall may be able to work things out now this stupid case is over. I'd be really, really upset to lose my friend! The shindig tomorrow with these guys here from the supermarket – you know there's going to be the usual bunch from the small farms, and you'll feel better once you've all had a good moan about how tough it is.'

Admittedly, Sarah did always enjoy Jimmie Gresham's parties. It was the only time she got to wear a posh frock, the food was always amazing and she enjoyed having the company of more interesting people than Niall. 'Is your uncle coming this time?' she said, very casually.

'Oh God, yes! If one has a big do, the other one always goes, then stands around criticising under their breath. Rob and I always swap notes afterwards – it's quite funny. And

I've ordered fish and chips canapés in little posh newspaper pokes, you should know – that would cheer anyone up.'

Sarah laughed. 'Oh, we won't be doing anything in a hurry anyway. And I'm quite happy to do my schmoozing bit to all the buyers.'

'That's my girl!' Briony said. 'Dad relies on you for that – they love someone a bit glossy and no one could say that about me.'

'Sterling qualities, though, darling – *sterling* qualities,' Sarah drawled, and they both burst out laughing; it was one of their running jokes. She'd been grateful for a friend to laugh with during the darkest months, even if she did have to be careful what she said. Briony took loyalty very seriously.

She had to hurry away after that and Sarah drove gloomily back to Eastlaw. She should probably have opened up the shop this morning but she'd been feeling a bit too raw. It had left her, though, with no excuse for not tackling the hen house that needed fumigating after an outbreak of ticks, but Niall had gone in for farm supplies and after she'd done it, she'd have the house to herself.

But as she drew up, she saw that there was a strange car parked outside and as she pulled in alongside it, a young woman got out and came over, holding up a warrant card.

'Ms Lindsay? DS Murray. I wonder if you've got time for a chat?'

Sarah's heart sank at the thought of having to go over it all again. 'Of course,' she said, a little stiffly. 'Come in.'

At least it postponed doing the hen house.

* * *

'It's an absolutely vile little place,' Sarah Lindsay said.

DS Murray had followed her through the front door of the Eastlaw Farm house and then to the kitchen at the back where she was now, sitting with a mug of coffee and a plate of Hobnobs in front of her. It had been sticky to start with: Sarah clearly felt she'd been ill-served by the encouragement Strang had given her to go after Muir and it had taken a lot of sympathetic murmuring before she'd even been invited to sit down. Once she realised that Murray's mission was to reassure her, she began to thaw, and after that there'd been no stopping her.

She'd told Murray all about their foolish belief that they could live on a view and then their awful realisation that no, you couldn't. Murray could heartily endorse that, never having been tempted to believe it in the first place, and after seeing the elegance of Sarah's shop, she was taken aback – shocked, almost – by the rural poverty she saw displayed here. The neighbourhood, with the slummy farm next door, and the dismal little house with the kitchen that didn't appear to have been touched since the seventies and was dark even on a bright day like today, was enough to leave anyone depressed. And Sarah undoubtedly was: she was a very good-looking woman, but her skin looked uncared-for, there were deep lines between her brows and she looked miserable.

Murray had heard all about their farming problems but at last she had managed to get her onto talking about Tarleton itself.

'The thing is,' Sarah was going on, 'it's two towns, really. There's the part the tourists like, and there are quite posh houses too – there's a good bit of money

49

around. That would be fine. But the end where I landed up, the Caddon – there's a sort of in-your-face brutal sullenness there. I couldn't say they made me welcome at the start, really, but they were civil enough and you have to make allowances for small communities being like that to incomers. They have their rules and after I was stupid enough to take on one of their own, it was like I was a bad smell.'

'Who makes the rules?' Murray asked.

'That's the thing. I've no idea. I've a good friend, Briony Gresham, who grew up here and she just quotes the local phrase, "Oh, it's aye been," and she sort of thinks it's funny. But it feels more than that, somehow.'

Murray filed all that away. 'Do you know many of the other farmers around here?'

'Yes, a few. The big man is Briony's father, Jimmie Gresham. He's totally into organic stuff and supplies to supermarkets. He obviously makes a bomb but it hasn't worked that way for us. It's only because he lets us sell through his business that we haven't gone under – at least, not quite. He's having a big do because there's buyers coming up and he invites all us small guys along so we can talk to them about how authentic we are. All our products are totally free from any of those dreadful pesticides – you know, the things that actually work.' Sarah spoke lightly, but the bitterness shone through.

'You're not just totally into organic, then?'

'No, I'm not,' she said with some vehemence. 'I couldn't care less. I'm sick to death of having to do everything the hard way. Look at my hands.' She held them out – well-shaped hands with long, slim fingers, but they were rough and reddened with ragged nails. 'I used to have a manicure every couple of weeks. Now I can barely afford proper hand cream.'

Murray made a sympathetic face. 'Sounds as if you're in the wrong business.'

'Oh, you think? But of course Niall can afford his nights in the pub – that's essential, apparently.'

Her tone was heavily sarcastic, but relationship problems weren't Murray's business. 'Which pub is this?'

'Oh, the Waterfoot down in the Caddon. Ghastly, spit-and-sawdust style. I'd be scared to set foot in it, after all this. I tell you, if you just went in and arrested the lot of them, Tarleton would be a crime-free zone.'

They were getting back to the point where Murray was going to have to apologise again, and Sarah was showing signs of restlessness. 'Was there anything else? Look, I've got stuff to do . . .'

Murray stood up. 'Thanks so much for your time.' But she couldn't resist adding, 'It's obviously really tough for you. What are you going to do?'

Sarah's lips tightened. 'Oh, we'll see,' was all she said, and now she'd gone to the door and was holding it open.

Murray had a lot to think about as she drove away. She could feel for Sarah; it was a rotten situation and behind those tight lips there was smouldering rage. She didn't think it would be very long till the volcano erupted.

When she arrived at Tarleton police station reception, she had little doubt that the woman PC who got up grudgingly from her seat at the back was the one who hadn't been considered likely to invite confidences. Stocky, grey-haired and granite-faced, she didn't seem to invite even the simplest of enquiries, like: 'Could I speak to DI Gunn, please.'

'Got an appointment?'

'No, but he'll be expecting me. Perhaps you could tell him I'm here. DS Murray.'

With a glare that suggested resentment at an unreasonable request, she went across to press a button on the internal telephone.

With a sidelong look at the visitor, she said, 'There's a DS Murray here – seems to think you're expecting her,' then, 'Right.' She put down the phone and went back to her seat.

DI Matthew Gunn appeared a moment later. He was young – about her own age, probably – and quite fit, but he seemed to be very nervous.

'DS Murray? Hello. Matt Gunn. Come this way.'

'Hi. I'm Livvy.'

As he closed the door to the reception area behind him, he said, 'I'm sorry about PC Thomson. She doesn't do welcoming.'

Murray laughed. 'I had noticed,' she said, following him down the corridor to his office.

'The trouble is none of us feel we can pull her up on it nowadays. She accused her previous sergeant of bullying and harassment. Everyone knew it was the other way round but none of the high heid yins wanted to hear that. The complaint was upheld and he was basically forced into retirement.'

'No point in picking a fight you can't win,' Murray agreed, sitting down. The light fell on Gunn's face as he took the chair behind his desk and she saw that he had the sort of marks of strain on his face that you wouldn't expect in a young man, and a tic was flickering at the side of his left eye. 'DCI Strang's sent me down to chat to Sarah Lindsay about what happened to her in court the other day. I don't think anyone had expected Doddie Muir would put up a top QC.'

He looked at her wearily. 'Not unheard of, actually, around here. Dunbar's got a reputation for seeing off the police.'

Murray was startled. 'Really?'

'Take that car theft a couple of months ago – open-and-shut, but Dunbar was representing that guy too and it collapsed for lack of witnesses. We're getting discouraged, quite honestly.'

He looked it, too. 'If you can't get convictions, you get to feeling it's a waste of time, I suppose.'

'Yes. The thing is—' He hesitated, then said, 'I don't know how to put this. There's something going on here, something I can't quite put my finger on. With the lockdown, everything went quiet but I don't think it meant nothing was happening.'

It seemed to be getting to him. Murray said soothingly, 'Well, I suppose crime does thrive on secrecy.'

He gave a short laugh. 'Oh yes, they're good at that here. It's been impossible to make progress even with the offences that actually come our way, and we know of plenty that don't. You won't see it reflected in the stats. Oh, there's always been a bit of low-level stuff, centred on the Caddon – that's almost a village on its own, all the old fishermen's houses round about the ancient harbour. Very picturesque, all higgledy-piggledy streets linking into each other – tradition has it this was deliberate, to give you a better chance of escape if the Excise was coming after you. But in general they were just what you'd call run-of-the-mill neds. Lockdown soured the atmosphere – not just in the Caddon either. Grassing on your neighbours got fashionable enough to keep us busy – "Jeanie So-and-So's had folk in for a party". You know the kind of thing.'

Murray nodded. 'And then you find that Jeanie and Jessie next door have been at it for years – probably their mammies were as well.'

'Yes, but it's got more like the informant culture in totalitarian states. Reporting someone seemed to be being used as a threat – ridiculous, because the most we'd give them was a gentle slap on the wrist. But there was one man came in and reported that he was being blackmailed but when we asked him what it was about, he took fright and said he'd made a mistake. We've had a lot more graffiti and vandalism, and even the owner of a popular Chinese takeaway beaten up, I guess because the virus came from China. He didn't want to report it and again we couldn't get any witnesses to come forward. It's like the neds feel they can operate with complete impunity. There were shockwaves when Ms Lindsay brought the case against Muir.'

'She's in a really bad place – very unhappy, angry, too. Eastlaw Farm's a miserable sort of run-down place and she told me she'd basically been picked on in the town here since then – she feels victimised and trapped. She talked about "rules" but she couldn't say who was making them. If they really exist, they'd have to be made by someone with a lot of clout, wouldn't they? Is there anyone you can think of?'

Gunn didn't hesitate. 'Oh, the Greshams, Jimmie and Andrew – this is their fiefdom. They're easily the major employers in town – Jimmie has a big farming cooperative and Andrew was a skipper and he's expanded into fish processing and all sorts of other stuff too. Not much love lost between them, though – the old sibling rivalry thing.'

'And would they have an interest in encouraging lawlessness?'

'Not an obvious one, I'd say – it's always seemed pretty much above board and it would be hard to see why they should. No, what I've wondered is whether one of the big guys is behind it but he's invisible – organised crime, like your boss was investigating.'

'Drugs?' Murray said. 'With all the boats coming and going, I'd have thought that might be one of your problems.'

'Oh, certainly, but that doesn't really come my way. We link up with the Cumbria constabulary and run a joint drugs unit – there's always sniffer dogs going round doing checks so it doesn't linger here – no doubt we miss quite a lot coming in but it goes out fast. It's – it's sort of worse than that.' The tic beside his eye was jumping again and he was fidgeting with a pen on his desk.

'What do you mean?'

'It just – well, it seems to have become a toxic place.'

The pen jumped out of his hand and his bending down to pick it up gave Murray a moment to think. He was clearly under considerable strain and when he straightened up, he was biting his lip.

Again, she found herself trying to reassure him. 'It's been bad for everyone lately. I suppose—'

He cut in, and he was actually shivering now. 'Yes. With

redundancies and business failures we've had suicides – inevitable, I suppose, and what must have been happening everywhere, but there was this particular one. Bizarrely, I was there when it happened. My day off, went up for a walk at St Abb's Head. Suddenly this car drove up and stopped, a young woman leapt out and ran straight to the cliff and jumped off. Didn't hesitate, just sprinted as if she couldn't get there quick enough.'

Murray felt a cold shiver herself. 'What a dreadful thing. Did she leave a note?'

'No, nothing. They said stress – she was a young doctor and they had a hard time, of course. But you see, she looked so eager, so happy. What could have made her life so wretched that a death like that was preferable? It's haunted me.'

And obviously, it had. Was he, Murray wondered, suffering from some sort of PTSD? 'It's been a terrible experience for you,' she said. 'Have you talked to anyone about it, Matt?'

He visibly pulled himself together. 'No, I'm fine, really – it was just, well – you know. Sorry, Livvy. I shouldn't be running on like this.'

'Not at all,' she said sympathetically, but she didn't think there was anything very useful she could say. Instead, she went on, 'My boss was interested in something you said about farm machinery thefts – some evidence you had?'

To her surprise, Gunn coloured up. 'Oh yes. Well, that's maybe putting it a bit too strongly. But I've been noticing that there have been reports of thefts right up and down the coast and across the Borders, and they have to get rid of the vehicles somewhere. We always have boats here that ply their trade right across the North Sea, even to the Baltic.'

'Have you anything to go on?'

'Er, no, not really. I was just hoping DCI Strang would be coming down.'

Strang would be disappointed that this very obvious conclusion was all Gunn had to offer. 'If something more concrete comes up, I'm sure he will.' She looked at her watch. 'It's time I was getting back. Thanks for all your help, Matt. That's been very interesting.'

She got up and he did too, but he was looking downcast as he said, 'Oh yes, of course. Er – is there anything you think I could be doing – about the situation here, I mean? I'm – I'm afraid they're actually becoming lawless. It's a morass of evil – anything could happen.'

Murray suddenly realised that this had all been a disguised plea for help. The man had clearly been traumatised by witnessing the young doctor's suicide and he certainly believed what he was saying about local tensions that could be dangerous. But did they actually exist, or was the tension within himself? He'd been hoping the SRCS could just come in to sort things out because he was floundering, and of course that wasn't the way it operated.

She said awkwardly, 'Well – keep your eye on it and let us know if anything useful comes your way.'

'Of course,' he said, but he looked so dejected that she added, 'Look, I'll give you my phone number. Keep in touch, Matt.'

Murray left feeling unhappy herself, as if she'd failed somehow, but there wasn't a lot she could do. Unless something did happen.

* * *

After Murray left, Gunn sat, head bowed, thinking. Victimised and trapped, Murray had said. Ms Lindsay was in a bad place – how much of this was she strong enough to take? He didn't know anything about her, couldn't tell if she was the sort of person who would say, 'Sod the lot of them' and tough it out, or if she'd let herself be driven out, or even if . . . He winced; he felt the tic by his eye start jumping and put up his finger to still it. If anything – well, happened to her, he'd never forgive himself.

Oh, as far as Muir was concerned, he'd no problem about making his life difficult – could take active pleasure in doing it, in fact – but he was helpless to stop the countless microaggressions that could make her life a daily misery.

The poor woman needed support – and of course! He knew just who might give it. On the thought, Gunn got up and walked out of the station with a nod to PC Thomson, who didn't turn her head, and set off towards the Caddon.

On this sunny day, the Caddon, given its name by the little Caddon burn that ran down from the hills behind into the old harbour, was looking like a postcard – neat stone fishermen's houses with brightly painted woodwork and the traditional whitewashed garden walls kept so bright they almost dazzled. Gunn opened a cheerful blue gate and went up the short path to ring the doorbell.

Rose Moncrieff's thin, worn face lit up when she saw him. 'Matt, how nice to see you,' she said. 'I'll just pop through and put the kettle on. Go on in.'

He went through to the sitting room. The small windows made it dark despite the pale paint on the walls but it was cleverly furnished and the cushions in jewel shades, as well as the fire burning in the grate, made it a very welcoming room.

He'd only seen her daughter Linden for those few brief moments before she jumped, but to his recollection she had looked quite like her mother, though Rose's fair hair was shading into grey and her blue eyes were faded. The responsibility he had felt after the tragedy had been illogical but he'd come round to express his sympathy and the friendship had grown. She'd been grateful for the chance to talk about her daughter and though he never shared his professional worries, when he felt things getting on top of him, a chat with her always seemed to help.

Rose wasn't popular either. There had been problems over the local surgery's practices during the pandemic and even Linden's death hadn't brought her the surge of sympathy you might have expected. And if anyone would understand Gunn's worries about a young woman being subjected to the sort of treatment Sarah Lindsay was suffering, it would be Rose.

When his hostess reappeared with coffee in pottery mugs she'd made herself in the little studio in the back yard, he said, 'Rose, I've got a problem. Can you help?', knowing what her reply would be.

'He's over there again,' Myrna Muir said. She was standing sideways-on to the window so that she couldn't be seen to be watching.

Doddie had just come in from work and was taking a beer out of the fridge. 'So?' he said.

'What's she telling him? That old bitch probably spies on us.'

'Not much she could be telling him, not at the moment anyway.' Doddie sounded wistful.

'Well – even so. I don't like having to live with a police spy right on my doorstep. She should have had the decency to move away, long ago.'

'You'll not get her out, you know.'

Myrna turned her sharp, spiteful gaze on him. 'You reckon? Haven't really tried, not properly. Yet.'

CHAPTER FOUR

DCI Kelso Strang was listening with considerable interest to DS Livvy Murray's account of her visit to Tarleton. He'd been there before but to him it had just looked like any other comfortably prosperous small town and, not for the first time, he thought how well small communities concealed that there were intense and frequently unhealthy currents swirling under the surface.

'That's pretty much it,' Murray said. 'But there's something bugging me. I'm not a hundred per cent sure that Matt's seeing this straight. He spent the whole time twitching. The girl killing herself in front of him totally spooked him.'

'It would, wouldn't it?' Strang said. 'Horrible experience. And they don't know why?'

'Just a young doctor, stressed with the pandemic. Seems OTT to me – you'd think there'd have to be more to it than that.'

'The fatal accident inquiry presumably checked it out. But anyway, tell me what he'd got on the machinery thefts? It sounded promising.'

Murray shook her head. 'Not really. Just, he'd thought with the boats that come in and out, it would be a good place to get stuff out of the country.'

It was a considerable disappointment. Strang said, 'Surely he didn't think we wouldn't have worked that out? I was hoping to put in a monitoring team if I'd got something to go on.'

'To be honest, I think he was just trying to get you down there.'

'Get me down there? What for?'

'To tell him what to do. I think he's out of his depth.'

Strang was puzzled. 'But that's not my job – he'd have to go through the usual channels, get mental help if he needs it.' It was definitely an odd one, this.

'I didn't know what to say, really,' Murray confessed. 'I think the trouble is he's got nothing proper to report because none of their cases go anywhere. When they've tried to nail someone, they can't get witnesses and if they do manage to get someone to court on circumstantial evidence, the big guy comes in and gets them off.'

'The big guy? Vincent Dunbar?'

'That's right. Matt mentioned a straightforward car theft where he was brought in to defend.'

Strang sat up in his chair. 'Was he? Was he really! I've agonised about the Doddie Muir case, wondering why anyone would go nuclear over that, and in particular wondering who was paying.'

The phone on his desk buzzed and he took the call, saying, 'Yes, I'll come now,' and pulling a face as he got up. 'I'll have to go. Nothing else urgent?'

'Don't think so.'

'Thanks, Livvy, that's been very helpful. Lots to think about.'

As he walked along the corridor to his meeting, he was indeed thinking. The police operation at Tarleton, at least in the person of DI Gunn, was clearly demoralised. If you could never make a charge stick, after a bit you wouldn't go on banging your head against a brick wall – and someone would have created a safe space where operations, serious and petty, could go on unimpeded. For any big player, a sympathetic QC's fees would be chickenfeed. But how could he find out who was actually paying them? The legal world was impenetrable to police questioning.

Then it struck him – tomorrow night he was taking Cat Fleming to an Italian restaurant to keep her from starving before the weekend. She would certainly know and she certainly didn't like her devil master.

He wasn't going to ask her, though. He was no more going to tempt her into treachery than he would offer Betsy ice cream to report on what went on between Finella and Peter.

It had been a slow morning. There had been one customer from one of the big modern houses up behind the main harbour who had looked through every one of Sarah

Lindsay's curtain sample books then left saying she was going to think about it. Which, being translated, meant she was going to check out the internet to see if she could find what she wanted cheaper.

Once she'd stacked all the books away, there was nothing to do but sit at her counter alone with her thoughts, idly aware of people passing, most of whom didn't even pause to look in the window. One or two, whom she recognised but couldn't name, directed an unfriendly glare at her as they went on their way.

The row this morning with Niall had been the worst they'd ever had and she was still feeling a bit shaky. She'd always prided herself on her composure, but there she'd been, shrieking at him.

It had all started with him reminding her about the Gresham's party tonight. 'You'll manage to pull out all the stops tonight, won't you? I was talking to Jimmie yesterday and he said he was relying on you to chat up the buyers.'

'Oh, I suppose so,' Sarah said. 'Under two conditions. One, you drive home afterwards. Two, we start working out how to sell this place and get out.'

She had known he would be taken aback. She hadn't realised he would be stunned. His jaw dropped; he stood stock-still as if what she had said had rooted him to the spot.

'But we can't!' he cried. 'We can't possibly!'

She'd started calmly. 'Oh yes we can.'

'No,' Niall had said flatly.

'I don't mean we have to do it tomorrow, but we've got to make a start soon on getting things moving.'

'It doesn't matter when it would be. We're not leaving.'

The temptation had been to start a yes-we-are-no-we're-not argument, but she controlled herself. 'It's not your decision to make. We own Eastlaw jointly, remember? We have to agree.'

'But I won't. We can't do it, Sarah, and you might as well accept that.'

'What!' She couldn't help her voice rising. 'Why can't we? Oh, I understand it might take us a while to find another sucker to buy it, but at least we could begin looking for one.'

'No,' Niall said again.

'You can't just say "no" like that!'

'I can. I'm refusing to discuss it.'

Sarah stared at him. 'For God's sake, what is all this about? I hate the place and if you're honest, so do you. You're a lousy farmer – Ken Blackford's scruffy slum is better run. Don't tell me constantly failing doesn't make you miserable, because I know it does.'

The way he looked at her gave her a bad feeling in the pit of her stomach. He looked – well, 'hunted' was the word that came to mind.

'Oh yes, I'm miserable. But we can't sell up.'

'I can't understand what this is about. Why not?'

Niall was chewing his lip. 'Too many threads,' he said. 'Threads, all criss-crossing like a spider's web.'

Such a weird thing to say! 'Explain to me what that means,' she said. 'You're starting to frighten me.'

'I can't. Just let it be, all right?'

That was when she had lost it. 'I won't let it be!' she yelled. 'We're staying right here till you tell me the truth about what's going on.'

Niall had given her a long, shuttered look, then walked out. She ran after him, shouting, 'Niall! Come back here! That won't solve anything.'

He'd acted as if he hadn't heard her, only lengthening his stride. She'd realised suddenly that Ken Blackford was standing watching with his usual sneer, and she'd retreated into the kitchen, still shaking with rage. Niall would have to come back sometime, and she wasn't going to let it rest. Sooner or later, she'd get out of him what was going on.

It wasn't pleasant, though, sitting through the long, quiet hours in an empty shop, with a sick feeling in the pit of her stomach, and the arrival of another customer was a welcome diversion. Sarah pinned on a professional smile and said, 'Hello! Do come in – how can I help you?'

The woman who came in was in her mid-sixties, Sarah reckoned, and wasn't one of the 'sixty-is-the-new-forty' brigade. The grey in her fair hair was definitely taking over, her face – thin, almost gaunt – was innocent of make-up and she was wearing jeans and a black fisherman's smock with a few ochre-coloured smears on it.

She smiled. 'I'm afraid I'm a fraud – I'm not really a customer. I'm Rose Moncrieff – I just came in to say hello. We're more or less neighbours.'

A lump came into Sarah's throat. It was the first time any of the natives had made any sort of overture of friendship, and her voice was husky as she said, 'How very nice of you! Do sit down. I can offer you a coffee but I'm afraid it's only Nescafé.'

'If there's caffeine in it, I'm good.' Rose took her seat by the counter and looked at the window display while Sarah boiled the kettle and set out mugs in the tiny back shop. 'I love that fabric! It just works, doesn't it? I'm an artist and I do enjoy good design.'

The streaks on the smock – Sarah suddenly made the connection. 'Oh, I know who you are now! I've seen your pots in the gift shop, haven't I? I'd have bought your lovely mugs if I could have afforded them, instead of these 80p ones from Tesco,' she said as she set them down apologetically.

Rose smiled. 'All you need is something that doesn't leak. I'd have dropped in sooner but I only heard what had been going on with you yesterday. I'm a social pariah so I don't get the gossip.'

'A pariah?'

'I know – sounds odd when you say it. It was a local policeman, Matt Gunn, who told me yesterday that you're another one.'

'Oh yes! I know why I am, but why are you?'

'It's a long and very sad story.' Rose paused, looking down at her coffee. Then she said, 'I'll give you a quick précis. My daughter Linden was a GP here and there was a lot of anger because the practice was sending out Do Not Resuscitate notices without consent from their elderly patients – there was even a sort of mob protest one afternoon. It all settled down eventually but later she killed herself – jumped off a cliff.'

'Oh no! I'm so sorry,' Sarah stammered.

'Yes, it was bad. Still is, really. There was no note and the fatal accident inquiry fixed on it just being stress, but—' Rose sighed. 'I still can't quite believe it.'

'Were there any other reasons?'

'None that I know. She had her own flat, and a boyfriend, but he was as bewildered and shattered as I was. He still keeps in touch, you know, though it's a year ago that it happened. We spend his visits trying to convince each other that it wasn't something we did.'

'It's a terrible thing for you to have to live with. And it's beyond belief that your neighbours wouldn't be sympathetic,' Sarah said.

Rose gave a wry smile. 'The inquiry caused a lot of trouble – police going round and interviewing people. And I think there's something about the climate here – those harsh east winds, the grey sea out there, the haars that smother the best of the sunshine – and it seems to make them a hard people. I'm what they call an incomer – I'm from the softer west coast myself and only came here after Linden got the job so I've felt very isolated.'

'Have you thought of moving?'

Rose's face twisted. 'Not really. I couldn't move away from the grief and my little house works well with the studio at the back. It's near Edinburgh where I have a lot of clients and being busy with work helps. I just keep myself to myself and go off to see old friends when I need a break. The important thing is not to let them get to me. But I've done enough talking. Now I'm going to listen to you.'

It was mortifying for Sarah that she burst into tears. Rose, unperturbed, waited until she'd finished crying and mopped up, then said, 'Tell me how it all happened.'

Sarah drew a long, shuddering sigh. 'Lockdown fever,

I suppose. I wasn't thinking straight – neither of us was. And now it's begun to feel utterly surreal, as if I'm not me any longer, as if some other woman's taken over and she's pushing me out and I won't be able to find myself again.'

Rose got to her feet decisively. 'We don't want to have this conversation here in full view. You can leave the shop for a bit – come over to my house and we can continue it.'

Sarah gave her a watery smile. 'Proper coffee and nice mugs?' she said.

'Absolutely,' Rose promised. 'I'll go over and get the fire lit as well.'

Sarah finished up, locked the door and followed. She was feeling better already.

Michelle Gresham sat in front of the dressing-table that stood in the window of the big Victorian house on the hill above the harbour, looking out to sea. It was a clear, golden evening, the sun was low in the sky and dancing reflections from the water were casting a merciless light on her face as she looked in the mirror.

She grimaced. She might be happier if she didn't subject herself to these daily encounters with relentless reality; on the other hand, knowing the worst encouraged you to do what was possible to improve on nature. She was a striking-looking woman but fifty was behind her now and she reached into her make-up drawer and got going with the concealer and illuminator.

She heard her husband coming in behind her, but he didn't speak and she didn't turn her head, carrying on with her make-up. She could feel his tension, though. He walked across to the other window and stood looking out for a minute, then paced back again to look at what she was doing. It wasn't helpful; she felt her finger slip and had to take a tissue to wipe away a smear.

He was looking at her dress too. 'Is that the one you wore to the last party?' he said.

No, of course it bloody isn't – do you think I don't know that Jimmie would say: 'I've always liked that dress'? she thought. 'No, it's a new one.'

'Right,' he said, 'That's fine,' though she doubted he had even noticed what colour it was – a warm gold that flattered her olive colouring.

With another critical look at the blusher she was putting on, he walked back to the door.

Then he turned. 'Will you be ready in time?'

'Yes, of course,' she said.

He grunted, and left. That was lucky; she needed a steady hand for her eyeliner. Giving a final brush to the thick dark hair that curled just below her shoulders, she went over to the pier glass to survey the final effect. She'd never been exactly pretty, with a mouth that was too wide and strongly marked dark brows, but she had good bone structure, good skin and thick-lashed, deep brown eyes. She narrowed them now as she looked at herself critically. Yes, she'd do.

Michelle had no illusions about what her job was on these occasions. The moment the brothers got into a room together, it was a competition and Jimmie was meant to feel a pang of envy when he saw Andrew with his glamorous wife.

She was fairly sure that was the only reason Andrew had married her. He'd been a widower for some time and it was only when Jimmie's wife had left him that he'd decided to regularise the informal relationship they'd had for a couple of years, when she was a secretary in the Arcturus Group.

There was a local rumour that he'd been devoted to his first wife but her own marriage, she had often thought cynically, was based on credit – she would be a credit to him, and he would never query the total on the credit card. She felt it was a fair enough exchange; Andrew was clumsy and often tactless, but he wasn't unkind to her. It was only on nights like this that his expectations became oppressive.

As the Gresham first-born he'd gone into fishing with his father, Robert, and was given his first boat, *Arcturus*, as soon as he was fit to skipper it. When Robert died, he'd inherited the boats and made the most of his opportunities, successfully expanding into processing and supplies. Jimmie, five years younger, had no taste for the rigours of the life and his legacy was a farm instead.

Fishermen in those wild northern seas, defying death as they rode the storms to bring back their silver treasure, were to Andrew real men; rejecting that life for farming was the mark of a weakling. Michelle knew he found it hard to disguise his contempt and the fact that Jimmie had been equally, possibly more successful in building a business, wasn't right, somehow.

As for Jimmie, he was the typical younger sibling, whose one aim in life was to catch up with the brother who had five years' life advantage, and preferably pass him.

Which, reflected Michelle, made it stressful for the women in their lives. And the odd thing was, in a way they were close, constantly in touch, but too similar in character for it ever to be an easy relationship.

She picked up her evening bag and wrap and went downstairs, where Andrew was already waiting in the hall.

They'd be going round to pick up Rob from the house in the Caddon that had once been hers but latterly a holiday rental, fortunately free at the time he'd come back to Tarleton. They'd be sharing the driving, naturally. Andrew would drive there; she would drive home. Rob would loll in the back.

It wasn't ideal – father and son hadn't had a happy relationship since Rob, too, had rejected the idea of going to sea, and Andrew resented the easy relationship Rob seemed to have with Jimmie. There would be tension in the car, but the traffic police around here were pretty savage and if Rob was done for drink driving, his father would go radge and she'd have to bear the brunt.

'Oh, there you are,' Andrew said, though in fact it was five minutes before the time he'd decreed. He strode out, leaving her to lock the front door, and the engine was running by the time she got into the car.

Another fun evening.

Sarah Lindsay, too, was studying her face with some anxiety, though the cramped bedroom was so dark that she had to stand by the little window holding a magnifying mirror in her hand.

What she saw there gave her no pleasure and she groaned as she reached for the stub of an eyeliner pencil and did what she could to emphasise the dark blue eyes that were her best feature.

She still had her Bare Minerals make-up – there hadn't been much call to use it – though she could have done now with heavier coverage to conceal the weather damage to her skin. Her hands – well, there wasn't much she could do about them, apart from neatening the nails. She had a lump in her throat as she looked at them – when had Sarah Lindsay ever gone to a party without painted nails? But the last thing she wanted was to draw attention to them.

She hadn't had her highlights done for years but luckily her hair was naturally honey-blonde. When she scooped it up into a knot, there were wisps that curled naturally round her face and when she had finished off with a slick of what was left of her precious Hermès blusher, she felt the effect was the best she could hope for.

Sarah was feeling better after her talk with Rose. They'd sat in her charming little sitting room eating toasties for lunch and now she was feeling more like herself. She had been losing all sense of proportion; she just needed to keep calm and work gently on Niall until she could persuade him to tell her what the problem was.

She was looking forward to the evening as a break in the dreary monotony of life, and she secretly admitted she was hoping that Rob Gresham would be there. Through Briony she'd met him a few times and he was more interesting than anyone else she'd met in this godforsaken place. She pined for civilised conversation!

She glanced at her watch, then frowned. Where was Niall? He should have been back and changed by now. It wouldn't do to be late for Jimmie's party – when the buyers came up as they did, from time to time, it was always a big deal and he liked to wheel them round the small farmers like themselves so they could impress the visitors with their zeal for everything organic. And of course a bit of cynical eyelash-fluttering at the middle-aged ones always kept them sweet.

She put away her make-up and went over to the long mirror on the back of the bedroom door for a final assessment. She had to move her dressing-gown aside to do it; she'd taken to hanging it there so that she wouldn't keep catching an unexpected glimpse of the sad, shabby creature she'd become. Now, though, she reckoned she'd scrubbed up pretty well, considering.

But where was Niall, FFS? They were definitely going to be late and Jimmie would be offended. Suddenly, she started feeling sick all over again.

Briony Gresham looked round the drawing room, just beginning to fill up with people, neighbours as well as professional contacts, since Jimmie liked a crowd. It was a long room on the first floor of the handsome farmhouse, built in the early nineteenth century for a gentleman farmer, and its long, low windows looked out to the Lammermuir Hills, bathed in the glow of the setting sun.

That earlier owner had been supported by the income from half a dozen satellite farms as well as his own, and it had been Jimmie Gresham's pride that he had the same number now under his umbrella, even if he didn't actually own them. Four of these would be represented tonight, one of the bigger ones and the other three fairly small, with owners like Niall Ritchie who were young and keen. One had even come all the way from Jedburgh to be here tonight.

Briony knew Jimmie particularly cherished those, which was why Sarah really must be talked out of selling up.

Another young farmer was standing in animated conversation with one of the buyers, along with his earnest-looking wife, who was wearing a sort of caftan-thing that looked as if she had run it up herself – very commendable, though perhaps a colour that wasn't purple would have been more flattering to the high colour in her cheeks.

For some reason, her father had been anxious about this evening. There'd been some sort of fuss yesterday – she'd heard raised voices and though she didn't know who Jimmie had been talking to or what it was about, she could tell something was still bothering him. He was always exuberantly genial when he was hosting a party but tonight he was overdoing it a bit.

Sarah and Niall hadn't arrived yet and nor had the other Greshams. The waiting staff were coming forward now with the dinky canapés – the promised fish and chips in their tiny paper cones, delicate tartlets gleaming with shrimps under aspic, little squares of rye bread topped with smoked salmon and trout caviar. The trays were emptying whenever they reached the guests and Briony saw Jimmie stop his glad-handing to give an anxious glance towards her. She masked her irritation with a reassuring smile, though for heaven's sake, he should know they wouldn't be going to run short.

And there were the Andrew Greshams now. They made a handsome couple: Michelle, tall, looking a million dollars as usual, Andrew rugged, six-foot plus. A man with the sea in his blood, Briony always thought, with grey eyes that looked as if he was scanning the horizon for storms. At the moment they would be scanning the room for any shortcomings in the provision for his brother's guests. Luckily at that moment a fresh lot of trays was borne in, with little cheese beignets, pheasant patties and prawn tempura, and Jimmie came across to them, gesturing to a waiter to bring glasses and indicating the plenty with a sweeping gesture.

'Come on now, tuck in! You've drinking time to make up. Some of this lot are well ahead of you!'

Behind them, Rob Gresham slipped in, making his way over to Briony, murmuring, 'Nice one he got in there, suggesting we were late. He's got Dad bridling already.'

Briony giggled. 'Has to make up somehow for being three inches shorter. I'll have to circulate – can't waste my time making subversive comments to you.'

'Who am I going to talk to, then?'

'There's Heather there – I could introduce you,' she said, indicating Purple Caftan.

'Gee, thanks.' He was looking round the room. 'Where's your pretty friend?'

'Don't think they've arrived yet. Oh no, there she is now! Sarah!' she called. 'Over here!'

Sarah was hovering on the threshold. There was no sign of Niall and Briony realised that she was looking stressed and made to go to her, but Jimmie got there first.

'Ah, Sarah! Good to see you – ravishing as always,'

he said, giving her a kiss. Then he half-turned, gesturing towards a plump man in an ill-fitting suit who came forward, beaming. 'I've got someone I want you both to meet. Ron here is one of these guys who makes sure we all keep up our organic standards. Ron, this is one of our idealistic couples with these farms that put us all to shame with what they do with very basic resources.' Then Jimmie looked around. 'But where's your young man?'

Sarah gulped. 'I – I don't know! He hasn't come back to the house. His car's there and I went out to look for him but I couldn't find him.'

Briony stiffened – Jimmie hated unpunctuality and she thought he was looking a little tense, but he only said, 'Now, now, my dear, don't worry. We all know a farmer's life isn't his own. Let's find you a drink and you can chat to Ron here until he arrives.'

Sarah produced a big bright smile and obliged, but Briony could see that she was on the verge of tears and hurried over. Once she'd managed to palm Ron off on another guest, she murmured, 'All right?'

Sarah's voice was shaking. 'No, not really. Niall wouldn't be late – he was fussing away about it this morning. Briony, we had the most terrible row today. I'm worried.'

'I don't think he'd deliberately miss the party because you had a row,' she said soothingly. 'He's probably just had to deal with a sheep that's landed on its back, like they do. He'll no doubt turn up later and he'd hate it if you'd made a fuss.'

Sarah was hesitant. 'Do you really think so?' she said.

'Absolutely. Come on, have another drink and circulate

for a bit and if Niall still hasn't appeared you can just slip away. He'll be back at the house by then and if he's worried about missing this you can tell him Jimmie will understand. If you have a "cowpit yowe", you have to get the poor beast back on its feet before you leave it.'

'It's certainly plausible,' Sarah said hesitantly.

'That's my girl,' she said. 'And look, here's Rob coming over to chat you up.'

Sarah managed a smile for him and Briony left them to it. But she was concerned; Sarah was blatantly unhappy at Eastlaw and if they were having dramatic rows, she could guess what they were about. Oh dear!

CHAPTER FIVE

Kelso Strang had given some thought as to where he should take Catriona Fleming and had chosen an Italian restaurant as the sort of place that would appeal to a young person with a hearty appetite. She'd been very appreciative.

'This is wonderful. I'll try to be delicate and not eat you out of house and home but Vincent kept me rushing around all through the recess so I haven't eaten since breakfast,' she said apologetically as the waiter came to take their order.

He assured her he could stand the strain. There were breadsticks on the table and he pushed them towards her. 'You can start with these. Difficult day, then?'

'Oh, he was in an absolutely stinking mood the whole time. He can see he's losing.'

'Oh dear. What went wrong?'

'The acting fiscal was a QC too and she's wiping the

floor with him, to be honest. The client's going to go down for quite a stretch and his brief's fed up – he's made his living out of representing members of that family for years and he'll be well ticked off if this makes them unsettled.'

'So they keep him busy?'

'Oh, yes. If you've ever watched *Rumpole*, they're the Timsons to the life. It's been a nice little earner for Vincent too so he had to be apologetic and chat up the solicitor in case he decides to take the business elsewhere next time, and Vincent hates being nice to anyone. He took it out on me and I've got a pile of stuff to do now before court tomorrow.'

'It's quite a demanding job, isn't it? What made you decide that was what you wanted to do?'

Cat nibbled thoughtfully on a breadstick. 'It just sort of crept up on me. I think it was partly to do with my mum – you know I said she was in the police?'

'Yes, I was interested. Tell me about her.'

'She was pretty cool actually. She was a DI and she did quite a lot of heavy-duty stuff – murders, sometimes, and she'd a big reputation for getting her man – or woman, of course.' She frowned. 'Perhaps you should say, "getting her person", but it wouldn't really work, somehow.'

He laughed. 'Not really. Is she still in the force?'

'No, retired a few years ago. She'd this idea that they could get into having continental holidays but Dad hates being away from the farm. Apparently all he did was check out the field management and livestock and compare them unfavourably with the standards at Mains of Craigie. The Sistine Chapel was wasted on him, apparently.'

'To tell you the truth, I was underwhelmed by it myself,'

Kelso confessed, 'but I'm careful who I say that to.'

'I'm good at keeping secrets. Mum basically gave up the struggle and retired and then someone grabbed her to go in when the police have mucked up an investigation so she can tell them what they've done wrong. It's a bit like Dad with foreign farmers, actually – she compares them with what it was like in her day in the Kirkluce CID.'

Kelso was amused by the idea. 'Can't say I've ever thought of the Police Investigations and Review Commission in quite that way, but it would explain a lot.'

'Oh, she's very bossy. I was the rebel, constantly taking her on. It was what made me do a degree in social work – it really riled her when I went on about you lot being all about punishment and what the bad guys really needed was sympathy and understanding.'

He felt obliged to defend his calling. 'Sure they do, but by the time they come our way it's too late to do a lot about their difficult lives and we're stuck in the middle with innocent victims who need sympathy and understanding too – and dare I say it, justice.'

Their starters arrived, but it didn't interrupt the discussion. Cat said, 'You know this, you'd get on with my mother. You must meet her sometime.'

Suddenly Kelso felt very, very old. 'Perhaps we just have the same professional outlook,' he suggested, a little feebly. 'But you didn't stay on in social work?'

'Er, no.' She was looking a bit embarrassed now too. 'Well, I realised you never really got anywhere – just bogged down in writing endless reports that didn't seem to make any difference. And if I'm truthful, I got a bit cynical. I began to realise that the understanding was all very

81

well but sometimes what the punters needed was straight talking rather than sympathy. There's this criminal defence advocate – he let me shadow him for a couple of weeks. His main aim was to keep them out of jail as long as possible and let them get a bit more mature, but he could be pretty damn ruthless if he was being mucked about. It just blew me away – he was achieving far more than I could in my work and by the end of it, I was – well, totally hooked. So I have to put up with the dreaded Vincent.'

Her eyes were shining as she said that. She was so young! That sort of idealism was very touching; he'd had it too, a long time ago, and it was sad that the hard realities of life tempered it as you got older.

'Well, good for you,' he said.

She gave him a sharp look. 'I really am all grown-up, you know.'

Kelso felt himself colouring. 'I'm sorry – did that sound patronising? It wasn't meant to be.'

'Not exactly patronising. Sort of benevolent, I suppose. And you're not entitled to rock benevolence until you're at least fifty so if you fancy it, you'll have a disappointingly long wait.'

'I'll take that as a compliment,' he said lightly but in truth the age gap between them seemed wider than ever.

The *coteleta alla Milanese* arrived. While Cat made appreciative noises, Kelso couldn't help wondering if she and the advocate were an item, but he couldn't really ask that. Instead, he said, to change the subject, 'And is your dad still farming?'

'Oh absolutely. You couldn't stop him – it's in the blood. But he's basically handed over to my brother Cameron to do the heavy lifting and he fills in the gaps.'

'Hang on,' Kelso said. 'Cameron Fleming – is he the rugby player?'

Cat pulled a face. 'Was. He was going to be in the British Lions squad, but he got an injury just a couple of weeks before.'

'I remember reading that in the papers. Terrible bad luck.'

'Yes, sort of. But there was an Aussie lass who'd come to help out on the farm while he was away, and now they're married and living in the Mains farmhouse. Mum and Dad have done up a couple of what used to be farm cottages. Mum's delighted – housework was never her thing.'

'I can imagine,' he said, just as the waiter came to take orders for puddings and he saw her glancing at her watch. 'Do you want to wait for that? I know you've a lot to do.'

'There's tiramisu,' she said wistfully. 'But if I waited for that I'd have to gobble and git. It'd be a bit rude.'

He burst out laughing. 'You're allowed. It'll give you energy for the night with the wet towel round your head. Will you get a breathing space after that or are you going to be plunged into another big case?'

The words were no sooner out of his mouth than he realised that was dangerous ground.

If she told him Vincent had another case from the Tarleton area, he wouldn't be able to ignore it, but he'd vowed not to be drawn into using her.

Fortunately, there was nothing of interest to him in Vincent Dunbar's upcoming briefs and once Cat had her pudding, she said, with what definitely looked like reluctance, that she must go.

They were headed in different directions. As Kelso kissed her on the cheek, she flung up her arms to hug him.

'Thank you so much! That was amazing. You've done your good deed in feeding the hungry and I had such a good time.'

He had too. But mindful of the advocate – and the fool he'd made of himself last time when he'd taken out a young inspector – he didn't suggest another evening, except in the most general way as they parted.

It was a pity she was so young. She was such an entertaining companion but cradle-snatching was distinctly distasteful – and he was still wincing at her comment about him getting on with her mother.

The farmhouse was in darkness when Sarah Lindsay arrived at Eastlaw. The weather had turned and a cold, determined rain was falling as she jumped out of the car and scurried to the front door.

She'd been feeling optimistic. She'd had more drinks than she really should have and Rob Gresham had cheered her up too, pointing out all the sudden emergencies a farmer might have to deal with. She knew what they were as well as he did, but when he spelt them out it had seemed a more rational explanation for Niall's absence than her own over-emotional reaction had been.

She'd let herself be convinced that she'd find him here, seething that he'd had to miss the party. She hadn't expected all the lights would be out but, of course, she told herself firmly, given that he'd be getting up at six he could just have gone to bed once he realised it was too late to turn up. Even so, her heart started to beat faster as she hurried upstairs to the bedroom and switched on the light.

Niall wasn't there. The room was exactly as she had left it, the day clothes she'd taken off still scattered on the bed.

She'd driven home feeling mildly tipsy; suddenly she was stone cold sober. Niall's car was still parked outside so where could he be? Round the farm, was the obvious answer. But now, after eleven, when it was pitch black out there? She peered out of the window, hoping to see the light of a bobbing torch, then ran downstairs and out into the yard.

There was nothing to see, only smothering darkness, and rain, falling more heavily now with a chilling breeze. Farms are dangerous places; Niall could have had an accident and be lying helpless somewhere. But where? Sarah called his name a few times but as her voice was swept away by the gusting wind, it felt futile. She retreated to the shelter of the house, with the fear she'd managed to push away earlier creeping back – a dark predator lurking just out of her line of sight.

She had dumped her handbag on the hall table as she came in and now she rooted in it for her mobile. She'd checked it a couple of times during the evening to see if there was a message from Niall. There hadn't been and there wasn't now. She called his number but it rang out.

Could Niall have left her a note, even sometime before the party, and she hadn't noticed it? If he had, it might explain what had happened – but that might be the worst news possible. She had to steel herself to open the kitchen door and switch on the light.

There was a mug she'd used upside down on the draining board where she'd left it.

Nothing else. No note. No sign that he'd come back to the house.

Her legs gave way and she collapsed onto a chair at the kitchen table. She needed to stop panicking. *Think, for God's sake, think!* But what was she to do? Where to begin?

The only certainty was that he hadn't left the farm. And then it hit her – it was even possible he hadn't left the house. She would have to check, open every door, terrified of what she might find. And she would have to do it now.

Sarah stood up, then sat back down again abruptly. She felt as if she was floating; she had to slump right down with her head between her knees until she felt confident that her legs would hold her. Then, shakily, she left the kitchen and went through to the sitting room.

In the glare of the overhead light, it looked bleak. It always did, despite her efforts to brighten it up; tonight, untidy and with a dead fire, it looked even worse than usual. But empty.

She'd seen the bedroom already. That only left the bathroom and the spare bedroom and as she climbed the stairs she was starting to hyperventilate. Was some horror waiting for her? And even if there wasn't, what would she do if he wasn't there either?

He wasn't.

Sarah was feeling so dizzy that she had to grab for the stair rail on the way down. She needed to get her head together. Tea – that was the traditional treatment for shock. At least it gave her something to do: she boiled the kettle, got out a mug and a teabag – no, two, and let it brew before she sat down at the table with her drink. The strong, scalding-hot liquid seemed to help and now she had to try and think it through. What could have happened?

Niall could just have had a brainstorm brought on by stress, forgotten about the party and gone off carousing with Blackford. But it wasn't comforting that this seemed better than the alternatives – and anyway, now she thought about it, she'd seen Blackford's jeep outside.

He might well have had an accident. If he had, he might be alive and lying injured somewhere and if he didn't get help he might die. But she didn't know where to begin to look – and he could be dead already.

And now she had to face up to the other possibility. What kept repeating in her head was the phrase, 'I hope he hasn't done something silly,' the phrase everyone used to avoid spelling the 'something' out. She'd been very uneasy when Niall hadn't come in to get ready for the party but it was still just a nasty feeling, and knowing the importance Jimmie Gresham placed on his parties, it hadn't seemed wise to piss him off by failing to turn up without a definite reason. Then when she'd got there she'd let herself be reassured by Briony and Rob.

But they hadn't known how bad the quarrel had been, or how weird Niall had sounded when he was talking about spider's webs. He had somehow felt trapped – and of course she felt that too, but she was willing to break free by selling up and leaving. He wasn't. He'd said they couldn't. So he'd no way out – except the way she was starting to believe he must have taken.

Outside, the wind was getting up, making an intermittent wailing sound like a child sobbing. Ken Blackford was next door but his lights too were out. Could she knock on his door, wake him, ask him to help her mount a search?

Eastlaw was a small farm, admittedly, but there would still be a lot of ground to cover – all but impossible, in these conditions. As if to make the point, a squall battered the window as if someone had thrown a handful of pebbles.

Was she just going to have to sit through the long, agonising hours of darkness until first light?

Then the phone rang.

Briony Gresham saw the caterers out, then came back through to the drawing room. It had been restored to order before they left and, as usual after a party, Jimmie was sitting in his favourite armchair with a final drink – a generous slug of Macallan – waiting for her to join him for their customary party post-mortem.

Briony poured a less ambitious one for herself and flopped down opposite, leaning back and stretching out. 'I'm absolutely shattered. It went very well, though, don't you think? I told the caterer the canapés were a triumph – everyone was talking about them. Even Michelle asked for the name of the firm, so no doubt they'll be copying us at their next party.'

Usually that was catnip for Jimmie, but tonight he barely noticed. 'Yes, yes, it was fine,' he said.

And thank you, Briony, for all your efforts, he didn't say. She tried again. 'Bruce and Heather are ever so keen, aren't they? They were obviously enjoying themselves – though I did think Heather might be wise to consider what alcohol and excitement does to the complexion! Her face was almost the same colour as that alarming garment she was wearing. I did offer to introduce Rob to her but he was reluctant, for some reason.'

'Yes,' Jimmie said, though Briony was fairly sure he couldn't have repeated what she'd said back to her. He was frowning down at his glass and she could guess what the problem was even before he said, 'Not really good enough, young Ritchie not turning up for the party.'

'Probably something cropped up on the farm,' Briony said. 'You know how it is – and Sarah came and did her stuff.'

'Yes. But I didn't think she was really her usual bright self. Problem there, would you say?'

Briony hesitated. 'I think she'd got herself a bit worked up. She said they'd had a row earlier and she was obviously worried about him missing the party, but I persuaded her to calm down – after all, the last thing Niall would want was a big fuss because something had cropped up to delay him, and she seemed to realise she was over-reacting. Actually, I was relieved that he didn't come – if they'd carried on with their domestic for the benefit of the assembled company, it wouldn't be a good look.'

'Certainly not. It was awkward enough already – Ron had been wanting to talk to Niall and I'd been going to suggest he went down there tomorrow morning for a cup of coffee and a chat. In fact . . .' Jimmie glanced at his watch. 'Sarah will only just have got back. If I checked with her tonight, I could tell Ron to head down there after breakfast. Got her number?'

Briony went to fetch her mobile. 'Do you want to speak to her yourself?'

'No, no. You just make the arrangement.' Jimmie sank back in his chair, closing his eyes.

'Sarah?' Briony said when the phone was answered.

'Well, has the wandering boy returned?' She had spoken lightly, but listening to Sarah, her smile disappeared. 'Oh no!'

Jimmie opened his eyes and sat up. 'Something wrong?'

'Niall's missing. She thinks something must have happened to him.'

One of the farm workers had to be summoned from his bed to take the Greshams across to Eastlaw: there was no way either of them would have been fit to drive for some hours yet. When they set off, the storm was blowing hard and Wattie Johnston, still sleepy and unfamiliar with the narrow, twisting roads, was cautious. By the time they reached the farm there was a noticeable lightening in the sky and the wind was dropping, at least a bit, though it was still raining hard.

At the first sound of the engine, Sarah rushed out and by the time the Greshams' car turned into the yard she was soaked through, with her teeth chattering. Briony jumped out almost before the car had stopped and ran across to put her arms round her. 'Oh, poor Sarah! Come on, let's go inside. You're shivering!'

'I–I don't know if it's cold or terror,' Sarah stammered, dropping her head onto Briony's shoulder. 'Thank God you came. I don't know what to do!'

Briony swept her through the back door into the kitchen. 'It's all right – Dad's here. He'll take charge and Wattie Johnston brought us so they'll both get out whenever it's light enough. Don't get too stressed – Niall could just have sprained his ankle, you know.'

Sarah turned as Jimmie Gresham appeared, followed by

the driver. Her kitchen suddenly seemed much smaller as the two big men came in, and now she felt, of all ridiculous things, embarrassed.

'Oh, I'm so sorry, Jimmie,' she found herself saying in a brightly social tone. 'Awful to have dragged you out like this. Thank you so much for coming over.'

He came over and patted her hand. 'Not at all, my dear. Don't worry, we'll find out what's happened. And don't you go assuming the worst! There's probably quite a simple reason – fallen awkwardly or something. And I know it was a bit of a wild night, but Niall's a fit young man and may even have managed to get himself to a bit of shelter. Now, have you any idea where he might have been working? Did he mention anything before he went out?'

'No,' she said. 'I was actually out for lunch and he wasn't around when I came back, but I only got a bit concerned when he wasn't there when we should have been setting off for your party.' She only just stopped herself from saying the automatic, 'Thank you for having me.' She was definitely losing it.

'Right,' Jimmie said. He bent to peer out of the window. 'I think it's pretty much light enough to see where we're going. Have you any torches, though?'

'I'll get the one from the car,' Wattie said and went out as Sarah fetched the two that were always kept in the cupboard by the back door.

Jimmie looked at them. 'One's Niall's – right? So he didn't go out after dark, then.'

There was a heavy feeling in her chest, making it hard to breathe. 'The thing is, there isn't any sign that he's been here any time today.'

The remark seemed to fall like a stone. Briony turned very pale; Jimmie said nothing for a moment. Then he said, 'Right, we'd better get going then, hadn't we? You wait here, ladies – make us a cup of tea, if you like.'

Sarah's bristling was instinctive. No one talked like that any more – but just for a minute she felt tempted into cowardice. She could stay here with Briony to hold her hand, waiting for bad news to come to her, if bad it was, instead of taking the risk of making some hideous discovery. But if she accepted, she'd think the worst of herself – and she wasn't exactly feeling good about herself right now.

'I know the farm better and I've got wet gear,' she said firmly. 'If you stay here, Briony, we can all call in to you.'

Briony made a token protest as she watched Sarah preparing, then gave her a hug as she got ready to join the men, putting on their own jackets and boots at the car.

'I'm sure he'll be fine,' she said robustly, but it didn't fool Sarah. Briony no more thought that than she did herself.

As she stepped out into the chilly half-light, she saw Ken Blackford walking across to speak to the two men. Farmers were early risers, of course, but she always had the uncomfortable feeling that she was being spied on and he'd arrived remarkably promptly. Still, it would make another body to help in the search and she forced herself to go over and look grateful.

When she reached them, Jimmie was asking whether he had seen Niall at any time the previous day, but the response hadn't been helpful. Ken had been away at a stock lamb sale in Kelso and had only seen him briefly near the house early on.

Together, Jimmie and Ken started laying out a plan,

heading off in different directions, while Sarah stood by herself, trying to fight down the sick feeling that was building. At last Jimmie turned to her.

'Why don't you check the barn – if you can tell what equipment he might have taken out with him, it would give us a steer, and you can call it in to Briony.'

She nodded, unable to speak. He was assuming that this was another of the regular accidents that happen on any farm, wasn't he, and he was still trying to protect her, but she couldn't believe he was right.

The more she had thought about it through those dark hours waiting for help to arrive, the more convinced she'd become that it hadn't been an accident. She'd gone to check the kitchen knives and none were missing. He didn't take medication. He didn't own a gun. If he had decided to take his own life, there was the barn right there, with the pulley and tackle for lifting heavy weights.

As Sarah dragged herself towards it, she noticed suddenly that there were hens around, picking their way out of the hen houses as the light strengthened. Niall couldn't have shut them up last night. If the fox had been around, there'd be carnage in there . . .

Too, she found herself adding. Nausea overwhelmed her and she vomited. Afterwards, gulping and coughing, she was thankful that at least the men had moved off – then she felt a prickle on the back of her neck and she swung round. Ken had been watching her humiliation; he only walked on when he saw her looking.

She still had to check in the barn and deal with whatever might be in it. Despite that policeman's warning, they didn't keep it locked – the equipment they had wasn't worth stealing – and she swung back one of the great wooden doors with shaking hands and stepped inside, the familiar smell that was a combination of dry hay and animal foodstuffs prickling her nose and her raw throat. High above her, the beams and the rafters soared and she closed her eyes for a moment in a silent prayer before she looked around for what she had expected to see.

But there was nothing. With her overactive imagination she'd pictured it so vividly – Niall's body swinging there in the great, airy space – that for a moment she was shocked, struggling to accept that it wasn't there. She'd been wrong – and now it looked as if Jimmie had been right and it was after all just another farm accident to add to the statistics. Not that it would make her feel better: what if he'd only been hurt, and if she'd sounded the alarm last night . . .

Time enough for guilt later. She scanned the equipment: tractor, quad bike, forklift truck – all there, nothing to suggest what Niall might have been doing. There was just the little store where he kept some tools to check on what might be missing from there before she went back to the house and waited for news from the others. Sarah went out and pulled the doors over behind her.

It was getting light and the rain was going off. She pushed back the hood of her oilskin jacket and, still feeling sickened by the disgusting taste in her mouth, she was glad of the fresh air on her face.

Ken was watching her, standing among the sheep in the near field. 'All right?' he called.

Stupid question, when it was so far from all right that it was taking all her strength to hold together. She forced a smile. 'Nothing helpful there.'

'Right. I'll carry on, then,' he said and walked on down the hill, but then she saw him give an apparently casual glance over his shoulder.

The shed was a tiny, ramshackle building with a corrugated iron roof, shelved and with barely enough floor space for a rotovator and some hand tools. It would only take a minute to check it and Sarah's mind was on what Niall might have been using yesterday that might help focus Jimmie's search when she reached it.

She hadn't been inside it herself for years. The door was on the latch and as she pushed it open, the first thing that caught her eye was a giant plastic bottle of weedkiller on a shelf, and she gave a gasp. That had no place on an organic farm – nor had the pesticides ranged beside it, nor the sack of chemical fertiliser on the floor. Stunned, she tried to open the door wider but it was sticking – well, not exactly sticking, it was just that something offered some resistance as she pushed it back to let her work her way round it and step in.

The something in the way was bobbing behind the door, something hanging from a hook in the low roof, something with a darkly suffused face, blood-red eyes and a purple, protruding tongue. Something that was, or had been, her partner Niall.

In the grip of horror, Sarah couldn't even scream. The world rocked around her and as she swayed, she heard Ken's voice behind her saying, 'It's all right, I've got you.' Then everything went black.

CHAPTER SIX

DI Matt Gunn had arrived at the Tarleton station promptly for his shift. He'd decided to work out of Tarleton today; he'd promised DS Murray to lean on Doddie Muir and it would do no harm to tweak the tail of a few other neds at the same time, so he'd some records to check first. But he'd only just sat down at the computer when the door to the office was flung open and PC Thomson marched in.

'Suicide at Eastlaw Farm,' she said.

'Perhaps,' he said, then stopped, with the rest of the sentence, *you could knock*, unuttered. 'What – what did you say?'

Thomson gave him an impatient look. 'Message from the switchboard. Suicide at Eastlaw Farm. Just been phoned in.'

He'd heard her, of course, and he cringed. He could hardly bear the thought of another young woman driven to despair. Rose Moncrieff had told him that she and Sarah had got on well and like a fool he'd put her out of his mind, believing that with Rose's comfort and support she'd be all right.

And he'd got it wrong. He had to swallow hard before he said, 'OK. How did she do it?'

'What do you mean "she"? It's not a her, it's a him.'

It took Gunn a moment to adjust. 'Him? What's his name?'

Thomson gave a put-upon sigh. 'I'll need to go back and look what I wrote down.'

He got up. 'I'll come with you. I'll have to get straight out there. What happened?'

'Found hanging. Some man gave the details.'

When they reached the front desk, she pointed to the log. 'It'll be there.'

Gunn picked it up and read what she had written down – barely enough information. Time of call, 08.04, five minutes earlier. Reported by James Gresham. Victim, Niall Ritchie. Address, Eastlaw Farm.

Surely there must have been more than that! She was being determinedly unhelpful. Still, getting involved in an argument wouldn't achieve anything.

'Right,' he said. His stomach might be churning but sadly it wasn't the first time he'd had to deal with a suicide so at least the routine was straightforward. 'Usual procedure – contact CID North Berwick and say I need appropriate support. I'll go right away.'

Heaving an elaborate sigh, Thomson picked up the

phone as he left. There was a Costa coffee on the desk along with a Danish pastry with a bite out of it and she'd clearly just been going to settle down to her breakfast.

He knew where Eastlaw Farm was but he'd never been there and the only other information he had was what DS Murray had told him. She hadn't mentioned Sarah Lindsay's partner's name but given the set-up she'd described, it was likely that he was this Niall Murray. An evil thing to have happened – and what would that do to a woman already seriously stressed?

He was always daunted by incidents like this and the tic at the side of his eye was twitching as he drove up the farm road in the grudging light of an overcast day, the air heavy with moisture, and turned in at the Eastlaw Farm sign. There were three cars in the yard in front of a small stone farmhouse that looked badly in need of maintenance: the external paintwork was blistered and he could see a slate on the roof that had slipped.

As he parked, a man who looked to be in his sixties came out, quite tall and broad-shouldered but carrying a good bit of extra weight. His face was grim. This must be Jimmie Gresham; Gunn knew him by reputation though they'd never met.

He came forward to introduce himself, and nodded as Gunn showed his warrant card.

'You're very prompt. I suppose I should explain – I've a farm business just south of Tarleton and Niall is – oh God, was, I should say, one of the young organic farmers I buy from to supply the supermarkets. This is a real tragedy.'

'Yes, sir. I gather Mr Ritchie was found hanging? Was it you who discovered him?'

'No. Unfortunately it was his partner, Sarah Lindsay. She's inside, distraught, of course. My daughter Briony's with her.'

Was there no end to the horror of these things? He braced himself. 'Perhaps you could give me some background before I go in to speak to her?'

'Of course. Just give me a minute, will you, to get it straight? I'm afraid we're all still in shock.'

'I'm sure. Had there been any indication that Mr Ritchie was suicidal?'

'Not as far as I know. He wasn't at a party I was giving last night, but I'd no idea there was a problem till late yesterday evening when I got my daughter to phone Sarah to arrange for a supermarket buyer to visit this morning and she told her Niall was missing.'

'And you said it was Ms Lindsay who found him?'

'Yes.' Gresham pointed across. 'Just over there – that little shed. Sarah had insisted on searching too and I suggested she should check the buildings for what Niall might have been working with – I reckoned there'd probably been an accident with machinery and they can be pretty messy, so this was meant to keep her out of the way. I was walking the sheep run, and one of my men was round the back searching the fields there. The neighbour from next door was helping too but of course—' He gave a grimace, spreading his hands wide. 'Nasty, very nasty. Do you want to see it now?'

He was glad to be able to shake his head. 'Not at the moment. There'll be a team coming. I just have to make sure that no one goes in.'

'Not a problem. Ken Blackford's gone back to his

farm next door and the rest of us are inside.'

With a glance over at the shed – the door was shut – Gunn followed Gresham into the kitchen.

There was a pretty, fair-haired woman sitting at the kitchen table. His heart went out to her; she was drooping over her folded arms and her face was so drained of colour that it had a greenish pallor. There was a pile of wet-weather gear dropped on the floor at her feet and she was wearing a flimsy flowered dress. A mug of tea sat in front of her, untouched, a silky film of milk forming on its surface.

As he came in, another woman, broad-shouldered and carrying a bit of extra weight, was holding a teapot and saying, 'Want a top-up, Wattie?' to the man in workman's clothes who was standing in one corner, looking awkward.

The woman at the table turned her head as Gunn came in, though she looked as if she was finding it hard to focus. 'I'm Niall's partner,' she said. 'Sarah Lindsay.'

'DI Gunn, Ms Lindsay. I'm sorry for your loss.' She didn't reply, and he said gently, 'Do you feel able to tell me what happened?'

She gave a great sigh. 'I suppose I must.'

Briony moved across to put an arm round her shoulders. 'Good girl! It's hard, I know, but we're here to support you.'

It wasn't what Gunn wanted. 'It would really be better to speak to you on your own, madam. Is there somewhere else we could go?'

Ignoring Briony, who was giving him a hostile look, Sarah stood up, a bit unsteadily.

'This way,' she said.

She took him through to the sitting room and sat down

in a chair at one side of the fireplace with its dead fire, a chair upholstered in what looked like an expensive fabric that was out of keeping with the general shabbiness of the room. It was very dark on this gloomy morning and quite perishingly cold but despite her bare neck and arms, she showed no sign of noticing.

'You'd better tell me where you want me to start,' she said.

Lack of sleep made everything weird, unreal. Sarah felt as if she was sitting behind a wall of plate glass watching what was going on – a woman being questioned by a police officer. The woman seemed to be talking perfectly coherently, which was odd without any input from the disconnected Sarah. She was telling him what had gone before last night, explaining quite smoothly why she had gone to the party and not started looking for Niall then, and he didn't seem to be blaming her, particularly. She didn't seem to remember much about the actual moment she saw him and the policeman wasn't trying to push her. In fact, after he asked if she could positively identify the body she had seen as being her partner's, he was saying that was all he needed at the moment and standing up.

Then he said, 'I don't think you should be left here. Can you go and stay with your friends, the Greshams?'

It was as if a stone had been chucked through the glass. Reality crashed in and Sarah was suddenly, and painfully, present. 'No!' she cried. 'Oh no, I can't.'

The policeman looked taken aback. 'I'm sure they'd want you to—'

'No,' she said more forcefully this time. 'It's just not possible.'

'Can you explain why?'

She took a moment to weigh her words; at least the brain fog was lifting and the plate glass had disappeared. Then she said, 'You'll see it anyway. We set up Eastlaw to be organic but Niall was a hopeless farmer, frankly. Jimmie Gresham threw us a lifeline by buying in our produce for Gresham's Farms – we'd have gone under if it hadn't been for him – but there were all these chemicals in that shed. I just feel I don't even want to see them again, let alone face them every morning.'

'Right.' The policeman was looking a bit stunned, but he persisted, 'I still think you shouldn't stay here. Have you family you could go to?'

'No. I'll be perfectly fine on my own here. My parents live in Spain now and we're not on the best of terms anyway. They thought I was a fool to come here – and how right they were!' She gave a little, harsh laugh.

He still looked unconvinced. 'Rose Moncrieff is a friend of yours, isn't she? Would you like me to ask her if you could stay with her meantime?'

She couldn't stop her eyes filling with tears at the mention of the name that brought up the memory of the warm living room, the warm food, the generous warmth of the welcome Rose had given her – and she realised now that she was cold, so cold.

Huddling down in her party frock, Sarah whispered, 'Yes please.'

Rose Moncrieff had been working in her studio in the backyard when DI Gunn's phone call came. The shock had the force almost of a flashback to the call she'd received herself, not so long ago: the one that had told her that Linden, the golden girl she had given life to, had so tragically thrown it away.

Would she really have the strength to walk alongside someone else through the wilderness of grief and pain that was still her own daily struggle? But as poor Sarah Lindsay began the lonely journey, Rose knew there was no one more qualified to help and to understand than she was herself. How could she say no?

She said, 'Of course, Matt,' turned off the potter's wheel, locked up and hurried into the house to wash the clay off her hands, light the sitting-room fire and put on the coffee machine. The spare bedroom was made up anyway, but she switched on the electric blanket and went out to snip some roses from the garden wall to put in a jug on the chest of drawers – old-fashioned, climbing yellow roses, with a heady perfume. A tortured mind might not register the pleasures of the senses, but it wasn't to say that they didn't have an effect.

When Sarah arrived on the doorstep carrying a holdall, she looked years older than the competent young woman Rose had met yesterday. She was wearing a sweater over a thin dress and she looked chilled, pale as a ghost, with indigo circles under eyes that were red and puffy with recent tears. It looked as if she could have been crying all the way down from Eastlaw, and it looked too as if it had taken a major effort to stop.

'You're so kind,' Sarah said. 'I'm sorry – I didn't mean to land on you, but—'

'Shush!' Rose said. 'Come on in. If you want to go straight to bed, it's ready for you, but I think you should just go through to the fire and get warmed up first. Have you had breakfast?'

'Not hungry,' Sarah said as she did as she was told and sat warming her hands at the blaze.

'Tea and toast,' Rose said firmly.

When she came back, Sarah had obviously been crying again, but she produced a ghost of a smile. 'It's so good of you to take me in.'

Rose handed Sarah the mug and set a plate of hot buttered toast on the small table beside her. 'Who was it said, "Fellow feeling makes us wondrous kind"? You must be in shock at the moment but I hope I can help when the pain floods in later. I know what it's like.'

Sarah sat very still for a moment. Then she said, 'I don't think you do. You loved your daughter. I told you yesterday that things had gone wrong between Niall and me but after we talked, I felt that we could at least sort something out that would be a way forward. But this has been so dreadful – agonising really. He didn't consider what it would do to me at all – didn't even leave a note – and now what I'm mostly feeling is raging humiliation. Niall has been lying and cheating all this time.'

Rose listened in some astonishment as she explained. It was ineffably sad: the young man who had the chance to live his idealistic dream and then found he hadn't the insight or the skills to make it a reality – or the courage to accept that and walk away.

'He must have felt such a failure,' she said.

'Yes, I think he did,' Sarah said. 'But he wouldn't discuss the problem, wouldn't even admit that there was one. If he'd been prepared to do that, we could have worked something out together. The trouble was the lockdown was so claustrophobic that the atmosphere got poisonous and we could hardly speak to each other without rowing. I carved out my own space once I was able to get the shop, and I suppose he just withdrew completely – and it was around then he got so chummy with our neighbour. Ken's always openly despised organic principles – it wouldn't surprise me if Niall got encouragement to cheat from him. He was furious with me for cooperating with the police case against Doddie Muir – probably his pals in the pub felt it might draw police attention to the grubby little underworld that's flourishing there.'

Rose hardly knew what to say. She'd been expecting to offer comfort to a woman who would be struggling with her loss but that wasn't the problem here. Sarah wasn't grieving; she felt betrayed and she was wounded – and angry.

'I can see how hard that must be,' she managed at last. 'So what are you going to do?'

Sarah had eaten some of the toast and was sipping the tea, but now she set it down.

'I – I don't know.' She had been sitting up, but now she slumped back in her seat and gave a huge yawn.

Rose stood up. 'I'm going to be bossy. Go straight up to bed and sleep, and we can talk about the practicalities later.'

With another jaw-dislocating yawn, Sarah went off and Rose cleared the dishes through to the kitchen. She hoped that her guest would manage to have a good sleep, because the practicalities she would have to deal with were daunting indeed – not least the immediate problem of live animals needing care.

'I'll put someone in to deal with the livestock and bring appropriate feedstuff,' Jimmie Gresham said. 'The sooner we start clearing the chemicals from the system, the better.'

'Thank you, sir. That would be of great assistance,' DI Gunn said. 'Would you be planning to farm it yourself? It seems unlikely Ms Lindsay would want to go on by herself.'

After Sarah left, they had sat down round the kitchen table while Briony produced more tea and he took their statements as Wattie Johnston's body language silently expressed his fervent wish to be somewhere else.

Beyond answering Gunn's questions, Briony had said little but now she burst out, 'She absolutely hated it here. It would be all Niall's idea – that foul stuff. She had nothing to do with the farm herself, nothing.'

Was that directed at him, Gunn wondered, or at her father? He couldn't read the other man's expression and Gresham didn't say anything.

Briony went on, 'I'm really upset that she wouldn't come back with us – didn't even come in to say goodbye. I'm not sure she was fit to drive, in her condition.' Her tone was distinctly reproachful.

'I did offer her transport but she was insistent that she would need her own car,' Gunn said, trying not to sound defensive. 'She just wanted to slip away without any fuss.'

'Where did she go?'

'I'm not at liberty to say,' he said but he was far from sure that Briony, a forceful lady, was going to leave it at that so he was relieved when he saw Ken Blackford walk past the window, and, with a perfunctory knock on the door, walk in.

He didn't greet anyone, just looked round and said, 'She gone, then?'

Gunn stood up. 'Ms Lindsay? Yes, she's gone.'

'Oh. Pity. I was wanting to speak to her. The stock isn't going to look after itself and I thought she'd rest easier if she knew I'd be taking it on.'

'We won't trouble you to do that,' Gresham said stiffly. 'I'll be putting someone in later today.'

'Oh? That's what the lady wants, is it? You've asked her, have you?'

Briony had been glaring at him ever since he'd barged straight in. His tone was impertinent and she was ready to meet aggression with aggression.

'She certainly wouldn't want to have anything to do with you, anyway,' she said. 'She's often told me you were a bully and a bad influence. She was scared of you. And you'd poison the farm with all the toxic stuff you use yourself—'

Blackford gave a sardonic smile. 'Judging by what was in that shed, it's poisoned already, isn't it? Given the land they've got here, it's the only way you could make a living off it. Organic, my arse. Rich man's game, that is. Anyway, I'm going to buy it off her. I could tell he wouldn't last long and I've fancied expanding the farm for a while.'

Briony's face had gone bright red but before she could speak, Gresham got up. 'I don't think this sort of crude antagonism is going to get us anywhere. DI Gunn, since Niall and Sarah had a supplier's contract with me, I feel I'm in a better position to deal with this until we have a chance to find out her wishes.'

There was no doubt that he had right on his side. Relieved, Gunn said, 'Mr Blackford, when next I speak to Ms Lindsay, I will tell her what you have said but she indicated to me that she was opposed to the use of chemicals so I think she would prefer Mr Gresham to deal with the farm meantime.'

As he spoke, he saw a personnel carrier drawing up in the yard. It enabled him to say, 'My colleagues have arrived. Mr Blackford, I must ask you to go back to your house and stay away from the area while we make our investigations.'

Blackford shrugged and stalked out. Gunn turned to the others. 'I have your names and addresses. Someone will come to take a formal statement for you to sign later, but for now you are free to go. Thank you for your cooperation.'

The Greshams stood up, making polite noises, but Wattie Johnston rose like a rocket and was out of the door before Gunn could reach it himself.

The police doctor, Stewart Drummond, was an older man who had seen it all before and had, in fact, assisted at two of the other suicides Gunn had dealt with in the past couple of years.

'Another one,' he said without preamble. 'Bad spell you've had. What is it this time?'

'Good morning, Dr Drummond. A hanging, I'm afraid.'

'No doubt about death, then. Well, let's get on with it and cut him down.'

'Of course.'

He led the doctor across to the shed while the

photographer and four uniforms unloaded equipment, feeling the familiar, sickening lurch in the gut when it came right down to the uglier part of police business. The tic started up again too and he put up a hand to quieten it as he said, 'I gather the body is behind the door. I'll take a look first, but it's a very cramped space and to give you room to work we'll probably need to take the door off.'

He directed the uniforms, choosing a burly older sergeant for the frontline operation and sending a young Asian constable – bright, but inexperienced and, Gunn noticed, looking a bit green around the gills – back to the transport to get tools. At times like this it was a rotten job and he felt almost overwhelmed by his own sense of helplessness. He sighed heavily as he returned to the doctor, who looked towards him.

'Oh,' Gunn said, 'it's just that it's awful having to deal with these tragedies and not being able to do anything to prevent them.'

Drummond gave him a hard look from under beetling brows. 'You're too sensitive, laddie. Not worked out yet that it's a hard world and you're not going to be the one born to put it straight? You're here to do a job, that's all. You can't get shaky, and agonising won't help.'

He was right, of course, but somehow knowing that didn't help. Keeping his voice level with an effort, Gunn said, 'Right – I'll just go and take a look.' He walked over to the shed and pushed open the door.

He had to edge round it and there the hanging body was – hideously close, that grotesque, bloated face fringed with a straggly beard only inches away from his own. His stomach heaved, and as he fought to control the nausea he thought of poor Sarah – what must it have been like for her? But he caught himself up; he'd no time for that, he must just grit his teeth and get on with the job that had to be done – and be grateful that what it dictated was backing out and supervising the removal of the door.

The hinges were rusty and it took only a minute with a crowbar before it fell and Niall Ritchie's dangling body was exposed, a rope noose tight around the neck as it hung from one of three sturdy hooks screwed into the rafters – relics, perhaps, of the day when there were bridles and reins to be stored. It was a sisal rope, thin enough to be flexible – the sort of rope you'd find in any farmyard.

With the doctor at his side, Gunn stood methodically checking out the visible evidence: the noose, secured to the hook with a basic-looking triple knot; the noose itself half-embedded in the dark abrasions round the throat; the empty packing case kicked over just below. But . . . Suddenly, he stiffened.

Drummond was moving forward and he put his hand out to stop him. 'Wait a minute,' Gunn said. 'I think there's something not right.'

'What do you mean?'

'The drop – doesn't look high enough, somehow.'

Drummond gave him an impatient look. 'Doesn't take much, you know. Just enough to tighten the noose.' Then he paused. 'The marks round the neck are very deep for that, though . . .'

'And it's the packing case.' Gunn's tic was flickering frantically now. 'It's cardboard, look, quite flimsy. If it had taken a man's weight, there would be signs of crushing. I certainly can't be sure this isn't a crime scene. We'll have to back off.'

'Don't know the procedure for this,' the doctor said heavily. 'Shouldn't we cut the poor bastard down?'

'It'll be a matter for the SRCS – the Serious Rural Crime Squad,' Gunn said. 'DCI Kelso Strang is in charge of that and I guess they'll get a squad here as soon as they can. I think I'd better get the door put back in place and seal off the scene. Sorry to have wasted your time.'

'Sorry it's come to this,' Drummond said, picking up his case. He paused, then said, 'You've had quite a bit of trouble down here, with one thing and another, haven't you? Nasty business with that young doctor.'

'Yes, it was.' Gunn had a lump in his throat as he escorted Drummond back to his car. There had been so much nasty business, and his unease – which was, as he'd said to DS Murray, like the discomfort you feel when there's a gathering storm – had been hideously prophetic.

But now at least someone would have to listen.

CHAPTER SEVEN

After spending most of the day after the party in troubled, unrefreshing sleep, Sarah Lindsay hadn't expected to drop off easily at bedtime and even the pill urged on her by Rose Moncrieff had only bought her a couple of hours before a dream full of nameless horrors jerked her awake with a cry. Yet she was tired, tired. Lying flat on her back, her eyes wide open in the darkness, she felt so paralysed by exhaustion that she couldn't even turn over to try to find a more comfortable position.

Her mind was energetic, though, leaping from worry to worry. At least the stock was being cared for – the police had told her that – but there were all the other practical problems waiting for her with daylight, like notifying the authorities, finding a lawyer, making arrangements for the funeral once that was allowed –

no, no, she shouldn't let herself go there. But even as she pushed the thought away, it began levering open the door she had barricaded with practicalities to keep out the emotion she would be struggling with for the rest of her life. Guilt.

Cutting herself off from Niall had started as self-defence, really. She'd been wounded that he seemed to prefer time down the pub with Ken Blackford and his pals to time spent with her, absorbed in her lonely misery as the flimsy relationship gradually died. Yes, she could see he was floundering but as he flatly refused to talk farm business, there was nothing she could do.

He'd talked Sarah into fulfilling his dream and the least he could do, she had told herself, was learn to be a better farmer, otherwise her whole life was being sacrificed to an ideal that had been doomed from the start. Once she'd started thinking that way, the blame game became shockingly addictive and the split between them had gaped wider and wider as they argued over the Doddie Muir case until she couldn't contain her resentment any longer. She was part-owner of the farm; she could force him to sell up, and she was going to do it.

So then he'd killed himself. She should have seen it coming. She'd known he was living with failure day after day. She'd seen her own misery reflected in his face but when he wouldn't engage with her, she'd given up.

One particular conversation came back to haunt her now: she'd asked, admittedly with an impatient edge to her voice, if there was something she could do to help when the lambing was going badly. 'No,' he'd said flatly, going back out again into the stormy darkness of a March night, and she'd shrugged. 'Your choice,' she'd said, and gone back to bed.

Even yesterday, after all that had happened, she'd still been nursing her rage but during the sleepless hours it had seeped away and now she was ashamed. A better woman would have overcome pride and resentment and persisted in coaxing him to talk about his feelings. Oh, perhaps it still wouldn't have made the difference between life and death, but that better woman wouldn't now be tormented by having failed in her duty to another human being, let alone someone to whom she had once declared her love. For the first time, the tears came, trickling down the sides of her cheeks and soaking into the pillows.

Eventually Sarah drifted into something between sleep and waking, full of brief, unsettling dreams. But she could wake herself up properly and get away from them, unlike the real-life nightmare that was waiting for her when morning came.

'No doubt about it at all,' the pathologist said. 'Stunned first, strangled and strung up later.'

After years of experience, DCI Kelso Strang was reflecting bleakly, you might expect to have become accustomed to the atmosphere of a morgue – the icy chill on the air, the smell of strong cleaning chemicals and formalin, the blank steel cabinets each with a life history behind them. He'd never managed it, though.

Helen Brown obviously had. She was cheerful as always; she'd told him once that pathologists were the only doctors not constantly riddled with anxiety about mistakes, since the worst had already happened to their patients. Now she was pointing out what she felt were the highlights of her examination – the blow to the skull, the two furrows, the petechial haemorrhages, the traumatic injury at the back of the neck that would not have been there in a suicide.

The body on the trolley looked mercifully more like a dummy than like something that had once lived and breathed, but even so, as Strang looked down obediently, he dropped his eyes so that he was looking past the trolley, concentrating on the glistening tiles beneath. He hoped she wouldn't notice; she'd mocked him mercilessly more than once.

Brown did, of course. 'Marks out of ten?' she said.

Strang looked up, frowning. 'What?'

'Shiny enough for you? I thought you must be checking that our floor cleaners were up to standard.'

He gave a reluctant grin. 'Oh, all right, Helen. Come on, you've had your laugh. Can we go through to where I can sit down without shivering and take notes?'

'Oh, very well. Go on and I'll be with you in a minute.'

As he left the morgue, the trolley slid the body silently back to its vault and he gave an involuntary shudder. You didn't need a skull on your desk as a memento mori when you were in police service; all too many of those came with the job.

Brown followed him through. 'Were you informed he's been ID'd? The girlfriend and someone called Gresham were each shown the video yesterday.'

'Yes, they passed that on to me. So, tell me what I need to know.' He had his notebook ready.

'Straightforward enough. There's a wealth of distinguishing marks to confirm strangulation – do you want me to go through them now? I'll be putting it all in my report, of course.'

'Just give me the basics for the moment.'

'Well, he was knocked out first: blunt instrument, stone, or wood perhaps – I'll have more on that later. The ligature furrow shows how he was killed. That was underneath the hanging furrow that was created when the dead body was suspended from the hook. Simple as that. There's the other evidence too that would be inconsistent with hanging.'

Strang looked up from his scribbling. 'So whoever did it didn't know enough to make a convincing job of it, then.'

'Far from it. Must have thought it looked convincing enough not to be checked.'

'Can I hope for a time of death?'

Brown shook her head. 'Nothing exact enough to help you. By the time I got to the body yesterday, he could even have been dead for twenty-four hours. Certainly not less than eight.'

'Right. And the head wound weapon – size? Shape? Give me a break – what should we be looking for?'

'You're the detective,' she said unhelpfully.

He made a face at her. 'All right, the rope, then – is it the one he was strangled with?'

'Hard to say. The rope round his neck is distorting the picture – we'll need to do more investigation to establish if the same rope was used to kill him.'

'Mmm. Right.' Strang shut his notebook and stood up. 'Many thanks, Helen. That's enough to be going on with. Get the report to me when you can and I swear I'll study it later, though I probably won't understand the half of it.'

Brown gave him a sideways look. 'Oh, yes? That's an

affectation, Kelso – you've come back with some quite penetrating questions in the past. Off you go and get on with it. Tell me what happens, anyway – it's not often you get a murder that's more sophisticated than some idiot losing their temper and sticking in a knife.'

DS Livvy Murray had driven down to Tarleton first thing, as the advance guard while DCI Strang went to the morgue in Edinburgh. When she reached Eastlaw Farm, there was no sign of police activity, beyond yellow strips of police tape fluttering in the wind tearing in from the sea. The sky was a leaden greenish-grey that threatened worse to come and she got out of the car and looked round about her with a shudder.

God, it was sinister, this place! It was perfectly understandable that killing yourself would be preferable to being forced to live up here, though given the sudden involvement of the SRCS it presumably wasn't what had happened here. She hadn't actually spoken to the boss but Angie Andrews had said he was being cagey and Murray reckoned 'suspicious circumstances' would feature in the next police statement.

There was nothing much for her to look at here for the moment, beyond the little ramshackle shed where apparently they'd found the body now being inspected by DCI Strang at the morgue. The door looked the worse for wear, with splintered hinges and a couple of struts nailed across it to prevent access. Activity would only start when Strang gave the nod for the SOCOs to move in.

There was a pick-up parked in front of the house and Murray could see a man working in the field just below, where there were hen houses and chickens scratching around outside. She'd been told that someone sent over by the Greshams would be working here and there was no reason to speak to him, so she went across to the house and knocked on the door. She didn't expect an answer; it was dark and gloomy and there were no lights on inside. She knocked again for form's sake and was turning away when a voice spoke at her shoulder.

'She's not there.'

It startled her; she hadn't heard him approach but there was a man standing right behind her, too close for it to be comfortable. She took a step backwards and turned round.

'Who are you?' she said.

He leered at her, displaying discoloured and uneven teeth. 'Depends who's wanting to know. Journalist?'

'No,' she snarled, reaching for her warrant card. 'Police. Now, shall we start again? Who are you?'

The transformation was almost comical. He took several steps back, saying, 'Sorry, sorry, OK? I've just been on the lookout for journalists, you know – Niall was a pal of mine and I wouldn't want his bidie-in upset by scum sneaking round to cause trouble.'

'Name?' Murray said flatly. The reaction had been interesting; she'd seen it often enough before and it usually meant that someone had reason to be nervous around the law. Making a mental note to get on to Records, she said, 'Is it your farm next door?'

'Yes, that's right. We're neighbours. Ken Blackford.'

She walked towards what was the boundary fence. There was a marked contrast between the neat garden here – Sarah's hobby, she guessed – and the ill-kept yard next door, which featured empty feed bags, rusting equipment and a tarpaulin-covered mound stabilised with discarded tyres, as well as a couple of thin-looking dogs watching them from a wire cage.

'Microchipped, are they?' she said, on the general principle of causing trouble.

It didn't work. 'Course,' he said, and worse, she realised he knew what she'd been trying to do and he was now looking cocky again.

'Want me to tell you about what happened that night?' he said.

'Not really. I've read the statement you gave yesterday – unless there's anything you want to add?'

'Oh, just what I didn't say – just I was worried about my pal Niall. I knew he'd a lot on his mind, stuff he wasn't wanting to talk about. Kind of defensive – know what I mean? Wasn't surprised about what happened, to be honest.'

'Did he say anything that suggested he might have been suicidal?'

'Not really – if he had, I'd have told him to get help, obviously! But he wasn't coping, that was the thing. Should have offered to buy him out, to be honest. Might have made a difference to the poor sod.'

That was the second 'to be honest'. Strang always said it made him think the speaker most likely tended towards the opposite. 'But you didn't try to buy Eastlaw at the time they bought it?'

A sour look came over his face. 'Wouldn't have been daft enough to pay what they paid.'

'You thought he'd have sold it cheap, did you?'

Blackford glared at her. 'Look, that's all I'm saying. To be honest, the man was useless and driving himself crazy – maybe it's as well for him that he's at peace now. Anything more you want?'

'No. Thank you, sir, you've been very helpful,' she said as she was trained to do.

He turned and stalked off. Murray took a final look round and got back in the car. She'd only come up here to fix the set-up in her mind and there was nothing more to do; the encounter with Blackford had been a bonus that gave her something more to think about as she drove down to liaise with DI Gunn. She drove away just as the rain started with a vengeance.

She parked as close to the entrance to the Tarleton police station as she could and sprinted in, dripping. PC Thomson was no more welcoming than she had been on the previous occasion.

'You again,' she said.

'Yes, that's right – DS Murray. Is DI Gunn in?'

'Just been hanging around since this all happened. What's going on, anyway?'

That was cheeky and Murray's response was cold. 'The SRCS is investigating events at Eastlaw Farm. I believe DI Gunn has been dealing with it.'

Thomson snorted. 'If you could call it that. No point in sending a bairn out to do a man's job, so I hope your lot know what they're doing.'

Gaping would be undignified. To stop her jaw from dropping, Murray snapped, 'Buzz DI Gunn, please, Constable. Rudeness is neither helpful nor appropriate.'

Thomson's hand had been reaching out to make the call

but she paused, turning her head to give Murray a cold stare.

Murray stared back silently and after a long moment the constable's eyes dropped and she made the call. 'That DS that was here – she's here again,' she said.

Murray raised her eyebrows. 'If you have memory problems, perhaps you should write down my name – DS Murray. We may be working out of here over the next bit.'

Thomson gave an eloquent sniff, but went back to the computer on her desk as DI Matt Gunn came through, looking, she thought, even more strained than he had previously. His welcome was effusive as he led her through to the office.

'I can't tell you how glad I am that you lot have been called in! Is DCI Strang on his way?'

'Probably,' she said as she sat down. 'I haven't spoken to him. You likely know more than I do – the first indications were that this was a suicide but we wouldn't have been called in if it was.'

'No,' he agreed. 'We were ready to deal with it from the North Berwick station, but there were a few odd features. Very unpleasant – horrible, really. And unfortunately it was Sarah Lindsay who found him.'

Murray hadn't heard that. 'Oh no! Poor woman!'

'So what happens now?' he said.

She was a little taken aback; he was the superior officer, and he'd had time to think about it so he should have a plan ready. 'I'm expecting to hear from the boss after he's talked to the pathologist and my guess is we'll be going public then about the "suspicious circumstances", but we shouldn't be wasting time. Have you a schedule lined up?'

'Well, not as such,' he said. 'If you want background, I suppose you could talk to the Greshams – the daughter, bryony, was a close friend of Sarah's. She can probably tell you if he'd been showing signs of strain—'

Murray had to try not to look impatient as she said, 'Of course it's not really his state of mind we'll be concerned with, is it? Not if it wasn't suicide.'

'No,' Gunn said. 'Of course not, when you think about it.'

And he hadn't thought about it, having known about this since yesterday? Murray looked at him sharply: he was very pale and his eyes were shadowed. She wondered if his experience yesterday had given him a sleepless night.

'We'll be needing an incident room,' she said. 'So we can start there. This office will do for DCI Strang, and, assuming he gives the nod, the technicians will come in and lay the phone lines and so on. Other rooms?'

'Some mothballed. There's good space in what used to be the CID room before.'

'You'll have to put a bomb under PC Thomson. She's going to have to cooperate with them.'

'Not sure she knows the meaning of the word,' he said bitterly.

Murray frowned. 'She's going to have to.'

Gunn gave a hollow laugh. 'Will you tell her or shall I?'

'Oh, I will. I'm not feart,' Murray was saying when her phone rang. She took it out and read the message, then stood up.

'Right, we're on. Homicide, and he'll be making a statement after he speaks to Sarah Lindsay. We've about an hour to get things organised here ready for the boss.'

'That's brilliant!' Gunn said. A little colour came back to his pale cheeks. 'Maybe he'll be able to get a grip on things.'

It was certainly time somebody did, Murray thought. Gunn seemed to see Strang as the miracle-worker, and though she'd be the first to say the boss was good at what he did, he wasn't that.

'If he tried walking on water he'd sink, same as everyone else,' she warned him, but from the look on his face she wasn't sure he believed her.

It was after ten o'clock when Sarah Lindsay woke up. The pill must have worked at last and she was feeling groggy as she tried to focus on the numbers on her watch.

The little house was very quiet. Her hostess must have gone out, or perhaps she was working in the studio in the yard at the back. Sarah got up, showered and dressed in the clothes Rose had found for her yesterday – her daughter's, perhaps, since Rose was inches shorter than she was. The dress she had worn to the party lay in a crumpled heap on the floor and she shuddered as she picked it up and put it on a chair. She'd never wear it again.

There was no sign of Rose but when she went through to the kitchen, there was a note propped up against the toaster: *You needed your sleep so I didn't wake you. Help yourself – you can guess where everything is. I'm in the studio if you need me.*

She wasn't hungry but she would need her strength for what the day might bring – the phone calls she must make, the visits she was pretty sure there would be from the police, who would want to talk to her about Niall: his state of mind, any suicidal threats, any indication of what he was planning . . . Yes, she must eat something.

Sarah finished the tea and toast dutifully, barely tasting them, and as she cleared away the dishes there was a knock on the front door. She tensed: the police? She'd better answer it, but as she walked into the narrow hall, the front door opened and to her surprise Rob Gresham walked in, calling, 'Rose?'

He was obviously surprised too. 'What are you doing here?'

'I'm just staying with Rose meantime.' She wondered if he knew about Niall, and saw him remembering.

'Oh, yes. I see. I'm so very sorry, Sarah. How are you?'

She grimaced. 'Not great. But Rose has been wonderful. You're a friend of hers, obviously.'

'Rose and I got very close over the last year. Her daughter Linden was my girlfriend and she and I have been propping each other up ever since she killed herself. She probably told you?'

'Yes, she did, and that she'd had a partner but she didn't mention your name. She sounded a wonderful girl – it must have been hard for you.'

His mouth twisted as he said, 'It was, and it still is. We have a lot in common now – if I can help you through the next bit, I'm glad to do anything I can. Rose is in the studio, is she?'

'I guess so. I was late getting up and I've just finished breakfast.'

'Look, you go and sit down and I'll tell her I'm here and you're awake.'

Sarah did as she was told and went through. It was dark

this morning; the sky was overcast, the rain was streaming down and without lamplight and a blazing fire, the room felt dreary and cold. She gave a little shiver as she sat down on the sofa.

Seeing Rob had reminded her uncomfortably of the evening she had spent enjoying his company and putting her own misgivings out of her mind when perhaps if she had gone home to see why Niall hadn't arrived, she could have stopped this happening.

Like Rose, he had made the wrong assumption about her feelings. Her sense of guilt was genuine enough, but there was no real sense of loss and having to pretend to grieve made her feel worse. She'd told Rose the truth, but then she'd been so angry at the time; confessing it now to Rob in cold blood, as it were, would be excruciating.

She could hear him coming back. 'She's just putting something into the kiln,' he said as he opened the door. 'I've switched on the coffee machine. It's a bit dismal today, isn't it?'

She watched as he went to switch on the lamps and unhesitatingly picked up matches from the drawer of a nearby table to light the fire, then took the larger of the two chairs that stood on either side. He was behaving like the son of the house – and perhaps that was what he was, or at least the son-in-law Rose might have hoped to have.

'That's better,' Rob said. 'I'm still taken aback to find you here. I heard about what had happened from Briony and I came in today because I thought news of another suicide might be upsetting for Rose. I didn't know she knew you, though. Briony was fretting about where you were, actually – she was all ready to scoop you up yesterday but the policeman said you'd gone. She and Jimmie are both very fond of you, you know.'

She didn't want to have to explain about her reaction either. 'It was DI Gunn that asked Rose to look out for me when he heard I was having a hard time locally – the Doddie Muir thing, you know – and she'd been wonderful. So . . . It just seemed natural.'

At the mention of Muir, he looked uncomfortable. 'Yes – that was difficult for you. And Rose would understand – there was a lot of resentment towards the doctors during Covid, you know.'

'Yes, she did.' Sarah wasn't sure that he did, though; 'difficult' was a weak word to use to describe what she had gone though over the last months. It was the 'it's aye been' attitude that made this town such a poisonous place to be. She just had to hang on to the thought that there would be a bad couple of days and then she could get away, put the farm on the market and never, ever come back.

'Jimmie's got the farm in hand, so don't worry about that. I'll tell Briony where you are . . .'

'No!' It was an instinctive response. She hadn't thought what reason she could give; it sounded churlish, and her face flamed in embarrassment.

Rob laughed. 'Don't worry, your secret is safe with me! Briony can be a bit much at times, can't she? After Linden died, she smothered me with kindness and I had a real fight to escape. I'll leave it to you to tell her when you feel strong enough to cope.'

'Thanks,' she said. 'It's not that I'm not grateful – so grateful, to them both, it's just that I want time to get my balance.'

'Of course,' he said soothingly. 'Oh, I think I hear Rose coming back.'

Rose's voice called from the kitchen, 'Here I am! Coffee for you both?'

There was a knock on the door. Sarah tensed up again – surely the police, this time? – and saw Rob giving her an anxious look. He got up, calling through to Rose, 'I'll get it!'

She heard someone speaking to him, then Rob's voice saying, 'Yes, she's here. Just go on through.'

She turned her head to look, and saw the inspector whose encouragement to take on Doddie Muir had caused her so much trouble, DCI Strang, coming in. Rob followed him and the two big men loomed over her as they made their way across the room. She gave a little gasp, as if she needed more air.

Strang said, 'How are you, Ms Lindsay? I'm very sorry for your loss.'

It was what people always said, but she found her tired mind playing with it – what had she lost? So, so many things . . . She managed to say, 'Thank you,' as Rose appeared, looking concerned, and sat down beside her.

While the introductions were being made, Sarah was trying to order her thoughts. He'd want to know if she'd had any advance warning of what Niall was planning, if there was any specific trigger for it. She would have to confess about their row, of course . . .

But there was something in the atmosphere, she realised. From the way Rob and Rose were looking at the policeman, they seemed to have noticed something she hadn't and Rose, sitting beside her on the sofa, had grabbed for her hand. Strang was turning his attention to her now and she studied his face, struck again by the ragged scar down the right-hand side.

'Ms Lindsay, I'm afraid this is going to come as a shock to you.'

He had said it heavily, and she suddenly realised what it was that the others had noticed. He'd mentioned the word 'crime' – the Serious Rural Crime Squad. Suicide wasn't a crime.

'We have reason to believe that your partner was murdered and we are opening an investigation.'

Murdered! Sarah couldn't speak. As she stared at Strang, the word reverberated in her head. The fire was still burning in the grate, the rain was still beating on the windowpanes, but it felt as if time had stopped. Niall was dead – though not because she had failed to stop him killing himself. This was absolution.

Then real life started again, with a jolt. Someone else had killed him. She heard herself saying, stupidly, 'But who did it?'

'That's what we're going to find out,' Strang said. He sounded very patient, sympathetic, even, but she could see that he was studying her face and a chill ran down her spine.

CHAPTER EIGHT

Myrna Muir had done the early shift on the supermarket till and was home in good time for a nice peaceful lunch and a read of the new *Hello!* magazine with the pictures of George and Amal's luxury pad – not that she liked them or anything, but it gave her something she could feel enjoyably aggrieved about. She'd just sat down with her Pot Noodle and a chocolate bar when the kitchen door opened and Doddie came in.

She looked up with some annoyance. 'What are you doing back at this time?'

'Forgot to take my piece.'

Myrna looked round the kitchen. 'There it's, in the corner.' She pointed to a Tupperware box. 'Lucky your head's stuck on.'

Doddie opened it and looked inside. 'Tuna,' he said. 'Don't really like tuna.'

'That all I had in. If you're wanting something different, you'll need to get it in yourself.' He looked as if he was going to take his sandwiches out and eat them there, so she said quickly, 'Well, you've got it now. You'd better away back or the others'll be finished their break.'

Doddie shrugged. 'Now I'm here, could you not make me something a bit better?'

Myrna gave a long-suffering sigh. 'There's a Pot Noodle in the cupboard, that's all. And you know where the kettle is – but after me making those sandwiches for you, you'll need to eat them sometime.'

'Oh aye, right enough,' he said, but she knew fine she'd find them in the food bin tomorrow.

He went to the cupboard, found the pot, complained about the variety, then switched on the kettle, staring out of the window as he waited for it to boil.

Myrna went back to her magazine, though he'd spoilt her moment, coming back like that and bellyaching. However, when he said suddenly, 'There's that policeman – he's just come out of Rose Moncrieff's house!' she sat up straight.

'What policeman?'

'The one that caused all the trouble – the one Vince saw off in the court.'

She was on her feet immediately, joining him to peer out of the window. 'She's likely complaining because folk aren't speaking to her. There's things you get done for these days just because someone gets huffy and says their feelings are hurt. I tell you, she'll be trouble as long as she's staying there. They'll start sniffing around here and you know no one's wanting that.'

Doddie's sharp, weasely face was screwed up into a

scowl. 'He's not just anyone, that's the thing. Gunn's a joke, but he's serious. And if he's not been scared off there could be trouble. I'd better away and tell them.'

He headed for the door. 'Don't forget your piece!' she called.

Pulling a face, he picked up the box and hurried out. Myrna settled back to her lunch but her Pot Noodle was cold and congealing now, and getting wrochit up about the unfairness of life wasn't going to change anything. She'd learnt all about that the hard way when her nan had died, thanks to that shameless woman's daughter, and her eyes filled with tears.

After DCI Strang had gone, there was an awkward silence. Then Rose said gently, 'Sarah, I'm so sorry. What an awful, awful thing!'

'Yes,' she said, her voice flat.

'He was very sympathetic, I thought,' Rose went on. 'These were all just the questions they have to ask, you know.'

'Yes.'

Rob leant forward. 'It's hard for you, but try not to read too much into it—'

She looked at him. 'I don't think I could read too much into it, really, could I? I'm the number one suspect. The partner always is. And I've told you, Rose, how I wanted to sell the farm and get out of here and he wouldn't, and how I was too angry with him to grieve.'

'But you were in a state of shock!' Rose protested. 'You weren't in any state to think clearly after such a dreadful experience – and I'm not about to tell the police anyway.'

'No? When he asks you to repeat what I told you when I came here afterwards? Or if you managed to skirt around it, what about when they put you on oath in the witness box – the truth, the whole truth and nothing but the truth, remember? And come to that, how do you know I didn't do it? I had the motive, the means and the opportunity – that's what they say they look for, isn't it? For the record, I didn't kill him. But then, I would say that, wouldn't I?'

'Oh, Sarah,' Rose said in distress.

'Look, I can go into the witness box to speak up for you,' Rob said. 'I saw you at the party. You were genuinely upset, and when he didn't arrive you were ready to go back. Perhaps I shouldn't have talked you out of it – I've been feeling bad about that ever since I heard what had happened, especially since you were worried about his mental state.'

'And isn't that exactly what I would have done, if I had killed him? I'd have had to be very cold-blooded not to be upset if I'd just butchered Niall, and telling you I was "worried about his mental state" could have been me preparing the ground for a verdict of suicide.'

Sarah waited for the reply that didn't come, then said, 'You see? I'm in serious trouble. Rose, I don't see how I can go on taking advantage of your good nature. I'll move out—'

'No,' Rose said firmly. 'Yes, I'd like to think I'm good-natured, but I'm not a fool. The other thing I'd like to think I am is a good judge of character, and we spent a lot of time talking. You were open and honest and realistic about your problems and it would be completely out of character for you to think that committing a horribly gruesome crime would solve anything. You can't go back to the farmhouse anyway – the chief inspector said they'll be busy there for the next few days. And he said there may be problems with journalists – at least if they find out you're here, I can answer the door and tell them to piss off.'

The way she said it, in her gentle ladylike voice, actually made Sarah smile. 'Rose, you're amazing. But I'm not popular here already and it's not going to be good for you if the neighbours have harbouring a murderer to add the slate of grievances.'

'I think you haven't noticed how incredibly little I care what the stupid, poisonous petty criminals who are my neighbours think – oh yes, Rob, they are,' she said fiercely as he made a murmur of protest. 'You and I both know they drove Linden to suicide and I won't be jerked around by them. Sarah, I *insist* that you stay, at least until things settle down a bit.'

Rob, looking uncomfortable, said weakly, 'They're really not all like that, you know. Most of them just don't – well, sort of notice. But I agree, you should stay here, Sarah. Now look, it's obvious you're going to have an awful lot of calls to make but I honestly think you'd feel better if you got a bit of fresh air first. The rain's gone off now and there's a good walk along the cliffs beyond the harbour.'

Sarah had been struggling for control after Rose's fighting speech. 'You know, I think that might be a good idea,' she said hoarsely.

'Excellent!' he said. 'Rose – you?'

She shook her head. 'I've got a batch of mugs to take out of the kiln. You go ahead and I'll have soup waiting for you when you get back.'

Sarah did feel better, feeling the wind in her face. Rob had been quite right. As they walked down to the harbour, she said, 'Oh, the boat's gone. There was a big one here yesterday when I walked along from the car park – foreign, I think.'

'Yes, that could be right. There's quite a lot of trade goes on here. Look, there's one there now – Polish, from the registration.' He pointed to it. 'Our firm exports quite a bit to them and Jimmie's does too. They're very keen on organic.'

It was an unwelcome reminder about the distinctly nonorganic crops that had been coming out of Niall's fields. 'Mmm,' she said, then, 'It's really quite windy now, isn't it?'

And they walked on.

Myrna Muir had eaten all she wanted of the now-cold Pot Noodle. She got up from the table to drop it in the bin and went to switch on the kettle for a cup of Nes to drink with her chocolate bar. She stared across, eyes narrowed, at the house of the woman she hated for her lack of shame.

As she looked, the front door opened and two people came out, two people she recognised. One of them she knew well, Rob Gresham. She'd known him since he was a wee boy but she'd thought none the better of him for taking up with that doctor, and worse, that he'd gone on visiting the mother after. Still, he was who he was.

But the other one – oh, she knew her all right. She was the cow who'd caused all the fuss about Doddie, and what was she doing there, with him, just after that fancy policeman had left?

She had no idea what it was about, but something was going on – Doddie had been worried too. Until *she* made trouble for him, they'd had it all going the way they wanted, never better. Rose Moncrieff had a brass nerve, squatting there ignoring what all the locals felt, and the other one was just the same – two witches together. Even thinking about it made her angry – very angry. It was time they spelt it out for them, the way they'd done before.

Immediately he had left the morgue, DCI Strang had called DS Murray, gone back to headquarters to produce a statement and actioned a team to head up to Eastlaw Farm before he set off for Tarleton. After he'd talked to Sarah Lindsay, he'd been able to pass on contact details for Ritchie's sister, who would have to be informed before the statement was released; he suspected Lindsay didn't realise that she herself wasn't the next of kin but it wasn't his business to tell her. Then he drove across from the Caddon to the police station where Murray, he hoped, would have got on with setting up an incident room.

She had warned him that PC Thomson didn't exactly have a reputation for being user-friendly, but when he arrived there, the woman, stout and distinctly stony-faced, greeted him with what he would have described as wary politeness and escorted him through to the office where DI Gunn and DS Murray were waiting for him.

'DCI Strang,' she announced as she ushered him in, then retreated, shutting the door behind her.

He saw Gunn and Murray exchanging glances as they stood up. 'Seemed perfectly user-friendly to me,' he said.

They both started laughing. 'Told you it would work,'

Murray said to Gunn. 'I said to her that you and the detective chief superintendent were just like that and that if she put a foot wrong she'd be up on a charge. This is DI Matt Gunn, boss.'

The two men shook hands and Gunn said, 'I'm so very glad you're here, sir. It's a great relief.'

For a moment he wondered if she'd been putting the fear of the DCS into him too and perhaps overdone it a bit, then remembered that Gunn had talked about hoping to lure him down here before. He said lightly, 'Well, we'll see how it goes. How have you been getting on here?'

'There's a local firm come in to start setting up phone lines and a router,' Murray said. 'And PC Thomson has actually been surprisingly helpful getting tables and chairs. I'll show you the room.'

He followed her along the corridor. These police stations, once busy hubs and now reduced to hollow shells, always depressed him; it was probably true that it saved money – and certainly the reorganisation had given him the job he loved – but he didn't believe it had improved policing. Where local officers would have known exactly what was going on and who was doing it, these part-time office-hours stations no longer knew what was going on in the community – and in fact, now he thought of it, this was exactly what Murray had said was troubling Gunn.

The incident room was starting to take shape already, with men moving furniture and cables around; he nodded approval and then went back to the office, where Gunn had a tray of coffee on the desk in front of him.

'PC Thomson brought it in without being asked,' he said. 'Hope you wouldn't have preferred tea.'

'Showing initiative, anyway. Yes, coffee's very welcome after an early start today.'

'It's all going full speed ahead, then, is it, boss?' Murray said.

'Yes, indeed. I'd better brief you both. I've informed the partner, Sarah Lindsay – they weren't married. She was almost rigidly calm – shock, perhaps, but she struck me as probably being quite tough. She looked very tired but there were none of the obvious signs of grief – swollen eyes, red nose . . .'

'From what she said when I came down to talk to her after the Muir case, she'd gone off him. Blamed him for her broken nails, I think.'

'You met her before all this happened. How did she strike you?'

Murray paused, thinking. 'The image that came to me was of a volcano about to blow. I have to say I didn't reckon to anything like this, but I did think there would be one hell of a row soon. And I suppose once you're into a domestic, anything could happen.'

'Mmm. Admittedly he had blunt force trauma to the back of the head, which could have been delivered in a temper, but he didn't die of it and the rest was calculated. Ritchie was strangled first, then he was strung up with the noose round his neck hiding the original ligature. It wouldn't be difficult to strangle someone who's unconscious, or even incapacitated, though you'd need a fair degree of physical strength to manhandle the body and string it up afterwards.'

'Lindsay's quite tall and fit-looking,' Murray was saying thoughtfully when Gunn chipped in.

'She didn't strike me as the kind to do that – not a typical woman's crime anyway, is it? She was in shock when I spoke to her, of course, but she told me very straightforwardly what had happened.'

Strang saw Murray give him a sideways look and he knew exactly what she was thinking: that you would be very unwise to generalise about what a woman might or might not do. He said, 'About the only thing we can say definitely is that whoever did it wasn't very professional. You saw immediately that it didn't stack up.'

'Yes,' Gunn said. 'The killer might just have been assuming that the cheating over the organic produce was the admission of guilt that would make suicide a natural conclusion. I was thinking that way until I noticed that he hadn't been standing on the cardboard box that had apparently been kicked away to allow the drop.'

'An important bit of observation,' Strang said. 'That could easily have been missed.'

Gunn beamed, but Murray, who had opened her mouth as if she was about to speak, shut it again, as if she'd thought the better of what she was going to say. Strang raised his eyebrows, but she shook her head and said it was nothing.

Making a mental not to ask her later, he went on, 'Well, there's no point in theorising until we see what the evidence tells us. The SOCOs should be getting on with the work at Eastlaw Farm now – Matt, could I leave you to organise a rota for a constable on duty there to keep a log of visits, and supervise the incident room? Livvy, you can come with me. I want to start by interviewing Gresham.'

'Sure, boss,' Murray said, but Gunn, who had murmured,

'Of course, boss,' looked disappointed, as if he'd been denied an anticipated treat.

When they got back to the car, he said to Murray, 'What were you going to say back there?'

She sighed. 'Oh dear. I was all ready to say, "They were probably quite sure they'd get away with it – they've been getting away with everything else," when I realised that wouldn't reflect very well on the way Gunn was running his patch. I want a brownie point for biting my tongue in time, boss.'

Strang laughed. 'Once upon a time you'd have come right out with it. You're learning, Livvy. So tell me, what do you think of the way he's running his patch?'

'Hate to say it, but he's not effective. Over-sensitive. Thomson was easy enough to quell, and from what she said when I told her she'd to be civil, she'd had enough of young, inexperienced officers who wrung their hands and didn't do a lot. She's waiting to see how you stack up, I have to warn you.'

Strang laughed, as he was meant to, but having to rely on an inadequate inspector wasn't an encouraging start to the investigation. 'Matt was a bit disappointed that you weren't the one to be left to the prosaic duties, I thought.'

Murray gave him a mocking glance. 'He was counting on learning from watching the great detective at work, you see. That's why he was looking as if someone had stolen his scone.'

Strang pulled a face at her. 'Not everything you're doing now is an improvement. Once upon a time you'd have treated your boss with proper respect, Sergeant.'

'Ah, but I wasn't a sergeant then, was I?' she said in triumph.

He said, 'Watch it!' but when he saw the grin that split her face, he couldn't help laughing.

'But where is she?' Briony Gresham said, not for the first time.

Her father moved irritably in his seat. 'There's no point in asking me again, when you know I don't know. Look, I've got work to do if you haven't.'

She had come through to his office because she was just too restless to get on with the job of cancelling engagements; you could hardly go on as normal when one of your colleagues had killed himself. It didn't reflect well on the business, for a start, and she was only grateful that the buyers had left before the story came out and they had the press around asking intrusive questions.

What was irritating her was that she couldn't find out what had happened to Sarah.

She'd been Sarah's best friend but she'd left message after message on her phone and got no reply; surely Sarah couldn't be blaming them for what had happened? Knowing how upset Jimmie would be if Niall sold up, she'd admittedly been very discouraging about that idea, but all she'd actually said was that Sarah should wait and see if things might settle down.

The other thing bugging her was that she couldn't remember any other occasion when she couldn't find out whatever she wanted to know about something that was happening in Tarleton. Somehow Sarah had just disappeared – gone back to Edinburgh, perhaps? The policeman obviously knew, but even when she'd phoned him this morning, she'd only got that irritating, 'Not at liberty to say,' guff.

Her father had gone back to his computer and Briony, with a sigh and a shrug, went back to her own office and started on the phone calls.

'Is that the councillor's secretary? Please could you pass through a message that Mr Gresham won't be able to keep the appointment this afternoon? Can you find a slot in the diary in a couple of days' time?'

She made the arrangement and was ready to start again when her father put his head round the door.

'I've just found out where Sarah is. One of the men mentioned it. She's staying in the Caddon with Rose Moncrieff – she was seen coming out of her house with Rob.'

Briony stared at him. '*Rob?* He knew where she was, and he didn't tell me? I talked to him last night and he didn't say a word.'

'Maybe he didn't know last night,' Gresham said. 'But anyway, you know now so you can stop pestering me.' He withdrew.

Briony was shaking. True enough, Rob might only have found out today. But what the hell was he doing in Rose Moncrieff's house anyway? It was a year since Linden Moncrieff had died, the woman who with her disgraceful practices had killed poor Myrna Muir's mother, and probably others besides. Surely Rob had moved on by now? If he hadn't, he should have.

At least now she knew where to find Sarah, but there was no way she was going to that house. She'd just have to wait until she chose to respond to her messages – and if she didn't, well, Briony had other friends. Some.

DS Murray was in high good humour as they drove out of Tarleton and down the coast to Gresham's Farm. The blot on her record after the last case they'd been on together had worried her but now he'd taken her, not the higher-ranking officer – surely a sign of forgiveness.

The rain had stopped and a feeble sun was making an attempt to break through the low cloud. Now Strang was saying, 'I've been to Gresham's Farm before, in fact. He'd reported a stolen tractor so that came across my desk. I saw him and then went round the local farms to warn them and that was when I spoke to Sarah Lindsay and the Doddie Weir business started. Frankly, I wish now I hadn't prompted it – went nowhere and she'd a very hard time because of it.'

'But that's what's been going on,' Murray said. 'Things have been ignored because it causes too much trouble if it's taken up. Then everyone just turns a blind eye to the trade in illegal cigarettes and booze and goodness knows what else. It seems it's gone on for years.'

'"*Watch the wall, my darling,*"' Strang quoted wryly.

Startled, she said, 'Sorry?' She'd no idea what he was talking about.

'Kipling,' he said. '"A Smuggler's Song". Great poem – I learnt it at school. Running in the brandy has been pretty traditional in small coastal towns ever since Robert Burns was an Exciseman. "*If you wake at midnight, and hear a horse's feet,/ Don't go drawing back the blind or looking in the street,/ Them that asks no questions isn't told a lie./ Watch the*

142

wall my darling while the Gentlemen go by." The "Gentlemen" smugglers were anything but gentle in their methods of dealing with anyone who didn't get the message.'

Murray was greatly struck by this. 'It's not just wee coastal places either. It operates in any criminal community.'

'This particular community seems to have become more criminal than most. I'm quite concerned about this one, Livvy.'

She couldn't remember him ever saying that openly to her before, though she'd often enough reckoned that was what he'd been thinking.

'It's really nasty, right enough – cold-blooded. Gunn was saying that when you opened the door to the shed, you were right up against the body and the face was just grotesque. Sarah Lindsay was shell-shocked, according to him. Of course, he's got kind of a sentimental attitude but she'd have to be a total monster to do that to her partner.'

'Let's keep an open mind, shall we?'

'I know, I know, until we see what the evidence tells us.'

He smiled, but didn't reply.

They had come a few miles south of Tarleton when he said, 'Here we are,' and she saw the smartly painted noticeboard at the bottom of the road that said in gold letters, *Gresham's Farms*. There was a sign directing lorries to turn off onto a service road looping round to the right while the house and the offices were straight ahead.

After so recently visiting Eastlaw Farm, the contrast struck Murray forcibly. This was farming as gracious living. Ancient trees lined the drive; the verges were well cut and the extensive fields on either side were lushly green, with sheep in one, nibbling away at their presumably organic grass.

The house itself reminded Murray of the houses that everyone made such a fuss about in the Edinburgh New Town – very plain, but you could see it was sort of classy. There wasn't any sign of farming activity to the front, just a well-laid-out garden with shrubs and the sort of lawn where you could take your afternoon tea in the summer and admire the flower beds, and she couldn't help comparing it to Sarah's scrubby little plot; life simply wasn't fair. Though, of course, if the woman really had killed her partner, she probably wouldn't be in favour of the sort of scrupulous fairness that would demand a life for a life.

Despite her own misgivings, Sarah had to be the prime suspect. The partner usually was and she'd seen for herself the woman's anger and resentment at what Niall Ritchie had put her through – and not only that, disposing of Niall was a logical way to solve the 'we'll sell' / 'no we won't' problem. And despite the boss always saying not to start from motive, she still believed it was helpful sometimes, as long as you didn't let your desire to be right adjust the evidence to fit. She'd been tempted by that in the past but of course she was experienced enough now to be professionally objective. Absolutely.

Another sign directed them round to the back of the house, where there were outbuildings and barns, sheds and stores as well as a large parking area, where a lorry was waiting while a couple of men loaded it with boxes and crates.

As they looked for a sign for reception, Strang stopped suddenly. 'Oh look,' he said, 'there's my friend Doddie Muir. That's interesting.'

Murray followed his gaze. Muir was an unimpressive-looking man with a ratty face – pretty much a typical ned. She could understand Sarah not taking him seriously, but these were often the type you had to watch out for. Small snakes were often more dangerous than big ones.

Busy at his work, he hadn't noticed them. As they walked on, Strang said, 'Might be an idea to check out his record.'

'On my to-do list already,' she said.

The building the sign directed them to was starkly functional in comparison with the elegance of the main house – just a standard office block. Before they reached it, a voice hailed them.

'DCI Strang!'

They turned. A man was coming towards them from a long, open shed housing farm machinery, several huge monsters. Murray didn't begin to know what anyone did with them, but she guessed the man coming towards them must be Jimmie Gresham.

As Strang introduced her, he said, 'I've been expecting a visit. Come this way – I'll take you straight to my office.'

It was large, but much less luxurious than Murray had expected, given the house. It was just the sort of place where you'd see your workers and meet reps, and the chairs, upholstered with wooden arms, showed the signs of wear – Gresham, for all his wealth, was clearly a canny man.

As they all sat down, he said heavily, 'I have to say from the start that though I was shocked, when I thought about it, I wasn't really surprised. The awful thing is, I blame myself.'

Was Strang going to tell him? Murray gave him a quick sideways glance.

He was looking impassive and he settled back in his chair as he said, 'Indeed, sir? Do go on.'

CHAPTER NINE

Sarah Lindsay stared at her phone, holding it at arm's length as if the words she was hearing were an actual physical threat. 'I – I don't understand. Are you saying I can't access my partner's account?'

'Look, I know this is hard for you, but we'd need to see a copy of his will.' The woman had obviously been chosen for the job in the bereavement department of the bank for her sympathetic voice, but she wasn't giving an inch.

'But we were partners; we co-owned the farm. I can't show you a copy of his will because he never made one. I don't have a will either.'

Sarah could hear a sharp intake of breath, swiftly repressed. 'The thing is,' the woman said, 'you actually have separate accounts, as well as the joint one to which, of course, you do have access.'

'That's because we had separate businesses. We both paid into the joint one for household expenses. But I need to know what the financial situation is with the farm. Surely as his partner the account reverts to me—'

The voice became even more sympathetic, but what she said was, 'The thing is, you're not his next of kin. His parents are—'

'But they're dead!' Sarah cried.

'Does he have siblings?'

'A sister – they don't speak. How can she be next of kin, when we've lived together for years? Doesn't that make me his common-law wife?'

'I'm afraid there's no such thing.' The woman cleared her throat. 'Er – did your contract for buying the farm stipulate that in the case of decease, ownership would revert to the remaining partner?'

'I – I don't know! I'd have to look it out.'

'Your lawyer would surely have made that a condition, to safeguard both parties. It's standard practice.'

'Right,' she said. 'I'll find it and get back to you once they let me back into the house.'

Sarah ended the call and slumped back into her chair. A conversation was playing in her head: Niall saying, 'I've got a pal who's training as a solicitor. He says it's dead simple and he'll give us mate's rates. If we did it through his firm, they'd charge for every phone call.' And, God help her, now she could hear herself saying, 'Sounds good to me.'

She'd taken it on trust. Niall was the accountant and she'd taken no interest in figures beyond what was needed to run her little business. Had the 'mate' been competent enough to set it up properly? She'd only met him a couple of times in the pub when he'd been the life and soul of the party – a nice enough bloke, but not someone who would immediately strike you as precise and meticulous.

Perhaps it was all right, but Sarah wasn't confident. It looked as if she'd never get access to Niall's bank account at all and any money the farm had made would go to his sister and possibly even half the farm as well. What a fool she'd been not to pay more attention to the accounts! She could find herself without a roof over her head and she gave a little shiver as the cold chill of fear that was becoming familiar returned.

Sitting here in her bedroom getting spooked wasn't helping. She had to get a grip. She could go for a run; she'd learnt during lockdown how with sheer physical effort she could obliterate the endless cycles of anxious thought. Today she'd have to run harder than ever, though.

Rose had made her a sandwich for lunch and insisted she ate it, then she'd gone back to work in the studio. Sarah let herself out of the house and set off along the lane at a cracking pace.

She'd only taken a few strides when she had that odd, prickling feeling you get when someone is staring at you, and she turned round, rubbing the back of her neck. There was a woman standing in the garden of the house opposite, putting something in a bin, and she was giving her a death stare.

Sarah didn't know who she was, though she recognised her as one of the women who had always blanked her since she reported Doddie Weir. Was the news of Niall's murder out now on the town grapevine, and was everyone going to look at her as if they knew she'd killed him?

And even if they were, there was nothing she could do about it. Except run. Run till it hurt.

'I knew he was struggling,' Jimmie Gresham said, 'and I was sympathetic, right from the start when the statutory inspection gave him a pretty poor score. He so truly believed in the organic principle, and that's what's wonderful about these kids that take on subsistence farming with the light of idealism in their eyes. I've dealt with several of these and one or two, admittedly, have bailed out but others have gone on to make a big success of it, even to expand, now organic is so popular. Niall's problem – well, he hadn't a real instinct for farming. I thought he'd learn and I've propped him up every way I could – even given him a helping hand a few times, but it wasn't coming right. He'd always say, "No, no, it's fine. I'm getting there" – too proud to admit he couldn't hack it and accept the big dream was becoming a big nightmare. In fact, I'd thought he'd been showing more promising signs latterly – better yields and so on. And then I'd a difficult phone call with one of the supermarkets.' He sighed.

'Problems with quality?' Strang suggested. He had been listening with watchful eyes and Murray had taken her cue from him, trying to work out whether the man actually knew already what they knew, and failing.

'Yes. They'd done one of the random spot checks they sometimes do. A consignment of carrots had shown up as having traces of chemical fertiliser and when we tracked it back, they had come from Eastlaw.'

Murray was interested. 'Does that often happen?'

'Oh, it's not unheard of. Usually it's a case of a contracted crop being poorer than expected and a farmer going out in a panic and buying cheap replacements to fill the quota. I'd a problem with that once before but it was an isolated incident and I persuaded the buyer to come down to the farm and see how hard the guy was trying and I didn't have to terminate the contract. Now his is the most successful of our small farms and it's never happened again. There's only been one where the farmer was actually cheating, and he was out on his ear. It never occurred to me that this wasn't a one-off – Niall was so completely dedicated to the principles. The terrible mistake I made was to call him to warn him about the complaint. I said I'd managed to persuade the buyer to have a chat with him at the party I was giving that night and that I was sure we could smooth it over if he could convince the man it had been a stupid panic, and let him see the way the farm was actually being run.'

'Did you see him after that?' Strang asked.

'No. I was flat out with meetings and preparations. God, I wish now I had! He might have come clean about what he'd done, instead of falling into despair. But at the time I was just upset when he didn't appear at the party, because it made it harder to give him a second chance. Now poor Sarah has to cope with all this. How is she? My daughter, Briony, has been trying to reach her but I suspect she's feeling embarrassed. Can you pass on the message to her that we're both worried about her and totally sympathetic – and indeed I want to say sorry that I didn't realise what was happening and do something about it.'

'Well, thank you for giving us the background, sir,'

Strang said. 'The thing is, it isn't evident that Mr Ritchie killed himself. There are suspicious circumstances, which we are investigating.'

Gresham looked stunned. 'But – but I saw the body hanging there myself—'

'Yes indeed, but there is disturbing forensic evidence. Can you think of any reason why someone would wish Mr Ritchie harm?'

'I–I can't think – what would anyone get out of that?' he stammered. 'I wouldn't have thought he'd an enemy in the place.'

'You must have been very shocked, angry, even, when you saw the chemicals he had been using?'

'Well, shocked, certainly. I wouldn't have believed it if someone had told me. But there was the poor lad, hanging there, so tortured with guilt that he'd killed himself, as I thought. So angry? No.'

'I see,' Strang said. 'Anyway, just as a matter of form, sir, can you talk me through your movements on Wednesday?'

'Let me think – it was a very busy day. Breakfast at the house with my daughter, then the office for the meetings I mentioned. I'd a couple of things to do in the town – spoke to my brother – or was that the day before? No, that's right, it was Wednesday. Then I was just here, around the farm, and checking everyone was organised for the party – car parking and so on. After the party was over, I suggested Briony should phone Sarah to prepare for the buyer's visit the next morning and then – well, you've probably read the statement I gave. But this is a terrible, terrible thing—'

'Yes it is,' Strang said gravely. 'Now, I think that's all for the moment. Thank you for your cooperation, sir.' He got up, Murray followed suit and Gresham escorted them to the door of the office. As they stepped outside, Strang gestured towards the machines across the yard.

'I see you've got a replacement for the tractor that was stolen.'

'Eventually,' Gresham said. 'Oh, it was insured, of course, but I was still left badly out of pocket, having to hire temporarily while we sourced another one. Working days lost cost serious money. Have you made any progress with the case?'

'The investigation is ongoing but it seems to link in to a wider network. I can only ask you to keep an eye open and pass anything on that strikes you.'

As they drove off, Murray said, 'He was gob-smacked, wasn't he?'

'He was certainly shocked – he didn't fake that reaction. But was he shocked that Niall had been murdered, or was he shocked that we'd found out?'

'Hard to say,' she said. But she reckoned Sarah Lindsay probably wasn't top of the suspect list any more.

When Jimmie Gresham left her office having broken the news, Briony sat at her desk staring into space. Was this why Sarah hadn't phoned her? She was uneasily aware that Sarah absolutely hated living in Tarleton, and when they'd talked about it last time, Sarah had actually indicated that if only she could persuade Niall, they'd just sell up. Briony had tried to talk her out of it; it really would be so ungrateful after all that Dad had done for them, and had kept on doing – she'd seen the books. But supposing Niall had refused to agree, what might Sarah have done then?

How desperate had she been to get away?

Oh, of course she didn't really believe that Sarah – her good friend, after all – could possibly do something so horrible. But she'd definitely been very upset about something when she arrived at the party – and of course it was probably only what she'd said, that she and Niall had had a row – a terrible row.

But the thing was, someone had to have killed Niall and a row could get out of hand; it could get physical, and the outcome could be a fatal accident. Supposing that had happened, wouldn't Sarah just phone the police and explain?

Briony knew Sarah's opinion of the police, though, after they'd encouraged her to take on Doddie Weir. She wouldn't trust them – and when she thought about it, if she did, they'd have no alternative but to arrest her anyway.

So was it possible that Sarah – the Sarah who had been her friend for years – could have done that dreadful thing, and then followed it through with a charade that Briony herself had been part of? Surely not! And yet, and yet . . .

She could phone Rob and tell him, see what he thought. Her hand was going out to her mobile when she remembered – of course, Rob probably knew already. Sarah would have been told the news before anyone else and if he'd been at Rose Moncrieff's house with Sarah, he'd probably heard at once.

And he hadn't told Briony that either. She'd believed they were very close, ever since Linden died, but he'd kept it secret that he'd gone on visiting her mother and now he was keeping it secret that he was in contact with Sarah.

It was hurtful. And Sarah – Briony had always been the

friend she would turn to, but now that seemed to be Rob. That was hurtful too. She was upset, very upset. She really hated disloyalty.

It was a dreich day as DCI Strang left Tarleton and took the climbing road to Eastlaw Farm, the cloud cover so heavy it was even catching the tops of the low, soft Moorfoot Hills, all dull greens and greys. The last time he'd been there, the sun must have been shining because it hadn't struck him what a dreary and isolated place it was; today he was thinking that living here could have a severe effect on mental health and stability.

He had dropped DS Murray off at the station while he went to see what the SOCOs had come up with, tasking her with getting her teeth into the background stuff.

'Research around every known contact,' he told her. 'You've got a real instinct – just follow your nose.'

Murray beamed. 'No problem, boss.'

'And ask Matt to commission bank statements and phone records ASAP – we're going to hit the weekend if we don't get them today – and find a constable to consolidate the information we have to date. We can't put out the statement until Ritchie's sister's been told so it may be that we won't have media interest until tomorrow. We've just said "suspicious circumstances" so it won't draw much attention yet.'

'It'll get round soon enough now Gresham knows,' Murray pointed out, 'but from what Matt's told me, we won't be finding lots of good citizens queueing up at the station to tell us what's been going on.'

He'd arranged for a briefing meeting before they headed

back and now he parked alongside the SRCS vehicles, looking for the officer in charge. A saluting uniform with a clipboard was at his side immediately and he nodded approval; Gunn had got on to that job with commendable efficiency.

There were SOCOs around a small, run-down shed – presumably where the body was found – and there was a huge old barn with its wide wooden doors standing open and another group working inside. He could see there was activity in the farmhouse too and headed towards it.

He must have been spotted. Strang was pleased to see that it was Steve MacRobert who was coming out to greet him; he'd worked with him before.

'So how's it going?' Strang said.

'I'd been hoping we'd find a signed confession left by the killer so we could get away home to our tea, but sadly not. Best we've come up with is a reel of rope in the barn that the guy could have been hanged with, though it's a pretty standard type – we've packed it up for forensics and they should be able to give a definitive answer.'

'What about the weapon that inflicted the head wound? Anything?'

MacRobert gave him a scornful look. 'This is a farmyard, mate – any idea how many potentially lethal weapons there are lying around this place? Stones, bricks, fence posts, implements? We're sending off a short length of sodden timber that was lying in one of the near fields, but I wouldn't get your hopes up. And there's death traps too just looking for them – one of the guys fell on his face down a bank when one of the bloody hens ran straight in front of him and then flew up into his face, shrieking.'

Following his pointing finger, Strang realised there were hens everywhere, pecking around the hen houses below.

'Scrambled eggs for tea, then?'

'There's a mannie working down there keeping a beady eye, more's the pity.'

'Anything from the shed?'

'Some scuff marks that could indicate dragging, but not beyond the obvious that we know already. There's a lad dusting for prints – some are most likely Ritchie's that we can match up, but dozens more that could go back decades.'

'And inside?'

'Lots of bumf from a desk upstairs in what looks to have been the farm office – we're packing it all away, and taking the computer for the boffins to gut. We've got his mobile too but we've been careful not to tamper with what looks like the woman's property – we haven't a warrant for that. I'm assuming she has to be a suspect and even if we found that signed confession, her brief could get her off on procedure.'

'Good man,' Strang said. 'I've got my team working to get as much info as we can before the weekend so we'll assess what we've got on Monday. Thanks, Steve.'

As he turned to get back in his car, he noticed there was a man standing watching what was happening on the other side of what presumably was the boundary fence with the farmyard next door – a surly-looking man with two-day stubble, wearing a dirty-looking waterproof jacket. Strang groped for the name on the statement he'd read – Blackford, that was it.

He walked across to speak to him but before he could say anything, Blackford said, 'You in charge? Like to tell me what the hell is going on here?'

'DCI Strang,' he said, automatically flipping out his card, which, unusually, was carefully scrutinised.

'Well, well – brought in the heavies, have they? Bit surprising for something like this, isn't it?'

Strang repeated the standard response – suspicious circumstances, investigating – while Blackford listened with narrowed eyes, then added, 'Do you have any reason to think that Mr Ritchie had enemies?'

'Him, enemies? Bit of a strong word with someone that couldn't blow the froth off his beer. But around here it's easy to get across someone without realising it.'

'Meaning?'

Blackford shrugged. 'Just – oh, there's aye this and that.'

'So did Mr Ritchie get across you?'

'Naah! We were pals – told him he was a mug with all the organic bollocks.'

'Were you aware that he was using pesticides?'

The pause suggested that Blackford was weighing up his response. 'None of my business. Gresham's business, though. You might want to ask him.'

Ignoring that, Strang asked him what he had done on Wednesday; the reply came without hesitation this time.

'Like I said when your lot asked before – left early for the stock lamb sale in Kelso, came back and settled in the stock I'd bought. Went to bed.'

'Did you see Mr Ritchie at any time that day? Or his partner?'

'Oh aye, saw the girl all right – off she went in some fancy clothes early evening. Never saw him. His car was there, though.'

'And you didn't see any sign of anyone else being around?'

'Not here to see them, if there was – I said, didn't I?'

'No lights in the evening, while Ms Lindsay was away?'

'Not till late when I heard Gresham's lot arriving.'

'Right,' Strang said thoughtfully. 'Thank you, sir – oh, just one more thing. Would you have thought Niall Ritchie might kill himself?'

His reply was scornful. 'Could have. Coward's way out, isn't it – poor, useless bastard.'

The miserable-looking dogs in the cage had suddenly started barking as one of the SOCOs passed and Blackford turned to shout obscenities at them. There wasn't much point in waiting; Strang didn't feel there was any more useful information he could get at this time and, with a farewell wave to MacRobert, he went back to his car.

There was nothing DS Murray liked more than a bit of ferreting and she was still glowing at Strang's compliment as she worked on Jimmie Gresham, and his brother Andrew for good measure, since they were mentioned so often together. They had no previous, apart from a few speeding tickets – the force around here were obviously trying to improve the poor crime stats with traffic offences. They featured on the business pages and in the local newspapers, mainly in reports of social functions and charitable events – indeed, Murray suspected that there was a certain amount of competitive philanthropy going on: when Andrew contributed to improvements to the swimming pool, it wouldn't be long before Jimmie donated to a local rewilding project. Respectable, well-doing citizens – kenspeckle figures, in the old Scots phrase. Nothing to get her teeth into – so far.

DI Gunn had been spending his time sitting on the phone to various departments of the banking system, muttering as he was yet again put on hold to listen to yet another irritating piece of music or a cooing voice that said, 'Please hold the line. Your call is important to us.'

'And that's a blatant lie,' he snarled. 'I'm being sent round in circles. I've had enough of this.'

Murray had been making sympathetic noises. 'Tell you what,' she said, 'do you think Thomson could be persuaded to bring us a cup of tea and maybe a biscuit?'

'Only if you could convince her that the DCS would take it as a personal insult if she didn't. I'll get it from the incident room. They'll be all set up by now.' He went out with some alacrity.

Murray looked after him thoughtfully. He was definitely looking more chipper since they arrived – less haunted or something, now it wasn't his responsibility. But she'd listened to him on the phone, thinking, *Oh, get a grip!* He wasn't forceful; she could hear that he was accepting their excuses too readily, not taking them on, not impressing them with the urgency of his enquiries. She was ready to bet that by now if she'd been tasked with it, she might not actually have access to the details but at least she'd have irritated senior management enough to get every junior jumping to find out for her what she wanted to know and get her off their backs.

Bank records told a story and if they'd managed to get them, they could have progressed things over the weekend. Phone and computer records would take time to be analysed and even though the SRCS had priority status, there was no chance of that sort of information until into next week so unless Strang had got something useful, it looked as if the inquiry would just stall.

Gunn came back triumphant with tea and a box of assorted biscuits. 'It's all looking good through there, but they're just dossing around. Not a soul across the threshold, not a phone call.'

Murray annexed a Jammie Dodger. 'Even in a place like this, it takes time for word to get around. I'm just going to run a check on Doddie Weir now – what do you know about him?'

'Save yourself the bother. Apart from the business with Sarah Lindsay and a few petty complaints that we never got anywhere with, you won't find anything. Do you know when the boss is likely to appear for the briefing?'

'Haven't heard from him. Are you going back to prodding the bank?'

'Do you think it'll do any good? One of them was muttering about a warrant and we don't have that yet.'

'Have another go at them,' Murray advised. 'Sound mean. You never know.'

Gunn sighed and picked up the phone again. She went back to her computer; despite what he said, she wasn't going to take his word for it about Doddie Weir. She got on to the records office and her eyebrows rose as she read what it said.

At that moment, she heard Strang's voice in the corridor. 'Thank you, Constable. I know my own way,' and she closed down the file. She'd have time to think about the implications later.

Driving back from Eastlaw Farm, DCI Strang had been reviewing the position. The formality of informing Ritchie's next of kin had apparently been completed and the statement, carefully worded, had been released; there were already media requests for more information. DCS Borthwick was handling that end and he would be reporting in to her later for discussions.

As far as interviews were concerned, there wasn't much more he could do here at the moment. He'd ordered checks on the movements of Jimmie Gresham and his daughter, and on Ken Blackford, but there wasn't at the moment anyone else in the picture. Unless Murray's researches had come up with a fresh angle, or someone came in off the street with something they could follow up, they'd just have to wait until the 'bumf' Steve MacRobert would send for analysis gave them some picture of Niall Ritchie's hinterland and they got hold of the bank information that would let him plot the next lines for investigation: 'follow the money' was always a good starting point, so he was hoping Gunn had been successful.

Banks were permanently reluctant to divulge anything about their clients, though, and as Strang went into the office where Murray and Gunn were working, he could hear Gunn saying with strained patience, 'It would really be very helpful if you could . . . Yes, I do see that. Thank you anyway.'

'No luck?' Strang said as Gunn put the phone down.

'Playing it by the book, sir, I'm afraid. And the person who knows most about this process has gone off for the weekend.'

Strang nodded, then turned to Murray. 'Anything useful?'

'Not so far. There's always more digging that can be done if you want, but it'd be kind of random – like a dog digging up the whole garden because he doesn't have a scooby where he's buried his bone.'

Strang smiled. 'I think you should put it on hold for the moment. The SOCOs are doing a very thorough job but the only physical evidence they've got is rope found in the barn that might, or might not, have been used, and a bit of wood that's the same. The records of one sort and another they're passing on for analysis. We're a bit stymied right now. The farm's very isolated; I've spoken to the neighbour, who didn't see anything, and there's no one else around for follow-up questioning. I'll be checking in over the weekend and if there's anything we can pursue down here we'll do that, but I've got to see JB today so I think we should pack it in now, unless there's anything else. All right?'

They both nodded, though Strang thought Murray was a little hesitant, and looked at her enquiringly.

'No, nothing,' she said.

'Right. I'll keep you informed.'

As he drove up the A1, his mind was on the weekend ahead. He'd go into the office, of course, to check on anything that came in, and Betsy had extracted a promise that he'd take her out for ice cream on Sunday, but he might indulge himself for once with a leisurely breakfast, and perhaps go to the gym in the afternoon. He'd been using the work excuse far too often of late.

Strang and Gunn left while Murray shut down her laptop and gathered up her things with a sigh. It felt very strange to be having a weekend in the middle of a case; when they'd worked together before, they'd always been on location, so to speak, and just going back home now felt sort of flat. It was true, though, that there was no point in investigating if you didn't know where you needed to go.

The police station was closed now and, letting herself out of the side door, she went to her car. At least she'd something to think over on the way north: an interesting thing had struck her as she checked the official records. She might check tomorrow to see whether the boss had indeed gone in to work and she could talk it through with him then.

She was driving along by the harbour when an idea came to her. There was, after all, something she could do, right now.

CHAPTER TEN

'Don't think we'll get a lot of media interest,' Detective Chief Superintendent Borthwick said. '"Suspicious circumstances" doesn't make much of a headline and by the time we confirm murder, it won't be hot news. A two-day-old cover-up crime doesn't have quite the same click appeal as "wolf attack" on Twitter.'

'Thank the Lord for that,' DCI Strang said with a reminiscent shudder. 'There's a lot going on in the background, though. Once we get started, I can't be sure what the spread will be, or where it will go. I get the impression the place has got a bit Wild West since lockdown.'

'A sort of general lawlessness, you mean?' she said.

'Yes. The police station runs on office hours, which I'm sure saves money, but at the cost of effective policing.'

It was true, but a bit of a bold statement. Finance was always a sensitive topic with JB, who admittedly was the one who had to argue for every penny, which wasn't easy. So he was waiting for her to change the subject now.

'Hmm,' she said. 'Anyway – suspects?'

'You know I'm always reluctant to start from there, but in this case there are two obvious front-runners – the girlfriend who was desperate to sell the farm while the victim was refusing, and the organic farmer who contracted to buy Ritchie's farm produce then discovered his own reputation compromised with his supermarket clients by the man using nonorganic methods.'

Borthwick frowned. 'A bit flimsy, no? The girl, perhaps – I could just about see that, I suppose, if she believed she could get away with it. But the businessman – an elaborately planned murder as punishment for nonorganic farm produce getting into the food chain? Seems excessive – he could just have terminated the contract rather than the man.'

'On the basis of the limited evidence we have, there isn't an argument to advance yet and until the reports come in, I'm afraid there's not a lot useful we can do.'

'You'll be working overtime once they land on your desk. Take a bit of a break, Kelso.'

'Right.' He got up. 'I've just got some desk work to shift and of course I'll check in to see if anything appears.'

As he went to the door, Borthwick said slyly, 'Fed any more starving young advocates lately?'

To Strang's annoyance, he felt his cheeks turn hot. 'Oh – er, no,' he said. 'Just a one-off. On much the same basis as

I'm taking my niece out for ice cream on Sunday.'

'Really?' Borthwick said, and he could hear her laughing as he shut the door.

DS Murray didn't really know where she was going, but she reckoned if she asked a passing local, they'd be able to tell her how to find the Waterfoot Tavern in the Caddon. She left the car in the harbour car park, grabbed a jacket and set off on foot.

The nights were starting to draw in and on this dreary day it was even darker than usual, and a light rain was falling. It was after Strang and Gunn had left that she had suddenly remembered Sarah Lindsay talking about Niall Ritchie's visits to the Waterfoot that she had so much resented, and it came to Murray that for the moment she was still pretty much anonymous.

It was a state of affairs that wouldn't last long; by the time the investigation picked up, she'd be a marked woman and conversations would die whenever she walked in. Now, however, the news that Niall had been murdered would be spreading and sitting quietly in the pub would be a good way to get a feel for the reaction. She was dead chuffed with herself for having thought of it. Strang couldn't help but be impressed when she reported—

On that thought, Murray stopped dead. She was at it again, wasn't she – thinking it was smart to take her own line, even after the number of times that had backfired on her. They were, as Strang had said wearily on previous occasions, a team, not a set of individuals, and he might, for instance, want to leave it so he could check out the pub himself later – though of course she didn't think that was

166

likely to be as useful as what she was planning now.

If she phoned to get authorisation, he might say no – and it was such a good idea! She walked on again slowly, wrestling with herself. She needn't even tell him she'd been – she'd just be getting a useful informal impression, not questioning anyone or anything. But then supposing she did pick up important information – how would she be able to feed it back without explaining how she'd got it—

And getting another black mark on her record. She stopped, then with a groan took out her phone and made the call. If it went to voicemail, it'd be a sign and she'd hang up . . .

'Oh, boss,' she said. 'Just wanted to run something past you. I thought it might be an idea to drop in at the Waterfoot Tavern before I drive back – folks won't know who I am yet and I could just sit in a corner with a Beck's Blue and earwig. Sarah Lindsay told me he went there a lot and word should be getting out about now.'

Murray held her breath as Strang said, 'Well, that's an interesting angle. I don't see why not. Don't try to get into conversations – we don't want them to know too much about the official side yet and you can't lie.'

'I'll take out my phone and get absorbed and then no one will bother me.' She was punching the air as she said it.

'Right. Report back tomorrow to tell me how you got on. Oh, and Livvy – well done!'

She could hear the smile in his voice as he rang off – it wasn't her idea that had won his pat on the back. She was feeling good about her discipline and maturity as she walked on into the maze of streets that was the Caddon.

The passer-by she stopped to ask for directions was

a middle-aged woman, who looked, Murray thought, surprised at the question, but pointed her along the narrow road that ran straight between the houses to the old harbour at the other end. She followed it down.

A small, stony burn ran down one side of the street until a tunnel took it under the road across the bottom to discharge into the harbour basin. The Waterfoot Tavern, squatting on one corner, didn't look appealing.

There was an old-fashioned Scottish pub style that had windows made of frosted glass with an inset ventilator and paintwork that always looked as if it was only there to stop the wood from rotting, and when Murray was young there'd been a quite number of those around Glasgow. Now they'd nearly all been bought over, tarted up and called something like The Prawn and Bagpiper – rubbish as pubs, but profitable. That this one was still going despite its lack of any sort of kerb appeal told her that it was still the watering-hole for a loyal local clientele – exactly what she was looking for.

The beery smell assailed her as she pressed down the old brass door latch and stepped inside. It was quite dark and she blinked for a moment as her eyes adjusted to take in the pitch pine woodwork and a bar boasting a range of beer pumps; there were stools round the bar and a few tables round the edge of the room.

It was, unfortunately, very small, and it wasn't going to be at all easy to carry out her plan of being inconspicuous – not least because it was early and there weren't a lot of drinkers yet. Not only that, nearly all of them were men and every head turned as she crossed the worn vinyl to place her order.

The barman, a bald, sour-faced man who looked as if he'd rather tell her to get out than ask her what she wanted, all but sneered when she asked for a Beck's Blue. Not the sort of thing real men would drink, of course.

'Don't stock it.'

He could hardly say he didn't have beer or lemonade for a shandy, so she ordered that instead. He made it grudgingly then took some pleasure in saying the van hadn't been when she asked if he had crisps. The message was clear – strange women weren't welcome.

Fortunately, there was an unoccupied table in the far corner so she slunk away to it, aware that she was still being regarded with hostile suspicion – Sarah Lindsay, she remembered, had said they were crooks, the lot of them. Murray had been preparing herself with bland replies to the normal social questions bartenders usually ask but the contrast between the lack of any verbal interest and the intensity of the silent scrutiny was disconcerting. All she could do was match the silence, and wait. She got out her phone and became instantly absorbed in it.

A couple of men came in and the tension dissipated. They were greeted and conversations started up again; apart from the odd glance sent in her direction, she was being pretty much ignored, which gave her time to take surreptitious glances round about.

There were only two women there. One was standing at the bar, middle-aged and with a cheap bleach job just growing out, and there was a lot of laughter in the group round her. The other was very different – not at all the sort of woman you'd expect to patronise a place like this.

She was sitting at a table with a much younger man –

quite buff, actually – and she had the sort of glossy finish that came in expensive – smartly styled dark brown hair, and a sharp-looking blazer paired with jeans and a cream sweater, an outfit that looked more suited to an office than a pub, particularly one like this. She was handsome rather than pretty and though she and her companion were involved in low-voiced conversation, they were interrupted several times by men who stopped by to chat to them both; they must be locals, so it wasn't likely that this was any sort of romantic relationship. Mother and son, perhaps, though she didn't look old enough to have a son that age.

Unfortunately, they were too far away for her to hear what they were saying. Added to that, it was looking as if the news of Niall Ritchie's murder had not yet got round locally – a disappointment. The only conversation she'd been able to hear clearly was about football and she was just deciding to give up when the door opened again and she saw, with some discomfort, Ken Blackford coming in.

He headed for the bar with the confident manner of a regular, just sweeping a glance round and nodding to a friend. Then he saw her. An unpleasant smile came over his face; he came across to stand directly in front of her and said loudly, 'Well, what do you know – Detective Murray! To what do we owe the pleasure of your company? Doing a bit of snooping, eh?'

Again, the room fell silent. It was an ugly silence; the sooner she got out of here, the better. Murray stood up, pocketing her phone. 'I just came in for a drink after work, in fact, but you're not a very friendly lot, are you?'

She shouldered her way past him. But on the way out she did notice that though there was general interest, the older woman and the man were staring at her and then looking at each other. By the time she reached the door, their heads were together across the table again in animated conversation.

On Saturday morning, the answer Sarah Lindsay got to her request to be allowed back into Eastlaw Farm wasn't the one she had been hoping for; it was apparently still a crime scene and permission was unlikely to be given before Monday.

Rose Moncrieff was sympathetic to her impatience, but thought it wouldn't be a good idea to go back anyway. 'It must all still be pretty raw,' she said, 'and it's so isolated. I really don't like to think of you there on your own, especially when there's a bedroom here standing empty.'

They were sitting over the breakfast table. Sarah put out a hand to touch Rose's arm. 'You're endlessly hospitable and you know how grateful I am. But until I get access to the records in the house, I can't find out what the position is with the farm – whether I'm even entitled to stay on there.'

'Have you spoken to Niall's sister yet?'

Sarah grimaced. 'Last night. She wasn't exactly helpful. I've only met her a couple of times and the meetings ended with the two of them having a stand-up row. Niall was the clever one who got a well-paying job and, because she's married to a deadbeat who keeps losing his, she thought it was Niall's duty to help provide for the two kids. And he did, but latterly we'd nothing to spare and she was furious. The last row was about how utterly selfish he was for being broke. The police had obviously told her she's his next of kin and all she wanted to know was how much would be

171

coming to her. "Farms must be worth a lot of money," she said.' Sarah gave a bitter laugh. 'Little does she know – with the mortgage and debts and everything, I'll be lucky if I come out of it £10 up – which I'll have to split with her.'

'Is there a lot of debt?' Rose asked, adding hastily, 'Of course, you may not want to talk about it . . .'

'Oh, why not? The trouble is, I don't know. At the start we had our separate businesses and I was lazy; Niall was good at all the figures and the paperwork you have to file with the government and I left it to him. Latterly I was sure things were going badly but he'd got very secretive and wouldn't let me look at the accounts, just said things were fine as long as we were careful. I didn't really believe him then and I don't believe it now. I didn't actually know him, did I?' There were tears in her eyes. 'I'm very sad for him, but I'm not truly grieving – just struggling with guilt over how little I did to try to save the relationship.'

Rose said gently, 'There's always guilt in the aftermath. I know intellectually that Linden's death was her choice and there was no way I could have stopped her, but still the if-only-I-hads keep cropping up. Rob says the same.' She blew her nose on a tissue.

'Oh, now look what I've done!' Sarah said. 'I'm sorry.' She got up. 'I'm going to clear the breakfast. And then I think I'd better go along to the shop. I'm not going to open it and I'll keep the blind down but I ought just to check for online orders.'

'That's a good idea,' Rose said heartily. 'I've got a batch of pots to take out of the kiln so I'll get on with that.'

'When I'm in the town, I'll pick up something for our lunch. Anything else you're needing?'

'That's kind. Now you mention it, a couple of things. I'll give you a list.'

Armed with that, Sarah walked along to her shop, grateful that it was still early and there weren't many people around to glare at her. It wouldn't be long before Tarleton was buzzing with the story, in which she would no doubt feature as the woman with blood on her hands.

But whose hands were they – the ones that had strangled Niall, then constructed the visible lie that he had killed himself? Someone she knew, or someone known only to him? He'd spoken to her of danger, of the 'spider's web' he'd somehow blundered into. And he'd been afraid. He'd linked it somehow to the Doddie Muir case – but what had he meant?

She'd need to repeat that to the chief inspector, who had spoken to her kindly – but had also looked at her with cool, appraising eyes. If he came to believe that she was guilty, she had no doubt at all that his pursuit of her would be ruthless. Perhaps there was no point in trying to keep her struggling business going. Her Majesty graciously provided board and lodging when you were staying at her pleasure.

Sarah had reached the shop but decided that the earlier she went to the supermarket, the better, and walked on. She'd been insistent that she would repay at least some of Rose's hospitality and as well as picking up the items on the list, she chose a selection of cheeses, a loaf from the in-store bakery and a carton of grapes for an easy lunch, along with a bottle of wine.

Her mind very much on her purchases, she joined the shortest queue. It was only when the customer in front moved on to start packing her shopping that she realised who was sitting at the till and gave an involuntary gasp. Her next step would bring her face to face with the woman who had stared at her with such hatred that she had almost felt it might burn her skin.

Sarah had a sudden wild impulse to turn and flee, leaving what she had chosen on the conveyor belt, but there was someone behind her now and it would cause a fuss that would attract attention, the last thing she wanted. To brave the woman's glare was the lesser of the two evils – after all, she was unlikely to follow it up with a physical attack in her workplace.

Myrna, read the name badge on her overall. The previous customer was having a chat as she presented her card, and Myrna laughed as she gave her the receipt. She was still smiling as she turned her head and saw Sarah.

The smile vanished and the woman's doughy face changed. She scowled, her deep-set eyes narrowed, her lips taut.

'Shameless!' she hissed. 'I know what you've done – and you coming here with your cheek to mix with decent folk when the poor man's body's barely cold!'

Sarah felt the blood drain from her head. Myrna had not lowered her voice and people were turning to stare. Feeling faint, she could only just manage to say, 'I don't know what you're talking about. Could you please just process my shopping?'

There was a buzz of conversation now, and the manager had obviously noticed. She came over and said, 'Is there a problem here?'

Myrna's face had gone red with anger, but she said hastily, 'No, it's all right. Just putting through this customer's stuff.' She began to do that, with practised speed, and the manager moved away.

Sarah moved along to pack it, avoiding looking at the woman, but she was uncomfortably aware that the man who was next in the queue was looking at her suspiciously and at the next-door till someone was having a conversation that included the words, 'saying he was murdered'.

She fumbled with her credit card as she took it out and in the seconds before she managed to complete the payment, Myrna took the chance to say, though in a lower voice this time, 'You'd better get out of here, you and her, witches the both of you. I'm warning you, we've had enough.'

Feeling sick, Sarah moved on, countering curious glances with a rictus smile. She'd better go to her shop and hide away there, until she had recovered her composure enough not to alarm Rose when she returned.

Niall Ritchie's suspicious death was reported on the local news on breakfast TV but there was no sensationalising. The wording of the official statement must have been very bland, Livvy Murray reflected admiringly. Police investigations were always easier when you didn't have the media breathing down your neck.

There couldn't have been any new developments overnight. Livvy was still in her pyjamas, eating cereal as she lounged on the sofa, and debating what she was going to do. Somehow it felt wrong not to be doing something to progress the investigation, but it was hard to see what she could do. She wasn't sure if Kelso would even go in to the station.

She could call up one of her mates and see if she fancied

mooching round the shops and having a bevvy or two, but it didn't really appeal.

She was disappointed that her foray into the dark hinterland of the Caddon hadn't yielded anything of use to report to Kelso. The news that Ritchie hadn't killed himself clearly hadn't been general knowledge by then, though when she thought about it, the older woman and the younger man had undoubtedly been having a rather intense discussion about something.

Blackford was a thoroughly nasty bully, and he would be an unpleasant neighbour for Sarah Lindsay once she got back to the house – hardly surprising she'd wanted out. Livvy had been inclined to be dismissive about Matt Gunn's worries, but she was beginning to feel very uncomfortable about the place herself.

That reminded her of the other thing she'd wanted to talk over with Kelso. Perhaps she'd just drop in at Fettes Avenue on the off-chance he might be there. She jumped up, switched off the TV and went to have a bath. Suddenly the day looked more interesting.

When Rob Gresham at last picked up the phone and called Briony, she was distinctly chilly.

'Good to hear from you at long last,' she said. 'I take it you've been in the centre of all that's going on?'

He was immediately defensive. 'That sounds like an accusation. What's your problem?'

'Oh, just I thought we were mates, but you knew where Sarah was and you didn't tell me. Then Dad tells me that you were at Rose Moncrieff's house when the police told her what had happened to Niall.'

'I suppose, guilty as charged. But I'm not sure why I should account for myself to you.'

Briony said, 'No, of course not,' but she went on. 'It's just – why would you be visiting Rose? She's not a popular lady here, you know – insensitive, really. There's people who feel upset with her squatting there and reminding them of what her daughter did. People like poor Myrna Muir.'

Tight-lipped, Rob snarled, 'Don't you dare talk about that! You and I both know what happened and the person who was blameless was Linden. Rose has gone through hell and if keeping in touch helps her, it's the very least I can do. All right? Otherwise I might—'

Briony backed off. 'No, no, of course I understand. I'm sorry, I didn't mean to sound like that. It's just I was really hurt that you hadn't told me what you were doing and I've been so upset with everything that's happened that it came out all wrong. The last thing I'd want to do is turn you against me. I couldn't bear that. We've been so close over this last bit, we're cousins – two of a kind, really.'

Rob's face twisted. 'God help us, I suppose we are. Chips off the old blocks, for our sins. Anyway, I thought you might want to hear how things are with your friend.'

'Oh. Well, yes, I do, of course.' But her voice still sounded cold.

He got the impression that Sarah might not be such a friend any more; Briony never coped well with rejection. 'Look, Sarah was feeling embarrassed and guilty because of what Niall had been doing – that's why she didn't get in touch with you. She feels Jimmie did so much for them and Niall had let him down badly.'

'Really? That's silly, of course we wouldn't have blamed

177

her for what Niall did. I just felt that Rose was her new friend and she didn't need her old one any more.'

'Not at all,' Rob said heartily. 'For goodness' sake, don't get all weird about it. I'll tell her it's all right and that you've been missing her – I'll be seeing her later.' As the words left his mouth he knew he'd said the wrong thing.

'Oh, will you?' she said.

He blundered on, 'She needs all the friends she can get at the moment, poor lass. I could bring her down to see you, if you like—'

'I'm not sure that's the best idea, just at the moment, with everything being up in the air. If she wants to speak to me, she knows how to get me.'

The penny dropped. 'You think she killed him, do you?'

'Of course not,' Briony said. 'It's just – well, somebody must have.'

Rob ended the call. He wasn't happy about where that left him, and he certainly wasn't happy about where that left Sarah Lindsay.

At that moment, Sarah was coming back from a run, her lungs bursting from the effort she had put in. She'd checked from the house before she went out to see that Myrna wasn't watching and headed up along the cliff path where she wasn't likely to meet anyone who knew her; she wasn't quite that notorious yet. All she could hope for was that before she was, she could get back to the farm, where she could run as far as she liked around the fields instead of finding herself confined to the house here. She'd never dreamt that she'd see the day when what she wanted to do was go back to Eastlaw.

With another anxious glance towards Myrna's house, she ran on to reach Rose's gate – and stopped dead, her stomach churning. There, daubed across Rose's pristine white garden wall was blood-red paint, running artistically down in droplets.

CHAPTER ELEVEN

Kelso Strang had meant to take a bit of a lie-in, but he had lost the art, somehow; he'd switched off his alarm, but he still woke before it would have gone. He'd planned on a leisurely breakfast and had even fetched croissants from the French bakery along the road, but once he'd eaten them he didn't quite know what to do next. He'd checked the news and the Niall Ritchie story had featured, but only briefly as yet.

At ten, he decided to go in to Fettes Avenue. If anything significant had come in he'd have been told already, and it looked as if Livvy Murray's pub idea hadn't yielded anything much either, but he was so restless that trying to relax had become stressful.

Needless to say, there was nothing on his desk from either the bank or the mobile phone company. Trying to put pressure on corporations was a thankless task and being denied the knowledge he needed was like an itch he couldn't scratch.

He'd seldom come across a victim who seemed to have so few contacts: his wife, his neighbour, the Greshams, presumably casual acquaintances in the pub. But the result of lockdown had been to isolate both Ritchie and Lindsay, preventing them from making friends locally, having left behind their friends in Edinburgh. He'd questioned Lindsay extensively about their social life and her first reaction had been a bitter laugh. 'Social life? You have to be joking. I exist in a vacuum.'

Where to start, without the financial facts as a pointer? Steve MacRobert had put in a preliminary report but it didn't say anything much more than he'd told him the day before. The SOCOs would be winding down the operation today; the pile of paper in his in-tray would wait, so why shouldn't he pop down there just to look it over again, even if it was nothing more than a displacement activity?

Strang was just about to move when there was a tap on the door and DS Murray poked her head round it.

'I wasn't sure if you would be in, boss,' she said.

'Not sure why I am,' he said. 'There's nothing new. Sit down anyway, Livvy. How was the pub?'

She screwed up her nose. 'Nothing to report there either, really, apart from the fact that Ken Blackford is a total oaf.'

'Not exactly fresh information, is it? What was the clientele like?'

'Unfriendly, to say the least. I felt pretty uncomfortable and I don't think it was because they knew who I was, just that I was a woman who had the cheek to walk into a private club uninvited. Sarah Lindsay said if you just arrested the lot of them, you'd have no more trouble with crime.'

'Was Doddie Muir there?'

'No, but it was still early. I'll tell you what I turned up about him yesterday, though, and about Blackford too – I just didn't want to say it in front of Matt Gunn. I'd told him I was going to check on Muir's record and he said there was no point, that he was clean apart from a few small things they'd never managed to pin on him. But I looked anyway, and it was only recently that his record was clean. Before the first lockdown, he'd quite an interesting slate – robbery with violence, ABH, reset of stolen goods, the lot. He's done time. So you have to ask yourself why the transformation.'

Strang was immediately interested. 'Can't see him getting religion. Love of a good woman – unlikely. Or . . .'

They looked at each other. 'Just – we stopped looking?' Murray said. 'That's almost what Matt said to me when I met him first – that they never got anywhere with the cases they tried to bring.'

'So should we be looking for someone behind all this? Someone who has no problem affording Vincent Dunbar when someone causes ripples? It's an interesting angle.'

'Can we find out who it is? You said you'd met his devil and she wasn't a fan – maybe you could work on her?'

To Strang's embarrassment, he found himself colouring. 'She'd be bound by legal confidentiality and I'm not going to use Cat Fleming as a spy.'

Murray looked at him with obvious interest but 'Right,' was all she said.

'Anyway, what about Blackford?'

'Handy with his fists, from the look of it. A trail of breaches of the peace over the years, six months for GBH, petty dishonesty. Not just the sort of neighbour you'd choose to have.'

'They're a charming lot around here, aren't they? I'll tell you what's worrying me – Gunn seems to be completely out of his depth.'

'He's definitely more confident now you've arrived, but he's not nasty enough – that's his problem. Believing folks are decent's a bad mistake. PC Thomson's got a brass neck but she's maybe right, talking about boys trying to do a man's job.'

'Perhaps you should have a chat with her. See if you can get anything out of her about what's been going on.'

'I *could*,' Murray said doubtfully.

'Is there anything else?' As she shook her head, he went on, 'I think I'm just going to take a drive down there and see how the SOCOs are getting on. Finishing today, I gather.'

'Oh,' Murray said, and there was such naked jealousy in her tone that Strang laughed.

'You're looking for something to do as well, are you? All right, come on then and we'll see if we can turn up something that will justify the petrol.'

Sarah was shaking and in tears as she came into the kitchen where Rose Moncrieff was making lunch. 'I only saw it when I came back towards the house. I'm so sorry, so sorry,' she kept repeating. 'I shouldn't have done this to you.'

Rose looked at her wryly. 'You think this is something

new? I keep a tub of white paint in the back so I can just cover it up when there's a message on the wall. And it's not as smelly as the buckets of stinking fish or even the dead rabbit on the doorstep.'

Sarah gaped at her. 'But you go on living here? It's – it's horrible!'

'The thing is, I'm old and I'm thrawn – I won't be bullied. When it happens, I call the police and for a while nothing happens, but of course then it starts up again. We all know who's behind it but there's never been clear proof. The worst was when she organised a mob and they went round to the surgery banging pans and breaking windows, but again, by the time the police arrived they'd gone. I've never really pursued it because I've real sympathy for her – the surgery's Do Not Resuscitate policy was inhuman, quite honestly. Linden was appalled but the partners told her that if they didn't follow it, hospitals would be overwhelmed and young people would die. It wasn't stopped until after Myrna Muir's mother had paid for the policy.'

The tears had dried on Sarah's cheeks. 'Was that what preyed on Linden's mind, do you think?'

Rose sighed. 'Oh, perhaps. Certainly not immediately: she apologised to Myrna and there weren't, as far as I heard, any more attacks on the surgery. Of course, she had her own flat by then and Rob says she didn't say anything to him about it. So who knows? Stress accumulates.'

'But why have they turned on you like this? You didn't do anything!'

'They hate me staying here, right in the middle of their evil fiefdom. I should have left in shame at having raised such a wicked child.' Her mouth was twisted as she said that.

'That's what Myrna hissed at me in the supermarket earlier – that I was shameless. She seemed to be assuming I'd killed Niall – I suppose lots of people will. She said we were both witches and should get out of here.'

Rose was unmoved. 'Oh, did she really? What a cow. Well, I've got the cauldron here – shall we add an eye or two of newt and give her chilblains or something?'

Sarah was forced to laugh. 'You're something else, Rose. Well, tell me where I can find the paint and I'll whitewash over it now.'

'No you won't,' Rose said firmly. 'I'm not going to ignore this – it only encourages her. I'm going to phone the police and get Matt Gunn to come and see what she's up to.'

Sarah grimaced. 'He was very kind when he came to the farm, but I'm not sure what he thinks now. I'm frightened of the police, to be honest.'

'We're by way of being friends. Look, Rob's taking you off somewhere this afternoon so you don't go stir crazy. I'll see if Matt can come down from North Berwick then and get her off our backs for now. Just put it out of your mind.'

Whatever Rose said, Sarah could see that her presence was making a bad situation worse and she silently determined that the moment the police agreed to let her back into Eastlaw, she would go.

There was a cutting east wind blowing today and even a bit of sunshine for once. You could see miles down the coast if you liked that sort of thing, always supposing you could stop your eyes from watering. DCI Strang seemed to be well into it, though, pointing out the Bass Rock far in the distance, but DS Murray turned away to speak to one of the SOCOs.

They were just packing up and when she asked if they'd come up with anything useful, he pulled a face. 'Not that I can see, though Steve may have ideas of his own. We did fingertip searches around the shed but there wasn't so much as a sweetie paper or a cigarette end we could send for analysis. They've dusted everything in sight so maybe once we get the prints run through there'll be something to go on, let's hope.'

'There's little enough of that at the moment,' Murray said and went over to join Steve MacRobert, who was talking to Strang on the threshold of the barn.

'It's an amazing building, really,' he was saying, and it certainly was, once she looked at it. It didn't match the scale of the farm at all and the small tractor that stood in one corner along with other bits of machinery, implements, piles of feedstuff sacks and a quad bike looked kind of apologetic, she thought. If it was her, she'd be flogging it to someone who wanted to do one of those barn conversion projects you were always seeing on the telly. They'd have their work cut out, though: no drains or anything exotic like electricity, just a hard mud floor and all those wooden beams that Kevin McCloud always went on about.

Strang was craning his neck, scanning the lofty spaces. 'Magnificent,' he said. 'But nothing for us here?'

'The only fresh information we've had is a match for one set of fingerprints – Blackford the neighbour has previous, but of course he's been in and out quite legitimately. Apart from that, no,' MacRobert said. 'I was just going to finish and lock up. You can tell the owner she's free to come back.'

'Always supposing she wants to. I wouldn't,' Murray said, looking across to the shed with a shudder.

'No, perhaps she won't,' Strang said, following MacRobert towards the door. Suddenly he stopped, looking down. 'Where did that come from?'

He was pointing at a clod of earth that was lying on the ground, quite a sizeable hardened chunk, deeply marked with ridges.

MacRobert turned to look. 'That? Just something that's fallen off a tractor after it's come in from the fields and the mud's dried out. Those are tyre marks. There's another one over there, look.'

'Yes,' said Strang. 'But they didn't come from that tractor, did they?'

Murray followed his pointing finger. What would have fallen off the apologetic little tractor's tyres would be a quarter of the size; the tractor that had dropped it must have been a monster.

MacRobert seemed puzzled. 'Could have been there long enough – maybe they'd a bigger tractor before. Or maybe they hired one of those big machines for harvesting or something.'

'Maybe they did,' Strang said. 'That'd be overkill for a farm this size, though, and Ms Lindsay told me the only farm machinery they had was clapped-out stuff. Maybe it was, shall we say, just passing through? Can you bag that for analysis, please – priority?'

MacRobert shrugged. 'Sure. Want us to check round for others?'

'Thanks.' He turned to Livvy. 'I think it's time we had another little chat with Ms Lindsay. She just might have something interesting to tell us.'

It seemed odd that this was something he would be getting excited about, and it was only as they went back to the car Murray remembered: when Strang had first met Sarah Lindsay, he'd been looking into the theft of valuable farm vehicles. If she was involved with that, it would put a very different complexion on the whole case.

The doctor had warned Myrna Muir about her blood pressure and she could feel it surging as she opened her door and saw DI Gunn standing there. Her face was bright red with temper as she said, 'What are *you* after?'

'Just a word, Myrna. We've spoken about this before,' he said.

She looked at him with contempt; they had indeed spoken before and she'd carried right on when it suited her. 'Oh, that Moncrieff wifie's been yammering on again, has she? What is it this time? Do you never feel embarrassed about being her wee puppy dog?'

'That isn't helpful,' he said. 'Perhaps I could come in to talk about it?'

She folded her arms. 'Perhaps you couldn't. Perhaps you could just stand there on the doorstep and tell me what new unfounded accusation she's come up with this time?'

'You know what it is, Myrna. Mrs Moncrieff's garden wall has been defaced again.'

'Dearie me. Who would have done a thing like that?'

'You, for one. In fact, just you.'

Cheeky sod! 'Proof?' she demanded.

'I haven't got it, at present, but we're going to start working on that. And now I have a witness who claims you used threatening language to her yesterday in the supermarket, which gives us something to go on.'

'Never said a word to her.' It was an automatic reaction, but she was annoyed with herself now for giving way to the pleasure of directing venom at the woman who'd caused all the trouble. She went on, 'Just her word against mine, isn't it? Reckon you can get any witnesses to come forward this time?'

It was a taunt that had been useful in the past, but now he said, 'It was said in the supermarket, not the Caddon, Myrna. There's quite a lot of decent folk around there.'

Myrna's face went redder than ever. By now, Gunn should have been backing off but for some reason he wasn't, like he usually did.

'Maybe they will, and maybe they won't,' was the best she could manage. 'Anyway, I never had anything to do with the woman's stupid wall.'

'I'm not accepting that. There's a history of persecution that I'm planning to lay before DCI Strang, including the events leading up to Dr Moncrieff's largely unexplained suicide. We'll leave it for the moment but it isn't going to rest there.' He turned away.

She managed to shut her door with a defiant slam before he was off the doorstep, but she felt as if she'd been punched in the stomach. She'd almost forgotten what it was like in the old days, being scared when the polis came chapping on the door. For a long time now, they'd got it organised so the power was in their own hands. If

189

that was changing, it was a problem. And if they started digging back . . .

It could get nasty.

'She's texted to say she's on the way and she'll be here about lunch time,' Marjory Fleming called to her husband, Bill, coming to greet her as she got out of the car and preceded by a young Border Collie that was dancing round in a frenzy of delight at seeing his mistress.

'Scott, that's enough. Down!' she scolded, with very little effect.

'Down!' Bill roared, and Scott, more or less obediently, sat.

'Ridiculous animal!' she said as they went inside the cottage.

The Mains of Craigie farmhouse, nestling in the soft hills of Galloway, had been handed over to their son, Cameron, and his Australian wife, Annelise, and Marjory sometimes thought it was the best thing they'd ever done. Two farm labourer's cottages, now unused, had been converted into a neat modern house for them, small but perfectly formed, as Bill liked to say.

The new kitchen wasn't large but that hadn't bothered Marjory; there was a Rayburn to make it cosy and she'd only ever cooked to prevent starvation. Domesticity had never been her strong point and having fewer rooms meant less housework, and she liked that too.

Her dark hair was salt-and-pepper now, but she still had the height and presence that had earned her the nickname 'Big Marge' when she was a DI in the Galloway Constabulary before the days of Police Scotland and she was, she reckoned, fitter now than she had been then, with more time for exercise.

Bill had been watching his weight since a heart attack a few years back, but he was still quite a burly figure. The hair that had once been fair like his daughter Catriona's was pure white now, and the present arrangement, where he still kept active on his beloved farm but had handed on the major decisions, and all the nightmare of paperwork, to his son, suited him perfectly.

'You'd think I'd been away for a fortnight instead of just into Kirkluce for the messages,' she said as they began unloading the shopping. 'Do you think he'll ever improve?'

'Not much. We couldn't have afforded one that had the makings of a working dog.'

There was a hint of sadness in Bill's voice, thinking of legendary Meg, who had been one of the family for so many years. 'He's not stupid, mind you, just daft. You're a good lad, aren't you, son?' He bent to ruffle the fur on Scott's head. 'So what time are we expecting to eat, then?'

'Cat thought about quarter to one. Is that all right with you?'

'They're dipping the sheep this afternoon so I said I'd go across immediately after lunch.'

'It's just a picnic so you can start when you like.' She put a baguette on the table along with cheese, ham and pâté. 'Annelise is making that Anzac Day diggers' stew for us all tonight. So clever of Cammie to marry a good cook!'

'Just as well there's one in the family to carry on your mother's mission to feed the hungry. Cat's always ravenous, poor wee soul.' He sat down and started making inroads into the cheese.

'At least she'd a good supper on Wednesday with that policeman. He seems quite interesting – I googled him, and he's had a few impressive results heading up the Serious Rural Crime Squad. He's a widower – lost his wife in an accident a few years ago.'

'Is he?' Bill asked, with a marked lack of enthusiasm. 'A DCI, she said? So what age does that make him?'

Marjory smiled. 'She's all grown up now, your little girl. She stays up late sometimes too, you know, without even getting permission.'

'Oh, for goodness' sake! It's just that older men can be predatory and all right, she's grown up but she's still not much more than a kid.'

'And will be to you, dear, when she's forty. Yes, yes, I know, but she's been out there in the big rough world quite a while now and she knows all about it.'

'Hmph. And I tell you the other thing – I don't like that Dunbar man. He's exploiting her and she's working all the hours God made doing what he's getting paid for.'

'It's just the system, isn't it? She's fascinated by the work and it's great to see her so sure about what she wants to do after all the dithering about.'

Scott, who had retired to his basket by the Rayburn, suddenly jumped up, barking, as a tall figure darkened the kitchen window and Cameron Fleming came in.

'Come on, come on, we can't have this kind of slacking,' he said jovially. 'There's work to be done, sheep out there looking for a shampoo and set.'

Bill got up, muttering subversively, with a slice of bread and ham in his hand.

'Ooh, you're a hard taskmaster!' Marjory said, adding,

'And leave enough lunch for your sister,' as Cammie leant forward to carve a chunk off the cheese.

He winked at her. 'See you this evening,' he said and the two of them left.

Marjory, wise to their ways of old, went to fetch what she had stashed in the fridge and replenished the depleted tray, thinking as she did so how lucky she was to have a close and affectionate family and a big-hearted daughter-in-law who had in her own way filled the gap in the family that her mother, Janet Laird, had left when she had, full of years and in her usual quiet way, slipped out of life.

As she sat down again at the table, she heard the sound of Cat's car arriving and Scott, once more alerted to his duty, rushed to the door barking.

'I thought a change of scene would do you good,' Rob Gresham said.

They had driven across the Borders in autumn sunshine to the little town of Duns and, after climbing up Duns Law to the ancient broch, were now sitting in a cheerful little cafe in the High Street.

Sarah sat back in her chair and gave a deep sigh. 'It's been such a help, just to have something else to think about and talk about. You've even made me laugh, and quite honestly in the last few days I've wondered if I would ever laugh again.'

He'd been keeping the conversation light but he was serious now as he said, 'You can't escape from what's happened, and the darkness gathers, doesn't it? You can't leave it alone either – replaying the regrets, the things you didn't do that you should have done and the things you shouldn't have done that you did—'

'The guilt,' Sarah said. 'My specialist subject, guilt.'

'Oh yes,' he said heavily. 'Guilt.'

There was something about the way he said it that made her give him a sideways glance.

'You shouldn't blame yourself,' she said. 'But it's true, I felt worse when I thought that Niall had chosen to kill himself, so I suppose everyone does, though I know from Rose how much you loved Linden and the love has extended into your affection for Rose. You're obviously the son-in-law she didn't quite have and that means a lot to her.'

Rob looked down. 'Hardly difficult,' he said.

'No,' she agreed. 'Rose is a complete star. Perhaps we're just pre-programmed for guilt, whatever happens. I'm tormenting myself with the thought that Niall must have made an enemy who was ruthless enough to kill him without me having a clue that such a person might exist, and that happened because I'd withdrawn myself. If he'd told me who he was worried about, I might not have been able to prevent it but at least I'd be able to tell the police now.'

'He didn't, though?'

'Oh, cryptic comments about spider's webs, but that was all. I'd no idea who he was meaning but I'm inclined to think the people he got to know in the pub may have had something to do with it.'

Rob shifted uneasily in his seat. 'Oh, don't let them convince you they're all villains in the Caddon. It's just a bit of an introverted community and they're not good at welcoming strangers.'

'That's one way of putting it!' Sarah said hotly. 'Doddie

194

Muir? And Myrna? Red paint on the walls and buckets of stinking fish?'

He was looking embarrassed now. 'Oh well, the Muirs . . . Doddie's a chancer and she's always been a right bitch. But it's not big-time stuff – they're harmless enough. There's always folk that try it on.'

She had to remember he was a resident himself, living in what he'd told her was his stepmother Michelle's house, and she bit back the hot words that came to mind, saying only, 'You mean, "It's aye been", like Briony sometimes says?'

'Oh dear, yes, perhaps I do.'

'I suppose I really should phone her. She's been leaving kind messages and I just didn't feel strong enough to deal with the whole situation. I don't want to lose the friendship, though.'

It was obvious something was wrong.

'I shouldn't?' she said, with a cold feeling in the pit of her stomach.

'Perhaps you should leave it a bit, until things sort of die down,' he said awkwardly.

'You don't mean, she thinks I did it? But she was there, she saw it all! She can't think I'm as good an actress as that!'

'No, no, I'm sure she doesn't really. It's more I think that she's feeling a bit miffed because I knew where you were and I didn't tell her, and you didn't answer her messages. She's annoyed with me too – she's always been pretty hot on loyalty and she feels our friendship with Rose is a little clique that's leaving her out.'

'But that's awful! I can't go to her and say it isn't like

that without her realising we've been talking about her behind her back, and that would make it worse.'

'Yes, I think it would. Just leave it for the moment.' Rob looked at his watch. 'Are you ready to set off back?'

'That's fine. Thanks so much for tea.'

As she walked back to the car, Sarah was finding it hard to believe that an hour ago she had been laughing and feeling better. She was feeling worse now, much worse. If her best friend could even in the smallest degree think that she was guilty, what chance did she have of convincing the community at large of her innocence, let alone the police?

Just as she got to the car, a text pinged in on her mobile, saying that she was free to go back to the only place she could call home whenever she liked. Even if she hated everything about it, she wouldn't be imprisoned indoors by fear of aggression or contempt the way she was just now. Whatever else, it would give her freedom and space to wrestle with her demons alone.

DI Gunn was feeling good as he walked away from his encounter with Myrna Muir. He'd let himself be too easily demoralised over these last awful years; he could see yesterday afternoon that Livvy Murray thought he was being a bit feeble with the bank and the phone company. Now with the backing of the SRCS he could tell himself that all the cards weren't stacked against him, and seeing Myrna Muir shaken for once did wonders for his confidence.

His final sally, the comment about Linden Moncrieff's suicide, hadn't been planned but after seeing its effect he was considering it now. He'd allowed the horror of her joy at imminent oblivion to haunt him when it should have inspired him to look into it further, even if the official case had closed with an umbrella verdict of stress. Perhaps it was indeed that monster in her own brain that had driven Linden to welcome death, but if the monster might have had a more human form – in the shape, for instance, of Myrna Muir – he wasn't going to ignore it any longer.

He had been the closest person to her in the last moments of her life; he owed it to her.

CHAPTER TWELVE

When Sarah Lindsay and Rob Gresham got back to Rose Moncrieff's house and she announced that she was leaving to go back to Eastlaw at once, a long argument ensued. Rose was horrified – 'Not tonight, surely – it's getting dark already' – and Rob, who'd been arguing with her in the car, warned that the house could be in chaos and the electricity might even have been turned off, the police not being famous for putting everything back neatly after a search.

Sarah, gritting her teeth so hard that her jaws ached, held her ground, though when Rob said he'd follow her up the road to see her in, she accepted his offer with only a token protest.

Rose assembled a survival pack for her and hugged her fiercely. 'Come back at once if there's any problem. Your room's always here. I'll miss you.'

Sarah had a lump in her throat as she hugged her back and drove off. Light was thickening now and the trees that lined the narrow roads were bending and twisting in the wind, drifts of leaves falling about the car. She'd always hated autumn with its sense of melancholy and decay and gathering darkness; that was all she could see ahead of her now.

Eastlaw Farm, when she reached it, had a derelict air. They hadn't cleared the strips of police tape that were purposeless now, flapping in the wind, and the shed with the struts nailed across it made her shudder. But there was nothing there now, she told herself, just an empty shell – in its own way, a graphic reminder of what their relationship had been. She averted her eyes.

Rob's car pulled in behind her and he jumped out. 'All right?'

'Fine,' she said, grabbing her bag and fumbling for the key to the front door. He took it from her and unlocked it; she wasn't sure how long it would have taken her to manage that, with her shaking hands.

The house was cold and dark and smelt fusty, but when she pressed the switch for the light it came on and, inside, none of the furniture had been displaced, though the surfaces were grimy with a greasy powder.

'I'll just go round and check that everything's all right upstairs,' Rob said. 'Then if you're happy, I'll take myself off.'

She felt obliged to offer to make tea, but was relieved when he was tactful enough to refuse. Suddenly she was very, very tired.

He came back downstairs. 'I think you'd maybe better

come up and have a look. The bedroom's all right but the worst mess is in what I think must be an office. I think they've probably taken stuff away.'

'Niall's office,' she said. 'I suppose they'd have to go through everything.'

Sarah followed him up. The computer hard drive was missing, the filing cabinets had been raided and left with drawers open. Papers they clearly thought hadn't been worth taking had been dumped in untidy drifts on the floor.

Her heart sank as she looked at it. Finding the legal papers that related to ownership of the farm had been her first priority whenever she got access; now she stared helplessly at the mess as Rob started gathering the papers into a pile.

'Doesn't look as if they've left much behind,' he said. 'Is that going to be a problem?'

'I suppose they'll have to give it all back when they've finished with it, but I really don't need this. There's a small filing cabinet in the sitting room where I kept my stuff, but that's probably gone too.'

They went back down. There wasn't much furniture in the sitting room anyway and it was largely undisturbed, though she could see that both drawers of the filing cabinet had been opened and not properly shut.

'I guess that's empty too,' she said wearily.

But when she opened the drawers, everything looked to be in order and when she investigated the labelled files, they were as she had left them. She pounced on the one marked *Legal* and riffled through it.

'Here it is!' she cried. 'The farm agreement.' Her heart was beating fast as she scanned it, expecting the worst

– but no, there it was: the clause that gave the survivor ownership rights. She took back all she had been thinking about Niall's helpful friend.

'It's all right,' Sarah said. 'At least I'm guaranteed a roof over my head.'

'They must have been careful about documents that were your property,' he said. 'So was there nothing of Niall's in there?'

'A few things, I think. There's a notebook here he used to work on some evenings. I'll check through later and give anything relevant to the police.'

He nodded. 'Fine. Well, are you all right now? Nothing else I can do for you? You do know you can go straight back if you're not happy.'

It wasn't easy to convince him she was absolutely fine, but Sarah managed it and waited at the door to see him drive off before she shut it.

The house was chillingly cold, heavily silent. At this time she could be sitting across the fire from Rose, with a glass in her hand, talking about something – anything! – that would take her mind off the ugly thoughts that were swirling now in her brain.

At least she could light the fire and be warm. And tomorrow she could run wherever she wanted to go, perhaps even drive down to the supermarket in Berwick to get supplies where no one would know her, try to establish some sort of normality – at least until the police came. As they would.

When a knock came on the back door, she almost jumped out of her skin. Surely not, at this time of night . . .

But it was Ken Blackford, standing on the doorstep. An

unwelcome sight – she'd somehow contrived to forget he would be around.

He looked at her with the smile that was almost a sneer. 'Back then, are you?'

'As you see,' Sarah said stiffly.

'Staying, or just dropping in?'

'I'll be staying meantime. What did you want?'

'Not very friendly, that, is it? I was just being neighbourly. But since you ask, Gresham's got his man working the farm. You're not needing him. Send him away and I'll take it on, preparatory to a sale agreement.'

'I haven't decided yet what I'm going to do. So if you'll excuse me—' She made to shut the door and found his foot was in the way.

'If you think you're going to set up a bidding war with Gresham, forget it. He'll do you over, like he does everybody else.'

Her phone was in her pocket. She took it out, hoping her hand wasn't too obviously shaking. 'You're threatening me. Move away or I phone the police.'

'I wouldn't do that if I was you,' he said, but he retreated enough to let her slam the door and she heard him swearing, then saw him pass the window on his way back to his house.

She shot home the bolts in the door and stood there, transfixed. She just wasn't thinking straight, was she? She'd let Myrna Muir's petty spite drive her away from the support of friends and now she was alone and unprotected from whatever Blackford might do to make her give him what he wanted – the farm.

And could she be sure that he hadn't taken earlier steps

to make sure it became available? He'd said that awful night that he'd been away all day – but had he?

Kelso Strang's niece, Betsy, had enjoyed her trip on Sunday afternoon to the little ice cream parlour, which was her idea of the height of sophistication and luxury, where the strawberry ripple was served in fluted dishes with a wafer fan on top and a flattened spoon that made it taste even better. She had worn her pink sundress to match, even if it wasn't entirely suited to a chilly autumn day, and had been a polite and charming companion, as Kelso Strang assured her mother when he returned her after their outing.

'It's not surprising, when you give her everything she wants and spoil her rotten,' Finella said. 'Just as well you haven't kids of your own. They'd be total brats.'

It always gave Kelso a pang when he thought about what might have been: the unborn child that had died with his wife would be a sturdy toddler now. As he drove away, he wondered if Fin was right that it was just as well: a child was such a hostage to fortune and the older you got, the more aware you became of the fragility of life. His little niece was enough for him and now he was no longer involved in her moral development, he could irresponsibly make quite sure that Unkie was her favourite person in the whole world.

He was still smiling, thinking about her, as he let himself into the cottage, found himself a beer and sat down by the window overlooking the Firth of Forth with his laptop on his knee to structure his priorities for the next day.

Nothing had come in since Friday and he'd stood down the incident room meantime. It was proving to be a

203

total waste of resources, with not a single witness coming forward. With what he knew of the Tarleton background, it was tempting to believe this indicated a conspiracy of silence, but it might only mean that as he had already discovered, almost no one had any contact with Niall Ritchie.

With any luck, tomorrow he would have proper information about Ritchie's financial affairs – if he didn't, he'd set Livvy onto them. She was really becoming a very effective officer and that she'd actually asked permission before her expedition to the pub was a big step forward, especially since it was entirely possible he might have vetoed it. Query: if he had, would she have done it anyway? Well, he didn't have to go there. The pub certainly merited further investigation.

And Sarah Lindsay: despite the temptation to go and find her yesterday, he'd decided to wait until he got a look at the figures – and possibly, even, until he got the forensic report on his discovery in the barn. They'd be able to establish the type and make of tyre, which would be a good pointer to the machine it had fallen off, and he had a file on his computer detailing every farm vehicle reported stolen. But how would it have come to be there?

Kelso was tempted to think he knew the answer to his own question. A massive, all but empty space, an isolated farm with few neighbours and the access along small back roads, twenty minutes from a trading port – perfect as a safe house until the operators got their ducks in a row. And then, off it would go, under cover of darkness, heading for Tarleton harbour, possibly even through the narrow streets of the Caddon where the culture of 'watching the wall' was ingrained.

Yeah, right. And how often had he pulled up Livvy Murray for constructing an elaborate scenario on the flimsiest of grounds and then making a crass mistake because she wanted it to have been right? Steve MacRobert had suggested the vehicle could have been brought in for some seasonal agricultural purpose but he himself had been so taken with his theory that he'd dismissed that, on the basis that it was such a small farm. But Ken Blackford's, next door, was bigger and they could, for instance, have combined on the hire, or he could even have commissioned one himself and Ritchie had allowed him to stable it in the barn as a neighbourly favour. It was certainly something to follow up about once the results of the tests came in, and surely he could hope there'd be info from the bank tomorrow, and the investigation could get properly underway.

Kelso was just closing down his laptop when his personal phone buzzed. His mother often phoned on a Sunday night and it was Mary Strang's name he expected to see when he picked it up, but it wasn't hers.

'Kelso?' Cat Fleming said. She sounded very tentative. 'Is this a bad time? I didn't really know whether I should call but I saw on the news website about that murder and your name was mentioned. Are you all right?'

He was touched. 'Yes, Cat, I'm fine. Nice to hear from you. Have you been down to Galloway to be fed and watered?'

'That's right. Stuffed, actually – my sister-in-law's catering is on an industrial scale. If I had a hump like a camel, I could live off it for a month, let alone a week.'

He laughed. 'Since you don't, perhaps I could suggest another visit to an oasis again sometime – I'm feeling in a very avuncular mood, having just taken my niece, Betsy, out for an elegant strawberry ripple in a gelateria this afternoon.'

'Sounds delightful,' she said.

He got the odd feeling that somehow he'd said the wrong thing, but she was going on: 'Actually, I was going to give *you* an invitation. My ma's really quizzy and I'm ashamed to say she's been googling you and now she really wants to meet you. Actually, I'll come clean – I'm hoping to be a fly on the wall while you get into competing over "cases I have cracked" and "villains I have brought to justice".'

'Not quite sure about that,' he said uncomfortably. 'But—'

She interrupted him. 'Oh, God, sorry, I got that so wrong, didn't I? Crass of me, really. There's too much black humour around the law courts.'

'There's a fair bit of it about in police stations too. Yes, I'd be delighted to meet your mother – and I think I now have a licence to google her back.'

'Absolutely! In fact' – Cat cleared her throat – 'I looked too. I'm very sorry about your wife.'

Taken by surprise, he stammered, 'Oh – thank you. Yes, it was a very sad accident.' For some reason, he found himself adding, 'That was how I got the scar on my cheek.' It was something he never said, unless he was asked a direct question, but – he just did.

Cat's voice softened. 'Yes, I guessed that.' But she didn't say any more about it, going on, 'I suppose you'll be busy, but if you found you were able, you could come down on Saturday.'

He was taken aback; he'd imagined Cat meant her mother would come up to Edinburgh and he stalled. 'The trouble is, I've no idea how the case is going to develop. I wouldn't like to make an arrangement I couldn't keep.'

'We're a police household – we understand. Anyway, I'd love you to see the farm – it's a really nice place. And Dad would like to meet you too.'

Kelso agreed in principle and finished the call, thinking, *I bet he would.* Any fond father would be keen to meet the middle-aged man who was taking an interest in his young daughter. And her 'quizzy' mother too – it probably wasn't only his professional background she was interested in. It could be a good idea to meet them and reassure them that he was perfectly well aware of the gulf of age and painful experience that yawned between them – that light-hearted comment about cases and villains!

It had been an odd phone call, in a way. The easy relationship he thought they'd established had shifted a bit, and he wasn't sure quite how he felt about it. It would take careful handling, but he'd certainly hate to forfeit the friendship that had given him – and her too, he hoped – so much pleasure.

On Monday morning, DS Murray was on the doorstep of Tarleton police station not long after it opened, despite the fact that rain was teeming down and as usual the Edinburgh bypass had ground to a standstill.

Talking to Briony Gresham hadn't been seen as a priority but processing would take some time even once the reports came in and DCI Strang had detailed her to do an interview.

'Ask her about possible enemies,' he'd said. 'I get the impression she hadn't a lot to do with Ritchie directly, but she might have picked up something from Lyndsay.'

The appointment had been arranged for ten, but remembering what Strang had said on Friday, she'd had it in mind to take on the challenge of chatting up PC Thomson first. She suspected that she might have useful things to say – if she could be induced to say them.

She'd given it careful thought and, on the way to collect a car from Fettes Avenue, she'd stopped off at a Greggs in Stockbridge. It was something of a challenge not to eat what she'd bought on the way down but with admirable self-control she still had two in the bag when she came into the police station, beaming engagingly at PC Thomson.

'Do you reckon you could find me a mug of coffee? I never got my breakfast and I've a couple of yum-yums here – you're welcome to one of them.'

Thomson didn't look overjoyed to see her. 'They're Greggs,' Murray said, holding up the bag and rustling it enticingly. There was no Greggs in Tarleton.

It was a master stroke. 'Well – don't mind if I do,' she said, actually getting up from her stool and going to switch on the kettle in the back office.

'Anything come in this morning?' Murray said, hospitably spreading the bag out like a tablecloth and laying her offering on it.

Thomson snorted. 'Not a thing. You'd need waterboarding to get anything out of this lot.'

'Why are they so hostile in the Caddon?' Murray said.

'I know nobody likes the polis, but this does seem to be something out of the ordinary.'

Thomson brought the mugs, sat back down and picked up a yum-yum. 'Bad blood,' she said, a little indistinctly. 'Bad through and through, the lot of them. Inbred, too – they're all related, one way or another. Criminal families with just the one idea – to get on with their nasty little businesses and not be interfered with.'

'What sort of businesses?'

'Cigarettes and booze, just for a start. Brought in from places like Poland along with the legitimate cargo – done that for years. A bit of a black-market with the fish when the trawlers have taken more than their quota. Scams of one sort and another. The odd bit of direct theft. But when we'd a proper station, we'd a grip on them – God knows what they're bringing in now. With this lot – we're a joke. I'm just humiliated.'

Murray was fascinated. 'When did it get out of hand?'

'Lockdown,' she said. 'They got a lot more professional, and we got wee boys, like I said. Him, for a start.' She jerked her head towards the office where DI Gunn would have been, if he wasn't still, presumably, in North Berwick. 'And just working office hours. They've seen them off.'

'Who's "they"?' It was the big question; she was almost holding her breath as PC Thomson absent-mindedly moved on to the other pastry.

'Who do you think? They're behind everything in this place. Careful to keep their noses clean, right enough, but scratch the surface and there's rot you can smell. We all know it, the decent folk here as well as the force, but there's something with all of that family, right back, every last one

– close-knit, and not a moral between them. Bad blood, like I said.'

'The Greshams? You think they could be involved in Ritchie's murder?'

Thomson didn't actually reply, just gave her a sideways look as she took out a tissue to wipe the sugar from her mouth.

'Acting together? Or separately?'

Thomson got up. 'I've been told often enough to know my place. You're meant to be the detectives. You could start doing a bit of that, couldn't you?' She picked up the mugs and the paper bag and took them through to a little pantry round the back.

The yum-yum truce was clearly over. Murray went through to the office they'd been using to wait for Strang, with a hollow feeling in her stomach where a yum-yum should have been. What she'd learnt hadn't been evidence, of course, but it chimed with what Matt Gunn had been saying. Perhaps he hadn't been imagining things after all.

When DCI Strang went in to Fettes Avenue, a report had come in: the bale of rope in the barn had been confirmed as the source for the rope around Niall Ritchie's neck – though it wasn't obvious what that suggested. There was nothing on the tyre cast yet; the farm accounts were being scrutinised as well as the phone and computer records – those would all take time.

Fortunately, the banks had belatedly been spurred into action and now he could bring up Niall Ritchie's financial statements on the screen in front of him. As he scrolled through them, he pursed his lips in a silent whistle of amazement.

It was like watching a slow-motion car crash, a month-by-month catalogue of accumulating disasters: mortgages and loans taken out, interest not paid, overdrafts, more loans, more problems. The payments from Gresham's Farms were irregular, presumably reflecting fluctuating production of goods, but they certainly weren't showing any sign of increasing over the years. There had initially been a standing order paid to Ritchie's sister, stopped some time ago. There was money paid in by cheque from James Gresham's personal account – the loans he had told them about, presumably – in the low thousands. Eastlaw Farm was, quite simply, sinking under an avalanche of debt.

This was Niall Ritchie's life written as a tragedy in three acts, Strang reflected: first, the early optimism when there was still money coming in from his accountant's job that allowed for the initial losses incurred in setting up at the farm; then, the shock of redundancy and the growing evidence that the farm simply wasn't a paying business; at last the collapse, with no immediate prospect of controlling the mounting debt and no hope at all of paying it off.

The man was an accountant; he must have seen what was coming. It didn't explain murder, but if he had in fact killed himself it wouldn't have been surprising. If he was a weak man who was afraid of confrontation, it could explain why he was resisting Sarah Lindsay's demand that they sell the farm, since she would then discover it was pretty much worthless, swallowed up by debt. He wondered how many of the later loans taken out she had even been aware of, far less consented to.

If she had found out, there was a powerful motive for murder right there. Lindsay was both tall and fit-looking; it would be perfectly possible for her to strangle her slight partner once he'd been rendered unconscious, especially if galvanised by the sort of volcanic rage Murray said she had glimpsed. Certainly, there was a lot he needed to ask that lady about.

As Strang looked at the pattern of money flow, it fell naturally into monthly payments into the partners' joint account for household expenses – meagre enough – and payments for farm expenses of one sort and another. They would need to look into how many of the firms listed had supplied chemical fertilisers and pesticides, and when the forensic accountants got busy on the tax returns there might also be some useful information there.

But there was something else, something very interesting. As well as all the standard banking transactions, there was a constant flow of random small amounts withdrawn in cash, and spaced out over the period, three much larger cash payments paid in – two £500s, and more recently a £600.

In these days of near-universal use of credit cards, cash transactions are unusual – and to any police officer, suspicious. Strang sat back in his chair and considered what this told him.

Initially, Ritchie had presented as a man with so few social contacts that it was difficult to imagine how he would have acquired such a deadly enemy, but looking at the life story being told by those statements, it wasn't hard to believe it after all.

* * *

DS Murray was just about to set off for Gresham's Farms when DI Gunn came in. He had a very purposeful look.

'Any word from the boss about a briefing?' he said.

'It may be quite a bit later. If the bank has got its finger out, he'll need time to check through it. I think he was hoping it might be eleven or eleven-thirty, but we'll get a text. I'm just going off to have a cosy chat with Briony Gresham.'

'Good luck with that. She's pretty aggressive – beat me about the head when I wouldn't tell her where Sarah Lindsay was staying. And you do know that Briony is a deadly poison?'

Murray laughed. 'I can't promise that I won't eat one of her biscuits if she offers. I'm famished – I bought a yum-yum for my breakfast but Thomson ate it. Two, actually.'

'What? She just ate it?'

'Too complicated – don't go there.'

'OK.' Still looking baffled, he went on, 'I was hoping I'd have time this morning to check up on something that happened at the weekend. You know Sarah's been staying with Rose Moncrieff? Her garden wall was painted with bloodstains after Myrna Muir – you know, Doddie's wife – threatened Sarah in the supermarket.'

'Nasty,' Murray said.

'But not unusual – over the years Rose has been hassled by the locals, egged on by Myrna Muir, stemming from the time Myrna's mother died of Covid and they blamed Linden. I want to nail Myrna and I might just get evidence this time. And I also reckon it's time to do a bit of digging. When Linden died, there was no doubt that it was suicide so they were ready to put it down to stress. There was no real investigation into the background, though both Rose and I felt that surely there had to be more to it than that. This gives me a peg to hang it on. If I'm not needed till later, I'll just go and interview one or two people and see what comes up. I told you I saw her face, so filled with joy at escaping, and I want to know why. I was standing right there when she died. I believe I owe it to her.'

'Well, it's your patch,' Murray said. 'But the boss is going to text when he's got something to tell us so don't get so involved that you miss it. You may find you don't have much time to pursue it after that.'

'Better get on with it, then.'

He went out and she looked after him thoughtfully. Since the SRCS arrived, he'd visibly gained in confidence. The little nervous twitch that had been so frequent seemed to have disappeared, at least for the moment, and perhaps even if he didn't get very far with an investigation, Linden Moncrieff's image might haunt him less if he had paid what he seemed to feel was his debt to her.

CHAPTER THIRTEEN

When you are a police officer, you become very good at reading body language. In extreme situations, it could mean the difference between life and death; out on the streets day to day it often helps you anticipate adverse reactions. First and foremost, though, it teaches you to recognise hostility, even when it comes with a veneer of politeness.

Briony Gresham was unmistakably hostile, from the moment she said, 'Oh!' in the offended tone of one surprised to find a tradesman with the nerve to appear at the company door to her house.

DS Murray produced her warrant card. 'I'm—'

'Oh, you needn't bother with that. I know who you are.' Then came the smile – the sort that turns the corners of the mouth upwards but doesn't crinkle the eyes. 'So – how can I help you? Do come in.'

Looking around her, Murray followed as Briony led her firmly past the social areas of the house – an elegant sitting room to one side, a dining room with a huge, polished mahogany table on the other – and through a door under the stairs that gave on to a corridor leading to the back door.

'I'm just taking you over to my office,' Briony said. 'I think you came here to talk to my father the other day?'

'Yes, we did,' Murray said, tempted to add, *As if you didn't know*. 'He was very helpful.'

Briony held open a door in the side of the Gresham's Farms building to let Murray in first. 'Well, yes, he would be.'

Now she was meant to feel gauche at having remarked on it. Unabashed, Murray took time before she stepped inside to look around the yard, which was quiet today; there was no sign of Doddie Muir and only a couple of men working in a barn on the farther side.

Briony went round to her seat at a plain wooden desk with a computer sitting on it, tiered trays on either side and a large diary opened in front of her. She waved Murray to one of the upright chairs opposite, ignoring the seating round the coffee table across the room.

'Since this is obviously business,' Briony said, 'I thought we could conduct it here. I'd appreciate it if it didn't take up too much of my time – I'm very busy woman – and I've made a full statement already.'

'Yes, I've read it. I just wanted to ask you about the things it didn't cover, madam.'

She bristled visibly. 'And what would those be?'

'Relationships, mainly. How well did you know Niall Ritchie?'

'Hardly at all. I mainly knew about him from what his

partner said, and his dealings with my father.'

'Let's take your father first. What did your father think of him? Were there problems there?'

She looked outraged. 'I can't believe you're asking me that. You spoke to my father and no doubt he told you. Are you trying to get me to say something that will contradict what he's said?'

'I'm not trying to get you to say anything, madam. We have to explore all the evidence we can. Perhaps we could return to what his partner said to you. Sarah Lindsay is a close friend of yours, isn't she?'

Briony crossed her arms, a classic gesture of rebuttal. 'Well – a friend, I suppose. It came out of the business contact with the farm and she was pretty desperate for companionship so we met for a coffee occasionally. She was always grumbling about Niall – said he was a hopeless farmer. If it hadn't been for my father, the whole thing would have crashed years ago.'

'He was anxious that it shouldn't? Ms Lindsay told me they were hanging on because your father wanted them to.'

Her faced flushed. 'Because they'd have been out on the streets otherwise and he believed they were really committed to the organic ideal. And then Niall betrayed him, using pesticides like that!'

'Was he very angry?' Murray said slyly.

'Oh, don't think I don't know what you're implying, and it's disgraceful. He was sad, if you want to know. But he thought it was a one-off – there had been a couple of problems like that before.'

'And what happened then?'

'One of them's still one of our farms, doing really well. The other one gave up, I think,' Briony said.

'Right. But Ms Lindsay – would you say that she was angry with Niall?' Murray asked.

'Oh, in a way she was quite angry, I suppose.' Briony sounded as if she was hesitating, reluctant to say anything more.

Murray, who didn't believe that, said nothing. Briony went on, still tentatively, 'I think there was, sort of, a lot going on – she didn't totally confide in me.'

Smart woman, Murray thought. *She's going to put the knife in now, isn't she?*

'Of course, I don't believe for a moment that Sarah could have done this – this horrible thing. She's not that kind of person, obviously. And she was in a total state that night when she called us – I can't believe she could have faked that. But I've tried reaching out to her and it seems strange that she hasn't bothered to reply to me. So . . . I don't really know what to think.' She shrugged.

Murray asked the question Strang had suggested – did she know of any enemies Ritchie might have had – and a few more on background stuff – could she suggest anyone else who might know something useful, had there been other signs of worries – to which the answer was always a cold 'no' as Briony moved restively in her chair.

'Look—' she said, and Murray left before she could be thrown out.

There were two lorries in the yard now, one with the name of one of the bigger supermarkets emblazoned on the side, and there were several workers going to and fro with sacks of potatoes. One, she thought, could have been one of the drinkers in the pub on Friday night, but she couldn't be sure.

As Murray drove back to Tarleton, she was thinking about Briony. Jimmie Gresham had been open and welcoming, his daughter the opposite. Why had she been so hostile? It seemed unlikely she believed her father had killed Ritchie because of a few pesticides in the carrots and was mounting a defence; it seemed more as if she felt she was entitled not to have to suffer the indignity of visits from the police, who should know their place.

And when it came to Sarah, again Murray didn't think Briony believed her one-time friend could have done it. That huffy little shrug – it was more as if she felt she'd been slighted and wanted to punish Sarah by causing trouble for her with the police.

Poisonous, indeed.

'Could I speak to the manager, please? Police,' DI Gunn said to a man who was stacking shelves. He was trying not to notice that Myrna Muir, seated at one of the tills, was directing the sort of look at him that could blister paintwork. The supermarket was still quiet, with only one other till open, but he was conscious of heads turning as he stood waiting.

A few minutes later, an anxious-looking woman appeared from the back of the shop. 'I'm Mary Mackay. Is there something wrong?'

Gunn introduced himself. 'Just a word, about an incident on Saturday morning, if I may?'

'You'd better come through to the back office.'

Myrna was ignoring the customer waiting for service as she stared towards the manager; he saw a glance go between the two women before they walked away and his heart sank a little. Had the Caddon mafia been at work already?

'Take a seat,' she said. 'What's the problem?'

'We have had a complaint about threatening language used to a customer by Myrna Muir on Saturday morning. Do you know anything about it?'

'Saturday? It's always kinda busy on a Saturday morning. I really couldn't say.'

'I'd like you to cast your mind back. The victim would have reacted with some distress.'

Mary Mackay raised her eyes to the ceiling in a pantomime of concentration, then shook her head. 'Can't say I remember anything.'

It was the old pattern; he could feel the sense of helpless frustration creeping up again. But he didn't need to be that person; he couldn't see Livvy Murray putting up with it.

'I'm afraid I'm not entirely satisfied with that answer, and I'm not going to leave it there. A competent manager would have been aware that there was some sort of disturbance, but you didn't notice anything?'

The woman was looking flustered now. 'Well – nothing that I can think of.'

'In that case, I shall need a list from you of the personnel who were on the premises on Saturday morning. We will be questioning them all. Perhaps you could do that now?'

'Yes – um, well, now I think about it, there was a lady customer complaining about something but that often happens and she went on to complete her purchase so I'd just forgotten about it. Sorry.'

'Did you hear what was said?'

'No, I'm afraid not. It was Myrna who was dealing with

her – perhaps she can help you.'

The woman was looking more confident now, standing up as a sign that the interview was over. There would be absolutely no point in citing her as a witness – yet again, he was meeting a brick wall.

But this time he wasn't going to give in. From what he knew of Myrna, she'd have created enemies who would be only too happy to see her in trouble.

'That list?' he said, and saw the manager scowl. She sat down at the desk with a bad grace, scribbled a few names on a piece of paper and thrust it at him.

Gunn left the store without looking towards Myrna. It was going to mean a lot of overtime to do the checks, but he wasn't going to give up. As he went to his car, he saw that the man who had been stacking shelves had slipped out of a side door and had ducked down on the farther side.

'Can I get in? I'm wanting to speak to you,' he said urgently.

He opened the car and nodded; the man sidled in, ducking down below the dashboard. When Gunn got in, he said, 'Don't want them to see me, or she'll get me the sack. But I heard what she said to that woman. Someone needs to stop Myrna Muir.'

'Would you be prepared to make a statement?'

'Swear on the Bible, if you want. Made my girl's life a misery when she was working here. I'll tell you where I live, but I'll need to get back before I'm missed.'

Feeling a warm glow, Gunn got out a notebook. Perhaps the tide was turning.

* * *

Sarah Lindsay had slept the sleep of exhaustion, aware when she woke that her dreams had been vivid and complicated, but unable to remember any of them. She got up late, feeling groggy, then lay in the bath that had peeling chrome taps and a brownish water stain round the plughole, forcing herself to be grateful that at least it was holding hot water, while she tried to get her head together about what the day might bring.

A police visit, certainly. 'The police are our friends,' her mother had told her when she was a little girl; she had nothing to hide so all she had to do was tell them everything she knew – after all, she'd got on really well with the chief inspector when she'd told him about Doddie Muir. He'd looked at her differently on Friday, though, his eyes watchful, telling her that he wasn't simply going to accept what she said.

And why should he? The more she thought about it, the more she could see that she was the stand-out suspect. Strang had asked her if she knew of enemies Niall might have had and she couldn't think of one, or any reason why he should have them.

But, improbably, someone had killed him. And that someone was still out there, and if she didn't know why they'd killed Niall, could she be sure that they didn't have some unknown reason to kill her too?

The bathwater was cooling and Sarah got out, shivering. The bathroom was icy this morning and she towelled herself vigorously, then hurried into her clothes. She was going to go and let the hens out but as she went down the stairs, she saw they were pecking around the field by the hen houses already and heard the rumble of an engine. When she looked, there was their little tractor being driven past the house, heading for the arable land round on the other side, driven by one of Jimmie Gresham's men, presumably; he really had been endlessly kind and she felt more embarrassed than ever that Niall had let him down.

She hadn't much appetite when she thought of the day ahead, but she made coffee and forced herself to eat a boiled egg. What she mustn't do, she told herself, was sit here waiting for something nasty to happen; she had to get on with life and if she wasn't here when the police arrived, they would no doubt come again later. Shop first, then tackle the house, with the promise of a run once it was clean as motivation. And perhaps Rob might come up to see how she was – he'd said he'd try if he could sneak out of work.

She was just washing her mug when she heard a car arriving, and a moment later a knock on the front door. Her stomach knotted: Rob wouldn't come to the front door, and nor would Ken Blackford. It had to be the police.

As well to get it over with. But when Sarah opened the door, it was Michelle Gresham who stood there, carrying a large bunch of white tulips and smiling.

'Sarah, Rob said you were here all on your own and when he said he was worried about you, I thought I'd just pop up and see how you were.'

'Hello, Michelle. How kind of you – do come in,' Sarah said. 'And what lovely flowers.' She was taken aback; she knew Michelle, of course, and she'd always been very nice but they'd only ever talked for a few minutes at parties.

'And do take these.' She produced a box of Florentines.

'Chocolate and flowers – my remedy when I'm feeling a bit down.'

Michelle was smartly dressed, as always, in an expensive-looking olive-green raincoat with the hood put up against the soft rain, and, when Sarah took it from her, she was wearing a wrap dress in an animal print underneath, with neat brown leather ankle boots. Sarah took her through to the sitting room, feeling humiliated by her own well-worn jersey and jeans – and even more humiliated by the state of the room.

'I'm afraid the police don't clear up after themselves and I haven't had time to do anything yet. But do sit down and I'll get the fire on. Would you like some coffee?'

'Never known to refuse. But if you need a bit of cleaning done, find a can of Pledge and a duster and I'm your woman!'

Sarah's eyes went to Michelle's immaculately manicured nails, wondering how long it was since she had done any of her own housework, but it was certainly a kind offer.

'It seems awful, to let a guest do my housework, but it's so cold you might be better to keep moving till I get the room warmed up.'

Michelle followed her through to the kitchen as she fetched the polish and a duster – an elderly duster, that hadn't been washed after previous uses – while her guest offered her credentials.

'I always cleaned the house in the Caddon where I grew up, even when I was letting it out – the one Rob's living in, you know? But Andrew's always had a cleaner so I'm a wee bit Lady Muck now. Do me good to do a bit of polishing.'

Sarah went out to chop kindling and fetch in some

logs for the basket. When she came back in, Michelle was indeed working with a will.

'You're showing me up. That table is positively gleaming,' Sarah said as she coaxed the fire to life and went back to make the coffee. When she returned with it, Michelle's face was quite flushed with her efforts and all traces of police activity had been removed.

'So how are things going?' Michelle asked. 'It must be so hard for you, like living a nightmare.'

Sympathy was hard to cope with, and Sarah's voice faltered as she said, 'Oh, just sort of putting one foot in front of the other, really. It's all I can do.'

'I'd really like to think there was something I could do to help. Is there more you're going to have to do in the house?'

There was, of course, but Sarah was feeling awkward enough already. 'No, honestly, I'm fine,' she said. 'It was so kind of you to take the trouble to come.'

'Not at all,' Michelle said. 'I just wanted you to know that we're here for you. And you know, we have a family lawyer that can always give you advice if you're worried about police questioning. The less you say to them, the better, you know – they've a bad habit of twisting what you say.'

Sarah suddenly began to feel uncomfortable. In her painful experience, it wasn't the police who twisted what you said, it was the lawyers. Michelle Gresham was, she had just said, deeply rooted in the Caddon, where no one, ever, had been taught that the police were their friends. And now she thought about it, there was something odd about the way she'd suddenly appeared on her doorstep when they barely knew each other.

She turned the conversation to talk about her gratitude to Jimmie Gresham and asked after Briony. When they had finished the coffee, she said, 'Now, I'm feeling bad about taking up your time. I know you're a busy woman.'

'Not at all,' Michelle said. 'I'm enjoying bunking off work in a good cause. Look, why don't we both just set to and get the house put to rights? Then you can relax.'

She stood up, and Sarah did as well. 'Thanks, Michelle – you've been far too kind. But to tell you the truth I want to have something to do – sitting idle gives me too much time for thinking.'

She moved across to open the door. She thought Michelle's lips had tightened but a moment later she was smiling again.

'Of course. I can understand that. I hope the rest of the day isn't too difficult for you. And remember, just lift the phone and I'll come out and keep you company any time.'

She was still smiling as she went out to her car. Sarah was smiling too, managing to hold it in place as she waved Michelle off. Once she had shut the front door, she went back into the sitting room and sank into a chair.

What had that been about? She realised that there was something odd about Michelle's dedication to housework, but what could it mean? Then she remembered the filing cabinet. She had told Rob there was a notebook of Niall's in there – could Michelle really have been looking for it?

She got up and opened the top drawer. It wasn't in disorder, or anything, but as she pulled it out, it caught on a label that was out of alignment. Almost as if someone had closed it in a hurry.

The fire was burning up nicely but she was feeling icy cold. Michelle hadn't got the notebook – she'd taken it upstairs herself last night to see if it might shed any light on what had happened to Niall. It hadn't; all it contained was dated columns with amounts of money and initials that certainly meant nothing to her.

Presumably it meant something to other people. If they cared enough, she would be in danger as long as it was in her possession. The best thing she could do was take it directly to the police, immediately.

Then make sure they knew she didn't have it any longer. It would be simple enough to do that – she'd only have to mention it to Rob when next he came. That hurt, that really hurt. She'd been fond of Rob, so grateful for his warmth and kindness. She'd been had for a fool.

And now she was afraid. The memory of Niall's bloated face, so close to hers, came up in a vivid flashback and she gagged.

DI Gunn was pleased with what he'd achieved this morning. For the first time he had a witness who was eager to testify and he'd arranged for a DC from North Berwick to come down to take a full statement. There was still no summons from DCI Strang, so he had time to make his next move.

The GP surgery was the obvious place to start. The senior partner had given evidence to the procurator fiscal but since there had been no suspicious circumstances, there had been no need for a fatal accident inquiry and there had been no extensive investigation, only a decision that she had been just another NHS worker broken by the strains of Covid.

Perhaps that was right, but he'd like to be sure. He bearded the stern-looking receptionist, who accepted his request to speak to the senior partner reluctantly, then sent him along to the waiting room, where he sat with a few patients until Dr Paton was free to see him.

Paton was tall and thin, in his mid-fifties, with frameless glasses and an austere expression. There was something faintly defensive about the way he asked how he could help.

'I'm just conducting a review of the enquiries related to the death of Linden Moncrieff, one of the GPs in your practice.'

'Oh?' he said. 'I understood that had been settled – a very sad case. We were all put under a great deal of stress at that time, as you will know.'

'Of course. I want to know if she had come to you beforehand, talking about her difficulties? There don't seem to have been any questions asked about that.'

The defensiveness was unmistakable now. 'The continual stress applied to us all, naturally, and we arranged counselling sessions for the whole staff on Zoom, particularly after that very distressing attack on the surgery. I do remember it reduced Linden to tears.'

'That happened after the death of Myrna Muir's mother, didn't it?'

Paton shifted uncomfortably in his chair. 'Yes. Most unfortunate. There was a national directive that the frail elderly should not be saved using scarce resources – later rescinded, of course, but I'm afraid Mrs MacPherson was a victim.'

'And were there others?'

'No – at least, not for that reason. In common with

everyone else, we sadly lost several of our elderly patients to Covid.'

'Did you talk to Dr Moncrieff about the situation?'

'Not specifically, no, but of course I was always there if she wanted help or advice. And it was quite a while after that when she so tragically took her life.'

'And you had no indication that she might have been having continuing problems because of that?'

Paton sighed. 'None at all,' he said firmly. 'At the time, the risk of infection was so great that we weren't having face-to-face meetings but if there had been further difficulties, she could have phoned for a talk.'

'But she didn't?'

'No,' Paton said, with marked emphasis. 'I'm afraid there really is nothing more I can tell you.' He looked pointedly at his watch. 'I do have a patient waiting . . .'

'Of course, sir. Thank you for your time.'

Gunn withdrew, disappointed. The receptionist looked up when he came out but didn't speak, only pressing an intercom button and directing a patient to go to Dr Paton's room. She didn't look the sort of person you would choose to confide in if you were an inexperienced GP with problems, but he had to try.

'Excuse me,' he said. 'I'm sure you're busy, but I'm involved in reviewing the background to Dr Linden Moncrieff's suicide and I wondered if you knew her?'

To his surprise, the stern face softened and her eyes filled with tears. 'Oh yes, I knew Linden. That poor girl! She suffered so much, and she was such a caring doctor. But it was just brutal – she was constantly getting phone calls, terrible pictures cut out from the papers and sent to her in the post, all sorts. It was just the once she broke down and told me, but she didn't want anyone else to know – sort of ashamed, I think. "My cross to bear" – that was what she said – "I should have had the courage to refuse to go along with it." She kept smiling, even though you could see the strain on her face.'

This was beyond expectation. 'Did she tell you who was doing it?'

'No. She didn't know herself, poor wee soul. But that Myrna Muir will be at the back of it, I've no doubt.'

Well, you couldn't have everything. He took the receptionist's details, thanked her and left, feeling almost dizzy at this confirmation of what had, after all, been only a feeling arising from what he had read on Linden's face.

A text came in on his phone just as he got back to his car. Strang wanted to hold a briefing at one-thirty, which would give him time now to try for an interview with Rob Gresham. According to Rose, he had been as shocked as she was at what Linden had done, but could that be true? Could she really have kept her pain concealed even from her lover?

He didn't know exactly where the man worked, but they would certainly be able to tell him at Andrew Gresham's office. He drove through the rain and up round to the other side of the harbour to the handsome Victorian building that housed the admin centre of Arcturus, a name that honoured the very first of Robert Gresham's trawlers. They had come a long way since then.

Sarah sat in the sitting room with the notebook in her hand, trying to make up her mind about what would be best to do. Yes, the police would certainly be coming to see her soon, but would it be better for her to go to them first? Would that make a good impression, convince them that she was keen to help them find Niall's killer – and that it wasn't her they should be looking at?

The trouble was, she wasn't sure how to do that. The police station in Tarleton was one of those part-time affairs, so you never knew when it would be open – you were obviously expected to make sure that you only needed help or protection within office hours. The person she was looking to impress was DCI Strang, and she'd no reason to suppose that he'd be there. If she just handed it to someone else, it might not reach him for days, and they might not make the point that she was keen to do anything she could to help them.

There was a car turning into the yard right now. She stood up and saw that it was indeed DCI Strang who was driving it, and the woman with him was DS Murray, who had interviewed her before. At least that solved the problem, but her stomach was churning with nerves as she went to open the door.

CHAPTER FOURTEEN

As they drove out to Eastlaw Farm, DS Murray told DCI Strang what PC Thomson had said, and reported on the interview she'd done with Briony Gresham.

'Let's put it this way – if she backstabs one of her friends like that, I'd hate to be an enemy,' she concluded.

Strang was interested. 'Is there something behind it, or is she just that kind of person?'

Murray considered it. 'My bet's on natural nastiness. The kind that goes in the huff about anything and sees payback like a kind of religion. Still can't quite see her stringing up Ritchie, though.'

'So – Sarah Lindsay. Any thoughts?'

'Just the obvious. Look, I know motive isn't everything, but she's the one who's got it. She wanted to sell up, he wouldn't hear of it, and from what you've said he's completely blown it and there's nothing but debts – if she found out, it could make anyone lose it. But I don't actually think it's her. And the cash payments could mean there are other hot suspects; we just don't have a handle on who they would be.'

'I'm hoping we can get something out of Sarah if we keep it low key and get her to chat.'

'It'd be good if she offered us coffee,' Murray said. 'And biscuits – I sacrificed my breakfast to Thomson.'

'Very noble. Anyway, I've told Matt Gunn we'll have a briefing at the station at one-thirty. Is he working in North Berwick this morning?'

'No, I saw him in Tarleton. He said that since he hadn't been tasked with anything, he was going to take the time to dig around Linden Moncrieff's suicide. Not sure why, but it's been a bit of an obsession for him.'

'Won't do any harm, I suppose. He won't have time for that later, though – I'll want him to contact the manager of Niall's bank and get him to talk him through the accounts just for a start. Here we are. She's spotted us arriving.'

Sarah Lindsay opened the door and was standing on the threshold wearing a nervous smile. 'Come in. I've been expecting you.'

'We just want to ask you a few things. It's not formal; we won't be recording it,' Strang said.

The fire in the sitting room was almost out, and she went through before them to put on a handful of kindling, then logs as the flames sprang up.

'I don't know if you want coffee. I could—'

'Let me,' Murray said. 'I saw where you kept things – you talk to DCI Strang.' She whisked out.

They both sat down and Strang said, 'Ms Lindsay—'

'Sarah, please,' she interrupted him. 'I know there's a lot of questions you have for me, but I want to hand this over to you first. Your men took all the papers from Niall's study but this was in the filing cabinet here where I keep my own records. I would have taken it in, but I didn't know how to find you.'

She was holding out a notebook, A3 size, with a red binding and a mottled cover. It was obviously much-used, the cardboard corners frayed.

He took it from her and opened it. The hairs at the back of his neck rose as he looked down the first page while she told him that on evenings in, Niall would sit jotting notes in it while they were watching TV. 'It was too cold to work in his study,' she explained.

The notebook was printed as an account book with columns for money in, money out. There were initials against each entry – a number of different ones. He couldn't be sure, but off the top of his head he thought they might well mirror the small cash transactions detailed in the bank statements; these entries could be a sort of profit and loss record. But what was the business?

'It looks like rough accounts. Do you know what these figures relate to?'

She shook her head. 'I did ask once, but he just said it was farm stuff. He dealt with all that and to be honest, I wasn't much interested. I had been involved originally but once I was able to get my shop in the town, I left all that side of it to him. So I don't really know anything about the finances and I'm told that because I'm not Niall's next of kin, I'm not allowed to know even now.'

'Did he ever talk about it – the problems and so on?'

'Not that I remember. We – er – didn't really talk much.'

Sarah had looked embarrassed as she said that. Was she thinking what a bleak picture this gave of the life they had been leading – the two of them, sitting silent in this unlovely little room, using the flickering pictures on the screen in the corner as plaster to cover up the gaping cracks in the relationship?

Strang held out the book, pointing to the heading on the first page. 'The start date for this – is that when you arrived here?'

'No,' she said. 'We came here about eighteen months before that, I think.'

'Can you think of any reason why he should have started keeping these records? Was there anything that had changed?'

Her harsh laughter startled him. 'Anything? Try "everything". With lockdown, we both lost our employment. It was growing obvious Niall just didn't have what it took, though he wouldn't face up to it. If Jimmie Gresham hadn't thrown us a lifeline, we'd have been out on the streets, which is why it was rotten of Niall to feed chemicals into the system.'

It chimed with what Briony Gresham had said, according to Murray. 'But to put it crudely,' he said, 'what was in it for him?'

'Oh, he's evangelical,' Sarah said. 'Niall was a member of the True Church and if he ducked out it would be a repudiation of the Faith. Jimmie loves giving those parties where he's the sun the little acolytes like us spin round.'

That was a strikingly shrewd and cynical assessment.

While she was speaking, Murray had quietly come in with a coffee tray and Strang saw her registering that remark as she handed round mugs and offered biscuits.

'So do you think keeping this record might have begun after the farm started losing money?'

Sarah leant forward to glance at the page again. 'That's probably right – this would be just after the second lockdown, wouldn't it?'

Murray said, 'I think you said to me that was when Niall started going off to the Watergate Tavern with Ken Blackford?'

'Yes, that could be right. But I can't see what significance that might have.'

She might not, but he did, and judging by the glance Murray shot at him as he handed her the book, she did too. She'd have heard the conversation from the kitchen.

'Now,' he began, but Sarah interrupted.

'There was something else I wanted to say—'

'I'll be happy to hear it, but I want to ask you one more thing first. We found dried mud in the barn that had clearly fallen off the tyre of a very large piece of farming machinery. Do you know where it could have come from?'

She looked completely blank. 'There's our tractor there—'

'This would have been much bigger. Did Niall ever hire anything for a specific purpose?'

'I can't think why he would. The farm's not big enough to need anything fancy.'

'And you never saw one in the barn?'

'No. But in fact I was hardly ever in there, after the

236

first few months, so I suppose I wouldn't necessarily have known if there was. It was really just the hens I was in charge of and there's a little store where I keep their stuff.'

'Fine,' Strang said. 'Now, there was something you wanted to tell me?'

'Yes.' She gave a nervous gulp. 'This could just be me being paranoid, and I don't want to make any sort of false accusation, but I am a bit worried.'

As she told them what had happened that morning, Strang stiffened. Murray, who had been quietly making inroads into the biscuits, stopped chewing.

'Right. With your permission, we are taking the book. You say that you are confident that you can get that information relayed to anyone who might be interested?'

Sarah bit her lip. 'Yes, I'm afraid so.'

'I would strongly suggest that you do that, but I'm very concerned about your staying here,' Strang said. 'You're isolated and very vulnerable. Is there anywhere else you could go, for your own protection? Would Mrs Moncrieff be able to host you again?'

'I was sort of hoping you'd tell me I'd be safe once you had it and just to lock my doors. Rose is endlessly hospitable but there's this woman who lives opposite carrying out a campaign of hatred against us both and it's horrible being there in Tarleton.'

'Oh? I haven't heard anything about this.'

'DI Gunn knows. He's a friend of Rose's and she said on Saturday she'd ask him to do something about it. It's happened to her a lot since her daughter's suicide – he's been trying to help.'

'I see,' Strang said. That perhaps had prompted Gunn to

revisit that case. 'I can certainly see to it that he continues to keep an eye on the situation.'

A glance at his watch told him that if they were to be back in time for the briefing at Tarleton, they'd have to leave – there wasn't time to get the whole story now.

'I think that's all. Just one final thing – you said when last we spoke that you couldn't think of enemies Niall might have had. Is that still what you would say?'

Sarah hesitated. 'I don't really want to point the finger. But Ken Blackford came round last night, being very pushy and aggressive about wanting to buy the farm and it did make me scared that he might have – well, done something about it. I don't really think he'd do anything to harm me, but—'

'All the more reason to take our advice. Please keep us informed about what you decide to do. We have your statement, of course, but someone will come to check through the details you gave us about your movements on the day when it happened.'

'I can't pretend to have an alibi. I was alone in the house all afternoon while I prepared for the party and you only have my word for it that I didn't see Niall at all then.'

She was looking as if she hoped for reassurance he wasn't in a position to give. He thanked her for her help and Murray thanked her for the biscuits and he gave her a receipt for the account book before they left.

As they went to the car, Strang handed it to Murray. 'Hold it carefully,' he said. 'It looks innocent enough, but actually I have a feeling that it's dynamite.'

* * *

238

DI Gunn, flushed with his successes, drove to the headquarters of Arcturus and walked up to the imposing front door. There was a vestibule floored with encaustic tiles and it gave on to a hall of positively baronial splendour where an ugly modern desk and steel-framed chairs arranged round a teak coffee table proclaimed a sturdy indifference to architectural aesthetics.

The receptionist was a plump, pleasant-looking middle-aged woman who was ready to be helpful, but she could only say that Rob Gresham would likely be down at the harbour.

'You're best just to go and ask around there. I think he said there was one of the skippers wanting to speak to him, and there's usually checks to be made at the processing plant.'

Gunn thanked her and walked off down the hill. The rain had stopped and the sun was making one of its tantalisingly brief appearances, like a diva determined to make sure of leaving the audience wanting more. There was a playful wind that was whipping up tiny waves in the harbour and in the marina the leisure boats were dancing at their moorings, their tackle chinking.

A good number of fishing boats were tied up in the main harbour today; it was Monday, of course, and they'd have been in over the weekend. Given the quota restrictions, they wouldn't be in any particular hurry to get the boats out and the place was quiet.

There were a few men working on the trawlers, though, among the ropes and nets, and Gunn approached the nearest one to ask if they knew where Rob Gresham might be.

'Oh aye,' one bearded giant said, 'I saw him away to

the plant a wee while ago. You'll probably find him there.' Then, with a suddenly suspicious look, he said, 'What were you wanting him for?'

He had obviously guessed that Gunn was the polis – some folk had an uncanny knack for that, usually folk who had reason to want to know. The activities on fishing boats didn't always relate strictly to fishing, particularly here.

He made the standard reply – 'Just wanting a word with him' – and had no doubt that the story would be out before he arrived at the processing plant at the inland end of the harbour.

He walked past the fish market – deserted today – and into the forecourt.

It was busy enough there, with boxes being loaded into several vans that were waiting, one from a restaurant whose name he recognised. Arcturus was certainly big business.

The smell of fish and the noise of machinery was pervasive as Gunn dodged through the workers, heading for a door that was standing open on a cramped little office. Beyond it he could see people in blue plastic overalls and caps handling fish onto a conveyor belt with considerable speed and expertise.

There was a high desk in the office, festooned with notes and posters, and the white-haired man behind it was deep in conversation with another man. Gunn had to shout his question to make himself heard, but the younger one immediately turned, saying, 'I'm Rob Gresham.'

Gunn introduced himself, and Gresham nodded, pointing outside. 'We'd better get out of here so we can hear ourselves think. What can I do for you?'

Gresham was a good-looking guy. He had an easy

manner, too, and it wasn't hard to see why Linden might have fallen for him; from the brief memory he had of her, they would have made an attractive couple. When he explained why he had come, Gresham's social smile faded and he looked sombre.

'I'd better take you to my office in the big house,' he said. 'I thought the police had drawn a line under Linden's death but if there's anything more I can help you with, I'll be glad to do it.'

Gresham's office, to the back of the ground floor, was smaller and more humbly furnished than Gunn would have expected accommodation for the boss's son to be, with only a small desk and three wooden chairs. But then Andrew Gresham had the reputation of being, if not exactly mean, considering his donations to charity, then of being careful not to spend a tenner when a fiver would do the job.

'Fire away,' Gresham said. 'Why are the police taking an interest again, after all this time?'

'I've known Rose Moncrieff ever since the tragedy occurred. She has always felt there was more to what Linden did than emerged at the time and I gather from her that you felt the same.'

His immediate reaction was cautious. 'Yes, perhaps, but as they said she certainly was very stressed by the work. Admittedly, despite talking about moving on, I could see she was more and more strained-looking and of course I was worried about her – suggested she get counselling, but no, she wouldn't. I believed she'd feel better given time – I certainly didn't realise at all what she was planning to do.'

'So it came as a complete shock to you?'

'Absolutely. And to Rose too.'

There was nothing Gunn could put his finger on, but mentioning Rose like that somehow rang a little false – as if Gresham was trying to use her to corroborate what he'd said. He pressed on.

'And you had no idea that she had been constantly tormented by anonymous phone calls and graphic newspaper cuttings being sent in the post?'

Gresham's shock was unmistakable. His eyes wide, he said, 'What? Who told you that?'

'I'm not at liberty to say. Are you saying that she never told you this was happening?'

His shoulders dropped and he sank back in his chair. After a moment, he said, 'Yes, I'm telling you that she never told me. I'm telling you I never saw her take a distressing call, I never saw her open anything like what you described. We didn't spend that much time at her flat, of course – my house has more space.'

'You have to accept that it seems unlikely that she wouldn't tell the person closest to her what she was going through?'

'Look, I'll swear on oath that she didn't tell me, if you like. Do you think I would have let it go on if I'd known at the time? And you can ask Rose – she and Linden were very close, but I'm perfectly sure she didn't hear about it at the time either.'

That was a telling point. Gunn knew for a fact that Linden had not said anything about this to her mother, and the receptionist at the surgery had said that Linden was determined to suffer in silence, almost by way of atonement for her patient's death. She had overestimated her own strength.

Time to move on. 'Are you aware of the harassment that Mrs Moncrieff has been subjected to over the years, and now Ms Lindsay too?'

'Oh God, yes. That's Myrna Muir. And you lot are to blame – you should have shut her down years ago. And if the implication is that she hounded my girlfriend to her death, then you'd better stop being feeble and do something about it, hadn't you?'

The direct attack was like a punch to the gut. 'Don't – don't think we haven't tried,' he managed. 'The Caddon has closed ranks against us every time. If you have evidence of what you just said, why haven't you given it to us?'

'Oh, I don't have *evidence*. It's just that everyone knows it. Perhaps your DCI Strang will be able to supply some much-needed backbone.'

Gunn could feel his confidence draining away. He'd never been good at confrontation but he needed to assert himself now if it wasn't to disappear completely; he had to stake out his territory. 'This has nothing to do with DCI Strang. He is in charge of the Niall Ritchie case. This is entirely my own investigation. Do you have Dr Moncrieff's mobile phone in your possession?'

'No, I don't. Your lot took it, I imagine. They certainly wouldn't be returning it to me, obviously, when Rose is her next of kin.'

He should have known that. He felt stupid, thrown off his stride, and he felt the tiny tweak of the nervous twitch by his left eye. There were other questions he should be asking but somehow they'd gone out of his head – and now he looked at the time, he realised he was in danger of being late for the briefing anyway, which gave him an excuse to stop.

'I have another meeting to go to, so I'll leave it at that, but I'll want to speak to you again.'

'You know where to find me. I'm usually around the harbour somewhere.' As Gunn left, Gresham added, 'Got anywhere with the murder inquiry? No? I thought not.'

At least he could comfort himself with the thought that Gresham had definitely looked shaken by what he'd said, but he'd been shaken himself by that sudden assault on his professionalism. The confidence he'd enjoyed earlier felt brittle now, and there were cracks appearing.

'You were thinking what I was thinking, weren't you?' DCI Strang said to DS Murray as they drove away from Eastlaw Farm.

'Waterford Tavern,' she said. 'It obviously hadn't occurred to Sarah, but I bet we can match up the initials to the regulars. I noticed KB for one.'

'And DM. Look, I think going across there to hold the publican's feet to the fire is a top priority. At the very least it will give me something to tell JB before she starts getting unhappy about the delay over the weekend. I'll get Matt to take the book to a face-to-face with Ritchie's bank manager – he must have discussed the borrowing at some stage and he might even be able to shed a light on some of the cash transactions. When it comes to the initials, Matt's local knowledge should be useful too. Meantime can you just jot them down, please, so we can confront the publican with them.'

'Sure, boss.' Murray got out a notebook and started scribbling. 'Don't think you'll find he's keen to be helpful, though.'

'Probably not, but he might be persuaded once I tell him that until we find out, there'll be a constable posted there indefinitely to question every punter who walks through the door. Wouldn't be good for business.'

Murray laughed. 'Fairly spoil the taste of your pint. But what are they, these accounts? Seem a bit random, really.'

'I was looking through it while Sarah was speaking. Pretty much every initial entry seems to have a smaller amount in the debit column and a larger one in the credit one, with a couple of exceptions I noticed where both sums were in the debit column. Interesting.'

Murray stared blankly at the book in her hand. 'Yeah, I suppose it would be, if I'd a scooby about what it means.'

'I don't *know*, of course, but given the activities around here it suggests to me that he was in some low-grade syndicate, where he'd buy a stake in some operation that would return a profit once the operation was completed – smuggled cigarettes and booze would be my guess. We're not talking drug profits here. What we do know is that Ritchie was strapped for money and getting desperate. Lindsay told me at the time of the Doddie Muir prosecution that he was pressuring her to drop it, and this would explain why.'

'And I suppose they wouldn't want him to pull out either,' Murray said. 'Poor guy!'

Strang grimaced. '"He who rides the tiger cannot dismount," as they say. They wouldn't trust him to keep his mouth shut if he escaped.'

'I suppose we're sure he didn't kill himself? Can't see much of a way out for him. No wonder he went on to Sarah about a spider's web.'

As Strang turned in to the Tarleton police station car

park, Murray said triumphantly, 'There! That's the complete list. I don't see Matt's car – he must have got held up.'

'Oh,' he said. 'That's a nuisance. I don't really want to hang around waiting for him. We won't want to go to the pub until two, when it'll be closed, but go and get something to eat. A diet of biscuits doesn't make for clear thinking. I'll just call to update him later. Leave the book at the desk for him, Livvy. Then we can get on with it.'

DI Gunn arrived at Tarleton police station in a fluster of apologies just as DS Murray was coming back out. She gabbled an explanation, and explained rapidly what Strang wanted him to do.

'Fine,' he said miserably. 'I'm really sorry—'

'Yes, you said. How did your morning go, anyway?'

'Oh, tell you later. You'd better go – the boss is waiting.'

Gunn's spirits sank; he'd been trying so hard to win Strang's approval and he'd be in the doghouse now. He picked up the book and took it along to his office. Murray had said his local knowledge would be useful and now as he opened it and flicked through the pages, initials leapt out at him. KB – Ken Blackford. He appeared regularly, on page after page. DM – Doddie Muir, less often. GS – that would be Doddie's mate Geordie Sinclair.

He hesitated over MG. There were half a dozen entries for that, and they were among the highest amounts, in both columns. He had seen Michelle Gresham in that pub several times when he'd had reason to call in, but surely with Andrew's money she wouldn't need to get involved in gutter crime like this? She was Caddon born and bred, of course – so why not? Money was always welcome.

And now he looked for it, there was RG as well. Rob Gresham? The two of them were known to be thick as thieves – which they probably were, without a scruple between them.

He felt a little shudder. There was so much going on, interweaving and shifting around so you couldn't tell what you were looking at.

Rob Gresham – he'd need to gather his wits and talk to him again, about this too. And now he remembered the question he'd been going to ask before he'd lost his focus. Was Myrna Muir the only person he knew of who might have reason to hate Linden?

CHAPTER FIFTEEN

As DI Gunn left, Gresham leant forward and put his head down on the desk, feeling sick. As if he didn't have enough problems already! He'd known at the time he'd taken a serious risk, but he was a gambler by nature and it had looked as if he'd made the right call. Until now. This was a serious threat.

Then there was Ritchie's notebook. He didn't know what was in it; it might be nothing more than stuff like how many sheep had the bots or something – he was happy to say he knew nothing about farming – or even philosophical maunderings about life, but he had a dark suspicion that the stupid sod was dumb enough to keep a record of the sort of transactions that no sane person would commit to paper.

And Michelle's idea hadn't worked. When he'd phoned

in a panic last night, she'd soothed him as she always did, like the mother he'd never had. 'Stepmummy will fix it,' she'd said – the phrase was a long-running joke between them.

She hadn't, though; she hadn't had enough time to check through the filing cabinet, and his first instinct had been to dash out to Eastlaw and try his luck, but Michelle had vetoed that – she'd told Sarah she'd come because he was working. The minute it was plausible to say he had come in his lunch hour, he'd been going to hurtle out there and just hope the police hadn't got there first.

Then Gunn had arrived. It had been almost funny to see that inadequate little jerk trying to throw his weight around – almost, if it wasn't for what he was doing. That wasn't funny at all.

Michelle couldn't help this time – he'd never confessed to her what had happened – but he couldn't deal with this himself. It was with some misgivings that he picked up his phone.

After the police left, Sarah Lindsay sat on, staring at the fire in the sitting room, taking deep breaths to try to stop her mind scurrying from one worry to another, like some trapped animal looking for the hole in the wall that would lead out to freedom. Her prison didn't seem to have one of those.

Handing over the notebook had been a smart move, though; that had definitely won brownie points, but Strang had markedly not commented on her lack of alibi – she was probably still number-one suspect. There was nothing she could do about that, except put it out of her mind – as if!

The more immediate worry was the decision she had to make about her own safety. Strang had taken seriously what she'd said about Michelle Gresham's visit, but if she followed Strang's advice and went back to Rose's house, she would not only feel stifled by the miasma of hostility that surrounded them but she might actually endanger Rose herself.

She'd really liked Rob, thought he was a good friend. It hurt that she was so sure that telling him the police already had the book would neutralise the immediate threat from there – and even now she was almost hoping she'd got it wrong – but if it was right, then she could, as she had said, lock her doors and stay on here, telling herself that Ken Blackford wouldn't really do anything while she was under the eye of the police. She might even convince herself, if she tried hard enough.

What she must do was tell Rob as soon as possible. She could even just phone him but she quailed at the thought of the coded conversation that would have to take place. She'd have to brace herself—

But there, right now, was his car, driving into the yard. Her heart seemed to leap into her throat; she felt breathless and a little dizzy. But she forced herself to the door, forced herself to open it and call, 'Rob! Good to see you!'

He was smiling his easy smile as he got out. He was clasping a bottle of wine and he held up a supermarket bag as he called back, 'Sandwich lunch!' and came over to kiss her on both cheeks.

'I thought you might need cheering up. Apologies in advance – it's not exactly Pret A Manger, but there was prawn and smoked salmon so I hope that's all right.'

Oddly enough, the exaggerated gesture made her feel better; this was a charade, and she too could play a part. Her racing pulse slowed.

'Oh, thank you. You're far too kind, spoiling me like this!' she said. 'Come on in. There's a fire in the sitting room.' She waited cynically for the first attempt to get her out of the room. It didn't take long.

Rob handed over the bottle, took the sandwiches out of the bag and sat down on the sofa. 'Now, why don't you go and look out glasses and plates and hunt out a corkscrew, while I release the sandwiches from captivity? I must admit I'm starving.'

'I'm hungry myself. I've had quite a stressful morning with the police here,' she said as she left the room, but not before she had seen that information hit him like a javelin. Sadly, she'd been right.

There was a momentary pause, and then he called through, 'Oh, poor you! How did it go?'

'No brutality, or anything – he's very civilised. Civilised but scary. If I'd done it, I'd probably just confess and not suffer being inexorably tracked down, hour by hour. My nerves wouldn't stand it.'

It didn't take long to assemble what was needed and he'd have had to move fast to open the filing cabinet, find the book and be back sitting down innocently with the sandwiches unwrapped before she came back in. As it was, his face was pale now and he obviously hadn't moved since she'd left.

'Here are the plates,' she said. 'Sandwiches?'

Rob jumped. 'Oh, sorry. Wool-gathering. There's been a lot on at work.' He handed her the bag. 'Now, corkscrew? Thanks. Tell me all about it, then.'

'They mostly just covered old ground – asked me if I'd thought of any other enemies Niall might have had since they spoke to me last, which of course I hadn't. Oh, and there was a question about mud in the barn from some big tractor. I don't know what that was about, but I remembered afterwards that DCI Strang had talked about thefts of farm machinery when he came here the first time. Do you know anything about that?'

'I've heard it happens, but nothing more. Do they think Niall may have had something to do with it?'

He handed her a glass. He was looking more relaxed; was he starting to hope that perhaps she'd forgotten about the notebook?

'I don't know – they keep their cards pretty close to their chests. Oh, and I gave them Niall's notebook. They seemed pretty interested in that.'

Rob turned so that she couldn't see his face and bent down to pick up the discarded sandwich wrappers. 'You don't want these lying around. I'll just put them in the bin in the kitchen.'

Sarah noticed his hands were shaking and his voice was forced as he called brightly, 'So, what was in it that was interesting?'

'Didn't make much sense to me,' she said, taking a sip of wine. 'I took it upstairs last night to look at it in bed, but it was just lists of initials and amounts of money. Then they went on about me being vulnerable out here. They seemed to think I should consider going back to stay with Rose.'

He came back in and sat down, picked up a sandwich and took a bite. 'Mmm – not bad, actually.' He didn't look as if he was enjoying it, though. 'Why not?'

'Do you think I should? Ken Blackford came round last night, wanting to talk about buying the farm and I'd a job getting rid of him.'

'Then you probably should – he's got a bit of a reputation, you know. You've enough on your plate without that. Is there anything keeping you here? You don't need to sort through any more papers to see if there's anything else of Niall's with your things, do you? I could help, if you like.'

It was so blatant, Sarah almost laughed. 'No, that was the only thing he kept down here. The police took everything else.'

'Right, right,' he said.

Time to change the subject. 'Have you seen Rose today? I hope she hasn't had more trouble with Myrna Muir. I was hoping my being out of the way might help so I'm a bit reluctant to take advantage of her kindness.'

He didn't seem any more comfortable with this line of conversation. He'd taken another sandwich and was eating it in quick bites, glancing at his watch. 'Oh, I'm sure it'll be all right. Look, I'm really sorry, I've just seen the time. I'll need to get back to work. No, don't get up. Just sit and enjoy your wine. At least I've seen you're OK – I'm impressed! You really are one tough cookie!' He bent over to kiss her and went out, telling her to call him if she needed anything.

Yes, she was a tough cookie, and getting tougher by the day. She had to.

The bald publican had looked at Murray as if she'd come in on someone's sole the last time, even before he knew she was polis. Standing behind the bar, still piled with glasses waiting to be cleared, he was looking even more hostile now, with Strang asking him to supply a list of his regulars.

'Not sure what you mean by that. Folks come in here all the time and there's none of them look as if they're underage, so I don't check their ID.'

He was looking pleased with his reply. Murray said, 'There's a list of initials here. Recognise any of them as matching any of the "folks" you do know that may just happen to come in?'

He took a cursory glance. 'Nuh. Can't say I do.'

Strang said, very smoothly, 'That's a real pity. We have reason to believe that an illicit business may be operating from these premises. Are you the licensee?'

The man scowled. 'Yes.'

'Your name, sir?'

'Joe Mackeson.' He spat out the words.

'Well, Mr Mackeson, as you know the conditions for keeping a licence are extremely strict. Any illegal transactions carried out on the premises would tell against renewal. The licensing board is very particular.'

'Never seen any sign of anything like that,' he said. But he had shifted uneasily, uncomfortable for the first time.

He looks like an old lag, Murray thought suddenly, just as Strang said, 'You are not obliged to answer this question. Have you a prison record? I do have to explain that if you refuse, we can go back and check.'

'Never let go, do you?' Mackeson said bitterly. 'It was years ago; I've done my time. They know all about it.'

'I'm sure. But as you say, we never let go. Perhaps I can ask for your cooperation now.'

'Or else you could get me closed down, is that it? And

even if I help you out and you set up some of my customers, I could still get closed down?'

'I'm not going to promise anything. What I can say is that if you don't, your denial of involvement won't seem credible.'

Mackeson was blinking rapidly now and licking his lips. Murray, who had learnt in her school playground that kicking a man when he was down might not be nice, but it was usually effective, said, 'There's a JM here.' She pointed to the list.

'Where did that come from? What's it a list of, anyway?'

'Not at liberty to say,' Strang and Murray said in unison.

'Initials don't prove anything.' The protests were getting feebler.

Strang said, 'An early plea to what seems like minor criminality would be very well received.'

'And if it led us to the main instigators, that would help too,' Murray added.

They left with names to set against the initials with only half a dozen missing, along with Mackeson's agreement to make a statement at Tarleton police station the next day.

'Great result,' Strang said, as they walked to their cars.

'I was glad to get out of there before he had a stroke,' Murray said. 'His face was getting more purple with fury by the minute.'

'He's right, of course – initials don't prove anything. But there may be others in the syndicate who'll crack under a bit of pressure.'

'I'll take these names and feed them through ACRO. Something tells me we may find quite a few of them featuring in the records.'

'Send me a copy. I'd better get back to Fettes Avenue and try to catch up with the DCS. It always pays to keep her in the picture, and I'll action opening up the incident room again too. It looks as if we're going to be busy.'

'That's good. I hate not having enough to do.'

Murray drove back in a good mood. It had even stopped raining; she was working more closely with Strang than ever before and it looked as if they might be in for an interesting time tomorrow.

That her thought had carried an echo of the words of the famous Chinese curse didn't even occur to her.

Detective Chief Superintendent Jane Borthwick was in a meeting, DCI Strang was told, but would call him when she returned. It was only a mild irritation; it would give him time to get his thoughts in order before he talked through the latest developments with her.

The copy of the list of initials, with such names as they'd been able to assign, pinged through from Murray and he read it with some satisfaction. There was a report from DI Gunn; the bank manager had indeed expressed concern to Ritchie about his finances and though his cash transactions had never been discussed, they were able to establish that none of the sums in the notebook's credit columns had been paid in; presumably Ritchie had quietly trousered the cash. That was all good stuff to show the boss.

His phone rang. 'The meeting's finished,' Borthwick said. 'Waste of time as they all are, frankly, but mercifully short. Come on up, Kelso.'

She was sitting looking expectant when he arrived. 'I hope you have something interesting for me. I could feel brain cells expiring from boredom this afternoon.'

Strang smiled. 'I'm happy to say I have. Evidence of what looks like a small crime syndicate operating out of the local pub. Sarah Lindsay handed in a notebook that shows Niall Ritchie was involved.'

Borthwick brightened. 'Now that's the sort of thing I like to hear. Is she still prime suspect?'

'Gut feeling is no, but she had motive and opportunity and no problem about finding the means to do it so we can't strike her off, though I would say there are others appearing in the frame. Can you call up the list Murray has put on file?'

As Borthwick tapped on her keyboard, he explained the context and his conclusions, drawing her attention to the Gresham names. 'What puzzles me is they're both big figures on the social scene in Tarleton and the sums assigned to the notebook are small – hard to see why it was worth the risk.'

She thought for a moment. 'Depends how much other punters paid in, doesn't it? Ritchie was skint but others may not have been. They could have been doing good business if they established a line from contraband coming into the port direct to one of the bigger players.'

'Livvy Murray is going to trawl ACRO. She checked out a couple that caught our eye before, and both of them had previous, but after lockdown they suddenly seemed to have gone straight.'

Borthwick raised her eyebrows. 'Meaning . . .?'

'DI Gunn said the force had got demoralised because even if they charged someone, they couldn't make it stick. Eyewitnesses wouldn't testify and in the odd case they brought using circumstantial evidence they came up against a top QC who made mincemeat of the fiscal. They've had it all their own way. Gunn's a decent man but not the most effective copper. But now we've got this, I'm sure we can get this whole operation mopped up.'

Borthwick said, 'Mmm.'

She was obviously thinking, so he didn't speak. At last she said, 'I'm sure you will, and I accept this is a breakthrough in those terms. But what I can't immediately see is how it relates to the murder that is the main focus. How do you plan to progress it?'

Strang couldn't think what to say. She was right, of course; the bloody woman always was. He'd been so worried that the 'golden hour' investigation immediately after the crime had yielded so little that he'd been carried away by this small success.

He could only be honest. 'I haven't any great plan apart from questioning all the names on the list – check out their movements on the day in question, see what comes up. If the Caddon criminal community is under the cosh, the neds may be more prepared to talk. And of course I'll be getting more from the forensic accountants when they've gone through Ritchie's papers. They're working too on the source of the rope that was used. It's not very sexy, I know, but . . .'

Borthwick shrugged. 'That's the job, isn't it? "It's dogged as does it," my sergeant used to say, and we're lucky in that the media hasn't really picked up on it – there's only been that one snide article about lack of progress today. Did you see it?'

'Yes,' he said. Oh yes, he'd seen it, and winced.

'I think it needs a bit of inspiration, Kelso. Step back from it tonight, take a look at it and tell me what you think tomorrow.'

'Ma'am,' he said as he left, feeling reprimanded and even a bit resentful that he'd been having to make bricks without straw. But as he left, he could imagine her retort if he'd been unwise enough to voice the thought – a crisp, 'Your job to find the straw.'

Sometimes DS Murray thought that her happiest hours were spent sitting at a computer in her favourite corner of the CID room, tucked away where the general bustle of detectives coming and going didn't bother her, while she lifted all the stones to see what little crawling things were lurking underneath.

She'd got a few squirming under the spotlight of investigation this afternoon. About half a dozen of the names on the list turned out to have previous convictions mainly related to minor crimes, carrying a fine rather than a custodial sentence, for petty dishonesty of one sort or another, but significantly they all seemed to have turned over a new leaf since lockdown. There was one who'd had a deferred sentence for domestic abuse but nothing else. Then there were the four who had done time.

Blackford and Muir she knew about already. Joe Mackeson, the publican, was also one, with a number of convictions for violence that culminated in nine months for GBH eight years ago, but nothing since. The fourth, though, was a real surprise.

Rob Gresham had spent eighteen months of a three-year sentence in Barlinnie as one of the less senior members arrested when a crime gang, with a long history of warehouse robberies, reset, car thefts – pretty much you name it – was busted by the Glasgow force.

From what she knew about Rob – that he'd been Linden Moncrieff's partner, that he'd been supporting Sarah Lindsay when Strang had first spoken to her, that he was part of a wealthy family – she hadn't expected anything like this. Out of the whole seedy lot of them, he was the only one who demonstrably had roots in organised crime. Her brain started buzzing.

Was Kelso still here? He'd only said he was coming in to report to JB, but he often had paperwork – there were always other ongoing investigations.

She called his number. 'Are you still in the office, boss?' she asked.

'No, Livvy. I'm at home. Did you want something?'

He was sounding a bit down. 'Doesn't matter. Tomorrow will do. Just, I found out Rob Gresham was jailed for involvement in a big Glasgow gang – thought you'd like to know. I've got an idea about that—'

'Do you, indeed!' His voice was suddenly brighter. 'I could come in, or – do you know where I live?'

Her heart gave a little jump. Of course she knew where he lived – she'd driven past the cottage a hundred times, wondering what it was like inside, wondering if she'd ever be close enough to the boss to merit an invitation to visit. 'Yes, I do,' she said. 'Shall I just pop over? I can pass the details through now.'

'Yes, do that, Livvy. It'll give me time to see what it suggests to me and then we can brainstorm. I'll have a beer waiting for you.'

Murray was almost breathless with anticipation as she sent off the notes she'd made. It was what she had always hoped for – that Kelso would see her as not just a problematic junior but a colleague and even – dare she think it? – a friend, now that he'd invited her to his home instead of coming back to the station for a formal meeting.

It was a gloomy evening with darkness gathering, but she felt so cheerful she could swear the sun was shining as she parked in one of the narrow streets behind the little square of fisherman's cottages. Strang's was an upside-down one and she had to climb a wooden staircase to reach the front door.

He had it open before she got there and ushered her to a seat by the window overlooking the Firth of Forth. She looked about her as he went to fetch the promised beers. She wasn't sure what she'd expected, some sort of bachelor pad, perhaps, but this was a charming room, with pale walls and a velvety grey sofa piled with cushions. There were a couple of striking pictures on the walls and two big table lamps were lit in anticipation of the coming darkness. More like a woman's room, she thought – and of course, it had been home to his dead wife. She felt a real pang of sadness for him; she'd never heard that he'd looked at anyone else since.

'Lovely house,' she said as he handed her the can.

'Thanks,' he said, but absent-mindedly; he was sitting down at the laptop on the table between them already. 'I'm feeling a bit bruised after my session with JB. She doesn't feel we've got very far and the Waterfoot Tavern stuff is very much a side issue and we're being diverted from what happened on the day Ritchie was killed.'

Murray bit her lip. 'Ah. Bit of a slap in the face, really.'

'I should have seen it coming. It's hard to think of a reason why the syndicate should want to kill him and set off a major police investigation – after all, they tried to get Lindsay to back off Doddie Muir so we wouldn't come sniffing around.'

'I suppose that's right. But look at this – the records are really interesting. Being picked up for pretty minor stuff was common, then suddenly that stops. If you look at the date, it seems to be just after lockdown, sort of like lockdown acted as a barrier that they'd managed to put up. After that, the police couldn't get anywhere. Did it just give them space to get organised or something?'

'Certainly something happened,' Strang said. 'We need to look at what changed. So Rob Gresham was involved in organised crime in Glasgow – what happened after he was released? That would have been three years ago. Did he come straight back home then, or did he only arrive to sit out Covid?'

'He'd know all about the Caddon and its ways,' Murray said. 'Sarah told me everyone knows, basically thinks it's a bit of a joke.'

'Right. At some stage, Gresham returns, sees a promising business that could do even better if it had a more professional outlet, and he was the boy to make the link. Lockdown's the ideal opportunity for organising behind closed doors, introducing *omertà*—'

'Probably had that already . . .'

'—reinforced with a heavy hand, if necessary. And if something went wrong and charges were brought, they could wheel in a heavy hitter like Vincent Dunlop, QC. I did wonder where the money for his fees had come from but that would be sweeties to a big crime syndicate.'

'No wonder Michelle was desperate to get her hands on the notebook.'

'Of course – she's MG. They must be in it together.'

'Now that fits,' Murray said slowly. 'I don't know what either of them looks like, but when I went to the pub before, there was this couple sitting together – good-looking older woman, much younger man, very absorbed in their conversation. I wondered if he was her toyboy, but they didn't act that way.'

She was puzzled that Strang seemed a little uncomfortable when she said that, but he didn't comment, only saying, 'We definitely need a long chat with Gresham. The small fry in the pub syndicate might not want to rock the boat, but if for some reason Ritchie was posing a threat to the whole business, the guys at the top would be ruthless. The incident room will go active again tomorrow and they can get busy on interviews. I think we need to show JB that we're not losing focus – get a spreadsheet up to map the movements of everyone we know about already and the ones we've turned up from this. And let's be positive – you never know what forensics will come up with.'

'Sounds good,' Murray said.

Should she make a move to go? It wasn't quite the same as a meeting in the office; she couldn't help hoping they might get into something more like a social chat but when he said, 'That's fine, then,' it was clear what he expected and it had all gone so well that she certainly didn't want to push her luck.

'Thanks, boss,' she said, and she had just got up when

his phone rang. She noticed that he had reddened a little when he glanced at the name.

He muttered, ''Scuse me – I'll just take this,' and she stood waiting as he said, 'Cat, I'm in a meeting. Call you back,' and rang off. 'Thanks, Livvy. That was great work. I really feel you've moved everything on – and I'll make sure to mention it to JB. She's one of your fans, you know.'

Murray should have been jubilant as she went down the wooden stairs. She'd impressed JB and the boss. She'd spent time in his house while they talked as equals. She'd even briefly let herself think that, with time, they might even get – well, closer.

Then the phone had rung. 'Cat,' he'd said. That was the name of Dunbar's devil, and she heard the way he said it. As she walked back to the car, it was almost completely dark, a biting wind was blowing off the sea and she shivered. She didn't fancy going back to her flat and sitting thinking; she'd call her friend Sacha and go out and get blootered.

When Gunn finished with the banker, he was quite pleased at how it had gone. He went back to the Tarleton station, hoping to report to Strang personally, but he and Livvy had left.

He was free to go back to North Berwick now, but it was still quite early to pack it in. He'd been planning to fix a time with Rob Gresham for tomorrow but with the pace of the investigation picking up, the next day could be busy and that might get crowded out. It would save time if he went along there now on spec; Gresham had said he was usually around the harbour somewhere. He'd thought of a couple more questions too, and he was determined not to be psyched out this time.

The days were shorter now and it was getting quite dark as he drove into the harbour car park. He looked around as he got out of the car and the place was deserted; the weather wouldn't tempt anyone to linger and though there were a couple of trawlers tied up, he couldn't see anyone working there. Perhaps he'd have to go up to the main office.

There was a car coming along slowly, looking for a parking place probably. Gunn stepped aside out of its way.

He hadn't even have time to think before he was flying through the air in an arc of death and landing head first on the deck of the *Silver Spray*.

CHAPTER SIXTEEN

He should really just have ignored her call. Kelso had seen Livvy ostentatiously not listening but he wanted to make sure Cat didn't ring off and go away; she'd been so anxious that she might be doing the wrong thing by phoning the last time. He felt, too, that he'd sounded awkward yesterday and he wanted to put that right.

'Cat, I'm sorry,' he said when she spoke. 'I was having a brainstorming session with my sergeant.'

'Oh sorry, sorry – I didn't mean to interrupt. Do you want to leave it just now?'

'No, she's gone now. How are you doing?'

She brushed that aside. 'Fine. But I just wanted – Well, it's maybe presumptuous, but I saw an article in one of the papers—'

'Oh, that article,' he said.

'It was just nasty and unfair and I'd feel really gutted if someone wrote like that about me and I thought if you needed someone to listen while you let rip, I could sit at the other end of the phone and make sympathetic noises.'

He laughed. 'That's a very kind thought but don't tempt me! If I started to tell you what I thought about the unfairness of the press, you'd be there all night. If you're in the force, you have to grow quite a thick skin and tell yourself it's no more than tomorrow's chip wrapping.'

'It's tough, though. I do hope you're all right. I saw Mum going through that too, you know, and I could tell it hurt.'

'I suppose it does,' he admitted. 'But quite honestly, what was more upsetting was that we'd had what I felt was a breakthrough and my boss wasn't impressed.'

'That isn't very good for morale.' She sounded quite indignant on his behalf. 'What's she like?'

He gave her the unexpurgated version of the description that usually concluded "firm, fair and effing formidable" which made her laugh. 'She was right, actually, as she always is. Something else has come in, though, so I'm hoping to have a new angle ready to present to her tomorrow.'

'And that's going to be a lot of work and I'm keeping you talking. I'm going now – lots of love.'

She rang off and he sat staring at the phone. He was very touched. His was a lonely job, and he couldn't remember the last time he'd talked to someone about what he was really feeling. He'd only known her for a week, but somehow he felt a closer connection to her now than he did to anyone else. He didn't even talk to Finella about his problems.

If only Cat was older, he wouldn't hesitate to . . .? He didn't know what they called it now; presumably no one used the word 'woo' any more. But she wasn't – and he had winced when Livvy mentioned 'toyboy' to describe a big age gap.

Anyway, he didn't even know if she'd a boyfriend of her own age, or even a girlfriend, and he had indeed a lot of work to do making sure the incident room was ready for action tomorrow, and he'd better get on with it.

Rob Gresham was sound asleep when his phone rang. He looked at the time on his radio alarm as he groped for it, and groaned. Just after six, still dark outside – it had to be trouble. He was always first contact.

When he managed to answer it, he couldn't at first make out what the man at the other end was saying, gabbling something panicky about a man on the dock or the deck or something. A boat problem, then.

'Slow down,' he said. 'Take a deep breath. Who am I speaking to anyway?'

'It's Jock Lowrie.'

Skipper of the *Silver Spray*, due to sail this morning. 'Something wrong with the boat, Jock?' he said.

'There's a mannie fallen on the deck. Like I said. Can you come?' He still sounded agitated, but at least comprehensible.

Rob swung his legs out of the bed and grabbed for his clothes. 'Is he hurt? Are we needing to get an ambulance?'

'I doubt you needn't bother,' he said. 'Not from the state of him.'

Rob froze, his jeans in his hand. 'Are – are you saying he's dead?'

'Aye, right enough.'

He swore. 'Be there in a minute. Don't touch anything. I'll put in a call to the police.'

He hadn't slept well and with being wakened like that, his head felt thick. He ran it under a cold tap, towelled it dry and ran out into the lane that ran through the Caddon, straight to the sea. He really didn't need this, on top of everything else; it had been promising to be a nightmare day anyway, and now he'd be snarled up dealing with this – probably some drunk staggering home from the Waterfoot. It had been known to happen – usually they only got a soaking but this poor sod must have got it wrong and toppled into a boat instead.

Lowrie was standing waiting for him in his oilskins and sea-boots. He seemed to have calmed down and embarked on a story that began with him getting out of his bed. When he got to the part where he'd seen the mannie lying on the deck and him saying to himself, 'Well, we'll not be getting the boat out today, I'm thinking,' Gresham cut him short.

'Where is he, then? Drunk, I suppose?'

'Didn't smell it off him. Here – we're tied up just beside the car park.'

They walked together along to the *Silver Spray*. The tide was going out and the boat was sitting low in the water. There was another crew member on board, standing beside the wheelhouse, looking awkward.

It had rained overnight. What Lowrie was pointing to looked like a pile of sodden clothing along in the stern. 'That's him there,' he said, and they both climbed down the iron rungs set into the wall and stepped on board.

Gresham walked the length of the boat and as he looked, he felt the blood drain from his head. He'd never fainted in his life but for a minute he thought he was going to.

The man was unmistakably dead. The crumpled body had one leg bent to an unfeasible angle, the arms flung out to either side, the neck twisted, the skull smashed. There was enough left of the face, just, to allow Gresham to recognise him as DI Matthew Gunn.

DS Livvy Murray was not feeling on top of her game as she drove down the A1 to Tarleton. The rain had actually stopped but there was a sullen sky suggesting it would be starting again any minute now; there were huge puddles on the road surface and lorries were throwing up great waves of spray.

She'd drunk too much the night before, which hadn't made her feel any better. She was old enough to know that it wouldn't, and that she'd feel rubbish in the morning, but she'd still done it, something that was depressing her as well. She wasn't going to think about why she had. That would only make her feel worse.

She must cheer up, think of the day lying ahead when they might start getting somewhere. If they could home in on links Rob Gresham might have with big guys in Glasgow, it was possible Ritchie might have done something that could have led to them sending someone round – or might he even have threatened to do something? Yes, she liked that. She could run it past Strang and see what he thought.

By nine o'clock when she reached Tarleton police station, she was in a rather more upbeat frame of mind. There were several cars in the car park; the incident room must have got off to a good start. She called a cheerful 'Good morning' to PC Thomson behind the desk and was mildly surprised when she didn't get a reply. Surely two yum-yums yesterday should be good for a 'Hello' today?

She turned her head and saw that Thomson was deathly pale and shocked-looking. 'For goodness' sake! What's the matter?' Murray exclaimed.

Before Thomson could speak, the door to the inner office opened and Strang appeared, looking grim. 'Livvy, come through,' he said.

Her knees were shaking as she walked along the passage. She could hear a buzz of voices from the incident room but he opened the door of the office they had been using.

'In here,' he said, then, as she shut the door behind her, 'I think you'd better sit down.'

Murray didn't try to speak, just sank onto a chair. Something awful must have happened.

'There's no good way of saying this. Matt Gunn is dead.'

But he can't be; I saw him yesterday. She didn't actually say it, but she wanted to. Perhaps that's what everyone thinks, because sudden death seems unreal, too dramatic for ordinary everyday life.

'What happened? Was there an accident?'

Strang was holding himself so rigidly that she could see the cords standing out on his neck. 'No,' he said. 'He was found having fallen onto a fishing boat, but there are signs that there was a blow to his back that pushed him off the dock. Probably a car, though we're not sure yet.'

'Oh no!' she said. 'Oh poor, poor Matt.' Then she was crying. 'Such a nice, decent, sensitive man. I don't think he should have been a police officer, quite honestly. He just wasn't hard enough – and now this. It's – it's not fair!'

Murray had sobbed the last words. Strang patted her

shoulder awkwardly and sat down himself, waiting until she managed to stop. She fished tissues out of her bag and blew her nose hard. 'So – what happens now?'

'Everything,' he said. 'Borthwick's on her way and the chief constable will be coming later. No doubt the media will be gathering already.'

'When did it happen?' Murray asked.

He shook his head. 'Don't know yet. They got to me around seven, and by the time I reached the harbour, the police doctor had been and certified death, so at least they could move the body. He wasn't prepared even to make a guess at time – it had been raining all night and probably there was spray coming off the sea. What they are going to want to know is how it relates to Ritchie's murder. The thing is, I wouldn't have said he'd been much involved – just doing background stuff, and talking to the bank yesterday.'

'But he told me yesterday he was going to try to revisit the investigation into Linden Moncrieff's death,' she said. 'You remember Sarah Lindsay said she'd been harassed and Rose Moncrieff had been getting grief too, and he said he was going to question one or two people.'

'Did he say who?'

'No, but he was sort of all fired up about it. Said he owed it to Linden to do a bit more to find out what prompted her to kill herself.'

'Try to remember the conversation and record it to pass on.'

'Sure,' she said. It would help her to get a grip on reality, which seemed at the moment to be getting blurred around the edges. 'And what are we going to be doing now? We can't exactly go on with what we planned.'

'No. We wait until they come and give us our orders.'

So they sat and waited, not really saying anything, both absorbed in the darkness of their thoughts.

It was as if a whirlwind had hit Tarleton. There were sirens, flashing blue lights, people carriers lining up in the car park, police officers swarming through the streets, visiting the shops and houses along the front in the hunt for eyewitnesses. An unruly scrum of press and TV reporters was engaged on a similar mission and a BBC outside broadcast van had taken up its position in the harbour car park, next to the *POLICE CRIME SCENE: DO NOT CROSS* tape. Crowds were gathering and being moved on and the owners of cars that had been left in the car park and were now being impounded for tests had formed a huddle where they muttered in carefully lowered voices about the inconvenience.

There wasn't enough space in the Tarleton police station car park for all the cars and the chief constable's Land Rover had to be parked on the road. DCS Borthwick had travelled down with him, clad appropriately in black. Did she keep it in a cupboard, Strang wondered as he waited to greet them, ready to be taken out when a tragedy occurred? Easier for the chief constable – his uniform was funereal anyway.

An entourage accompanied him and, after a brief word of sympathy, he went immediately to the incident room, while Strang took the DCS, as requested, into the office where Murray, hunched and red-eyed, was waiting.

Borthwick's eyes were kind as she briefly studied their faces, then she said, 'I don't need to ask you how you're

273

feeling. It's as bad as it gets, isn't it? But I do want to know if you're all right.'

They both did the nodding, murmuring bit though Strang was pretty sure that Murray's inner voice was shrieking, as his was, *No, I'm not!*

'We're fine, ready to do whatever we can to get whoever did this,' Strang said.

'I know you will be, and we're going to pump you for every scrap of information you have towards that end but I'm afraid we're pulling you out meantime, until the situation steadies. We can't risk having our officers picked off one by one.'

Strang was horrified and he saw Murray quiver, as if she'd been struck. 'But—'

'You don't need to tell me. You want to leap into action out of feeling for your fallen comrade. It's understandable, even admirable in a way, but it's the shortest possible route to a miscarriage of justice. You will be seen as vengeful, however professional you try to be – and in fact, you probably would be, and the investigation would not be well-directed. I'm taking overall charge and the Chief has appointed DCI Brian Campbell from Glasgow to be senior investigating officer. I don't know if you've met him?'

Strang hadn't, but he'd noticed a burly, grey-haired man coming in with the chief constable and he asked if that was him.

'Yes. He's got a reputation as a safe pair of hands, which is what we need now. He'll take charge of questioning you, but first I wanted to ask if you've any feel at all for what might have provoked this – either of you.'

Borthwick looked from one to the other. Murray had

been silent, sitting with her arms wrapped round herself as if for comfort.

Strang prompted her, 'Livvy, you were saying Matt had been pursuing a line of his own, outwith the murder investigation. Those notes you made – I think they could be relevant.'

'Yes, they could be.' She picked up her notebook from the desk and found the page. 'You see, we haven't had anything to do with this, so it would be all wrong to take us off the case. I don't care how good DCI Campbell is; he won't be as good as DCI Strang, and that's not right – Matt Gunn deserves to have his killer brought to justice and that would give him the best chance.'

She had been looking limp earlier, but now she was fired up. It wasn't perhaps the best idea for a lowly DS to rebuke the DCS, but Borthwick smiled. 'That's impressive loyalty and I don't necessarily disagree. I'm not taking you off the Niall Ritchie case completely, but DCI Campbell will direct the investigation into what happened to Matt Gunn. I'll speak to the next of kin myself. Apart from anything else, you're both in shock. Whenever you've given your reports to DCI Campbell, I'm standing you down meantime. It's all going to get a lot worse. Stay in so we know where you are and try to get some rest – and that's an order.'

When Borthwick looked like that, it was seriously unwise to say anything other than, 'Yes, ma'am.' Strang was afraid that Murray might try, but she only shrank back in her seat and he could see the tears in her eyes.

'Don't think I don't understand,' the superintendent said as she left. 'We've lost a member of the family.'

'That's – that's just cruel!' Murray burst out as the

door closed. 'The only thing that would help is to get busy nailing the bastard who did this and now I'm going to have to go back to an empty flat and stare at the walls until I start climbing them.'

Strang was feeling hollow inside himself. 'I hate it, but she's right,' he said. 'The defence will scream "personal bias" anyway because he was a cop and we don't want to give them more ammunition. We need to do as we're told and hope that the golden hour works for them this time and people come forward.'

Murray looked up blearily. 'From the Caddon? You think?'

'Surely there must be some honest people in this hellhole,' he said, but even to his own ears it didn't sound convincing.

After Rob Gresham had left, Sarah Lindsay had tried to fill the day with practical activities – housework, chatting to the man Jimmie Gresham had sent and cleaning out the hen houses so he didn't have to, going for a run, even crossing the Border to Berwick-on-Tweed for shopping.

She'd been tired at night and another encounter after she got back with Ken Blackford had been the last thing she wanted. This time he had decided to try what passed for charm instead of threatening – 'A pretty lassie like you doesn't want to be stuck away up here – terrible waste! Just say the word and you could be off with the money in your pocket' – but it actually sounded more sinister, especially when she caught the look on his face as she said, 'No thank you,' and shut the door.

But was he actually dangerous? Probably not: if anything happened to her, he would know he'd be top of the suspect list and she now was pretty confident that the Greshams wouldn't be back. She could stay here and not make things worse for Rose, but what had kept her awake through another broken night was the dark reality – someone had killed Niall, and how could she be sure that they didn't have a reason to kill her too? Despite the hours spent thinking, she still hadn't come to a decision.

The woman who looked back at her from the mirror as she brushed her hair in the morning looked gaunt and years older than the woman who had prettied herself for Jimmie Gresham's party less than a week ago. What would she look like a week from now?

Sarah grimaced and went downstairs. It was such a dark morning that she had to switch on the light; the haar had crept in from the sea overnight and the kitchen window was a small opaque white square. It was bitterly cold too and she went through to the sitting room to light the fire while the coffee brewed. She couldn't face anything more, though her clothes were hanging off her and she knew she ought to eat.

She'd just poured out the coffee when she heard a car arriving and her heart gave a heavy thump as she went to the sitting-room window. What next?

It was Rose who came hurrying out of the mist. She looked dishevelled and she barely knocked on the door before she burst into the hall.

'Sarah, where are you? Are you all right?'

'Here, Rose,' she called. 'I'm fine, just having coffee. Do you want some?'

Her face cleared. 'I was so worried . . . No, no coffee. I've just come to take you away.'

She had phoned twice since Sarah had left for Eastlaw, trying to persuade her to return. 'Rose, I don't think—' she said.

'We're not arguing any more. I've something terrible to tell you. Let's sit down.'

Light-headedness was becoming a familiar sensation. Sarah sat down obediently on the sofa beside her friend.

'It's Matt Gunn,' Rose said. 'You know, the lovely policeman, who was always so kind to me, and to you too, I think.'

Still bewildered, Sarah agreed that he had been and Rose told her the story that was leaping like wildfire all round Tarleton.

'I'm horribly afraid it's because I asked him to do something about Myrna Muir. The police are everywhere and they're going to interview me later this morning so I'll have protection, but out here you're vulnerable. How long would it take you to get your things?'

Numb with shock, she was too stunned to argue. 'I can do that now,' she said, getting up and going to the door.

'That's good. I'll phone Rob and tell him what you're doing – he'll want to know where you are—'

Sarah stopped. 'No, Rose. Wait. I – I don't want you to tell him.'

She raised her eyebrows. 'Really?'

She could guess what Rose was thinking – 'Those young people with their squabbles!' – but she had to be blunt and tell her the full story, though she almost regretted it when she saw Rose's hurt.

'But he's been like family to me! Oh, they weren't married, but I've always counted him as a son-in-law. He made her so happy and he's been such a help to me, such a support over this last terrible year.'

'I don't know what it is that the police are doing with the notebook but them trying to steal it left me feeling really scared.'

'I can see why. Oh dear, how dreadful! Anyway, go and get your things.'

Upstairs, Sarah packed a bag, straightened the covers on her bed and took a quick look round. She was thankful the decision had been made for her and if she could manage it, she'd never set foot again in this place where the very walls seemed to reek of the years of misery and the tragedy that had followed them.

Rob Gresham buzzed his stepmother in her office. 'I need to see you,' he said urgently. 'Can I come up now?'

Michelle didn't sound encouraging. 'I think, quite honestly, right at the moment it might be better if we stay apart and keep a very low profile. The police have the notebook and that'll cause trouble enough, even though I don't think it has anything to do with this sorry mess.'

'Well, it might. Sort of. There's something else, something you don't know about. Please, Michelle!' He knew he was sounding panicky.

There was a frozen silence at the other end. Then, 'Oh, for God's sake!' she said. 'Just come up, then. But be ready with some sort of story if Andrew drops in. He might well – he's been down with the police at the dock all morning.'

He really didn't want to involve Michelle in this. They'd made a brilliant team; he couldn't believe his luck when he came back to Tarleton and found that not only was there quite a nice little earner operating on his doorstep just asking for economic development, it was his stepmother who was running it and was more than happy to link it to his contacts, and import their business methods too. Lockdown had played into their hands and Michelle had said once that in all her years in the Caddon, she'd never known everyone to be so cheerful and united.

As yet they hadn't been able to discuss what they were going to do to deal with the flak from the dumb bastard's notebook. Michelle had been working all day and then Andrew had taken her off to some charity do. He'd been counting on Michelle, with her devious mind, to come up with something.

That was one thing. This was quite another.

Rob was dreading having to confess to her what he'd done but he was desperate. They'd always got on very well; she'd thought it was a bit of a laugh to have a stepson like him. He was under no illusions, though; she was hard as nails.

As he took the seat on the other side of the desk and saw the look on her face, he almost quailed, told her some temporising lie. But he simply wasn't strong enough to deal with this on his own.

Michelle listened in awful silence, her gaze piercing as a gimlet. Then she spoke in a furious undertone. Her mother had been a fishwife with a famously rich vocabulary but even she would have been forced to admire her daughter's fluency.

* * *

It was past midday by the time DCI Campbell had finished interviewing Strang and Murray and afterwards even she had been forced to admit grudgingly that even if he was a bit pompous, he seemed to know what he was doing. He'd kept the emotional temperature low, which made it easier to think clearly about the information that might be most useful, though he wasn't to be drawn into committing primarily to the line of enquiry that Murray had been urging upon him.

Afterwards she was inclined to be indignant about that. 'He'll waste his time looking into Ritchie's murder all over again,' she said, but Strang had pointed out the virtues of an open mind.

'You never know, he might spot something we missed,' he said, and – ignoring her subversive '*Might!*' – went on to say that at the end of his interview, Campbell had promised to keep him in the picture with whatever developments there might be.

'Well, bully for you,' she muttered.

'Bully for you, *sir*!' he said with a hint of an edge. 'Livvy, we're both pissed off at being sent out of the room while the grown-ups talk, but behaving childishly isn't going to help.'

Murray looked abashed. 'Yeah, I suppose. I was out of order – sorry, boss. I'm just dreading being shut in with nothing to do. I've never been into daytime telly.'

Strang knew how she felt, and he wasn't returning to a one-bed rental. He thought for a moment of suggesting she came round to the cottage for an hour or two to break up the day, but it wouldn't be appropriate.

'Tell you what,' he said. 'I promise I'll phone with any

scraps that Campbell puts my way. And we've both still got access to our laptops, and time to review everything that's come in already.'

She brightened a little. 'I suppose so. And I could get some mates round to mine for a drink in the evening – I don't think any of them are planning to murder me. At least I hope not.' Then she paused. 'Not that funny, though, is it? Oh, poor Matt!'

They parted soberly. The fog was thick on the motorway and on the outskirts of Edinburgh there was congestion; a car had obviously stopped and the one immediately behind hadn't, but it only looked like bent metal and Strang was back at the cottage just after two, feeling as bleak as the weather.

There was no view at all from his favourite window today and, muffled by the haar, the usual sound of traffic was muted to something like white noise – odd and disorientating. The day's events had left him feeling uncharacteristically helpless; Tarleton was getting to him, somehow. Perhaps this was what poor Matt had been feeling – 'a morass of evil' was the way he'd described it to Murray. He'd felt demoralised, unable to see a way forward. That danger was lurking now for Strang himself.

He rarely drank during the day and then usually beer, but now he poured a Scotch instead for the comfort of its fiery warmth. Matt's death had been a brutal reminder of the risks they took daily in policing a violent world – and he hadn't been able to prevent it.

He hadn't said anything to Murray about what would happen now. The internal inquiry into precisely how the SRCS had managed to get an officer killed would be formal, prolonged and painful. He didn't know what the procedure was, but no doubt someone would inform him. Nothing he could do about it now, anyway.

With a sigh, he sat down in his usual seat with his personal phone and started flipping through the messages, though he didn't plan to pick any up until he'd had time to get his head straight. His mother and Finella featured, of course; they'd have heard the news, and would be anxious so he'd have to call them soon. There were two or three others from friends, though they were probably standard social calls.

And there was another from a number he didn't recognise. He was extremely careful who he gave that number to; the media were always on the lookout for an 'in' and it would be irritating to have to change the number again. He was frowning as he pressed 'Play'.

The voice at the other end was warm and confident, but the message began apologetically. 'I'm Marjory Fleming. I hope you won't feel I'm being impertinent or intrusive, but my daughter Cat gave me this number and encouraged me to call you when she heard the horrible news about your officer. I know the desolation you must be feeling because one of my officers died taking a bullet intended for me and if you think I can do anything to help, if only because I've been through the formal process, call me back. If not, please ignore this and accept my apology.'

It only took a moment's reflection to decide to call her back.

CHAPTER SEVENTEEN

Myrna Muir kept making mistakes – keying in the wrong amount, muddling the codes and forgetting to ask for the loyalty card before she rang up the total. The supermarket was busy and the customers had chosen today to be even more annoyingly stupid than usual so she was snarling indiscriminately at everyone, alarming hapless OAPs slow to dig out their credit cards with her ferocity.

Mary Mackay, the manager, was eyeing her anxiously. The whole town was buzzing with the news about the policeman being killed and Myrna had been the subject of a complaint he'd been investigating. She'd asked her if she was all right and got her head bitten off, but she was beginning to wonder if it would be best to tell her to take the day off rather than having them coming in to arrest her here. She wouldn't put it past Myrna to have given the man a shove if he'd spoken to her again when she was in a bad temper.

With deep roots in the Caddon, Mary knew the rules and of course she wouldn't talk out of turn – she certainly wasn't going to volunteer anything – but denying that the policeman had been asking questions about Myrna and what she'd said to that Lindsay woman was pointless when too many people knew what had been happening. It was getting to the stage when she had to think about safeguarding herself.

By the time DCI Campbell and the uniformed officers came in, she was standing ready to unpick Myrna's clinging fingers from the side of the lifeboat and tip her off.

Myrna cast a desperate glance at her as she was ushered out in a silence that became a tumult of sound as the automatic doors swished closed behind them.

The Police Investigations and Review committee meeting in Edinburgh had finished at lunchtime and, as usual when they met in Edinburgh, Marjory Fleming had arranged to take the daughter who always claimed to be starving for lunch.

Today there had been hushed voices at the news of the latest police fatality, and by the time they met it had been all round the courts as well. Marjory hadn't fully appreciated that Cat's DCI was involved, but before Cat had even picked up the menu, she was urging her to phone him.

'He might not welcome a strange, retired copper butting in,' she'd protested, but Cat had an answer for that.

'Oh, you're not all that strange, only mildly eccentric. And the thing is, you know what it's like – remember that poor woman who saved your life.'

Indeed she did; she couldn't possibly forget what she had done, even if it had been something close to suicide-by-villain after the death of her daughter.

'And it's such a lonely job – he'll be needing someone to talk to,' Cat urged.

'Maybe he's got a girlfriend – or a close associate, like Tam was for me,' Marjory said fondly – Tam MacNee, the sergeant who'd been at her side throughout, was now enjoying his retirement in Glasgow.

Cat looked thoughtful at that, but she said only, 'Go on, just leave a message, then he can follow it up if he likes. And I bet he does.'

She was right, and now Marjory was driving down through Leith and along the shore to the little harbour at Newhaven, with Kelso Strang's address. There was poor visibility with the sea haar thicker down here, though a breeze was stirring and it was starting to clear in places.

She looked with considerable interest at the man who had so captured her daughter's interest as he opened the front door at the top of the wooden staircase. He was tall and well-built, fit-looking too, with dark hair and hazel eyes, but the scar down one side of his face definitely marred his looks. Perhaps Cat felt it was romantic.

He got plus points for meeting her eyes and greeting her with a warm smile and a firm handshake – Bill always set great store by that. The coffee he had ready for her was good coffee too – another plus.

They made the usual polite social noises and agreed that Cat was a very managing young woman, but it wasn't long before Marjory said bluntly, 'Tell me how I can help. This is the worst thing that can happen to you as an officer.'

He bowed his head. 'Oh God, yes. I feel I failed him. I knew he was struggling with policing this place and to be honest I didn't rate him. My main concern was investigating the murder of Niall Ritchie and I have a very effective sergeant, so I chose to involve her in interviews rather than him. It meant he had time on his hands that let him embark on a new sort of unofficial investigation that I'm virtually certain made him a target.'

'Don't blame yourself too much. You weren't responsible for the decisions he made and your duty was as always to concentrate on the task in hand – investigating Ritchie's murder. I said I could tell you from bitter experience what happens next, if that's what you want, but if you want to talk about the case first I'm happy to be a listening ear.'

'If it was just "a case",' Kelso burst out, 'I'd know what to do. This seems to be two or three separate cases and I'm not seeing straight. I don't know any more which are linked and which are distinct. Matt Gunn felt defeated by the general lawlessness and criminality and I'm beginning to feel beleaguered too. They've brought in DCI Campbell from Glasgow and it's probably just as well.'

Marjory said, very gently, 'Just break it down for me. One section at a time.'

Kelso drew a long breath. Then he began: the ongoing inquiry into the theft of foreign vehicles that had led to the prosecution of Doddie Muir; the murder of Niall Ritchie, who initially had seemed to have no enemies apart from, possibly, the unhappy Sarah Lindsay; the breakthrough notebook that had disclosed an organised petty crime syndicate in the Caddon; the abuse of Lindsay and Rose Moncrieff that had led to Matt Gunn reverting to questioning

Linden Moncrieff's suicide that had so haunted him.

Making only prompting noises, Marjory had listened with considerable interest. She hadn't missed the bureaucracy or the anxiety or the relentless demands of policework, but she had missed the mental challenge of sorting the strands of an investigation into a rational pattern.

When Kelso ran down at last, the emotional intensity had left him shaking. He stood up, looking awkward, saying, 'More coffee, I think,' and went over to the kitchen area to make it.

Marjory sat quietly, assembling her thoughts. When he brought it over, he was looking embarrassed. 'I'm sorry to have dumped all that on you.' But she waved it aside.

'Divide and conquer, don't you think?' she said. 'DCI Campbell's dealing with Matt Gunn's killing, right? It sounds to me as if the notebook investigation is likely to go ahead quite satisfactorily with solid legwork that you can deputise. That would give you scope to concentrate on the Ritchie case, wouldn't it?'

'That's more or less what DCS Borthwick said,' he admitted.

'Oh, Jane Borthwick? I've known her for years. She's good. And having time to go into the history of his farm could be interesting. Speaking with my other hat on as a farmer's wife, I can tell you that organic is seriously big business. We have a hill farm that's run on principles close to organic, but the demands made by supermarkets are very exhaustive – they probably put quite a lot of pressure on the main supplier. Even so, I can't see the man being killed just because he cheated – dropped, yes; killed, no – but there's maybe an angle there.'

'Looking at it now,' Kelso said thoughtfully, 'I think what's bedevilled the whole investigation is that I've been trying too hard to find a one-size-fits-all solution. The Waterfoot syndicate seemed to be a real breakthrough at the time but it was a distraction. If Ritchie had somehow got across one of the big players, I can't see them bothering with such an elaborate scenario rather than putting a gun to the back of the head and then vanishing.'

'What about the partner?' Marjory said. 'Classic prime suspect.'

'Doesn't present that way,' he said. 'But I would judge she was physically capable of doing it – he was quite a slight man – and she certainly had the opportunity and the means, so there may be more than meets the eye.'

She gave a short laugh. 'Isn't there always? Anyway, do you want me to fill you in on what happens now?'

He pulled a face. 'Doubt if I want to hear this, but it's better to be prepared.'

She outlined the procedure – the form-filling, the interviews, the appraisals. 'It's not comfortable,' she said, 'but you get through it. I was in a more difficult position since the officer was under my direct command at the time. DI Gunn was acting as a free agent, remember. The hardest thing is to learn to forgive yourself.'

He still sounded doubtful as he said, 'I suppose so,' but she sensed that some of the tension had gone out of him as he went on, 'I'm really grateful for all this, though. It's as if you've broken up a logjam and so I can see clear water ahead.'

Marjory smiled. 'My pleasure. I'd better get going,

though – the rush hour will be building up and it's a long way back to Kirkluce.'

'Oh, I'm sorry,' Kelso said. 'I've taken up far too much of your time. Thanks for listening.'

As she went to the door, she said, a little mischievously, 'I'll have to report back to Cat, of course.'

He reddened. 'Look, I don't quite know how to say this, but I just wanted you to know that I enjoy her company very much but I'm fully aware that Cat's not much more than a child. You needn't worry that this is anything more than a friendship.'

'I'm more worried that you may feel she's stalking you!' Marjory said as she stepped outside. 'Good luck with the inquiry.'

As she walked back to the car, she was smiling. She had taken to Cat's Kelso Strang; she was glad she'd been able to give him a chance to unburden himself. She'd always had Bill at her back, but being on your own could make it a brutally cruel job when things went wrong.

She was amused, though, by his naivety in thinking of her sassy, savvy daughter as not much more than a child; she'd always known her own mind and if Cat saw this as nothing more than friendship, she'd be very surprised indeed.

'You couldn't say he'd been anything other than polite and professional,' Rose Moncrieff said to Sarah Lindsay when DCI Campbell and his sergeant had gone, 'but the way he looked at you with those dull grey eyes made you feel he'd decided already that you were on the wrong side of the law, even though I was the one who was making a complaint.'

'I felt vulnerable, quite honestly. I know I'm under suspicion but I reckoned Chief Inspector Strang would be fair – this guy's scary. And I don't have an alibi for poor Inspector Gunn's murder either, if I'm in the frame.'

'I don't think he was looking at you that way,' Rose said soothingly. 'The questions were all relating to Myrna Muir and all the things she'd done.'

'Yes, I suppose so. Perhaps I'm just being paranoid – it's this long hang-on without knowing what's happening.'

'I know.' Rose got up. 'It makes me fidgety. If you don't mind, I think I'll go out to the studio and throw some pots. I've got an order to fill and I really ought to get them in the kiln tonight.'

'Of course,' Sarah said, though with some envy. How good it would be if she had something to do other than sit here with her unwelcome thoughts. She got up and walked restlessly across to the window.

It was still foggy but she could see there was something going on at Myrna Muir's house opposite. There were a couple of police cars parked outside, the door to the house was standing open and while she watched a policeman came out carrying a pot of red paint, swathed in plastic. There was no sign of Myrna herself and she could see that there were officers examining a car that was parked in the lane outside.

She was just wondering what this meant – good news, surely, since the red paint had formed part of the complaint – when her mobile rang and she fetched it without enthusiasm. It was hard to think who might be phoning her that she would want to speak to.

It was Briony's name that was showing. She answered it cautiously; Rob had warned her that Briony was being a bit antagonistic at the moment, but she sounded friendly enough.

'Sarah! I was just wondering how you are.'

'Nice to hear from you. I'm all right – upset, obviously, about all that's been happening.'

'Oh yes – that poor policeman. Terrible,' she said, though without any great conviction, Sarah thought. 'Have they been round asking questions?'

'Yes. DCI Campbell has just left. He's in charge, I think.'

'I expect he'll be getting round all of us. What sort of things does he want to know?'

'Oh, just general things.'

'Like?'

There was something odd about her persistence and Sarah's reply was guarded. 'Nothing you'll find it difficult to answer, I'm sure.'

'You know they've arrested Myrna Muir?' Briony said.

'Really? No, I didn't.'

'It's quite ridiculous, of course. I don't believe the poor woman's done anything at all.'

Sarah was tempted to give her chapter and verse but contented herself with saying, 'Someone must have killed him.'

'Do you think so? Probably he just tripped and fell but now they're making something out of it. Anyway, I'm glad you answered me this time. You didn't before.'

She hadn't, of course. 'I'm sorry, Briony. I really wasn't fit company for anyone at the time.'

'I thought that was what friends were for – to be there

when there was a problem. But of course you'd another friend by then, didn't you?'

The attack took Sarah by surprise. There was real venom in Briony's voice. 'No, I—' she stammered.

'No? What about Rob? You've got very friendly with him recently, haven't you?'

'Not–not really. He's been very kind—'

'Oh, kind, is he? That's nice. In fact, he's probably there with you now. I can't get him at the office and he's not answering his phone – would you let me speak to him?'

'I can't! He isn't here.'

There was a silence, then she said, 'Is he just refusing to speak to me? Is that it?'

'No! I promise you, he isn't here. I'm staying with Rose Moncrieff.'

'I suppose you both are. And there's not much point in speaking to you, is there?' The line went dead.

Sarah stood staring blankly out of the window, trying to make sense of what she had just been hearing. Across the road, the police cars were driving off, but Myrna Muir had been arrested – unfairly, Briony had said. And she'd accused Sarah of being too friendly with her cousin – if only she knew! She was obviously jealous – but was it because Rob had taken her place as Sarah's friend, or because Sarah had somehow taken her place as Rob's friend? She wasn't entirely sure, but it sounded as if Rob was avoiding Briony anyway.

This was all she needed – to find herself in a kind of cat fight over a man she wanted nothing further to do with, a man she believed to be a villain. There was something wrong with that family, and somehow she was getting involved. Niall had talked about a spider's web; she could almost feel the sticky strands clinging to her.

DS Murray had spent the day switching from one news programme to another, trawling for scraps of information. She heard about Myrna Muir's arrest on the early evening news so presumably Strang knew as well, though he hadn't contacted her.

Surely that meant they were safe enough to get back on the job? Campbell had obviously been very effective, but it was frustrating that everything to do with Matt's murder would still be in his hands. From the questions he'd asked her, he seemed to be thinking of it in terms of a completely separate case and he didn't plan to involve them at all – and to be fair, it could be true that the harassment of Sarah Lindsay was more or less coincidental.

Strang had suggested they could occupy themselves by reviewing such information as they had so far, but there was nothing they hadn't gone into already and her bright idea about some crime boss taking care of Ritchie for some unspecified misdemeanour actually felt a bit clunky when you looked at it closely. A professional wouldn't bother to make it look like suicide.

Why a professional, though? Ritchie could be posing a threat to someone nearer to home – someone like Rob Gresham, for instance. Or even Blackford – he was right there on the notebook list, of course, and when she thought about it, Sarah Lindsay had said he was pushing her to sell him the farm. The more she thought about it, the more she liked it. Yes, they needed to take a much closer look at Blackford. She could enjoy watching Strang pinning him to the wall.

Had Lindsay taken the advice not to stay at Eastlaw? If she hadn't, she could be in danger. She'd hate to be at Blackford's mercy, herself. Accidents were always happening on farms.

It was a shock when the *BBC News at Six* reported that Myrna Muir had been charged with harassment and then released. She stared at the screen in dismay. What use was that? While she was at large, they could still be considered to be under threat, and though it would be a risk she was perfectly happy to take if it meant she wasn't going to be shut up here till the walls actually closed in on her, it wasn't up to her.

Strang phoned just after the item had finished. 'Disappointing,' he said. 'And they're saying there probably isn't any chance of finding a damaged car since contact was probably at a slow speed – the back injury was very slight.'

'Bit of a disaster, really,' she said gloomily.

'I wouldn't put it quite as strongly as that,' he said. 'Just a setback.' He was sounding a lot more positive than she felt as he went on, 'Campbell called me and they've got solid evidence relating to the graffiti on Rose Moncrieff's wall and threatening language towards Sarah Lindsay. Nothing more as yet, though. They're still pursuing it, but she apparently has a heavyweight solicitor on the case.'

'But that's just what Matt said always happened!' Murray exclaimed.

'Yes, I know,' he said. 'Anyway, Campbell said he'd advised JB that he believed it was safe enough to go on with our original investigation – he's got Myrna under surveillance. So a briefing at Tarleton tomorrow at nine?

I'm figuring out a new direction.'

'Sure, boss.'

It was good news, but as she rang off, she was puzzled. It was definitely odd that he'd just dismissed what she'd said about Tarleton reverting to its familiar pattern of bringing in threatening lawyers. Then she remembered. The 'Cat' who had been phoning – she was Vince Dunbar's devil. Strang was about to find himself in a very difficult position.

That was his problem, not hers. He'd sounded quite upbeat in general, though, and she liked the sound of a new direction. They certainly needed one.

It was almost dark when there was a knock on Rose Moncrieff's front door. She had just come in from the studio and was in the kitchen washing the clay off her hands.

'I'll go,' Sarah called. She tensed up; she had a nasty feeling that it would be Rob Gresham and she hadn't worked out what she was going to say next time she saw him.

But when she opened the door, it was Briony who stood there. The haar was still lingering; the yellow street lamp outside had a blurry nimbus and in the wet her hair had frizzed out to make a sort of nimbus of its own.

'Briony!' Sarah said. She was going to say, mendaciously, that it was good to see her, but she didn't get the chance.

'He's here, isn't he?' she said brusquely.

'Do you mean Rob? No.'

But Briony was pushing past her. 'I don't believe you. Rob!' she called.

'For goodness' sake, Briony—' Sarah was protesting,

just as Rose came through from the kitchen and confronted Briony.

'Rob's not here,' she said. 'I don't know why you think he should be.'

'Because he always is. Because you and that murderous daughter of yours have sunk your claws into him.' She turned on Sarah. 'And now you too!'

Rose had gone very pale. Sarah stepped between them. 'Briony, I think you'd better get out. You can't come in here and sling abuse like this.'

She ignored her, going to the foot of the stairs and shouting, 'Rob! Rob!'

No one spoke, and when she turned round there were tears in her eyes. 'He's blocking me but I need to speak to him. He knows why. If I go now, will you talk to him and persuade him to call me back?'

'I promise you Rob isn't here,' Sarah said helplessly. 'You can go up and see for yourself, if you like. Briony, I think you're not well.'

Briony's eyes narrowed. 'Is there no end to your lies? It's not me that's sick, it's the two of you. If he wants to stay hiding upstairs, there's nothing I can do now. But tell him I'll be watching.'

She went out, leaving the door open. A little wisp of mist crept in as Sarah went to look out after her, then came back in and shut it.

'She's just driven off in a car,' she said. 'Oh, and Myrna Muir's back at the house – I didn't think they'd lock her up, more's the pity.'

'Indeed it is. But dear God – Briony! What was all that about? Was she drunk, do you think?'

Sarah shook her head. 'I'd have smelt it. It was just – crazy. I wonder if she's having a breakdown?'

'I feel quite shaky after that. She's certainly delusional. I've got some brandy somewhere – I think we need it.'

As they sat by the fire, nursing their glasses, Rose said, 'You know, Linden had a bit of a problem with her when she was with Rob. Jealous, she said, though I don't think there'd ever been anything between them except that as cousins they'd once been very close and she probably felt she'd been elbowed out.' Rose sighed. 'Then, of course, there was the dreadful Do Not Resuscitate policy and Briony definitely sided with the locals.'

Sarah looked at her friend with sympathy. 'It's been so hard for you – you don't need this. What seems clear is that Rob is trying to avoid speaking to her, for some reason. What do you think we should do?'

'If poor Matt Gunn was still here, I'd have phoned him, but I don't fancy dealing with the Campbell man. Anyway, I wouldn't know how to get hold of him. If I phoned the police, I'd just be put through to speak to a central switchboard, so I don't see the point.'

'I think I should just phone Rob, little though I want to, and tell him what's happening and that he'd better speak to her before she comes round here again. Just another swig of Dutch courage, and then I'll do it.'

The haar was lifting at last and the sky was clear and cold, with a tiny thumbnail moon. It was fully dark now and the lights along the harbour were reflected in water black as pitch. Most of the fishing fleet had gone out but there were arc lights and activity still around the *Silver Spray*.

It was all spread out below Michelle Gresham as she sat at her desk on the first floor of the Arcturus office, but she barely noticed it as she wrestled with the problems presented by the man who sat on the other side of it, looking abject. They'd sat there for hours as she tried to find solutions and he made pointless apologies and came up with nothing that even faintly resembled an idea.

'If only I hadn't done that, but you know—'

'Yes, I know,' she snapped. 'Family solidarity – you said that. Several times. Yes, sure, it's bone deep in all of us – we know what we know but we don't tell.'

He seized on that. 'Exactly. So we cover—'

She held up her hand. 'Up to a point. We're past the point.'

'But it would drag us in.'

'Not us. You. And don't think I wouldn't dump you in it if I needed to.'

'Oh, I have no illusions,' he said bitterly.

'But I was just thinking it could be a sort of bargaining chip. Niall Ritchie, may he rot in hell, has done for us with his notebook, but we can look at damage limitation. We're the only ones who know it was more than petty crime and we can discourage the small fry from yapping their heads off.'

Rob looked at her. He was just saying, 'What are you suggesting? Do you think—' when his mobile rang. He groaned. 'That'll be her again.'

Briony had phoned intermittently all afternoon, but it wasn't her name that showed.

'Sarah Lindsay,' he said, raising his eyebrows. At Michelle's nod, he answered it, injecting warmth into his voice as he said, 'Sarah! Good to hear from you. How are you, love?'

As he listened, Michelle could see his face change. 'Right,' he said. 'I see. Yes, how difficult for you – I'm sorry. You know, she's always been a bit, well, nervy, I suppose. I'll try to talk her down, see it doesn't happen again. All right?'

'So – what fresh hell is this?' Michelle asked, tight-lipped.

'Briony's flipped. She went round to Rose's claiming I was there hiding from her. I suppose I'd better phone her.'

'No.' Michelle's response was decisive. 'You don't want to have any contact with her right now. Delete whatever calls you've made to her. The way she's going on, the police will get on to her soon. We need to talk to the police tomorrow, while there's still value in what we have to offer.'

He looked at her pitifully. 'Hand ourselves in? I don't think I can bear to go through the jail horrors again.'

'You must have missed the memo that said "If you can't do the time, don't do the crime",' she said acidly. 'Too late now. There's no alternative that isn't going to be worse.'

'What about getting in the lawyers?' he bleated.

'Are you mad? They'd operate for the others' benefit, not ours.' She stood up. 'Andrew will come looking for me if I don't go now. See you back here in the morning.'

Sarah Lindsay stirred in her sleep. Her throat was dry and she coughed, but she was tired, so very, very tired that she couldn't rouse herself to get a drink of water. She moved her muzzy head from side to side, muttering a little, but then she sank back into the pillow and let sleep take her again.

The smoky fire had been smouldering for some time in the overstuffed sofa where the petrol-soaked brand had landed, but as the wind got up outside, the draught from the open window fanned it into vigorous life. It began to race greedily from sofa to floor to chair to curtains until the little room was a raging tempest of flames.

CHAPTER EIGHTEEN

'I thought you'd have phoned me before now,' Catriona Fleming said plaintively.

'Cat, I've only just taken my coat off. It was a foul journey – the Edinburgh bypass locked solid, then fog and roadworks on the motorway,' Marjory Fleming said, subsiding into the chair by the Rayburn as she fended off the pup's hysterical welcome. 'Haven't had a thing to eat yet and your father's only just pouring me a drink – thanks, Bill.'

Her husband rolled his eyes as he handed her the glass and sat down with his own at the kitchen table.

'Did Kelso talk to you?'

'Yes, we had a long chat.'

'And?' Cat prompted. 'Is he all right?'

'He's certainly an improvement on your last two or

three – your taste must be improving.' She winked at Bill.

'Oh for goodness' sake, Mum! I meant – you know, it must be so awful and I'm really worried about him. Are they getting anywhere? I don't like to ask him about it.'

'How wise. I'm sure he wouldn't tell you and I'm not going to either.'

There was an offended silence. 'Oh, very well then, be like that. But if he told you stuff I suppose you must have got on pretty well.'

Marjorie smiled. 'Yes, I think I could say we did. He's a nice guy.'

'He is, isn't he? Anyway, if you're not going to tell me anything else, I've got work to do. Night!'

'It's late! That man works you far too hard.' She put down the phone, shaking her head.

'Right,' Bill said. 'You can tell me now about this bloke that's pursuing Cat. I don't think it's at all suitable.'

'He agrees with you. He was very anxious to assure me it was just a casual friendship.'

'Hmm. Might have started that way, maybe. That reply sounds a bit sleekit to me.'

'I'm a pretty good judge of character and there was nothing devious about the way he said it. I can assure you that the only pursuing is being done by Cat. And when it comes to him being too old, I can only say she's been fussing about him today like a mother hen.'

Bill looked horrified. 'That's not a good sign – and don't encourage her! She should be enjoying her youth, just having a good time.'

Marjory laughed. 'Will you never learn? I don't know if anything will come of this, but you should know your daughter well enough by now to be sure that she'll do what she wants without paying any attention to what we say.'

'It's true, but it isn't a comfort,' Bill said darkly.

The woman PC gave an enormous yawn. 'I am so bored my whole head is numb. It's an hour now since they went to bed and there's not a sign of movement. Do we really have to stay here all night, Sarge?'

'Tell me what the orders were, and you've got your answer,' he said unhelpfully.

'I'd be able to keep awake if I'd something to eat. I could get chips from that chippie by the caravan park while you go on staring at nothing.'

It was a tempting offer. 'OK, but don't be long or I might fall asleep myself without your sparkling conversation.'

She jumped out of the car immediately as he settled to wait with resignation, but she was back a minute later.

'Fire brigade, category red! House across there!' While he put in the call, she rushed back, but until the hoses arrived it was obvious there wasn't much they could do.

No one could have slept through the sirens. The whole of the Caddon was roused; Rob Gresham in the next street along woke in a panic that only grew when he threw on some clothes and went out to see the fire brigade working on Rose Moncrieff's house.

They were managing to confine the fire to the ground floor, but the damage there was extensive. He was in time to see two women being carried out to the ambulance but no one seemed to know what state they were in and of course the rumours going round the gathering crowd became more extravagant by the moment. With the lurid light of the flames and the belching smoke, there was a sort of theatrical unreality about the scene.

It wasn't unreal, though. Rob was feeling dizzy and sick. She'd done it, hadn't she? She'd thought he was in the house and refusing to speak to him, and this was what she had done. He was meant to be one of the victims and he didn't even know if the other two would live.

He had liked both of them. If they died, it would be because he had ducked out of making that phone call last night, knowing how ugly it would be. And if he hadn't done what he could see now was a wicked thing, that detective would still be alive.

Michelle would be horrified at what he was going to do but now it had got past – way past – talking about bargaining chips. He needed to tell the truth before someone else died.

Several police cars had arrived but Rob didn't recognise any of the officers. He wanted to speak to Strang, who had treated Sarah so respectfully. He looked up to the house on the hill where Andrew and Michelle lived; there were lights coming on and no doubt they would be here too very soon.

He moved into the crowd, muttering apologies as he worked his way through until he could very quietly disappear.

Sarah Lindsay came round in the ambulance, struggling against the mask that was being held over her face, coughing and choking. The pain in her head was excruciating and she couldn't think where she was or what was happening.

A paramedic in a green gown was holding down her flailing hands. 'It's all right, dear, we've got you. You're OK.'

'Am I ill?' she croaked.

'Just smoke inhalation. There was a fire, but we got you both out. Lucky there was a patrol car on the scene.'

'Both?' The word 'Rose' came into her head, but she couldn't relate it to the vehicle she was in that was speeding through the streets, making a noise that cut into her aching head like a knife.

'Don't worry,' the soothing voice said again. 'Just you shut your eyes and take deep breaths.'

It was too difficult to think any more and Sarah drifted back into an uncomfortable half-sleep.

DCI Strang had driven down to Tarleton that morning feeling purposeful. It had been an extraordinary experience, talking to Marjory Fleming. He'd only ever talked difficulties through with JB or, latterly, Murray, but Livvy acted mainly as a sounding board and he could never forget that JB was his boss. Marjory Fleming was a highly experienced and very successful operator, as he'd found out when he'd looked her up before, and she'd seen the situation so clearly that he could see it now too. He arrived in Tarleton station determined to allow nothing to divert him from drilling down into everything relating to Eastlaw Farm.

Murray arrived as he was getting out of his car at the police station. Since he was no longer on Gunn's case, there had been no official reason for Strang to be informed about the developments overnight. He'd briefly switched on the BBC news but a small house fire, rapidly extinguished, with no serious injuries, hadn't made the headlines.

So it was quite a shock when they walked in and PC

Thomson took considerable pleasure in giving them the bad news and informing them that DCI Campbell was there already. 'Up half the night, they said he's been,' she told them. 'No arrests, though. Could have been murdered in their beds, those women.'

There was quite a bit of activity in the incident room; phones were ringing, uniforms were conferring in small groups and Campbell's magisterial manner was much less evident this morning.

'It's been a bad night, Strang, though it could have been worse – no fatalities, fire brigade on the spot in minutes, mercifully.'

Keen to be tactful, Strang said heartily, 'Good work, then. So – looking for pointers as to how it happened?'

'"How" is easy – window not latched, burning substance chucked in. "Why" and "who" are a whole other thing.'

Strang could see Murray almost exploding with questions and shot her a forbidding look. 'Oh?'

'I told you we'd arrested the Muir woman, but we couldn't make anything stick other than the harassment charge. A witness did come forward to say she had told Gunn the previous day about abuse of Linden Moncrieff before her suicide, but Muir flatly denied having anything to do with that. Then last night we'd a car on surveillance and she never left the house. So we're a bit stymied.' After what looked like a brief struggle with himself, he said, 'I'd welcome any information you might have.'

Strang looked at Murray, but she didn't seem to have any more to offer than he did. 'I'm sorry. The trouble is we'd no idea what Gunn was doing,' he said.

'I see. Don't worry about it, then – you've no doubt got

enough to do. Once the women are fit to answer questions, we may get somewhere and I've got someone checking through such cameras as there are – not very many, unfortunately. I'll keep you informed about developments.'

Interpreting this as a dismissal, Strang and Murray went back to the office.

'What's with this place?' Murray said. 'I'm beginning to think that being shut up in my flat may not be the worst thing that can happen. I just keep thinking of what Matt said at the start – that the way things are here meant awful things would happen.'

'He was right there, anyway. But this isn't our business now, remember? I want to start looking a lot more closely at Niall and the farm. They've followed up alibis for the Greshams and Blackford and they checked out to the extent alibis ever do, when there's no precise time frame. It's all but impossible to say, for instance, that Blackford didn't slope off from the sale earlier than he said or that Jimmie Gresham couldn't have put in a quick visit to Eastlaw, but we've no actual reason to believe they did.'

'But who goes round setting houses on fire?' Murray demanded. 'You have to look at . . . Oh. Sorry.'

'DCI Campbell's problem, right? Our focus – Eastlaw Farm. I'll summarise: no DNA results as yet, but let's assume the wood off-cut the SOCOs found was used to knock Ritchie out – no fingerprints, they're saying, but a possibility of a DNA match if we find someone to link it to; the rope in the barn matched the rope round his neck; no information as yet from suppliers who might have sold Ritchie the chemical stuff – legwork ongoing there. So where does that leave us? I'd like to see the whole

308

background to Ritchie and Lindsay's purchase of the farm – what was Blackford's situation at the time? If he wanted it, did he offer for it and lose? How angry might he have been about that? Then there's the set-up with Gresham's Farms – how do they operate? Gresham mentioned a farm that had previously had a problem, and about one that had given up – what can we find out about them?'

'Perhaps I could go and talk unofficially to one of the other ones,' Murray suggested. 'They might know what happened and I could find out what they say about the Greshams. Sarah Lindsay's always sounded very positive – very grateful to them, I think.'

'Good idea. You could ask what they thought about Ritchie, and her too – we have to remember she's still a suspect, whatever may have happened to her.'

Murray wrinkled her nose at that, but she didn't argue. 'Want me to get on to that now?'

'Yes, absolutely. I'm going to have to make a report to the DCS to assure her I'm keeping out of DCI Campbell's hair and that we've got lots of ideas for making progress on Ritchie's murder.'

At the start of the case, she'd done research on Gresham's Farms and she accessed it even as he was speaking. 'They're spread out over quite a wide area,' she said, running her eye down the list. 'There's quite a big one near Duns. Would that do?'

'Why not?' he said absently, starting to scribble down points on a piece of paper.

Murray gathered up her bag and left.

* * *

Strang was just about to pick up the phone when there was a perfunctory knock on the door and PC Thomson came in without waiting for an answer. 'There's a mannie here says he's wanting to speak to you. Will I let him?'

The effect of Murray's pep talk about his extraordinary importance seemed to have worn off. 'What does he want, Constable?'

'Wouldn't say.'

It would only waste time if he let her start an argument with the man. 'Oh, show him in anyway.'

You got them every so often, the 'wouldn't say' ones, and sometimes it was a vital, shy witness who hadn't come forward before. Sometimes, of course, it was someone looking for an opportunity to rehearse their grievances with the entire national force, but you had to take the risk.

When Rob Gresham appeared, Strang was surprised that he hadn't just given his name, and even more surprised by the look of the man. He was deathly pale and trembling and he looked as if he'd just thrown on his clothes; he certainly hadn't shaved that morning or even combed his hair, from the looks of it.

When Strang greeted him and waved him to a seat, he didn't respond in kind, just slumped down on the chair as if he was afraid his legs wouldn't hold him up.

'I've got something I have to tell you,' he said. 'Something awful.'

'If this is a confession—' Strang began, but Gresham cut in.

'Not exactly. I just need to tell you about something I did. Don't stop me or I might lose my nerve.' He took a deep breath. 'I did a wicked thing, after my partner killed herself. It wasn't that I didn't love Linden – I did. She was a wonderful person, far too good for trash like me and I was totally gutted when she died. I'd known she was stressed, of course, but she never told me the whole truth – that she was constantly being sent press photos of Covid victims and getting anonymous phone calls – and it was only afterwards when I checked her phone to see if she'd left anything that might explain why she'd done it that I recognised the voice of the persecutor – my cousin Briony.'

This was the point at which Strang undoubtedly ought to say, 'You should be telling DCI Campbell this, not me.' On the other hand, the man had said if his confession was interrupted he might never tell the whole story – and if that was special pleading, so be it. He could always bring in Campbell later.

'You don't need to tell me what I should have done,' Gresham said, 'I know – tell the police and have her arrested. But – well, she's family. We'd been close and I felt bad that she'd felt hurt when I fell in love with Linden and pretty much ignored her for a while. And Linden was dead – what would be the point of wrecking Briony's life as well?'

The point would have been, Strang thought with cold fury, that Matt Gunn wouldn't have been at this moment on a slab in the mortuary, and that two women wouldn't have very nearly joined him there.

'So I told her I knew, and she said she'd only been trying to drive Linden away and she was totally horrified at what had actually happened – she's always been, well, nervy, you know. I sort of held it over her head, told her I'd go to the police if I ever heard of her doing that sort of thing again, but I believed she wouldn't.'

Strang took the risk of asking what had happened to the phone.

Gresham shrugged. 'In the sea. We just needed to forget it and move on. Briony was on a much more even keel and until she started behaving oddly about Sarah, I wasn't worried. Then of course—' He stopped, gulped, then after a pause that had Strang on the edge of his seat, went on, 'Gunn started questioning me about Linden.'

'And you told Briony.' That just came out; Strang couldn't stop himself.

Gresham bowed his head. 'Yes, I told her. I didn't want to see it dug up again – it was pointless anyway, and all so long in the past now. I only wanted her to be careful what she said. She's – well, family, you see.'

It was chilling: he'd said that already and perhaps that said it all. Pretend everything is all right, watch the wall and say nothing.

He had stopped meeting Strang's eyes and his voice was flat as he went on, 'She came down to see me that afternoon. She'd parked in the harbour car park.'

And you didn't think of mentioning this to us? Strang had to clamp his lips tightly together to stop himself saying it.

'Of course, I don't actually know what she did. When I phoned her afterwards she didn't tell me anything, only reminded me that I'd always stood by her. But then – last night. Something's gone wrong with her. She's flipped again and she's dangerous.'

That word 'again' was interesting. 'I'm sorry,' Strang said, 'we can't continue on this basis. I'm going to have to take you through to DCI Campbell.'

Gresham's head shot up. 'No! I wanted to talk to you, because I thought you could see to it that Briony was stopped before she could do more damage. I won't say anything official – I'll just walk out.'

'I'm afraid you won't. Robert Gresham, I'm arresting you on suspicion of perverting the course of justice. You are not obliged to say anything . . .'

For once it was a sunny morning as DS Murray drove across to Blackstone Farm. There had been a touch of frost during the night and suddenly the trees were flaming with autumn colours, palest amber right through to deepest red, but she was in no mood to notice them, eaten up as she was with frustration at being side-lined from the main action.

Yes, Niall Ritchie deserved to have his murderer brought to justice, but she felt that at the moment this was a waste; with what she knew about Tarleton, she'd have been more likely to tap useful witnesses than a detective, however senior, from Glasgow.

Still, that wasn't her job. Hers was to try to find out the inside story of Gresham's Farms. Jimmie Gresham had clearly built up a little organic empire, and by his own account – and from what Sarah Lindsay had said – had been very supportive of the young novices even if they got it wrong to start with. From her own observation of Jimmie Gresham, she reckoned he got quite a kick out of being the emperor.

Blackstone Farm was jointly owned by Bruce and Heather Duncan. Had they too found it difficult at the start? she wondered, as she drove up the farm track. If they had, that time was well behind them – the contrast with Eastlaw was striking.

Murray was no expert but the fields on either side looked well-kept, with neat fences and a lot of sheep doing sheep stuff, while at the top of the track was a smart, modern house. The farmyard beyond had new-looking outbuildings and the Land Rover parked there had a recent registration. *Doing very nicely, thank you*, she thought as a man approached her car, looking enquiring.

She stepped out and introduced herself. 'I wondered if I could have a word with you? We're investigating the murder of Niall Ritchie.'

He had a pleasant, rather gentle face, she thought, and he'd been smiling, but when she said that he was immediately serious. 'Oh yes, of course. Such a horrible tragedy. I'm Bruce Duncan. You'd better come in. How is poor Sarah?'

She made a suitable reply as they went to the house. He opened the front door and called, 'Heather! Can you come?'

A woman emerged from the kitchen, a large woman with a florid complexion, wearing jeans and a mauve home-knitted sweater with a butcher's apron tied on top. Her hands were floury and she looked curiously from the visitor to her husband.

'Sorry – I was just making bread. Can we do something for you?'

'This is Detective Sergeant Murray – about poor Niall,' Duncan said.

Heather took charge. 'Come into the lounge, then. We've all been so shocked in our little farming community. And poor Jimmie – this must have been frightful for him.

Especially when they found all those chemicals Niall had been using – he must have felt very let down.'

It seemed Gresham had another fan here. Unprompted, Heather talked on about how much support he always gave them and it was clear that, while giving a nod to Niall's death, she hadn't had much of an opinion of him anyway.

'You could tell he'd just been an armchair farmer and he wasn't much use practically – and of course I don't think she ever really put her back into it.'

The unsaid words, 'not like me', hung in the air. Murray asked if they had found it hard to begin with and it was Bruce who responded.

'Well, yes, I suppose we did. Organic farming's very demanding—'

Heather had bridled. 'Oh Bruce, only in the first five minutes! Jimmie was so helpful and before long we were getting along fine – expanding the farm, able to pull down the old farmhouse and build this.'

'I understand that it wasn't the first time there had been a problem with nonorganic food sent to the supermarkets?'

Heather's face went bright red. 'I don't know what you mean. Whoever told you that was just repeating idle gossip.'

As Murray said, 'It was Mr Gresham, in fact,' she had time to notice that Bruce was looking acutely embarrassed. No prizes, then, for guessing which the farm was that had screwed up but gone on to success.

Heather muttered, 'I suppose I wouldn't necessarily have heard.'

'So you didn't know anything about a farm that had closed down?'

'Certainly not.' She got up. 'Is there anything else? We didn't really know Niall and Sarah except very casually and I ought to get on – and so should you, Bruce. If you're dipping this afternoon, you'll need to check the pens.'

Bruce meekly got up and Murray found herself being escorted to the front door; as she went to her car, Heather shut it firmly. But just as she was about to drive off, Bruce appeared from round the side of the house and, with a nervous glance over his shoulder, approached her. She opened the window.

'You might try to find Graham Letham. Had a farm a bit north of Tarleton – Greencraig. Don't know where he is now.'

He walked quickly away and when Murray called him, he didn't even turn his head, as if, she thought, he was afraid Heather might be coming after him with a rolling pin. Well, if there was one thing the police force was good at, it was finding out where people were. She put in the request for a trace, and drove on.

'We'll be discharging you both today,' the nurse said, pausing briefly at the foot of Sarah Lindsay's bed. 'Mrs Moncrieff could maybe do with a wee while longer but we're short of beds. Just keep an eye on her and she'll be fine.'

She was already moving away when Sarah said, 'But her house burnt down!'

The nurse looked irritated. 'You could go to a hotel or something. The insurance'll probably pay. The beds here are for folk that need them.' She walked away.

Sarah's throat felt as if it had been scraped with sandpaper. She wheezed when she breathed and her headache made it painful to hold her eyes open. She didn't feel like someone who was unnecessarily hogging a bed, but it was true she was recovering. When she'd gone through to see Rose, she was looking even worse than she felt herself – paper-white and frail. She'd definitely need nursing and in a hotel you'd have no kitchen for making hot drinks or scrambled eggs.

They'd said it was only Rose's sitting-room that had been wrecked, thanks to the quick response from the fire brigade, but the fumes would still be toxic. Her stomach turned at the thought of going back to Eastlaw – cold, dark and rank with bad memories – but it looked as if there was no alternative.

She could get a taxi to take them back to Rose's house and she could put on a mask to go in for extra blankets and heaters and fetch her car. Rose could stay in it with the engine running and the heater on until she'd time to light the fire and fill hot water bottles.

What they needed was someone who could do that before they got there, get in supplies for them. But there wasn't a soul she could ask in that vile little town and the only neighbour was Ken Blackford. She'd been sorely tested already, and everything was about to get worse.

PC Thomson came into the incident room where DCI Campbell and DCI Strang were watching Rob Gresham going through the formal processes before being taken to Edinburgh. As usual, she favoured the informal approach, ignoring Campbell's look of annoyance and walking straight up to him.

'There's a call come in from the switchboard. James

Gresham's reported his daughter's missing – never came in last night. Says that's not like her.'

Strang heard a gasp from Rob that was almost a groan and realised he had gasped himself, though more quietly. Beside him, Campbell had gone rigid.

Thomson stood looking from one to the other. 'Am I to do something?'

Someone would certainly have to, with a homicidal woman somewhere out there, Strang thought, though what that something should be was not immediately apparent to him.

CHAPTER NINETEEN

Murray had meant to return to the Tarleton station while she waited for information on Graham Letham – apart from anything else, not knowing what Campbell was doing was like an itch she couldn't scratch – but in fact the result came through well before she got there.

There was a Graham Letham on the voters' roll with a previous address given as Greencraig Farm. His current address was near St Abbs, and she keyed in the postcode and started following the directions.

She was ten miles away when the message came through from Strang. He sounded very much on edge as he asked her where she was and directed her to meet him at Gresham's Farms.

He didn't wait long enough for her to ask what it was about so Murray had to drive on with her mind racing. Did it mean there was going to be an arrest? Matt Gunn had said to her that it was the Greshams, Andrew and Jimmie, who had all the power in Tarleton, and PC Thomson had talked about criminality running like bad blood through that entire family. Had they found out that Jimmie had gone into a rage because Ritchie had let him down and killed him and then hanged him as a cover-up?

She took the bypass rather than driving through the town and she began to notice that there was a lot of police activity – patrol cars going in both directions. There had been cars working from the police station since the previous day but it looked as if there was something going on. She tuned in to the police channel and sure enough there was an APB for a car, citing the number.

That was interesting – you didn't put out an all-points bulletin just because someone hit eighty on the motorway. Did that have something to do with Strang's summons?

When she reached Gresham's Farms, there were two badged cars there already. Strang was leaning in through the open window of one of them, giving instructions of some sort and whenever he straightened up, it drove off. When he saw her, he came across immediately.

He gave her a quick-fire summary of what had happened since she left. He didn't leave time for comments, which was just as well since she was so stunned she couldn't think what she would have said.

'We're going to have to take this carefully,' he went on as they walked towards the front door of the farmhouse. 'Jimmie Gresham thinks that we're here to begin a search because he reported that his daughter didn't come home last night and that's totally how we play it. You do the platitudes about how adult women do sometimes take off – yadda yadda yadda – and I draw him out on her contacts and habits and say that of course we're taking it seriously. Right?'

'Yes, boss.'

The front door was opened the moment they rang the bell. Jimmie Gresham was looking strained, but he greeted them with a rather forced smile and, 'Good of you to come so promptly, Chief Inspector. Do come in. I know I'm probably just being an over-anxious parent, but she's my one chick, and this is totally unlike her.'

He took them through to the sitting room that Briony had so pointedly marched Murray past before. When they sat down, she noticed he was sitting right on the edge of a cream leather armchair, his hands locked round his knees.

'Mr Gresham, I know it's very worrying for you,' she said, 'but it's a common thing for a woman to go off without notice and in almost all cases they come back when they're ready. It could be they just forget to explain—'

He was shaking his head but she carried on, 'Or perhaps even there was a row, or a misunderstanding—'

'No!' He was vehement. 'You don't understand. Briony isn't like that. And there was no row. She wouldn't do this to me. We're very close and she would know how worried I would be.'

'Sometimes,' Strang said gently, 'a sensitive person might overreact, sir. Would you say your daughter might not, well, be seeing things straight?'

Gresham hesitated, his brow furrowed. Murray could read the thought on his face: he didn't want to say anything to suggest that his daughter – *his daughter* – was less than perfect.

'She does sometimes get, well, a little agitated. She had a bad time after my mother died – she was devoted to her – but she's mostly fine now.'

Murray noted that admission and was sure Strang had as well, though he was saying, 'Was it a Covid death?'

Gresham gave a great sigh. 'Yes. And Briony blamed herself – she had brought it into the house.'

'I'm sorry. How very sad.' Then Strang said, as if casually, 'Not as a result of the Do Not Resuscitate policy, I hope?'

'No, no.' Gresham sounded dismissive. 'Never reached hospital, poor old dear. But we're wasting time. What are you going to do about finding Briony?'

Murray produced a notebook. 'Perhaps you could help us by giving us an idea of what she was doing yesterday. Are there friends she might have seen? Perhaps she stayed the night with one and forgot to tell you.'

Gresham gave her a look of contempt. 'You think I haven't phoned round everyone I could think of already? The only person I haven't managed to speak to is my nephew Rob – they've always been good friends – but he isn't answering his phone. Her car was gone when I came back from work but I've no idea where she might have gone – she could be anywhere.'

'We've already put out an alert for the car registration you gave us,' Strang said.

'That's something, I suppose. But—' He broke off and gave a half sob. They waited and after a moment he went on, 'What if she's been – well, hurt?'

'We know all too well that these are violent times,' Strang said.

Gresham's face went very still and his voice was harsh as he said, 'I suppose they are. But my concern at the moment is all for my daughter.'

'Of course,' Murray said soothingly. 'And you know, if anything has happened to her we would hear about it. It's bad news that travels fast and no news is good news.'

She did have a feeling of guilt as she said it but she'd never been burdened, as she saw it, with the scruples that affected her boss and she ignored Strang's sideways glance.

He was getting up now. 'You can be assured we're doing all we can. If you think of anything helpful, do contact us at once.'

'Of course,' Gresham said, getting up to show them out.

He looked completely crushed. Murray had seen that look before, in cases like this: against all reason, people tended to pin their hopes on it being 'all right' once the police came and realising that no, it wouldn't be, was devastating.

She could see in her rear-view mirror that he was watching them as she drove away.

Michelle Gresham called the number again and swore under her breath as there was no answer, yet again. She hadn't been able to concentrate on anything this morning and Andrew had been distinctly terse when he wanted to sign off on a contract she should have prepared for him.

He'd glared at her. 'You're seeming a bit skeery this morning. What's the matter?'

'Oh, I'm just all over the place today,' she said. 'You know, this stuff that's been happening and now Jimmie saying Briony's missing too.'

Only Andrew, she thought, could look surprised. 'Oh, well, she'll be back when it suits her,' he said vaguely. 'Nothing we can do anyway. How long is it going to take you to get this licked into shape?'

'Give me half an hour,' she said, and he nodded and left her office.

She looked at her watch. Half-past two – and she still hadn't heard anything, though she could see plenty of police activity in the town below. What the hell was Rob playing at?

They'd agreed to go to the police first thing; he could at least have told her he'd got cold feet and given her time to come up with an alternative plan.

But now, she was feeling ill with nerves. Briony was not only in one of her weird moods, but no one knew where she was – or more importantly, what she might be doing.

'Nothing useful to indicate where she might be, I'm afraid,' DCI Strang said to DCI Campbell, 'but he said Briony sometimes gets "a little agitated" and had difficulties after her grandmother died of Covid.'

He was careful to present the information as bare facts without drawing conclusions from them; he'd only been offered the chance to interview James Gresham because they wanted him to believe it was a misper investigation they were conducting.

'Ah,' Campbell said. 'Now you see, that would perhaps go some way towards explaining her hostility to Linden Moncrieff.'

Out of the corner of his eye, Strang could see Murray, who had come into the incident room and ensconced herself at a computer terminal well within earshot, mouthing, 'Duh!' to a nearby PC, who grinned.

It was unfortunate that Campbell had such a patronising manner; even Strang could feel his hackles rising as he was briefly thanked and dismissed. Tact be blowed!

'Has anything else come in this morning?' he said without moving. 'Were the women fit to give you any more details?'

Campbell looked put out. 'Oh yes, the women – well, they're still in hospital so we don't want to risk complaints about pressure. I understand a full recovery is expected.'

'But nothing from the cars?'

'Not as yet, but I'm sure they'll get her soon,' he said stiffly and moved a pointed few steps away. 'I've no doubt you've got a lot on your plate too. I'm just off up to Edinburgh to assist at Robert Gresham's interrogation.'

'Of course,' Strang said. 'I'll be around here if there's anything I can do to help.'

As he left, Murray slid quietly out of her seat and joined him in the office that had become their unofficial headquarters.

'Don't think I didn't notice you,' he said, and she looked abashed.

'Well, it was the way he was stating the effing obvious as if it would never have occurred to the rest of us.'

'Hmm. I admit the lack of urgency worries me.'

'It sounds as if he's just relying on the APB to find her – and maybe in Glasgow it would, but he hasn't a scooby about what the back roads are like around here – and the farm tracks. And the victims of a fire – wouldn't you reckon it's worth at least asking if they're ready to talk?

They could always say no, they aren't well enough. That woman's somewhere out there – she could just be hiding up until dark to do something else.'

'I agree I'm not happy. But looked at rationally, the aggression seems to have been directed at Rob Gresham, Rose Moncrieff and Sarah Lindsay. He's in custody and the women are both in hospital.'

'But Briony could go to the hospital in visiting hours, say she was a friend,' Murray argued. 'I'm sure I heard about that somewhere.'

Strang was not entirely convinced. 'In any number of TV crime series, I suspect, and I'm not in a position to station someone on guard. On the other hand, since Lindsay is still a suspect for her partner's murder, I think if necessary we could claim that this was why you went to the hospital to talk to her.'

'Yes!' Murray said. 'Right now?'

'Not Rose Moncrieff,' he warned. 'That case is nothing to do with us, remember?'

She was on her way to the door when she turned. 'Oh, I meant to say – I had an interesting talk with the couple at Blackstone Farm. Very defensive, Jimmie was absolutely wonderful, and I reckon they were the ones he talked about that went on to success after a bit of cheating initially. On my way out, the man slipped me the name of the one who cheated and got dropped – I was on my way to see him when you called me in.'

'Now that is interesting. Where is it?'

'Up towards St Abbs. I might have time to go after I've seen Sarah.'

'If not, you can cover it tomorrow. Good luck!'

When she had gone, he wondered about phoning JB. He'd thought she might have phoned him, as she usually did when a lot was happening and the media was in full cry – which it certainly was at the moment. She'd been on the national news last night.

Since she hadn't, it must mean they were taking ownership of the case at headquarters and keeping the SRCS out of it. In a way, he was relieved; it was a hideously difficult high-profile situation and if mud ended up being slung, he'd be happy enough to dodge it. On the other hand, Matt Gunn had been one of his temporary officers and, certainly so far, Strang hadn't been impressed by what he'd seen of Campbell's operation. It would be hard to sound enthusiastic about it if JB asked him.

On second thoughts, he'd wait till she chose to phone him, and meantime he could start working through the forensic accountant's report on Ritchie's papers, which so far had been both unenlightening and indigestible. He sighed as he clicked onto the file.

'He's been *what?*' Jimmie Gresham bellowed down the phone. 'For God's sake, what in hell has your son been done for this time? I thought he knew he had to keep his nose clean.'

'I don't know.' Andrew Gresham's voice was taut with anger. 'He wouldn't say. Just asked for a lawyer – said he was needing one. I'm not party to all his . . . interests.'

'What about Michelle? She's always mothering him – does she not know?'

'She says she doesn't. I don't believe her.'

'She's a dark horse, your wife. I told you that when you

married her.' There was only a stony silence at the other end of the phone, and Jimmie sounded placatory as he went on, 'Well, water under the bridge and all that. But with her contacts she may know someone who knows.'

'She very well may. She won't tell me.'

'I daresay beating it out of her would be frowned on these days,' he said drily. 'But dear God, it's the last thing I need today, with all the worry about Briony.'

'She's not back, then?'

'No,' Jimmie said, then with sudden suspicion, 'It's not anything to do with Rob, is it?'

'Can't think why it should be,' Andrew said. 'Michelle says she's probably just gone walkabout. Rob claimed she was acting a bit strange again.'

Jimmie said heavily, 'I can't bear it if she's gone back to that. She gets so unhappy. She'd been fine until that business with Ritchie and afterwards I know she was hurt that Sarah had basically cut her dead – very ungrateful. And Rob wasn't as supportive as I'd expected him to be either, with them being such pals.'

'Yes,' Andrew agreed, though without much conviction. 'There's really nothing more I can tell you, Jimmie.'

'I'm worried. All we can do is keep our heads down and hope the storm blows over.'

'Looked at from the bridge, it's shaping up to be a north-easter,' Andrew said, putting down his phone. He thought for a moment, then went to look for Michelle.

She was sitting in the lounge watching a travel programme on the supersize TV that took up most of the side wall and painting her nails a brilliant coral. She didn't turn her head as he came in.

'I've told Jimmie about Rob,' he said.

'Did he have a fit?'

'For God's sake, we're all having fits, even you, for all you're trying to look relaxed. Has Rob never told you anything that might give us an idea what this is about?'

She shrugged. 'Rob has his little secrets.' She got up, picking up her varnish, and turned to look very directly at her husband. 'But then, we all do. Don't we?'

As Michelle walked past him, he noticed there was a smear of coral on her right thumb.

DS Murray hadn't quite realised how far it was to the Borders General Hospital at Melrose, where the fire victims had been taken. By the time she arrived, it was quite dark with an overcast sky; the rain that was falling was getting steadily heavier and, with a couple of ambulances lined up waiting, she had to drive round the car park several times to find a space.

She went in the front entrance. A lot of people were milling around; it looked as if visiting time might just be ending. There were a few people waiting at the reception desk but when she reached the receptionist and showed her warrant card, she got prompt attention.

'I'll just check the ward for you,' the young woman said, turning to tap on her computer. She looked up, frowning. 'No one of that name, I'm afraid.'

'I was assured that the ambulance brought her and another woman here after a house fire last night,' Murray said. 'Smoke inhalation, I think. Is there a special ward for that?'

The woman was still shaking her head. 'Perhaps she's

been discharged – I'll just check that list. Ah, here we are – yes, left the hospital at 14.23.'

That wasn't good news. Chancing her arm, Murray said, 'There was another victim, Rose Moncrieff – is she still here?'

'No. She's on this list too at the same time – I suppose they must have left together.'

'I see. Where have they gone?'

'I'm afraid we don't have a record of that. There will be medical records of their home addresses, of course—'

'No, we have those. I need to speak to the person who discharged them. Could you arrange that for me?'

The people behind her were getting restive and a man pushed forward, giving Murray a dirty look and saying to the receptionist, 'Are you going to let the polis shove us all out the way? I've an urgent query.'

The poor woman looked flustered and Murray said hastily, 'Just tell me where they were and I'll ask there.'

Armed with the ward number and followed by a triumphant smirk from the creep behind her, she navigated her way to Ward 7. A couple of nurses were at the ward station when she came in.

They were very ready to be helpful, but they'd both just come back on duty and had no idea where Sarah and Rose might have gone. Murray was about to give up – perhaps with Rose's house wrecked they'd gone to Eastlaw Farm, and she could find them there – when one of them said, 'I could look for Ali – he was on earlier,' and came back a few minutes later with a young man in green scrubs.

'The two ladies with smoke inhalation? Yes, I was on

the ward when they left but I didn't speak to them myself. It was Janette who processed them. I think she said they'd be going to a hotel, if that's any help.'

'I don't suppose she said which one?' Murray said.

She was right; Janette hadn't. There were any number of hotels and guest houses in the Borders and there was less than no point in trying to track them down. By now it was really too late to go on to the St Abbs address and she drove back to Edinburgh feeling thoroughly frustrated.

As Sarah Lindsay drove towards Eastlaw Farm, her spirits sank, even though her headache was lifting and she wasn't wheezing quite so much. There was no alternative, though; the sympathetic taxi driver who had dropped them at Rose's house had been horrified when he saw the gaping hole that had been a window and the ruined furniture dragged out into the yard.

'You'll not be planning to stay there, surely, dearie?'

Sarah, shuddering herself, assured him she was only dropping in to see what could be salvaged and gave him as much as he would allow her to pay, though she had protested that it wouldn't even cover his petrol.

There was *DO NOT ENTER* tape across the front path but there was no one around and she had ignored it, taking a deep breath before she went into the blackened wreck that had been the pretty little house. She'd been ready for the soot and the blackened walls but not for the water damage – stupid, really, because how else could the flames have been extinguished? There was a deep layer of sludge in the hall and she'd had to wade through it to reach the kitchen. It was little short of a miracle that the fire hadn't spread beyond the sitting room, but the acrid smell was everywhere.

Rose had stayed in the car. It hadn't been difficult to persuade her; she was too exhausted to make an effort and had drifted back into sleep while Sarah raided the kitchen for food supplies and the bedrooms for underwear and warm clothes. They stank of smoke but at least there was a washing machine at the farm.

The autumn afternoon had settled into a dreary sort of twilight as they set off and by the time they arrived at Eastlaw, darkness had fallen, the sort of deep, implacable darkness you only find in the heart of the countryside. Sarah had always hated it, felt almost smothered by it, and for once would have welcomed the lights being on in Ken Blackford's house.

They weren't, and his jeep wasn't there either. Gone to the Waterfoot, no doubt. She didn't like the thought of him coming back later drunk – and with a sudden qualm she recognised how vulnerable they were, though at least she could be pretty sure that Myrna Muir wouldn't even know where Eastlaw Farm was.

She'd been concentrating on the challenge of caring for Rose, who was looking so worryingly frail and hadn't even wakened when the car stopped. Now she was wondering whether a hotel would have been better – but it was too late now.

Switching on the torch on her mobile, she got out of the car and hurried into the house. She felt better once she got the lights switched on, and a couple of electric heaters began their job of warming up the icy air. The first priority was hot water bottles; fortunately, she was well-equipped and she got water heating on the stove as well while the kettle boiled.

There was no point in lighting the fire in the sitting room. Rose needed to get straight to bed, with something to eat if she would take it, and Sarah wasn't exactly planning a late night. Rose could sleep in her room and there was a single bed in Niall's office where she could sleep herself, but she'd have to look out sheets.

Rose still hadn't stirred by the time her bed was ready for her. She looked almost limp as she sat there slumped and Sarah knew a pang of alarm as she opened the door and reached in to pat her arm.

But Rose opened her eyes and struggled up, saying, 'Oh my dear, I'm sorry. You've been doing everything—'

'Not a problem,' Sarah said with huge relief. 'I'm feeling much better. Now let me take your arm, and we'll go upstairs where there's a nice cosy bed waiting for you. I'll bring in the bags with our pyjamas and you can change while I make toast and tea.'

When Sarah came up with a tray, Rose had got into bed and was asleep already. She thought for a moment; sleep was probably more important than food just at the moment and she took it back to the kitchen.

She didn't feel quite ready to go to bed herself. She was feeling nervous about Ken coming back from the pub and she wanted to be alert enough to deal with whatever might happen. She could find something to watch on TV, and perhaps at the same time lay the fire so it would be ready to light in the morning.

Sarah picked up some kindling and went through to the sitting room. It was like an icebox; she shivered as she flicked on the light – and dropped the kindling in shock. Someone was sitting in the chair by the dead fire.

'Briony!' she exclaimed. 'You gave me the fright of my life! What on earth are you doing here?'

CHAPTER TWENTY

There had been half-hearted showers off and on all day but as night fell, the rain gathered conviction, teeming down and orchestrated with the faint ugly whine of a rising wind. Kelso Strang had drawn the curtains over his favourite view to blot out the depressing weather, but he could hear it even so.

He was finding it hard to settle to anything. Whatever resolutions he had made about ignoring the investigation that he'd been firmly told was nothing to do with him, he kept thinking about the missing woman.

In weather like this, where was Briony Gresham? She had to have taken shelter, or even gone home – and perhaps she had, since there was no reason for anyone to have informed him – and though it was a pity that, according to Livvy Murray, Lindsay and Moncrieff had been discharged from hospital, an unnamed hotel was as safe as anywhere. He needed to put it out of his mind now.

Yet he couldn't resist switching on the evening news to see what was making the headlines. The search for the murderer of the police officer had slipped to third item, so clearly Brian Campbell hadn't thrown them any red meat and the connection with the house fire didn't seem to have been made.

Stop it, Kelso told himself. He went to make a cup of coffee; he had a new William Boyd so he could distract himself with that. No, he couldn't. His eyes followed the words on the page but his mind was elsewhere. There was no point in ruining a good book.

He fetched his laptop with a sigh and opened up the files for the case he should be concentrating on with a notepad at his side. He'd time on his hands now to do an evaluation of what information they had gathered so far and, importantly, what was still missing.

The interview with the failed organic farmer could open up a new avenue of enquiry – shame that Livvy hadn't had time to do it this afternoon. The sifting interviews with the people whose initials appeared in the notebook were starting tomorrow and when Campbell had finished with Rob Gresham, he'd get his own turn to interview him about what had gone on there – he was tolerably certain that Rob would crack open like a nut. He was fundamentally a weak man rather than an irredeemably wicked man; even damaged, perhaps, given the home he'd come from.

What he needed to do was go right back to the beginning, to Gunn's narrative of what had taken place at Eastlaw

Farm, and he read it frowning in concentration. Then he looked up, thinking.

There was a question that hadn't been asked, a question that was central to the whole thing. One person should be able to answer it, and he wrote the name in block capitals on his pad, with an exclamation mark.

First thing tomorrow morning, then. And if the answer was what he was now thinking it could be, and the results of the ongoing forensic tests were what they hoped, the road to justice for Niall Ritchie might at last be opening before them.

Briony Gresham's nose was blue with cold even though she was wearing a thick overcoat and was huddling in a chair with her hands tucked under her armpits. She blinked, screwing up her eyes against the sudden light.

'Oh, for goodness' sake, get that fire on before I freeze to death!' she snapped.

Sarah stared at her. 'Briony, I don't understand! How did you get in?'

Briony gave a high-pitched giggle. 'Key on top of the doorframe, stoopid!'

It was true; they were casual around here and there was always one there in case they locked themselves out. But there was something very wrong with Briony; her eyes were wild and glittering and she'd started beating on the arms of her chair, chanting, 'Fire! Fire! Fire!'

It was easier to light it than to argue. Sarah gathered up the kindling she'd dropped and knelt on the hearth, laying the fire as she tried to get things straight. Briony had certainly been strange yesterday evening but until now she'd assumed the house fire was another stage in Myrna Muir's hate campaign. It hadn't been, though, had it?

The little flames were licking eagerly up now and she bent over them, feeding in smaller sticks. Without looking up, she said, 'Why are you here, Briony?'

'Where is he?' she said. 'Is he coming later?'

'Who do you mean?' Sarah asked. As if she didn't know.

'Rob, of course. He still won't speak to me, and I'm not having that. It's betrayal and it makes me angry, very angry. And you see, I know now you're trying to keep him to yourself and I won't have that either. So you all deserved to be punished, but then you escaped.' She was scowling. 'You weren't meant to. I went back to see, after, and I was cross about that – but ooh, what a mess!' With a sudden change of mood, she gave that disconcerting giggle again. 'Goodbye, little house! So you would have to come back here, and then he'd come too.'

'I didn't see your car.'

'No, I hid it. Down the track, where a path goes off. Clever, eh? If you'd known I was here you'd tell him to keep away. And I want him here. I want all of you together.'

The fire was blazing now but it did nothing for the chill that had seized Sarah. Briony had blue circles under her eyes and that papery look you get when you're unslept and she had just given a little twitch, as if she was fighting to stay alert. But she seemed to be in the grip of some sort of mania and Sarah could almost smell the barely suppressed violence.

She must talk Briony down. Her phone was still in her pocket; if she could get through to the kitchen . . .

She stood up. 'You poor soul!' she said. 'You must be

338

absolutely freezing, waiting for us here. I'll make a hot drink – are you hungry as well?'

The too-bright eyes bored into her. 'No. I told you – all I want is to get Rob here. He has to pay – and so do you. Give me your phone. He'll answer it if he sees your number, won't he, and then I can explain to him why he needs to come.' She bared her teeth in what was more a grimace than a smile. 'For your sake. And hers too.' She pointed at the ceiling.

This couldn't be real. This was a nightmare she'd wake up from any second now – but it wasn't. Briony was holding out her left hand. And as she moved, Sarah saw that the right hand, the one that was still tucked under the coat, was clutching something with a wooden handle. Sick with terror, Sarah recognised it: the heavy knife Niall had used to kill chickens when necessary.

She tried to stop her hand from shaking as she handed over the phone. Perhaps it was for the best; if Briony said that to Rob, there was no way he wouldn't alert the police before he came. Briony muttered away, scanning her phonebook until, with a triumphant smile, she made the connection.

The phone rang out and as it went to voicemail, Briony's smile faded. She scowled and switched it off.

'If I leave a message, he'll ignore it. You do it, and when he's picked up, pass it on.'

It was all she could do. She was on the point of redialling when a light swept the room. Briony was on her feet instantly and now the knife was clearly visible, squat, heavy, with a blade that had always been kept razor-sharp.

'What's that?' she demanded.

Sarah made herself sound calm. 'It's only my neighbour, coming back from the pub.'

'Put out the light!' Briony ordered. 'And sit down, over there.'

She did as she was told. By the light of the fire, she could see where Briony was now – standing between her and the door. She couldn't get past her and if she screamed, she didn't think Ken would even hear her. If he did and came to her aid, she'd be dead before he could reach her.

'Will he come in?' Briony said.

'No. He's just gone past to his own house.'

Briony was pacing to and fro now. 'He'd better not come round.'

'He won't,' she said confidently, then to her dismay a moment later saw the light of a torch bobbing along the path outside.

Briony made a sound like the hissing of a snake as she darted across the room. 'I warn you, don't betray me. I'm going upstairs now, and if I have to use this knife on Rose Moncrieff, her death will be on your conscience forever – not mine.'

The knock came on the door as she went out and Sarah, weak at the knees, went to open it, feeling Briony's eyes watching her from the upstairs landing.

It was very wet outside and the man's hair had become plastered to his head, even in the short distance from his house to hers.

'Oh, hello, Ken! How are you?' she cried, as if she was greeting a long-lost friend.

She got a grunt in response, and, 'Saw you were back.'

'Good to see you – how nice of you to drop round,'

she gushed. 'How are you doing? I've been away for a few days, you know, but it's lovely to be home.'

She could see puzzlement on the man's face. 'Yeah, well. I just thought I'd tell you – saw someone lurking round the house earlier. You all right?'

She mouthed, 'No!' but said brightly, 'Oh yes, absolutely. And whoever it was isn't here now. Probably some journalist, you know what they're like. But I know I can always rely on you to chase them off, can't I?' She mouthed, 'Help!' this time, and saw comprehension dawning.

'That's all right then. I'd better get to my bed – bit of a heavy evening.'

'Naughty man!' she said with a flirtatious laugh. 'Still, as long as you had a good time. Night, Ken!'

Briony was coming down the stairs as she turned round. 'All right,' she said. 'But he could be dangerous. We need to get on with the plan. You phone Rob. You have to leave a message, all right, and then, when he picks up, you know, you give it to me and then . . .' There was a hysterical note in her voice and she trailed off as if she'd lost her train of thought.

'Yes, of course,' Sarah said. 'But you know he could be driving or something – he might not be able to answer his phone.'

Briony looked at her as if this was shattering news. Her lip quivered and she wailed, 'But he has to come! Otherwise . . .'

'Otherwise what, Briony?' Sarah said gently.

She had slumped back down in the chair, crying, 'I–I don't know!'

For the first time, Sarah felt a flicker of hope. 'I'll do the

341

message and say he has to come, and we'll see. Then we can have a cup of tea while we wait.'

It was a mistake. Briony leapt up again, holding the knife now in a threatening position. 'You're trying to trick me, I know you are. You've all been conspiring against me from the start. But I can be tricksy too. I could tell him you were here, even if you were dead – that wouldn't be a lie, would it?' She laughed again, that high-pitched manic laugh.

Sarah's flicker of hope died. Even supposing Ken Blackford did raise the alarm, how could anyone get past the crazy woman holding the knife? At least it would be quick; she'd carefully sharpened it herself to make sure, at the time when it was only a chicken that would reap the benefit.

Kelso Strang had packed it in and gone to bed early but he'd fallen into the sort of sleep where you're never quite sure if you're awake or not, almost as if he'd been waiting for the phone call that came just after eleven-thirty. So he came to quickly, but what did take him by surprise was the voice at the other end.

DCS Borthwick said, 'Kelso? Sorry it's so late but we've got a situation.'

He swallowed hard. 'Bad?'

'Yes. Serious problem – Sarah Lindsay is at Eastlaw Farm and her neighbour—'

'Ken Blackford,' he said grimly. He'd been worried about that.

'You know him? That's good. He called emergency to say that he thinks there's a hostage situation there. He went round to tell Ms Lindsay he'd seen an intruder hanging around earlier and she was talking oddly as if someone was listening and mouthed "Help!" That's all we have.'

It took him a moment to adjust. 'Good God!' he said blankly, then, 'Have they picked up Briony Gresham?'

'No. So I think we can assume that she's somehow involved. DCI Campbell is in Glasgow – in fact, he's in Helensburgh, where he lives. We can't bring him in by chopper for a situation like this so you'll need to take over. How long before you get there?'

'An hour, with blues and twos on the motorway. Are Armed Response on alert?' He was pulling off his pyjamas as he spoke.

'Assembling now. Do you know the territory?'

'Yes. I'll liaise with them about where we can meet – any approach to the farm could kick it off. A negotiator?'

'Being summoned now. Into your hands, Kelso. Keep me in the picture.'

He was all but dressed by the time the call finished. There was body armour and outdoor protective clothing waiting in the car and he went up to the kitchen to grab water and a couple of energy bars – who knew how long he might have to stand outside, and it was a filthy night now. With adrenaline surging, he leapt down the wooden outdoor staircase to reach his car and took off for the bypass, carving through the late-night traffic with lights and siren.

Don't think about what might be happening to Sarah Lindsay, he told himself sternly. *Go through procedure. Remember the basics. Clear instructions for the guys. Calmness at all times. And a very, very cool head if it comes to going in.*

* * *

Briony had changed her mind. 'Don't tell him that about coming to protect you and her. I'm not afraid he'd tell the police, because we're family. I know he would never, never betray me to them – he's proved that. But he might not care what happened to you, you see? Maybe he's not as fond of you as you like to think? You and that woman' – she jerked her head upwards in a contemptuous gesture – 'and her snake of a daughter, you all coiled yourselves round him so he couldn't think straight.'

'So what am I to say to him, then?' Sarah said as calmly as she could, given the knot of terror twisting her guts.

'Just say you want to see him. Act lovey-dovey, the way you usually do. Go on!'

Her encouraging smile wouldn't have fooled anyone. 'I don't,' Sarah said bluntly. 'If I did, he'd think there was something wrong.'

Once again, confronted with a setback, Briony crumpled. 'What are we going to do, then?' she wailed.

Sarah took the risk of going to sit on the chair opposite, facing the window. 'Let's talk about it, Briony. You know how we always used to talk about everything together, and you used to listen to all my problems – remember?'

Briony was watching her warily, but her eyes were drooping and she gave another of the little twitches.

'You must be so tired,' she went on gently. 'Just so tired!' She managed a yawn and saw Briony catch the infection, giving a yawn so huge her jaw almost cracked.

Perhaps if she just went on talking . . . 'Remember how you tried to cheer me up, telling me about the mini fish and chips? So clever, the way your parties always were . . .'

The room was warm now and she made her voice

softer, softer, almost hypnotic and was rewarded by seeing Briony's head drop forwards. Trying to seize the moment, she leant forward, reaching for the knife she was holding in her hand.

Too quickly. Briony's eyes shot open and she tightened her grip. 'You were trying to get it off me. I'm not going to let you.'

She got up and, standing with the knife blade directed at Sarah, pushed her chair across till it was blocking the door. 'If I drop off, I'll wake up the second you move.'

The brief spark of hope flickered and died. 'So what are we going to do now?' Sarah said dully.

'It's your job. Leave a message for Rob that will make him come.'

Sarah's mind was racing as fast as her pulse. What could she say? If she spun it out, would that give Blackford time to get help to her – always supposing he'd tried? She called Rob's number.

He didn't pick up and she began her message. 'Rob, it's Sarah. Sorry to bother you, but you did say if I was worried about anything to let you know. I'm getting sort of panicky out here at the farm and I keep hearing footsteps. Could you bear to come out and tell me I'm being stupid? There's a Scotch in it for you.'

Briony was nodding while she was speaking. 'That was good,' she said when Sarah finished. 'That'll bring him all right.'

Then they waited. After a few minutes, Briony started getting restless. 'Why isn't he calling back?'

'Could be out for the evening,' Sarah said. 'Or could be driving, like I said.'

345

'Oh no!' She was looking ready to break down again – and if she totally flipped, who knew what would happen? Sarah couldn't go on being passive. She'd feel such a fool if she ended up dead and she'd just sat there.

'What do you think will happen to you afterwards if you – well, hurt us?'

With one of her lightning changes of mood, Briony perked up. 'Oh, I've thought of that. I just walk away. They won't know it's me any more than they know it's me set that bitch's house on fire. Anyway, I'm a Gresham. The police don't dare to touch the Greshams.'

It was so blatant, Sarah almost choked. She couldn't afford to react, though. 'Tell me how that works,' she said, fixing her gaze on the knife, waiting for the moment when the grip might loosen. If a kick knocked it away, she'd back herself to reach it first. Briony had never been athletic.

Perhaps it had been a mistake to ask. Briony seemed to have wakened up as she talked family history. It gave Sarah time to think and it wasn't comfortable. Even supposing help came, how could they reach her in this room with its tiny window that no one could come in or get out through? All she could do was wait and listen to the rain and wind that was battering the house – and pray, perhaps, though she'd a feeling God might be surprised to hear from her after all this time.

Strang stopped his car at the edge of a short, rough path some way below the Eastlaw farmhouse – a path where he saw another car had been parked, a neat little silver Audi A3. A car whose number he recognised. His ugliest suspicions confirmed, he left the car to walk on up to the

346

farm. She wouldn't be making a quick getaway from there, anyway, especially with Armed Response moving into position across the track behind him, waiting for him to reconnoitre and report back.

It was a night well up to the standard of the worst Berwickshire could offer, making a mockery of the term 'weather protection uniform'. There was not a glimmer of light in the sky and his attempt to avoid the puddles and the quagmires met with indifferent success.

As always before an operation, he was experiencing that familiar twist of anticipatory fear for what he might find – and what level of threat he might face. He hadn't seen Briony Gresham, but in any sort of direct encounter, a woman would be likely to come off worse – though recalling his previous case, Kipling's comment about the female of the species did forcibly come to mind.

There were lights ahead. In Blackford's farm, further on, there were house lights showing and outdoor lights had been switched on that spread almost as far as the garden around the Eastlaw farmhouse – useful for the approach, and luckily leaving the area round it still in darkness.

There was a light showing in what could be an upstairs hall, and there was a patch of light spilling out round the back too; the kitchen, he found when he eased his way round, and though it appeared to be empty, he didn't risk stepping close.

The only other inside light was fitful, coming from the sitting room: firelight, flickering. It was a very small window and this time he would have to get up close to be able to see. Strang lined himself up against the wall beside it, angling his head to get a view and trusting to the cloak of outside darkness.

It looked unalarming – a cosy domestic picture, two women chatting by the fireside in the small room. Sarah Lindsay was looking distressed, sitting in a chair looking towards the window but her attention was fixed on the other woman – Briony Gresham, presumably – who was facing the fire and talking, though he couldn't hear what she was saying.

She was facing the fire, yes, but the odd thing was that her chair was placed right across the door of the room as if she was acting as a jailer. Had she a weapon?

He edged another half-inch forward to get a better look – and froze. Lindsay had caught the movement. Even across the room he saw her eyes widen involuntarily, but she didn't jump and as he drew back, he saw her switch her gaze smoothly back to Gresham.

Strang edged silently back out of sight. He'd seen the knife, the heavy butcher's knife held in Gresham's hand, and it was potentially a very volatile situation. It would take a negotiator some time to arrive and by then it could easily be too late for talking. He hurried back down the track to where the superintendent of Armed Response was standing ready beside the people-carrier.

'Knife-edge stuff, literally,' Strang said, 'and we'll have to busk it. I know the house. Room to right of front door. Female holding a serious knife in a chair, blocking the door. Awkward angle for a shot. Hostage further in, knows I'm around. So I'll spearhead, your lot encircle – operational silence. I get the front door and let your guys through. I reckon if they crash the room door off its hinges it should take her out without fatal results. Risky, but we can't wait – she's killed before and it could go very wrong in seconds. Right?'

'Your call,' the super said, thumping his fist on the side of the van and instantly the armed officers, sinister in their helmets and visors, were jumping out. 'Anyone else in the house?' he asked.

Strang paused. Of course, there well could be; he'd seen Lindsay in immediate danger but he hadn't thought of Moncrieff, who might have come to Eastlaw with her. 'Likely upstairs,' he said, 'but not in the room. Right, lads. Here we go!'

They had come! Sarah hadn't dared to believe it, but someone was definitely there, though she only caught a brief glimpse of a face. What could they do, even so? And was there anything she could do that might help?

They'd be trying to surround the house. But if they made a noise, Briony would realise that her clever plan for walking away wasn't working, and what would she do then? Perhaps she would just crumple, as she had before, but perhaps she might lose it completely. She wouldn't like to bet which way it would take her.

'So you see, that was how the whole Gresham family thing came about,' Briony said, and Sarah seized her moment.

'That was really interesting. Now, since we have to wait, I tell you what – I've got Spotify here, and I'll put it on so we have something to listen to as we chat.' She went back to her phone, found the app and switched it on before Briony could object.

She looked suspicious, but she didn't react and Sarah could see her start to sag in her chair.

Perhaps she wouldn't need help after all, if she just let the music, the warmth and exhaustion do its bit. And at least it would cover up whatever noise the rescuers made.

It was a few minutes later that she not only heard a sound; she saw the door handle turn and then Rose's voice was saying, 'Sarah? Are you in there? I think the door's stuck.'

Briony was on her feet immediately, pushing aside the chair, opening the door. 'Well, well, Mrs Moncrieff! How gracious of you to join us. I thought you were fast asleep upstairs, but maybe it's better to have you here where I can see you.'

Rose looked completely bemused as she let herself be ushered in. 'I heard the music and I came down. But – Briony, I didn't know you were here?' She looked across at Sarah, who was sitting with her head in her hands.

'Sit down,' snarled Briony.

'But I don't understand—'

'Sit!' she snarled again.

'You'd better,' Sarah said tiredly. 'She's got a knife.'

Rose, who was still looking very frail, collapsed onto the sofa as Briony, standing over her, said, 'I don't think he's going to come at all, do you, Sarah? I think this is all taking too long.'

And there was silence, apart from a voice singing, with hideous irony, something about being crazy.

CHAPTER TWENTY-ONE

As Strang approached the house for the second time, he was surprised to hear music. It was a pop song he vaguely recognised and it took him a moment to realise that Lindsay must have provided it as cover. Clever woman!

That would be a considerable advantage but he'd have to do a final recce before they put the plan into action. He'd been feeling more upbeat, so he got a nasty shock when he actually looked in.

The door that was to have been weaponised was standing open now and the chair that had been across it was empty. He could risk taking a better look since only Lindsay had a line of sight towards the window; Gresham was standing with her back to him.

She was leaning over someone on the sofa that Strang couldn't see and the way she was holding the knife was threatening; he saw too with alarm that Lindsay had jumped up, as if ready to defend either herself, or her friend. The music still playing was seeming more macabre by the minute.

Gresham might turn round. He retreated to the more concealed position, sensing rather than hearing the black figures gathering beside him and he held up a hand to slow them.

Gresham seemed to be agitated, pointing towards something at the further side of the room. Strang couldn't see that corner but Lindsay walked over towards it, then back to the visible centre of the room with her phone held ostentatiously. She started fiddling with it, fiddling and fiddling.

He heard Gresham shouting but not what she said. It wasn't hard to guess, though – the music was to be turned off. But the sitting-room door was standing wide.

With a gesture, Strang drew the silent cohort in behind him. The front door creaked loudly, but it opened a bare moment before the covering music stopped.

And by then the black figures were surging past him, like a visitation from hell in the flickering firelight. There was a piercing scream and as Strang followed in, a knife went spinning across the room to clatter into the fireplace. Briony Gresham was struggling violently; it took two officers to throw her to the floor but then she was pinned there, the handcuffs were on and all she could do was scream and swear. As DCI Strang stood watching, Sarah Lindsay all but knocked him off his feet by casting herself on him in a fit of hysterical tears.

* * *

'It was quite a risk, Kelso,' Detective Superintendent Jane Borthwick said, looking tired after a late and anxious night. 'You hadn't covered your back. It could all have gone wrong and you hadn't waited for the negotiator to try and talk the woman down.'

Strang had gone straight to headquarters after the operation at Eastlaw Farm had been wound down and he wasn't feeling at his best either. 'Yes, I accept that,' he said. 'But when you have a killer with a knife in a developing situation, it could all have gone wrong very quickly and I don't think citing correct protocol would have covered me if there had been two dead women and no action taken to protect them.'

'True enough. The outcome was certainly impressive – well done!'

'The AR guys did a great job. Shock and awe, really – the Darth Vader styling always helps. Briony Gresham was decked before she knew what was happening and they've taken her in and put her on suicide watch. We got Sarah Lindsay and Rose Moncrieff back into hospital for check-ups but I don't think there's anything wrong with them apart from shock. The car has been picked up for forensic tests, though given that it was only a minor impact that knocked Matt Gunn off the dock they may not find much.'

'That's going to be difficult, unless we get a witness who can put her at the scene – not impossible, given that she's well-known. *Omertà* may not work quite so well once the news of all this gets out,' she said.

'I think there may be quite a few people very anxious to save their own skins – Rob Gresham for one. I'm looking forward to that interview.'

Borthwick nodded. 'Campbell's softening him up for you this morning. Anyway, my name's on this one so it's my problem and I'm certainly grateful for such an efficient operation. If you can get a full report to me, that will wrap it up, and free you to focus on the Niall Ritchie case. And don't worry – in the circumstances, I'm not going to so much as ask you if there's any progress there.'

'Not exactly progress,' Strang said cautiously, 'but a promising line of enquiry I set up yesterday. Then I had quite an interesting chat with Blackford late last night after we got the Eastlaw situation sorted out.'

'That's the neighbour who gave the alarm?'

'Yes. The neighbour, incidentally, who will also be answering questions about those unofficial business activities that took place at the Waterfoot Inn. I asked him if he'd noticed the artificial fertilisers had begun producing better crops for Ritchie but he hadn't seen any sign of that, though according to him, the man would have been a rubbish farmer whatever he did and he was getting desperate, with Jimmie Gresham being hard as nails when it came to delivery. That's rather at odds with the way it was presented to us – Jimmie being an idealist keen to help a young man with a dream to get on his feet.'

'Hmm,' she said. 'There are remarkably few highly successful men who are in the making-dreams-come-true business. Bit of a red flag, that one, I would say.'

'I've got Murray digging around the background to the small farms like Ritchie's and she was planning on talking to a farmer who failed this morning. I'm just hoping our luck keeps running.'

Borthwick sighed, putting up a hand to her head. 'We

354

still need it on this one too. It's not enough having Briony Gresham charged with arson – I want her nailed with Matt Gunn's murder and sentenced accordingly, even if she serves it in a secure hospital. Thanks, Kelso. A good night's work.'

DS Livvy Murray got up promptly on Thursday morning. She wanted to get the visit to Graham Letham done and dusted so that she could get back to Tarleton and see what might have happened overnight. Provokingly, there wasn't anything on the morning news bulletin, not even that there was a search on for a missing woman. Campbell must be playing this one close to his chest, but you couldn't do that forever.

She had to make a fine judgement about the best time to catch someone in. First thing in the morning was usually the best bet, but she was hoping to engage this man in helpful conversation and getting him, and possibly a partner if there was one, out of bed was not a good beginning. On the other hand, if he was employed as a farmworker, as he could be, nine o'clock could virtually be lunchtime. So Fate, and the Edinburgh bypass, might as well decide.

In the event, it was quarter to nine when Murray arrived at a small and shabby-looking terrace flat in a back street of St Abbs. The paintwork was flaking, which might just be lack of money, but it didn't cost anything to clean your windows and doorstep so she wasn't surprised that the man who opened the door to her was a poor-looking specimen with thin, gingery hair that needed a cut, a face that needed shaving and clothes that could definitely do with a good wash. She'd like to think the egg stains on the T-shirt had come from this morning's breakfast but she wouldn't have wanted to put money on it.

Over the years she'd become a bit of a connoisseur of reactions from the public to her warrant card – the uneasy look from the ones with something on their conscience, the cheesy beam of the householders keen to show support for law and order, the weary resignation of those who'd known what she was long before she'd ever offered it – oh, the list was endless. But this was about the first time she'd seen utter indifference.

Letham listened to what she had to say, then shrugged. 'Come in if you want to,' he said, leading her through a dark, narrow hallway to a tiny kitchen at the back where dirty dishes were piled by the sink and the table, with its oilcloth, still had crumbs lying on it, and even a smear of butter. The narrow window looked onto an alleyway.

The odd thing was the hothouse smell. Perched on every shelf and the surfaces all round about were pots and pots of plants – bare plastic pots, but filled with riotously green things growing. Letham, with his narrow, hunched shoulders and his worn-out trainers, looked as if all his energy had been drawn from him and into them.

It had a real *Little Shop of Horrors* vibe and Murray was almost reluctant to sit down herself, just in case. Eying the largest of them warily, she said, 'You do like flowers, don't you?'

Letham gave a shrug. 'I like any growing thing.'

He had, she noticed, sad eyes like a spaniel that's been kicked too often. 'You were a farmer, weren't you?'

'I was.'

'But not now?'

He gave a bitter laugh. 'Oh no, not now. Farmhand, if I get lucky.'

Clearly a sensitive subject; just the sort of thing to pile into with hobnailed boots. 'So what happened with the farm, then?'

For the first time he seemed to connect. 'Look, what is this about?'

'You were involved with Gresham's Farms, weren't you? We're investigating the murder of Niall Ritchie at Eastlaw – did you know him?'

She'd caught got his attention. 'That poor bastard! No, after my time. No doubt selected as another of Gresham's victims.'

It was fair to say he'd caught her attention too. Startled, she said, 'Gresham's victims? What do you mean by that?'

He gave a long, drawn-out sigh. 'Oh, the king of organic farming, right? Makes his fortune that way, except he takes every shortcut in the book when it suits him. It's hard to make any money at all with a small-holding, done right, but he absolutely insists on it – for everyone else.'

'Do you mean Jimmie Gresham cheats?'

He was getting animated now. 'Course he does. I reckon most of the big commercial operations do when necessary and often it suits the supermarkets to turn a blind eye to make sure the shelves stay full.'

'Did you?'

His face flushed scarlet. 'Never! Unlike some of the others, I totally believe in it. Even if you're just scraping along, you're doing the right thing for the planet.'

'So what went wrong with your farm?'

'Nothing went wrong with it! Not until . . .' His

shoulders sagged again. 'Oh, what's the point? I know I'm a nothing – all this is pointless.'

He really was infuriatingly spineless. 'Look, sir,' Murray said firmly, 'I'm getting the impression that somehow Mr Gresham cheated you out of your farm. I need you to tell me what happened.'

Letham gave her another spaniel look. 'No one would take my word against his.'

'I might. You're saying that your farm foundered and you see yourself as Mr Gresham's victim. Is that right?'

'More scapegoat, really. That's what we're all there for, the small farms. Act as cover.'

She was puzzled. 'What were you meant to cover?'

'The cheating, of course. You see, every so often the buyers do run a test and something nonorganic crops up with produce coming from Gresham's Farms. He has to keep his spotless reputation so of course it always turns out to actually have come from one of the small farms and the farmer says sorry and Jimmie fudges it over with the buyer and we all go on fine.'

It was all falling into place. 'You weren't prepared to do that?'

'No!' he said fiercely. 'I wasn't going to have my good name trashed. When he came to tell me what I had to do, I refused – there was never anything nonorganic used on my land. He threatened me – he'd see to it I'd never be able to sell my produce again. Then he got angrier and angrier – I really thought he was going to hit me, but my girlfriend happened to come in and he left in a temper. So then he called in loans he'd given me earlier and that was the end of the farm – and the girlfriend.'

No wonder the poor sod looked demoralised. The whole pattern of Jimmie Gresham's business plan was being laid out before her: the disposable small farms, controlled by the loans he so generously gave them, the terms being that whenever chemicals were found in Gresham's Farms produce, they would take the blame. It had paid Bruce and Heather Duncan handsomely to fall into line; Graham Letham had lost his livelihood because he hadn't – and Niall Ritchie? Had a refusal cost him his life?

'Would you be prepared to make a formal statement to that effect – that Jimmie Gresham had actually threatened you?' she asked.

Letham stared at her. 'Would I be prepared . . .? If I can get anyone to listen, I'll shout it from the rooftops.'

He was looking like a different man. Murray smiled. 'I don't think we'd ask you to do that, but it could be of considerable importance. You'll be hearing from us.'

'I can't tell you what this means to me. You're the first person who's listened and believed me.' As she got up to leave, he reached down a pot and said, 'Here – thanks for what you've done.'

It was a large, fleshy plant with an angular bloom that was zebra-striped with yellow. Concealing her dismay, Murray took it with appropriate expressions of gratitude and carried it out to the car. She put it in the far corner of the back seat, just to be safe; she'd only have to share her living space with it for the half-hour it would take to reach the Tarleton police station. Then she could present it to PC Thomson, who probably hadn't seen *Little Shop of Horrors* and wasn't the kind to be intimidated anyway.

What she hadn't expected was that DCS Borthwick

would be coming out to the relentless clacking of cameras and flashing light bulbs. She was ignoring them, heading for her car, but Murray's face flared scarlet at her look of astonishment as she passed the detective sergeant and her strange and interesting plant.

Some mildly positive information had at last come in. The pathologist's report confirmed that the length of wood found near the site showed traces of Ritchie's blood, but as they'd suggested before, it hadn't taken fingerprints and any DNA evidence would be likely to be of poor quality.

Reading it, DCI Strang sighed. Supposing they did get a result, it would be after a considerable delay at best, and even then the same problem arose as with the extensive fingerprint evidence they had already – how could you link it to a suspect when you had no viable reason to test them?

He was increasingly sure, though, that he knew who had killed Niall Ritchie. He even thought he knew how the scenario had played out and had ordered tests accordingly – but he still felt there was something not quite right, some sort of imbalance. He'd told Murray often enough that motive wasn't their business, yet here it was niggling at him – the reaction seemed wholly disproportionate to the offence. But he should be getting on with his report for JB instead of wasting time on speculation.

Strang was working on it when he heard DS Murray's voice in the corridor; someone must be bringing her up to speed on the night's events because she was exclaiming. She'd taken Matt Gunn's death very hard and she'd be upset at having played no part in the arrest of his killer.

To his surprise, though, when she came in she was cocka-hoop, barely pausing to compliment him on the result before she burst out with, 'Just wait till you hear this!'

Strang listened with astonishment as Murray recounted what Graham Letham had said. He'd envisaged the lashing out in anger and the cover-up; he'd even, after what Blackford had said, reckoned that the chemicals in the shed were a plant, to give a motive for the ostensible suicide. What he hadn't figured out was why it mattered so much that Ritchie had taken the sort of shortcut Gresham had said occasionally happened.

'It could mean his whole business empire down the tube,' Murray said. 'If Ritchie said that he was going to tell the buyer that it was Gresham who was cheating, it would reach the others in minutes. According to Letham, he was doing it regularly.'

'Presumably the supermarkets' testers wouldn't always agree to play ball and a small organic farm would be forced out of business but it's a hard life, so no one would be asking questions.'

'Gresham certainly made it worthwhile for the ones who took the rap for him. Bruce and Heather Duncan are doing very nicely, thank you.'

'Right. But tell me – Letham's prepared to give sworn evidence of what he said to you?'

Murray grinned. 'Can't wait.'

Strang got up, abandoning his report. 'I feel an arrest for uttering threats coming on. By midday we'll have his prints on file and then we can turn to the questions of homicide and fraud. It's going to be a busy afternoon. Let's go!'

* * *

Andrew and Michelle Gresham drove in silence from the house by the harbour out to Gresham's Farms, the air in the car thick with secrets. Michelle turned her head once to glance at her husband but he was looking straight ahead, granite-faced.

She wanted to tell herself that all that had actually happened was that Briony, a spoilt brat who frankly should have been drowned at birth, was going to be charged with attempted murder, and very probably murder too, if they could dredge up enough evidence, which needn't affect them. Rob's arrest was more of a problem; he wasn't stupid but he was weak and she couldn't trust him not to break under pressure, though the thought of the revenge his pals in Glasgow would take if he grassed might stiffen his spine.

She'd been hearing the rumours of other regulars at the Waterfoot being questioned and she wasn't naïve enough to think she wouldn't be implicated. Still, with luck, she could fudge her involvement to the point where Vincent Dunbar would be able to deliver a deferred sentence for her.

That would be unpleasant and embarrassing enough but that wasn't the fear that was holding them both in its icy grip. It was the sense that everything was falling apart, that the enemies were at the gates of the kingdom they had ruled for so long and the walls that had kept them at bay were crumbling.

Jimmie had been all but hysterical when he phoned. He couldn't believe it, he'd bring a case against the police for false arrest, they were covering up for their failure to find Briony when she was missing . . . Andrew had actually shouted at him. He was the older brother and that seniority

362

still counted and Jimmie had agreed to wait until they had talked before doing anything.

Now, as they turned up the drive to the farmhouse, they noticed that the yard was looking very quiet and the one man they had passed on the way in had steadfastly looked at the ground rather than waving a greeting.

Andrew walked straight in, calling, 'Jimmie!' and her brother-in law appeared from the kitchen, looking dishevelled as she'd never seen him before, grey-faced and red-eyed.

He was literally wringing his hands. 'Oh my God, Andrew, what are we going to do?'

'Get back in there and sit down while you tell me exactly what happened – calmly!' Andrew snapped. 'Michelle, make a cup of tea. And put a slug of brandy in it.'

She was glad to have something to do, while Jimmie sobbed the story out to his brother. She watched as Andrew's expression got bleaker and bleaker but it was only when Jimmie began suggesting that Rob was to blame for not looking after Briony that he intervened.

'That's enough,' he said. 'In this situation, all we can do is not make things worse. Get on to that psychiatrist she saw before, get him to make representations. See that they're getting Dunbar lined up for advice. And make bloody sure this doesn't unravel any more or we'll be needing him too.'

As Michelle brought the mugs to the table and sat down with them, Jimmie was sounding calmer.

'That's true,' he said. 'She's just at the mercy of her illness, poor girl, and after all the women were unharmed. There's no reason why it should involve us.'

'That's right. We're as helpful as possible to the police

363

and make sure we've got the firewalls in place. It will all settle down and fortunately there's nothing pending.'

Michelle was facing the window. 'That's a car drawing up now,' she said. 'The woman that's getting out is that detective who was in the Waterfoot the other night. There's a man with her.'

Jimmie turned his head. 'Oh yes, that's DCI Strang. They came when I reported Briony was missing. I'll go and meet them.'

The doorbell rang as he went through the hall. Michelle heard him open the door and then she heard the chief inspector say, 'James Gresham, I am arresting you on suspicion of uttering threats. You do not have to say anything . . .'

When they had gone, Michelle sat looking down at her hands that were clenched so tightly that the knuckles had turned white, waiting for Andrew to speak.

After several minutes, he said, 'Uttering threats. There's something going on there that I don't know about. What has my brother done?'

'I – I don't know,' she stammered. 'Will it affect you?'

He gave a groan. 'Who knows? It depends where this all goes, but it's still just possible that it won't. It's going to be every man for himself.'

CHAPTER TWENTY-TWO

'His prints were all over the bags of chemicals in the shed and on the walls so we were able to go straight to a homicide charge,' DCI Strang said as he and DS Murray reported to DCS Borthwick in her office in Fettes Avenue.

'Excellent,' Borthwick said. 'The chief constable is delighted with the results.'

'In fact, there's another little kicker. When we were in the huge barn at Eastlaw Farm, I happened to notice a lump of hardened mud on the floor that had the imprint of a much larger tyre than for any machine Niall had. I sent it off to forensics and what they came back with is pretty interesting. They couldn't pin the tyres to any specific type, but the only one on my "reported missing" list that was fitted with them was the one Jimmie Gresham claimed had been stolen. And, strangely, it was just at the time that

£500 in cash was put into Niall Ritchie's bank account.'

Borthwick's eyebrows shot up. 'Really? Rent for use of the barn until a shipment could be arranged, you think?'

'It's a fair assumption – and there were two or three similar payments at other times. It isn't proof yet, but it looks like a point of departure for a major new investigation.'

'That was what Matt Gunn said right at the start,' Murray put in, 'that there was a good route for stolen machines, with all the boats that go to and fro trading with places like Poland.'

'It looks as if he was right, then,' Borthwick said, but she was sounding abstracted and it was a long moment before she spoke again. 'You know what all this means, don't you? With all the aspects of the Gresham family's activity that you've exposed, it takes things far beyond the scope of the SRCS.'

'Yes,' Strang said flatly. He'd realised, and it didn't make him happy. Murray was looking dismayed.

'Oh, I know it's not easy,' Borthwick said. 'We all get possessive about our cases, but as I said, the chief constable is very pleased and you'll certainly get credit for it at least. And if it's any comfort, you are both being recommended for excellence awards.'

Murray's face flamed and he could feel his own cheeks getting hot as they stammered their thanks. As they went out, Borthwick said, 'Kelso, I know it's not pretty behaviour to say "I told you so", but I told you so.'

He grinned and as they went along the corridor Murray said, 'What did she tell you?'

'Oh, she tells me lots of things,' Strang said vaguely. It

was the first time that they'd got through a case without her going off at a tangent and he didn't want it to go to her head.

DS Murray knew she should be feeling elated. A brilliant result and the promise she'd be recommended for an excellence award – she should be walking on air. But it had all happened so fast and now everything had been snatched out of their hands, there was nothing more to do except go back to the CID room and write up her notes for someone else to take forward.

She wanted to stamp her foot and say, 'It's not fair!', and telling herself that was childish didn't help this time any more than it had helped every previous time she'd tried it, and her steps were dragging as she walked down the stairs. She was feeling way too restless to sit down at her desk; the adrenaline was still coursing through her. She needed an excuse to do something, to dash off somewhere. There must be loose ends that needed tying up . . .

Then it came to her – Sarah Lindsay. The poor woman had been the prime suspect for her partner's murder and it would be no one's job to tell her she was off the hook now.

Murray could act in a family liaison capacity to make sure that she didn't still have that particular worry on top of the trauma of the previous night.

When last heard of, she and Rose Moncrieff had been taken to hospital for a check-up. She didn't imagine they would still be there but she called to make sure and then set out for Eastlaw Farm.

At least it wasn't raining today, just gloomy, with a sharp east wind fluttering the trailing crime scene tapes. The place looked almost derelict, with the battered shed and the little garden weed-choked and soggy with browning vegetation. The only signs of life came from the chickens pecking around the hen houses and a pair of squabbling seagulls that flew screaming overhead.

Murray knocked on the front door. There was no immediate response and she realised she was being scrutinised from the window on the right. After a long moment, Sarah Lindsay opened it.

'Oh, it's you,' she said dully.

Murray could hardly recognise her as the woman she had first met – could it really have been only a week ago? She looked as if she hadn't eaten or slept since and there were deep hollows under her cheekbones.

'I just came to see how you were, Sarah? And is Mrs Moncrieff all right after your ordeal?'

Sarah made no move to admit her. 'More or less, I think. She's gone to stay with a friend in Glasgow.' She gave a little, hard laugh. 'She didn't fancy coming back here. Not that I did, either.'

'No, I can understand that.' It felt awkward having the conversation on the doorstep but Murray didn't want to ask if she could come in and be refused so she ploughed on.

'I wanted to let you know that Briony Gresham has been charged.'

There was no sign of softening. 'I imagined she would be.'

'And I was keen to tell you whenever I could that James Gresham has been arrested for the murder of your partner, Niall Ritchie.'

The only visible reaction was her eyebrows rising. Then she said, 'I see. So you've got round to realising I didn't do it after all.'

Murray hadn't been naïve enough to expect anything approaching thanks but she hadn't expected to have to be defensive. 'I'm sorry, but I'm afraid suspecting everyone, no matter who they are, is a professional duty.' She would have liked to add, *Actually, I never really did think it was you*, but it wasn't that sort of conversation.

Sarah gave an unforgiving nod and started to turn away. Murray spoke quickly. 'Will you be staying here?'

Again, Sarah gave a short laugh. 'Oh no. I'll be selling, probably at a serious loss.' She took a step back, closing the door over.

'What will you do?' Murray said.

'Oh, crawl back to my parents in Spain. Admit I'm a total failure. Of course, I can cheer them up by telling them I haven't been arrested after all.'

The door shut firmly and Murray had no alternative but to turn away. She went back to her car in a sombre mood. When you were celebrating the successful ending of an investigation it was easy to forget about the wasteland strewn with human wreckage that had been left behind. Poor Sarah, poor Rose and poor gentle, sensitive Matt, who hadn't lived to know that he had got justice for Linden Moncrieff.

She'd never had a particularly vivid imagination but now she shuddered as she drove away, feeling now what Matt had been living with: a sense of the evil of a tainted family that had poisoned a whole community.

Catriona Fleming appeared in the kitchen, looking for breakfast, greatly to her father's surprise.

'Dear me! Got insomnia, have you? I thought Saturday

didn't dawn till midday as far as you were concerned.'

She gave him a withering look. 'I shall treat that with the contempt it deserves. Yes, good morning, Scott,' she said, petting the collie that was dancing frantically round her. 'Yes, you're a good boy – well, you're not really, are you? Sit!'

Clearly recognising the word, Scott made a sketchy bob towards the floor as she sat down, then jumped up to paw at her. 'No!' she said sharply. 'Not at the table. Basket!'

Giving her a wounded look, he went over to his bed beside the Rayburn, then got distracted by the smell of the bacon Marjory was cooking and moved to sit down at her feet, looking up beseechingly.

'No, Scott,' she said automatically. 'Cat, what do you want for breakfast?'

'Whatever's going. I'm starving.'

'Ah! That explains it!' Bill said. 'I wondered why we were being honoured with your presence so early.'

'You should know perfectly well why, Bill,' Marjory said. 'Kelso Strang's coming this morning. She's probably been awake half the night with excitement.'

'Oh, *Mum*!' Cat jumped up to get some coffee, turning so that they couldn't see her face going pink.

'Oh, he is, is he?' Bill grunted. 'Well, I'm finished. I'll just get off round the farm.'

When he stood up, it set off another frantic round of enthusiasm as the dog said his farewells, doing his best to make sure that no one felt hurt by having been neglected.

'That dog is a perfect nuisance,' Cat said, pushing him down. 'Too much of a good thing, Scott!'

Bill paused on his way to the door. 'Aye, right! You'd

do well to think of that yourself, and not get carried away. What time's lunch?'

Cat looked at her mother, who was bringing over a plate to put in front of her. 'Is he going to be like that the whole day?'

Marjory sat down. 'He doesn't like the thought of you dating a much older man.'

'We're not dating, more's the pity. I think he thinks I'm far too young for him.'

'He's probably right. And Dad thinks it's just a crush.'

'Oh, for God's sake! What age do they think I am? I'm a mature, professional woman, for heaven's sake! All I can say is, stick around. Unless Dad puts him off. Or there's someone else just waiting in the wings.'

Marjory looked at her daughter's anxious face. 'Do you remember what Gran used to say – what's for ye'll no go by ye?'

'Mmm. But Dad's not being fair – I have played it cooler this week, you know. I was dying to know how he was getting on when it's all been so dramatic, but I didn't pester him. It was him that phoned to say was the invitation still open to come down here, you know.'

'That sounds promising from your point of view, I'd say.'

'Yes, but – well, the only thing is, he sounded more as if he was hoping to talk to you.'

'Oh? Of course, I'd be delighted to do that,' Marjory said, trying without much success to conceal her gratification.

'I know he won't tell me any background stuff, but supposing I leave the two of you to talk after lunch – I can say I have work to do, which I have, actually, and then you can tell me how it's been for him afterwards. And picking up the unspoken stuff is your particular skill, isn't it? You could maybe suss out what he really thinks about me.'

With her mature, professional daughter looking at her with the hopeful expression of a hungry baby bird, Marjory laughed. 'I'll do my best.'

Kelso Strang had driven down to Galloway on a perfect autumn day when, after a sharp frost, the trees seemed to be in a competition for the most outrageous combination of deep gold, orange, pale yellow and flaunting red. It was good to get away; knowing that his fate for the next few days would be to sit in his office and write up reports had been an unappealing prospect and a depressing anticlimax after all the fevered activity.

They had been his cases, now they weren't any more, and even though he knew it was unreasonable, he felt aggrieved and flat. He needed something to distract him, cheer him up. Of course, he'd thought of phoning Cat and asking if she was hungry, but he was afraid he wouldn't be able to keep off the subject uppermost in his mind and the last thing he wanted was to have her think of him as a moaning old man.

It was then he'd remembered the invitation to the farm. He could have the fun of Cat's company and even manage to get a therapeutic half an hour on his own with Marjory, who would understand how he was feeling – might even have been there herself.

Cat had been touchingly pleased when he'd asked if he could accept the invitation. He wasn't sure how relaxing it would be, though, when it came to meeting the rest of family; he'd be pretty cynical if a grown-up Betsy appeared with a considerably older 'friend' – perish the thought!

But it was such a happy, relaxed morning. Cat took him off round the farm, and apart from giving him a long, anxious look and saying, 'Oh well, you look as if you've survived – you must be tough!', she didn't mention his work, just kept him amused with stories about her bolshie teen years and her battles with her mother.

'Just too alike in some ways, I guess. By the way, she's hoping to lure you away so she can tempt you into serious indiscretion about the case I know you won't tell me about,' she said with a sideways glance. 'Oh, there's Cammie feeding the stirks! Come and meet him.'

It was just so easy. He liked Cammie, he liked Bill, and though he'd got a hard stare from him straight out of the Paddington playbook, he reckoned that by the end of Annelise's lunch – catered on a lavish scale – Bill had thawed. Kelso was beginning to feel strangely at home here, despite it being as different as it could be from the home he'd grown up in, dominated by Major General Sir Roderick Strang.

Part of his mission today had been to show Cat's parents that he wasn't looking for a relationship with their young daughter, but however much he told himself that what he felt for Cat was mere friendship, it was a pretence that was wearing thin and he doubted if it was convincing anyone.

He'd created a protective shell after his wife had died and to admit to himself that he was falling in love with Cat would leave him open to the sort of pain he dreaded ever feeling again. He could get addicted to the happiness he felt when he was with her – but she was too young to be ready to settle and even if she was giving him every sign of encouragement, he was still a novelty and she might well change her mind when that wore off. He wondered too about the advocate, her 'inspiration' to go to the bar; perhaps he was another 'friend' and perhaps when it came to it, she would realise he could offer more than a widower twelve years older than she was.

He could think about that later – indeed, once he got back to Edinburgh he would probably find it hard to think about anything else. But right now, Cat was saying she had work to do and had flitted upstairs while Marjory showed him to the sitting room and poked the stove into a blaze.

It was a room that was cosy rather than stylish. It spoke of relaxing after a busy day, of easy conversation over a glass of something, of the comfortable confidence of the Flemings' long and happy marriage, and he felt a sharp pang of envy.

Hastily, he said, 'Don't make it any warmer. My eyes are drooping already.'

Marjory laughed. 'Oh, Annelise's lunches are notorious! If you want to do anything afterwards, you're as well to avoid pudding.'

'Now she tells me! But Marjory, I'm really glad to have a chance to thank you for putting me on the right track on Tuesday.'

'If I did put you on the right track, you certainly followed it up effectively. It's been something of a triumph, going by the column inches. And as we both know that's all that matters to the high heid yins.'

Kelso pulled a face. 'Too right.' He told her briefly about the way things had worked out, then said, 'But what dawned on me after speaking to you was that it wasn't just one disease: Tarleton was an unhealthy organism that had bred different illnesses in the different parts of the communal body. Matt Gunn knew there was something terribly wrong but he was up against a wall of silence.'

'Can the place recover, after all this?' she said.

He thought about that. 'The Caddon has been ignoring the law for centuries and you won't change that. It's a "watch the wall" culture, if you remember the poem.'

'Indeed I do. Learnt it at school, and it applies to every flourishing criminal community, from the Outer Isles to the Glasgow backstreets.'

'The trouble is, these places have got much more vulnerable, just ripe for takeover for enterprises like county lines. There's so little contact with the police, with the local stations that worked in the heart of the communities reduced to office hours two days a week.'

'Oh, don't get me started on Police Scotland,' Marjory said. 'You should have heard my sergeant Tam MacNee on that subject.'

'The victims of the pandemic weren't only the ones who suffered from Covid – the lockdown made it easier for a wealthy and corrupt family to enforce their rules, with a bit of intimidation. There's even a belief that it started with a previous generation – a local constable talked darkly to my sergeant about "bad blood" in the family and right now it looks as if none of the current generation escaped it. Still, it's out of my hands now. It's all being kicked upstairs and no one's going to ask me about how it should be progressed and what might be done to break the chain of corruption, and naturally they won't handle it the way I would have.

Of course, I know it's none of my business . . .'

Marjory looked at him with a slight smile. 'Do I perhaps detect just a touch of bitterness?'

'Too damn right you do!' he said, turning down the corners of his mouth, but the smile seemed to be infectious and it became a rueful grin. 'Oh, I know perfectly well the scale of the operation they're embarking on and the one-man-and-his-dog operation I'm in charge of couldn't begin to run it but I did think I could have been involved somewhere, in fairness.'

'And you still think the authorities are interested in fairness, after how many years of service? I actually ended up suspended after I'd brought a very difficult case to a successful conclusion.'

Strang was interested. 'Really?'

'Oh no,' she said. 'Let sleeping grudges lie – and Cat will be down any minute. I hope she's giving you space to breathe. She can be a bit too single-minded.'

'Oh no, no, absolutely not!' he said. 'It's been an amazing piece of luck, getting to know her. I'd almost forgotten what it felt like to be light-hearted. Of course, she's very young, and I'm sure she has lots of other friends.' He took a deep breath, then said, 'I know there's one – he's an advocate, I think. She talked about him being her inspiration and I just wondered if . . .'

Marjory frowned. 'An advocate? There's no one she's mentioned to me. Inspiration? Oh, wait a minute! You don't mean Dominic? I got to know him when he was a struggling young advocate hanging round the courts desperate for briefs. When Cat was struggling with being a social worker, he was a top Glasgow QC and he basically talked her into going to the bar. Retired now, and had his golden wedding last year, in case you're interested.'

He tried to sound nonchalant. 'No, no, I didn't mean . . .' But there was another smile starting and he couldn't stop that one either.

Marjory shook her head. 'I don't know – maybe you two should just try talking to each other and see how it works out instead of going all round the houses.'

'And – you wouldn't object? Your husband?'

Marjory laughed. 'After lunch, Bill said to me, "Seems a decent enough bloke, actually." That's high praise, from Bill.'

There was the sound of feet on the stairs and Cat came in, her eyes going anxiously from one to the other. 'Have you had a good talk? You know, it's funny. I was just going through the papers for Vincent next week, and one of the cases he's giving advice on is that woman from Tarleton that was arrested last week – Briony Gresham, I think it was.'

Then she stopped, suddenly aware that the other two had frozen. 'What? What did I say? What's the matter?'

Kelso said painfully, 'I'm going to be the principal police witness in that. I can't associate with you until it's over.'

Consternation showed on Cat's face. 'But that could be a year – very possibly more.'

'Indeed. At least, the way the courts are at the moment.'

Marjory got up. 'Look, Kelso, I think you should be going. Why don't I leave you to talk to each other properly first? It might help if I tell you that I have the firm impression you're on the same wavelength.'

* * *

377

As Marjory went out, Bill came into the hall from the kitchen, calling, 'Where is everybody?'

'Shh,' she said, ushering him backwards as she pointed at the sitting-room door. 'Young love,' she said, 'and older love too, if I read it right. In accordance with tradition, it's not running smooth at the moment, but I've every confidence they'll work it out.'

'She could certainly do worse,' Bill admitted. 'After all, he got a trial for the Army 1st XV when he was serving.'

'Oh well, *that's* all right then,' Marjory said, rolling her eyes.

Kelso Strang drove back to Edinburgh in the golden autumn evening, feeling an extraordinary mixture of elation and dismay. He'd been able to take Cat in his arms for the first time and it had felt so right – as if it was *meant*, she had said – even as he was having to dry her tears as they said goodbye.

There should have been time to get to know each other in the new context – long, lazy weeks of courtship – but there was no time for that now and it was more than strange how certain both of them had been about what they wanted when the professional thunderbolt hit them. But absence presented quite a challenge to a relationship that had as yet no real roots and he'd left himself with no defence against the agony he'd suffer if she changed her mind.

Yet somehow, he didn't think she would. She'd been fierce with him when he'd talked about her being so young, saying scornfully, 'Don't be silly. Everyone knows a woman's emotional age is at least ten years more than her real age and a man's is ten years younger, which makes us equally mature, right? In fact, that might even work out as me being older than you are.'

It made him smile again as he thought of it, but it still wasn't going to be easy. She'd said she'd just walk out on Vincent – 'such a horrible man anyway' – but he'd managed to persuade her to stick it for the sake of her career; pupillages were hard to come by and in fact she'd only six more months of it to complete before she could set up her own plate – and then, in defiance of the cab rank principle, only take cases he wasn't involved in. They had agreed that they could risk writing careful letters but other means of contact were best avoided, at least for the moment. 'Quite like old-time sweethearts,' Cat had said, her lips quivering.

There was nothing to lift his spirits in the week ahead. He could invite himself to Finella and Peter's for Sunday lunch, and Betsy's demands would stop him having time to brood. He could always make a chart like a schoolchild to score off the days and plan for the celebration they'd have the day Cat shook the dust of Dunbar's office off her feet, but unless he got another interesting case for the SRCS, the days were going to drag by.

But it was only a fortnight later that his phone rang and he saw Cat's number displayed.

He answered it gingerly. 'Cat?' Surely she hadn't just broken, and quit?

'Did you pull strings about Vincent?' she said bluntly.

'Vincent? No, not guilty.'

'It's just that suddenly some detectives arrived and they've been asking all sorts of questions about the dealings we've been having with the Gresham family and Vincent's got all hot and bothered and now he's told us that we're not to accept any more instructions from the Gresham family's solicitors.'

'What? I wonder what on earth's going on? I must ask around.'

'For heaven's sake, Kelso, don't get yourself involved in that next!'

'No, no, of course not,' he said hastily, as joy swept through him and everything was all right again. 'By the way, are you hungry, by any chance?'

ACKNOWLEDGEMENTS

My thanks go, as always, to my agent Jane Conway-Gordon, my publisher Susie Dunlop and all at Allison and Busby.

ALINE TEMPLETON grew up in the fishing village of Anstruther, in the East Neuk of Fife. She has worked in education and broadcasting and was a Justice of the Peace for ten years. She has been a Chair of the Society of Authors in Scotland and a director of the Crime Writers' Association. Married, with a son and a daughter and four grandchildren, she lived in Edinburgh for many years but now lives in Kent.

alinetempleton.co.uk   *@Aline Templeton*